SORROW HILL

SORROW HILL

BEOWULF - SWORD OF WODEN

C. R. MAY

COPYRIGHT

ISBN-10: 1495927989
ISBN-13: 978-1495927980

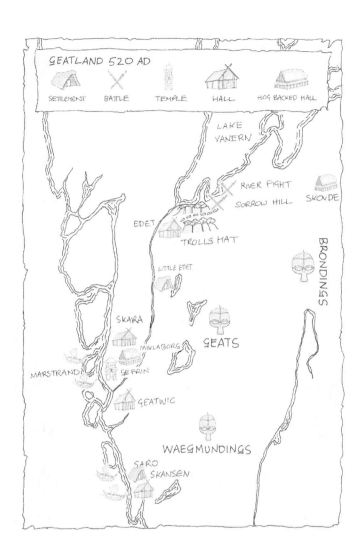

GEATLAND 520 AD

| SETTLEMENT | BATTLE | TEMPLE | HALL | HOG BACKED HALL |

LAKE VANERN

RIVER FIGHT

SORROW HILL

SKONDE

EDET

TROLLS HAT

LITTLE EDET

BRONDINGS

SKARA

GEATS

MIKLABORG

MARSTRAND

GEFRIN

GEATWIC

WAEGMUNDINGS

SARO

SKANSEN

There was no one else like him alive.
In his day, he was the mightiest man on earth;
High born and powerful....

1

The boy stood at the base of the tree and cocked his head, listening. With the daylight almost spent he would need to hurry, but now the old familiar ghosts began to gather around him, unbidden, unwelcome. He *could* just turn around and ride home, back to his life of privilege and comfort and none would be any wiser. Or he could face down his demons, push on and risk a violent and lonely death. His head whispered return home, his heart seize the day. He knew which path his father would have taken. Ecgtheow was a great warrior, one of the king's leading men, an *ealdorman*. With a troop of hearth companions, the grizzled veteran of countless shield walls was a generous ring giver, a man whom any warrior would be proud to serve and call his lord, but it was a truth that the boy felt overwhelmed by the expectations placed upon him by his father's greatness.

Disturbed by his sudden appearance, a wood pigeon clattered from the branches above him. Rising into the cool spring air, the boy watched as the grey bird spread its wings and glided beyond the tree line. It was a god-sign that the killers were away, and the young Geat smiled and touched the small hammer pendant at his neck in thanks. There *was* no choice to be made he knew, he could not go back now to live a life of obscurity, forever the boy. His decision made, the ghosts of self-doubt retreated back into the shadows. Today he would begin to carve out a reputation for himself, one which would give the *scops*, the guardians of folk history, cause to recount the deeds of a new hero in the smoky halls of his people. That story would begin at this place, on this day; men not yet born would wonder at the deeds of Beowulf Ecgtheowson.

Struggling from his thick travelling cloak, Beowulf wrapped it tightly around his body as his eyes scanned the lower branches. Darkness was already beginning to envelop the land, and he would be thankful for it soon enough if he were to spend a night in the tree, poised for his assault early the next day. Looping a small bag around his shoulder he gave the strap a sharp tug, pulling it securely to his body as he decided on the likeliest route upwards. The shadows were lengthening quickly now, the time available to him slipping away as he launched himself at the branch. Weary hands found a grip and he grunted with effort as he began to haul himself up into the foliage, feet scrabbling for a toehold as he slung an arm across the bough and held on tight. At last his efforts paid off, and a boot wedged into one of the many runnels which lined the old trunk. With a final heave he was there and, safely aloft, he moved swiftly upwards as the sounds of the forest faded beneath him.

Clear of the lower levels the branches were densely packed, and he made good progress as he pushed his way through. The sweet smell of pine resin quickly replaced the mustiness of the forest floor as, branch by branch, he climbed towards the canopy. As Beowulf rose higher the limbs crowded in, clutching at his clothing as he forced his way towards his goal. A flash of brilliant light startled him as without warning he burst from the canopy into the full glare of the setting sun, but a fear filled glance was enough to tell him that the killers were still elsewhere as he jerked his head back into the shadows and listened. Nothing came but the sounds of the forest; a gentle breeze caressing the treetops, somewhere in the middle distance the dog-like bark of a vixen carried to haunt the greenwood.

It was a mistake born of exhaustion but it could so easily have cost him his life, and the young Geat cursed his sloppiness as he made his way back to the place he had marked to spend the night. The sun's dying light was struggling to pierce the canopy now, and he still had one last task to perform in readiness for the assault. Unslinging his pack Beowulf loosened the ties, removing several small strips of cloth and laying them out carefully on his thigh. Snapping off one of the small twigs from the nearest branch the boy gently stroked each one, gradually coating them in a thin layer of sticky resin, before popping them into a small leather purse and stashing it away.

Finally set, the young Geat stifled a yawn as the trials of the day overtook him, but he was satisfied that he had made all the preparations that he could for the dawn, and he settled his back against the bole of the tree as he gnawed hungrily at a hard wedge of cheese. A piercing screech told him that the killers had returned but he had chosen his hiding place well, and Beowulf allowed himself a small smile of satisfaction as the last rays of the sun slowly paled, leaving him in a world of darkness, silence, and bitter cold.

$\approx$

THE EYRIE LOOMED ABOVE HIM, enormous and menacing, as he prepared to climb the last few feet. He had planned as well as he could for this moment, tracking the adult eagles back to their nest over many weeks to discover which one of the several nests in the area the pair had chosen to lay their eggs in this year. From talking to his father's falconer he had determined when the best time to raid the nest had been. Too early and he would find only eggs, too late and the chicks would be too strong to take.

Beowulf had stepped up his visits to the area soon after the harsh northern winter had begun to give way to the gentler days of spring, and as soon as the birds had begun to return with food for the chicks he had finalised his plans. Now the moment had finally arrived, and Beowulf braced against the trunk, nervously scanning the sky for any sign of the adult birds returning. He had chosen this part of the day to make his assault on the eyrie carefully. Svip, the falconer, had told him that the parents would spend each night at the nest and at first light they should both leave together in search of food. At two weeks the eaglets would be large enough to see off predators such as crows or gulls, enabling both parents to satisfy their own hunger before returning to the eyrie with food for their offspring. Beowulf hoped that this would give him just enough time to remove the chicks and regain cover before one or both of the adults returned. The chances that a fully grown man would survive an attack were slim; a boy who had only just lived through his sixth winter could expect only a swift and savage end.

Beowulf quartered the skies above as he forced down a fear which threatened to overwhelm him. An invisible force seemed to have reached out to hold him in its grip, anchoring his body to the gently swaying branches. He knew that he must overcome it or regret this moment for the rest of his life.

With a last gulp of air he steeled himself, breaking the mental chains as he forced his body forward.

Now!

With a racing heart Beowulf grabbed the edge of the eyrie, swinging himself over the lip and onto the surface of the nest. Ahead of him two chicks stood among the remains of last night's meal, too busy squabbling over the pelt of a rabbit to notice the danger which had landed in their midst.

Tearing open the bag, Beowulf quickly laid out the leather pouch containing the tacky strips and made a grab. Scooping up the nearest chick, he quickly bound the razor-like beak with the material before stuffing the struggling body away. Spooked by the intruder and the disappearance of his brood mate, the remaining chick scrambled away as the boy's eyes cast a fearful look skyward, and his mind raced as a whimper of fear escaped his lips. The surface of the eyrie was a mess of sticks, as rough as an old man's beard and strewn with skulls, bones and pelts: the pathetic remains of previous meals. Unbalanced on the rickety lip of the bowl, Beowulf lunged and missed again. A wave of fear threatened to over-whelm him as he thrashed among the debris, well aware that time was short and his life hung in the balance. Desperate now as the daylight brightened, Beowulf scrambled across and snatched up the remaining chick, quickly binding its beak and shoving it inside the sack with its sibling.

Away to the East the horizon flared as the wolf-grey light of the pre dawn was chased away, and the eyrie shone a burnished bronze as the sun broke free of the world's rim. As if to mark the moment a piercing screech from above tore into his mind, and the boy gasped in horror as a shadow flitted across the surface of the nest.

Panic stricken he swung his legs back over the rim, his feet desperately searching out a foothold as the bird dipped a wing and turned back. The eagle, its wicked talons glinting in the sun, bore down on his exposed head as he clung helplessly to the side of the nest. There was only one thing that he could do to stand any chance of surviving the adult's attack, and in desperation he released his grip.

As the giant bird flashed through his vision the first strike crashed into his back, knocking the air from his body as he tumbled down through the canopy in a series of heavy blows before coming to rest on a large branch winded, bruised, scratched but alive. As Beowulf's senses returned in a rush he heard the piercing cries of the adult eagle as it searched for him. It would take only moments before the bird found him, as peering skywards he could still see a slash of grey through the trail of broken and twisted branches which marked the path through which his body had fallen.

A moment of fear as he scrabbled for his knife, but hope flared within him as his hand closed about the handle, the blade still in its scabbard after the long fall. High above cries of alarm still cut the air, and in a moment of clarity Beowulf instinctively knew that the only chance that he had to survive the day was to attack and silence the eagle as quickly as possible, before its urgent cries brought its mate rushing to its aid. He looped the bag containing his catch to a bough as he tore off his cloak, wrapping the woollen sheet tightly around his shield arm as he drew the dagger and edged into the open.

Almost immediately the air around him became a maelstrom of beating wings and slashing talons as the eagle attacked.

Beowulf retreated before the ferocity of the parent's onslaught, back into the canopy of the tree, frantically using his improvised shield to fend off the enraged bird. As he had hoped, the thick cover of the branches were not only good for concealment, they snatched and pulled at the bird's great wings as it forced its way into the crush. Lord of the air and a perfect killer in its element the eagle was becoming entangled, and Beowulf knew that if he could just stay out of reach and remain calm, an opportunity to win the contest would present itself.

First one wing snagged and then the other, and he knew that he would have to act quickly to seize his best chance of surviving the encounter. Beowulf edged forward in a last do-or-die attempt to trap and kill the bird before it regained its freedom, and he forced down a gut twisting fear as he thrust forward his arm.

With a sky ripping screech the eagle took the bait, its legs flying forward as the talons sank deeply into the material of the cloak. Instantly Beowulf twisted his arm, ensnaring the bird in the heavy wool, tugging the eagle back into the thicker press of leafage. The great bird thrashed the air in an attempt to free itself, but drawing deeply on reserves of strength which he had never tapped before the Geat hurled it onto its back, pearls of blood misting the air as he stabbed and stabbed.

THE LIGHT WAS GONE, the long day a memory when Beowulf ventured from his hiding place. A petal of flame flickered into life in the twilight, and the boy's spirits rose as he retrieved his mount, forded the beck and guided the horse towards the grove. The promise of warm food and warmer flames drew him on, and he was soon within hailing distance of the buttery circle of light. A solitary figure sat within it, his back resting against an aged trunk, and Beowulf called out as he grew nearer.

"I am approaching the camp, friend."

He had been on enough hunting trips into the wild wood to know of the dangers of approaching camp fires unannounced. Folk were skittish enough alone on the moors or in the great forests of Geatland at night, without seeing shadowy shapes coming at them out of the gloom. The figure replied without raising his gaze from the dancing flames.

"Yes, I know that you are boy. You are welcome at my fire."

Slipping wearily from the saddle, Beowulf secured the horse to a nearby tree and approached the camp of the stranger.

"My name is Beowulf. I am the son of the ealdorman, Ecgtheow," he announced. "I ask for your hospitality for this night."

"I offer it gladly," replied the man. "I have travelled far and wide and have been known by many names, some men call me Hrani. I trade in curious things and gather knowledge. You look as if you may have a tale to tell, I should be interested to hear it."

Hrani gestured to a place next to the fire and Beowulf gratefully took it. Even the hard earth was an improvement over a precarious branch.

"Have you eaten, Beowulf Ecgtheowson? I have already, but there is plenty of food left in the pot for guests."

Hrani produced a bowl from the pack lying at his side, ladling in a meaty stew from the smoke-blackened pot nestling at the edge of the fire. Beowulf thanked him and wolfed the broth down, feeling the warmth and renewed energy coursing through his body. When he had eaten his fill, Beowulf sat back and regarded his host for the first time.

Hrani sat with his back to the wizened trunk of what, the boy decided, must be the oldest tree in the forest. A cloak of the finest wool was gathered at his neck and a wide brimmed hat typical of the well travelled was pulled low, casting his features into deep shadow. Although he could not see the man's face clearly, Beowulf sensed an amused and keen intelligence in his companion.

"So what brings the son of an ealdorman out on a night like this? Travelling alone through the domain of wolves and trolls; where are your hearth companions, Beowulf?"

"They are... nearby," Beowulf replied cautiously, suddenly aware of his vulnerability. If the man really was a *wulfes-heafod*, a wolf-head, an outlaw, he would give a good account of himself before he fell, despite his weariness.

Hrani chuckled, and Beowulf had the uncomfortable feeling that the man could read his thoughts. Laughter danced across the older man's features as he indicated the leather sack containing the chicks.

"You will need to feed them soon if they are to survive. Even eagles enjoy Hrani's stew."

Beowulf gaped in surprise. "So, you saw me?"

Hrani remained silent and took a sip from his cup as he studied the boy closely. Beowulf shifted uncomfortably as the mood in the clearing subtly changed. As if in response, the sounds of the night seemed to diminish and the shadows crept closer.

"I see many things Beowulf, sometimes I am lucky and I see something special, maybe a boy with the potential for greatness." He gave a small shrug. "Those days are all too rare, but when they do come along it makes my journeying through the lands of Middle-earth all the more rewarding."

The air felt heavy, cloying, and Beowulf blinked in surprise as a coterie of mice scampered from the long grass and disappeared inside his host's shirt. His lids felt heavy, and Beowulf dimly came to realise that he had been hexed. He cast an anxious look at the bowl of food and saw Hrani follow his gaze with undisguised amusement, but gentle laughter rolled from the man and the spell was instantly broken. Hrani continued brightly as if nothing untoward had occurred. "But I also recognise the sound that a hungry chick makes, and yours are very hungry!"

Unnerved but excited in equal measure, Beowulf retrieved the pack from the horse and returned to the fireside. He had met several wizards and cunning women before, but none had come close to matching Hrani's aura of wisdom and power. Unfastening it, he withdrew the larger of the chicks and bound its legs tightly with the resinous material before removing the binding to its beak. The chick began to tear hungrily at the meat as Beowulf tended to its sibling. Hrani watched the birds as they ate.

"The smaller of the two looks like it has been roughly handled. May I look at it? Some consider me to have certain skills where injured creatures are concerned."

Beowulf hesitated for a moment before handing over the chick but decided that the man could easily kill him and take them both if he had a mind. In reality he had little choice. Hrani purred softly as he examined the eaglet.

"Beautiful! I have watched the Goths use these birds to hunt and kill wolves, even drive off bears."

As he spoke he slowly ran his hands over the body of the chick which had become still and calm, almost as if it were entranced. Returning the bird, Hrani watched as Beowulf fed and returned them to the bag for the night. Hrani filled a cup and handed it to his guest.

"It is wine. I hope that you like it. It is not so easy to find in the North but I always try to obtain enough to last me when I am in the warmer lands to the South."

Beowulf took the cup and drank deeply. In truth he preferred the honest taste of good ale to wine, 'a drink for

Francs and women' his father had once told him, but he was thirsty and he did not wish to offend his host. Hrani waited until he had drained the cup and, reaching forward, refilled it to the brim.

"So," he continued, "tell me how a young man comes to be travelling alone at night carrying two eagle chicks, and I will consider it a handsome payment for the use of my food and fire."

Beowulf recounted the story of his raid and the planning which had gone into it as Hrani sat back and sipped his wine. The older man nodded at the conclusion and seemed impressed.

"That is a tale fit to grace any hall, Beowulf. Are you Woden born?"

"My mother's father is King Hrethel of the Geats, so yes, the Allfather's blood flows in me, but I fear that I am not living up to the hopes of my own father." Beowulf smiled thinly and looked into his cup. "I am his only son and I know that I am a disappointment to him."

Hrani snorted and shook his head.

"All sons feel that way at some time my friend. We have a night ahead of us and I sense the potential for greatness in you. Let us talk and I will see if I can share some of my wisdom with you. Ask away, for no better burden can a man carry on his journey through life than a store of common sense. Believe me," he chuckled, "it can be worth more than a bag of gold in a strange and unfamiliar place."

Beowulf looked up.

"How can I prove my worth to my father and my kin? That is my dearest wish Hrani."

Hrani snorted again.

"That is easy little one. Be true to yourself Beowulf, you have no need to prove anything. It would be no true father who said only pleasant things. Ecgtheow may seem aloof but he has many worries and responsibilities. He protects you from the troubles of the world until you are old enough to fend for yourself. It is what fathers are meant to do, and if you were honest with yourself you would not want it any other way."

The fire flared suddenly as Hrani pushed a branch with his foot, releasing a cloud of sparks which curled lazily upwards. Settling back he sniffed and continued.

"I will give you good advice on how to live your life, advice you would be wise to heed. Remember Beowulf, generous and brave men live best but a cowardly man is afraid of everything. Be thoughtful and cheerful, brave at the clash of shields. The foolish man thinks that he will live forever if he keeps away from the fighting, but death will still seek him out just the same." Hrani leaned close, and Beowulf was startled to see that one of his eye sockets was withered and empty. The old man fixed him with his remaining eye and the boy trembled under the intensity of his gaze. "Mark these words above all Beowulf. They are the most important that you will ever hear. All things eventually die and pass from this world, but glory and reputation never die for the man who is able to achieve it in his lifetime."

Hrani entertained Beowulf long into the night with tales of the gods, how they had tricked the wolf Fenrir and left him bound and gagged where he lies in wait for the chaos at the end of the world. Tales of the gods Tiwaz and Thunor, of the *eorthan modor* Nerthus, and of how he should use their teachings as a guide to live his own life.

As the night drew on Beowulf sat entranced as Hrani regaled him with tales of honour and wisdom.

"You have been a noble and generous host and I have

been found wanting in my payment to you," Beowulf declared after Hrani had talked long into the night.

Rising to his feet he made his way across to where the bag containing the eagle chicks had been placed near the fire for warmth. Reaching inside he removed the larger of the chicks and held it towards his host.

"Hrani, I should like to make a gift to you of this eagle, in gratitude for the hospitality and advice which you have given me."

Hrani's face beamed with pleasure at the gesture.

"It is a noble gift and worthy of your character. I accept it, gladly."

Hrani produced a coarsely woven bag from inside his cloak and placed the chick inside. Beowulf watched as the older man hesitated. He was clearly thinking deeply on a matter of some importance to him. Finally he seemed to have reached his decision and he turned back.

"There is one more thing I wish to do for you, Beowulf Ecgtheowson."

Picking up the staff which lay at his side, Hrani broke a short piece from it and handed it across to him.

"Keep this on you at all times and it will help to keep you from harm. Look on it as a loan. One day we will meet again and you can return it to me." He nodded towards a cleared space beside the fire. "Now you must sleep Beowulf. You have had a tumultuous day and I have kept you up far too late. Tomorrow you have a long ride ahead of you if you are to regain your father's hall before sunset, and you will need to make an early start."

Hrani moved back against the tree as Beowulf rested his head, the old traveller merging with the shadows as sleep finally reached out and claimed the boy.

BEOWULF AWOKE as the first rays of the sun splashed pink on the eastern horizon. It had been a cold night and a hoar frost had dusted the ground around him and painted the branches of the trees a milky white. Casting about, he was unsurprised to find that his host had already departed and he was once more alone.

Struggling from the folds of his cloak, Beowulf stretched and rubbed his muscles in an attempt to instil some warmth into them. His foot brushed gently against something and, glancing down, he noticed a supply of raw meat and food had been left for him. Beowulf chewed on a piece of meat, softening it, before removing it from his mouth and feeding the chick. The eaglet hungrily bolted down the offering and called for more as Beowulf held him close.

The chick seemed far more comfortable being held today. Svip had said that golden eagles were trainable but Beowulf had been sceptical, especially when the falconer had been forced to admit that he had never seen a tame example himself and he had, he claimed, travelled through many lands in the North plying his trade.

Keen to put as many miles between the eyrie and his prize as soon as possible, Beowulf doused the fire and secured the bag to his saddle horn before untying the gelding's forelocks and leaving the site of his strange encounter.

Riding south along the track, Beowulf was able to reflect on the events of the previous night. Hrani had said more to him in a few hours than any adult had ever taken the time to say before. The boy had felt for the first time that he had been part of a conversation and not the subject of a lecture.

He passed the time by attempting to recall the main

lessons he had been taught, 'a framework for a good life', Hrani had called them.

He decided to try and list the main points before they passed from his memory and fortunately, despite the number of tales which Hrani had used to illustrate each piece of advice, they seemed to fall quite neatly into a list of dos and don'ts.

Beowulf closed his eyes, allowing the warmth of the morning sun and the rhythmic movement of his horse to relax his mind, and he amused himself as the words returned like swallows in the spring.

Use the years you have been given wisely. *Obviously...*

Build a reputation before age or death brings you low. *Definitely!*

Be generous and cheerful in all your dealings. *Maybe...*

Make and keep good friends. *Yes...*

Honour and protect your kin. *Always...*

Never drink to excess or be a glutton. *Hmm...*

Don't amass wealth for its own sake. *Never...*

Or trust the words of a woman...

A shout interrupted his thoughts. Beowulf quickly scanned the tree line and was relieved to find Bjalki, one of his father's shield men riding towards him.

Bjalki called out cheerfully as he drew closer.

"I wouldn't like to be you boy. Not when we get back!"

Grinning, Bjalki's features radiated warmth and good humour, and Beowulf could not help but return the smile as he fell in beside him. He was glad that Bjalki had been the first to find him and couldn't help but think that Hrani would have approved of the jovial warrior.

"Where have you been? Your mother thinks that a troll has taken you and your father's getting ready to ride out against the Wuffings to rescue you!"

Bjalki reached across and tousled his hair affectionately.

"What's in the bag, little man?"

"An eagle, big man."

Bjalki laughed at the retort, and Beowulf's heart leapt at the sound. It was as warm and homely as his father's hearth or his mother's spindle, and the boy shot the big man a grin as he replied. "You'll see."

2
_____

The familiar sounds of a camp stirring itself back into
life slowly began to enter Beowulf's consciousness.
Coughs and groans, the steady splash of water falling on soil.
Outside the warriors made ready for the day and began to
make their way over to the place where the thralls had already
prepared breakfast.

Beowulf swung himself up from the bed and pulled on his
woollen cloak. Unfastening the leather thong which secured
the tent opening he made his way eagerly over to the fire. A
heavy set warrior looked up from his stool and grinned at the
approaching boy.

"Beowulf! I trust that you slept well?"

"I did", he replied. "I find that a day in the saddle always
helps, Bjalki."

"You'll be wanting this then," Bjalki added jovially,
holding out a steaming bowl of porridge and sausage.

Beowulf had turned seven earlier that summer and had
begun to be weaned on the duties of an ealdorman. Of course
returning with a dead eagle and a live chick done no
harm to his reputation, and although his father had accepted

the gifts with his customary aloofness he had seen the excitement in the ealdorman's eyes for a brief moment before he regained his composure. Now he had been sent with a dozen of his father's best warriors on a journey to the land of the Danes to deliver gifts to their king, Hrothgar. It was a mark of how far he had risen in his father's estimation to be entrusted with such a task. "We'd best get moving if we want to make the coast this morning," said Bjalki. "If we can sail today we will. There's no sense in spending longer than we need to in that place!"

Leaving the thralls to break camp the troop mounted up and formed into a column with the pack horse containing the tribute placed safely in the centre. Although it was unlikely that anyone would be foolish enough to attack a dozen of the Waegmunding's finest shield men it would show that they were prepared for any trouble should the need arise. Leaving the thralls to follow on once they had broken camp, the troop of warriors rejoined the road which led to the coast.

They rode in silence for a time, Beowulf and Bjalki at the head of the column, as they moved through his father's lands. The forest began to open up as they neared the coast, allowing the light to penetrate the former gloom. Borage began to cover the clearing with a haze of blue while cherry trees, heavy with white blossom, began to show in the glades between the oak and elm. The skies were full of swifts and swallows and the call of the cuckoo was already a thing of the past. Lost among the trees a woodpecker beat out its familiar staccato sound. Beowulf was the first to break the spell as he turned to his companion and questioned him.

"There is something I don't understand, Bjalki, why does my father send tribute to the king of the Danes when the Waegmundings are part of the Geat nation?"

Bjalki rode on for a while in thought before answering.

"I don't know if it is really my place to say, Beowulf, but you should know the reason for our visit and, in truth your father has asked me to mentor you so I will explain. "A long time ago, a *very* long time ago," he smiled to himself, "there was a feud between the Waegmundings and the Wuffingas. The Wuffings became over proud and began to take game from our lands near their border. While the elders debated what should be done and petitioned King Hrethel for a Geatish force to restore our lands, your father rode out with a troop of his companions and killed the Wuffing hunters. Just as they were returning home a party of Wuffing warriors arrived and challenged them over the killings, demanding wergild be paid for the hunters with additional compensation for encroaching on 'their' land. There was one particularly big bastard called Heatholaf there who, to give him his due, looked bloody frightening in his war glory. Words flew like arrows and tempers rose. Your father told this Heatholaf where he could... well let's just say that he disagreed... and the next thing Ecgtheow and Heatholaf are fighting each other between the two forces."

"You were there?" Beowulf gasped in surprise.

"I was, I was holding the horses and offering fervent prayers to the Allfather that your father prevailed. I was just a small lad out on my first trip with the warriors and I certainly picked a good one eh? Anyway your father and Heatholaf were pretty well matched and the fight swung both ways for a good time but eventually your father feinted and took his head clean off. I have been in a few fights since, but I have never seen a move like it. It seemed to happen quicker than the eye could follow, it was a beautiful stroke. The Wuffing shield wall was stunned for a moment and then a great cry went up and they charged our wall. They fought well but we outnumbered them and in the end the party was wiped out.

We left the bodies back on their side of the border and told one of their thralls who was watching some pigs nearby to carry the news back while we returned to our hall.

He chuckled at the memory. "As you can imagine this wasn't what the elders had had in mind and it caused quite stir. Ecgtheow and half a dozen of his most faithful companions were told to leave until a way could be found to avert a full scale war. He couldn't go to King Hrethel even though the king's sons supported him, because it would have complicated the negotiations, and he couldn't go to the Swedes because they are two faced weasel shit eaters as we all know, so he took ship and sought sanctuary at the court of the new king of the Danes, Hrothgar. Eventually tempers cooled and Hrothgar shipped a load of treasure over to the Wuffings to enable your father and his companions to return home."

Beowulf nodded but was still far from satisfied with the explanation. He probed again in his effort to understand the workings of the adult world he would one day inhabit.

"Why would the king of the Danes deplete his hoard in order to keep peace in a foreign country?"

"Ah, you have much to learn of the workings of lords and kings," replied Bjalki, "I can see why you have been entrusted to my wise care. Hrothgar had only recently taken the crown of the Danes and such a time is always tense as men jostle for favours and influence with the new king. The kings of surrounding people often test the mettle of the new king, border disputes, shows of strength that sort of thing, so it suited Hrothgar to spend a little treasure to obtain your father's oath. He knew that he was a friend of the Geat æthelings and with King Hrethel getting older he could see a time when a store of goodwill on his eastern borders could be useful. The Danes see the Jutes, Engles and Saxons as their main threat, even the Frisians and Franks for that matter, so treasure spent cultivating friends in what they see as their rear is money well spent to them." Bjalki paused as, rounding a bend Beowulf marvelled at his first sight of the sea. The morning sun reflected off its surface as it lay spread out before them the colour of hammered iron. Below them a settlement hugged the coast from which the smoke of dozens of fires rose lazily into the air. "Beowulf, I present the sea!" Bjalki announced with a flourish. "You can't drink it, it's bloody cold and it can be as dangerous as an argument with Thunor, Old Red Beard himself, but I promise you that you will grow to love it."

"Never been to sea!" exclaimed Hudda.

"Then I don't suppose that you know much about these then," he continued, pointing at the large ship resting on the foreshore.

"I'll give you a quick lesson before we get some food inside us, there are no idle hands on the *Griffon*, even noble hands, and if I tell you to go up forward and you shimmy up the mast we are both going to look stupid aren't we?"

Hudda strode off across the strand as Beowulf hurried along in his wake. Hudda had an honest, open face and the bluest eyes that Beowulf had ever seen set within a tanned and lined face which clearly told the story of a lifetime exposed to sun, wind and rain. Beowulf liked him immediately.

"This great big thing is called a ship," he began, "and this is the hull," he said slapping the sides of the ship with his huge tar stained hand. "That pointy end is the bow, which is the front end to landsmen, and the other pointy end is the stern. You can tell them apart because the stern has this great thing which is the steer board where I guide the ship when we are under way. The hull is made of overlapping planks of oak called strakes, attached to..." he grabbed the side of the hull and pointed inside, "these cross frames which give the hull its strength. Along the top edge of the hull is known as the wale and these curving pieces of wood along the top are row locks."

"Is that the sort of language to use in front of the young lord?" a voice carried from the strand.

Beowulf looked over to see a huge, grinning man, carrying supplies aboard.

"And that lump of gristle is called Tiny," Hudda added with a smile.

"Make sure that you listen carefully to anything he has to say and then do the opposite," he chuckled as he continued with his lightning paced tour.

"Despite what *some* so called sailors may think," he grinned, "row locks or thole pins if you prefer, take the oars, which are those long round pieces of wood with flattened ends that you can see tied to those frames called cross trees which you can see at the base of the mast. The mast of course is that great big thing pointing straight up out of the centre of the ship. The right hand side as you look forward is called the steerboard side because that is where the steer board is always fitted, while the other side is the larboard, and the flat planking which forms the floor of the ship is called the deck, and is often used by lazy sods like Ucca there to lie on while everybody else is readying the ship for sea."

Beowulf smiled at the prone figure of a sailor which was relaxing on a large knot of ropes.

"Just checking the caulking Hudda," Ucca replied with an obviously well practised look of innocence.

"Ah the caulking, that's moss and strips of hide mixed

with tar which we drive into any gaps we can find in an effort to make the vessel watertight. But that is a job that the son of an ealdorman will never need to do eh?" Hudda said with a friendly wink.

"Got all that? Great, let's go and eat. I'll send you down a nice fat rat Ucca!" he called back over his shoulder as they set off back up the beach to find Bjalki and the others.

After they had eaten the pack horses were brought through the settlement to the strand and the gifts for King Hrothgar loaded aboard. Ecgtheow's thralls had arrived by then and were busy loading the supplies of salted and wind dried fish which were part of the tribute collected yearly from the settlement by their lord. They would return to Ecgtheow's hall with the fish and return with the horses in good time to meet the returning warriors. Gulls swooped and cried noisily overhead as the party prepared to get under way.

Hudda gripped the stern post and cried outboard.

"Heave away!"

The small group of fishermen gathered at the stern of the ship lent their weight against the hull and manhandled the vessel into the water. Tossing the men a small silver coin, Hudda turned and took up position on the steering platform.

"Right, let's unship those oars and get under way," he cried to the ships company.

Slipping the oars into the thole pins the crew took up position and looked expectantly at Hudda for the signal to begin.

"Right, PULL!" he cried.

As one, the oars entered the water and with a grunt the crew pulled the first stroke. Slowly the ship gained headway as it fought to gain momentum. A bevy of swans glided silently out of their path to pass slowly down their larboard side as the oars rose and fell in unison, lines of foam from the disturbed water marking their progress.

"How long will it take us to reach Dane Land?" Beowulf asked.

"A good question, lord," Hudda replied.

"If we have a following wind we could be there late tomorrow evening, but it is more likely to be the following day if you ask me. Then again the wind could drop away and we will all be bending the oars for a time. That will add a day or two. Never mind it'll put some muscle on your bones, a warrior can never have too much of that, eh?"

For now Beowulf remained on the steering platform with Hudda. It was a mark of his rank, and to a lesser extent his youth, that he had been spared duty at the oars for now. He watched with interest as the waterway slowly widened as they drew steadily away from the settlement until it became an indistinct smear against the expanse of green and blue, before finally disappearing as they rounded a bend. Ahead, beyond the rocky outlines of the skerries which girded the coastline lay the mouth of the fjord and beyond that, the sea. The crew pulled rhythmically at their oars as the sun shone steadily out of a cloudless sky.

The sound of gulls thrashing the waters nearby drew Beowulf's attention to a string of fishing vessels as they made their way back up the estuary after their nights work. As he watched he saw one of the boats detach itself from its companions and head towards them. As the boat neared the *Griffon*, Beowulf could see one of the crew waving at them to attract their attention.

"Back oars boys!" Hudda called, "let's see what Tofi thinks is so important."

The *Griffon* slew to halt within a boat's length and waited for the smaller vessel to draw level.

Hudda called down as the fishing boat bobbed below the level of the shields fixed outboard the *Griffon*'s hull.

"Tofi, I trust you haven't stopped a ship full of warriors on their lord's business to discuss the fishing?" The fisherman jumped onto the wale of his boat and rested his elbows on the *Griffon*. He and Hudda were clearly old friends thought Beowulf. The man shook his head. "Not this time Hudda. At first light, as we passed Skraeling Island, I could see the beast heads of at least two draccas moored for the night beyond the point. They are obviously not Geat ships or they would not be mounting their beast heads in home waters. I was going to report it to you when we got in but seeing you now I think that it's too much of a coincidence. What do you think?"

"I think that you have done both us *and* your lord a great service today old friend. We carry gifts for Hrothgar, the Danish king, not to mention young Beowulf here, Ecgtheow's only son. Do you think that they saw you?"

Tofi shook his head. "I doubt it, the sun was just rising behind them so they were backlit and we were still in the gloom, plus the fact that we are much smaller. Unless their watchmen could see in the dark I would think that they were still lying in wait for their victim, you know, maybe something like a ship carrying a king's treasure and a young lord they could ransom. It's not something which happens along every day I'll grant you, but you never know their luck!" he exclaimed with a mischievous smile.

"And all they got was a gap toothed bundle of rags that smells worse than a month old herring!" Hudda chuckled. "Send up a bucket of your best catch, smoke the rest and take it up to my hall when you get in. I'll stand the ale when I return."

"Don't you always?" Tofi grinned.

The fish were hauled up by one of the crew and Tofi pushed his boat away.

"I'll sacrifice for your safe return, Hudda," He called as the vessels drew apart.

"You'd sacrifice your mother for the promise of free ale!" Hudda replied with a wave.

Tofi laughed and returned the wave as the boat made its way back to its companions.

"Bjalki, we need to speak," called Hudda.

Bjalki made his way to the steering platform and stood with the ship master. Beowulf made to move away to let them speak in private but a hand on his shoulder stopped him.

"Stay," Bjalki said. "You need to learn how decisions such as these are taken."

"I assume you heard all that," Hudda said. "What do you think?"

"How many draccas were there?" Bjalki replied tersely.

"What's a dracca?" Beowulf interrupted.

"A dracca is a ship with no other purpose than to carry warriors, Beowulf, and if it is not one of ours then what is it doing here and what does it want?" Bjalki replied.

"I think that Tofi's right. It seems too much of a coincidence that they turn up where they are, just as we are due through." He rubbed his hand thoughtfully through his beard. "My men and yours can take any ship's company on, on land or sea, maybe two, but we don't know exactly how many there are. Tofi said that he saw at least two, there could be more."

"I can take us out to sea. With luck we should make the island of Anholt before dark. The inhabitants recognise King Hrothgar as their lord so we should be welcome there. If not we can lay to for the night. It's only a few hours this time of year and with any luck the moon will give us enough light to make a safe headway, save us half a day that way."

"I agree," said Bjalki. "We are not tasked with hunting vikings but delivering our cargo safely, if they start to cause trouble in the area King Hrethel will deal with them."

Bjalki returned to his bench and at Hudda's command the oarsmen resumed their labours. Soon the *Griffon* cleared the headland which marked the head of the estuary and entered the waters of the Kattegat. Once clear of the shelter of the land a steady breeze came from the north west, sending a fine spray flying from the tops of the darkening waves.

"Ship oars, boys," Hudda called. "Let's get that sail up and make some decent headway, the quicker we get there the quicker we eat."

The crew quickly unshipped their oars and lashed them to the cross trees which Hudda had pointed out to Beowulf on the strand.

"Get that yard up, before we lose headway boys," Hudda called.

"That's the long piece of pine with the sail attached," he explained to Beowulf with a friendly pat on the shoulder. "I forgot that one earlier!"

Within moments the yard had been swung out and hoisted to the top of the mast. Already unleashed by the crew, the sail unfurled with a clap and was sheeted home. Immediately the wind filled the sail with a crack and the *Griffon* leapt forward, the timbers of the hull creaking and groaning under the strain. Beowulf watched as the coastline diminished on the horizon until it was little more than a smear of grey and green before becoming completely lost from sight. He looked on in wonder as shearwaters darted to and fro inches from the tops of the waves.

"Welcome to my World, Beowulf," Hudda murmured.

"Come up and try a spell at the steer board and feel the power of Aegir."

Aegir was the god who, together with his wife Ran, was responsible for both the good and destructive forces of the sea.

"Grip the tiller with me and just feel the power flow through you."

To his surprise Beowulf found that he could not move the steer board at all without Hudda's help.

"Not as easy as it looks is it?" Hudda said with a smile. "You wait until you get some muscle on those arms and shoulders and you will love it as much as me, this is the feeling of true freedom," he smiled.

The hours passed by swiftly as the *Griffon* sped south under a freshening wind, and by early evening land again came into view ahead. Bjalki came up to the steering platform.

"How do you think we should play this one, Hudda? Is there a port or shall we look to beach ourselves?"

"There is a long sandy coast all around the island so we can stop there if you think it would be better." Hudda responded.

Frowning, Bjalki looked out to sea as he pondered his decision. Turning back he replied.

"Unless you think that we might need any extra warriors during the night, I would rather stay away from the town. They all smell of shit and fish, we'll be much better off alone."

"If it is those draccas you are thinking about, even if they eventually guessed our heading they would be miles away, we made good time today. I doubt they could be here before tomorrow morning and we would be away by then."

"That's good enough for me," Bjalki smiled. "Find us a

28

nice stretch of beach, as far away from the settlement as you can. We don't want visits from overenthusiastic reeves in the night come to collect their taxes do we."

"We are a bit early in the day really." Hudda replied, holding up his hand and spreading his fingers as he measured the distance between the sun and the horizon. "I'll stand off to the east for a bit and make doubly sure that we weren't followed. That will give any watchers on shore time to get home to their ale as well."

Hudda pushed on the tiller and guided the *Griffon* eastwards, before coming about and trending west again.

"Ratty, up you go and have a good look around," he called.

Immediately a short, wiry member of the crew left his companions and scurried up the mast.

"We call him Ratty because he can climb anything as fast as Ratatosk." Hudda smiled to Beowulf.

Ratatosk was the name of the squirrel which ran up and down the World ash tree Erminsul, a good name, Beowulf thought with a smile. There was still no sign of any other ships as the sun finally settled in the West and Hudda brought the *Griffon* expertly to land.

"Make a camp in the dunes," Bjalki ordered. "We don't want our fire to be seen."

While some members of Hudda's crew collected driftwood for the fire, others brought ashore barrels of salted beef and ale for the evening meal.

"Get the food on, Tiny," Hudda called as the big man strode up the beach, a barrel held on each shoulder. "And leave some for us this time. Remember we have important guests!" Hudda glanced down at Beowulf. "He's a fine cook is Tiny but we do tend to lose a lot of the meat during cooking as he 'tests' to see whether it is done," he grinned.

Soon the smell of roasting meat was added to the smells of the beach as Ecgtheow's hearth warriors and Hudda's crew began to slake their thirsts on the first of the evening's ale. It had been a long day but they had made good time and spirits were high. Bjalki came over to Beowulf as he ate with the warriors.

"I want you to stand a watch tonight, Beowulf," he said. "Orme here will give you a shake when it is time. I want you to stay with him and stay alert, we are in a foreign land without permission and I don't want any surprises, nasty or otherwise."

Orme flashed Beowulf a friendly smile. "Wrap up well, it can get cold and windy near the sea at night, lord."

Beowulf nodded, he was already tired from the day so he decided to leave the men to their ale. Clearing a space of stones, sticks and the shell of a long dead crab, he wound himself tightly in his cloak and was soon asleep.

"BEOWULF, IT'S TIME."

A hand shook him awake after what seemed like no time at all. He pulled the cloak from his face and found himself looking up at Orme.

"Let's go."

Stretching, Beowulf rose and followed him out, past the guttering flames of the fire and into the blackness of the night.

"Griffon," Orme called softly as they approached one of the dunes with a distinctive tuft of grass marking its crest.

"Ran."

The two made their way stealthily towards the figure they could just make out to the right of the dune.

"You took your time!" the figure hissed as they reached it.

"Would I let you down? I saved you a nice warm patch of sand," Orme chuckled.

Beowulf could sense the trust and friendship which had developed over many years between the two warriors, even though it was too dark to see their faces.

"Look after him, Beowulf," the shadowy figure whispered as he made his way back toward the camp. "He's not as young as he used to be!"

Beowulf followed Orme as he made his way to the position just vacated by the previous warrior.

"Why don't we stand up on the dune, we could see much further up there?" Beowulf asked innocently.

"Shhh, keep your voice down!" Orme snapped.

Beowulf was taken aback. He had never been spoken to in that tone by a man of lower rank before.

"Sorry, lord, I didn't mean to speak so sharply to you," Orme whispered apologetically.

"Sound carries for miles on a still night like this one and you must understand that we should not be here. At the very least we should have gone to the port and announced our presence and no doubt paid the reeve duty for permission to stay on their land."

They stood in silence for some time, staring out into the blackness before a chastened Beowulf spoke again.

"I am sorry, Orme. Would you teach me how to stand guard correctly?"

"Of course, lord, that is why you are here." Orme replied.

Beowulf could sense affection in the big warrior's voice and felt grateful that he had not ruined the evening by his inexperienced clumsiness.

"The first thing to remember on a night like this one with such a big, bright, moon is never to look directly at it.

Remember you are not here to look at the pretty sky but to keep your sleeping companions from having their throats cut. Keep your eyes in the shadows at all times and you will be surprised at the things you will see once they get used to the gloom."

Beowulf could not help but flick a quick glance up at the moon. It hung, full and bright, to the South, its wan light painting the landscape in hues of black and grey.

"If you ever think that you see something out there try not to look directly at it," Orme continued in a whisper. "If you look off to one side you will find that you can see the object clearer, give it a try."

Beowulf picked a small indistinct bush some way off, almost completely hidden in the shadows. He looked slightly to the right of it and concentrated on his peripheral vision. To his astonishment he found that Orme was right, he *could* see it far better.

"That's incredible, Orme. I can see it much clearer than before!"

"Just one of my little tricks," Orme replied with obvious pride.

"Can you think why we might be down here in the shadows and not further up like you suggested earlier?"

He didn't need time to think of the answer, it was so obvious that he could feel his cheeks redden in embarrassment. He was thankful that the darkness would hide his discomfort.

"We could see better, but anyone out there could also see us," he murmured.

"Of course," Orme replied warmly. "There's no point in being able to see further if they see you first. They will either sneak up on you or go for help, neither of which tend to have particularly healthy outcomes for lone guards. The key to guard duty is concentration, Beowulf. Find a dark spot with a good field of view and stay as still as you can there. If you don't move you will be practically invisible to someone standing only feet away. It can save your life and the lives of your friends. Protect your night eyes by never looking at lights of any kind and listen. You would be surprised at how much noise a warrior will make as he moves, even if he is trying to be quiet. If he is unaware you are here a practised ear will be able to hear even a lone warrior at a surprisingly great distance. Right what do you do?"

"Concentrate. Stay still and use your eyes and ears." Beowulf could just make out Orme's smile in the darkness. "You've got it, lord, now let's practice what we have learnt shall we?"

Beowulf and Orme stood guard until the pale light of the pre dawn began to creep, almost imperceptibly, into the eastern sky. As the full light of dawn burst onto the eastern horizon they heard a slight noise from their rear. Orme motioned for Beowulf to withdraw into the heart of the shadows. Softly, a voice called the password for the day.

"Griffon."

Orme put his finger to his lips and winked at Beowulf. Beowulf understood and remained frozen in the shadows.

A figure crept past them, spear at the ready, obviously beginning to grow anxious at their apparent absence. Orme waited until the figure had passed them and then, slipping from the shadows, he tapped the man smartly on the head. Bjalki whirled around, his spear poised to defend himself, only to be confronted by the grinning figure of Orme.

"You silly bastard, what do you think that you are doing! Didn't you hear the password?" he spat.

"Sorry Bjalki," Orme sniggered. "I was just demonstrating to Beowulf how easy it is to fool even the greatest of warriors if you keep quiet and still in the shadows."

"You are lucky that I didn't run you through, you oaf! You wouldn't have got any breakfast then would you?"

Orme's face lit up at the mention of the word, 'breakfast'.

"Get yourself back to the camp and get some hot food. We will be away soon. They are already loading the ship. I will cover for you here until we leave. Off you go you two."

Orme and Beowulf picked their way through the dunes, back to the camp. As promised, Bjalki had organised two bowls of porridge for them. As he sat there next to Orme, Beowulf reflected on his first experience of guard duty. Despite the cold and discomfort he had to admit to himself that he had enjoyed it immensely. He had experienced the unspoken comradeship of the warrior band for the first time and had enjoyed being in a position of trust. He had even enjoyed the experience of spending a night in the open. For the first time ever he had stood and observed the world outside the hall fires and had found that it was not the realm of trolls and werewolves after all.

"Come on, time to go boys!" Ucca called as he raced past. "You had better get on board quick or we will leave without you. I am just going to get Bjalki and we will be gone!"

Spooning the last of his porridge into his mouth, Beowulf rose and trotted to the *Griffon*.

"Sail, to larboard!" Ratty called down from the masthead. "No wait, two...three sail running South!"

"Keep your eyes on them Ratty, I want to know all about them," Hudda called up.

Bjalki made his way back to the ship master and shot him a look of concern. "Trouble?"

"It could be, we'll know soon enough," he replied. "If they get any closer Ratty will be able to see the hulls of the ships and we will know whether they are traders or draccas. Sharpest eyes I've ever known that boy, I'll edge over to steer board a bit, with any luck they haven't spotted us yet."

"They've turned towards us!" Ratty cried from above. "I think that I can make out dragon heads."

"There's your answer, looks like our friends from yesterday *were* after us after all."

"Will they catch us?" said Beowulf.

"It depends on the wind, lord," Hudda replied. "If it blows as steady as it has done so far we should outrun them easily but if it drops off and we have to take to the oars then they are bigger than us, and bigger means more oars and more oars means they will be up on us in no time. Unfortunately those oars will be manned by warriors who appear to want us dead, so best we trust that Corpse Gulper keeps flapping those wings."

Seeing Beowulf's questioning look Bjalki explained. "Corpse Gulper is the giant eagle which flaps its wings and creates the wind. You haven't done anything to upset eagles I trust, lord?" He smiled before flicking a look over at Hudda. "We'll get ready just in case," he added grimly and called down the deck to his men. "If this wind drops we'll have work to do boys so let's get ready to dance!"

Making their way to their sea chests the warriors took out and unrolled their mail shirts, helping one another as they wriggled into the tight fitting garments. Taking out their sharpening stones they ran them lovingly along the length of the blades restoring the keenness to their cutting edge. Beowulf marvelled at the change in the warriors' demeanour.

In an instant they had gone from a group of relaxed, joking, friends out on a trip to a group of serious, highly skilled killers.

For almost two hours Corpse Gulper beat its wings and a steady wind came down from the North driving the *Griffon* ahead of it to safety. Suddenly a call came from above.

"Land ahead, Hudda!"

"Are we there already?" Bjalki turned and asked Hudda in surprise.

"No, that will be Hesselo," he replied. "We still have about another twenty miles or so to go before we reach Dane Land, about another hour if this wind keeps up."

The draccas were gaining on the *Griffon*, their sails were now clearly visible to those on deck, but they were entering Dane controlled waters now and they must have been on the point of abandoning the chase when Corpse Gulper decided it was time to take a rest.

"Unship oars," Hudda called as soon as the wind began to drop and the vessel began to lose way, "and drop that spar, we need all the speed we can get. Ratty come down and help, we can all see them now."

Looking back Beowulf could see the same process being repeated on the chasing draccas, the sunlight glinting on their oars as they slid out proud of their hulls. He watched as they began to stroke the waves, reminding him of a trio of swans as they beat their way laboriously into the air.

"Keep the strokes steady, lads," Bjalki called out, "keep some strength for the fight."

"If the gods are with us it may not come to that," Hudda murmured, leaning on the tiller and guiding the *Griffon* towards the island of Hesselo.

"Is it inhabited?" Bjalki asked.

"Only by a few Danes posted there to keep a look out and light a beacon," Hudda replied.

"We can't fight them on land without help," Bjalki said, "there are too many of them, they will outflank our shield wall and roll us up in no time."

"I know," Hudda replied, "and if we fight them at sea they will double up on us and still have a ship spare to come in over our stern. But if I can pull off what I have in mind, there won't be a fight at all."

Hudda steered the *Griffon* straight for a rocky beach at the western end of the island.

"What are the draccas doing Beowulf? You'll have to be my eyes for now."

Beowulf grasped the stern post and peered aft.

"The smaller two are bearing off to the South. It looks as though they are going to pass to the other side of the island. The larger one is still following us. It looks as though they are trying to catch us in a giant net."

"Beautiful!" Hudda exclaimed. "They are not half as clever as they think they are. It's a shame they didn't all follow us but this should still work. Ratty, get back up the mast, Ucca up in the prow, quick as you can boys. Let's show these vikings how real seamen can handle a ship. Oarsmen, when I call out 'Now', I want you to put your backs into it, we need a short burst of speed. Tiny, distribute the cargo evenly around the ship as quick as you can." Hudda called ahead to the newly positioned lookouts. "Ratty and Ucca, there is a sand bank up ahead like a great tail coming off the Island leading out to two smaller Islands off to steer board, see it?"

"I can see it," Ratty called down.

"I can see where the water is disturbed as it flows over it," Ucca called back.

"Just off the rocks there is a narrow channel which is a bit deeper than the rest, I am heading for that. If I look to be missing it sing out you two."

"Right then." Hudda inhaled as the men manning the oars waited for his order.

"*NOW!*"

With a collective grunt the oarsmen redoubled their efforts and the *Griffon* shot forward. Beowulf glanced back at the following dracca.

"They are quickening their pace to match us," he reported to Hudda.

"Good, we don't want them thinking too deeply at the moment," he replied.

Beowulf watched as Hudda concentrated on the way ahead, his eyes darting from left to right and back again as he aimed the *Griffon* for the small tell-tale patch of calm which marked the narrow channel of deeper water.

"Looking good, Hudda!" Ratty called down.

"Spot on!" Ucca called from the prow as the *Griffon* bore down on the gap.

"Right oarsmen when I call out 'now', keep your oars moving but don't let them bite the water until we get through the gap."

"We are there!" Ucca called out from the bow.

"Right, *NOW!*"

The oarsmen changed their strokes from deep to shallow as the *Griffon* shot through the channel.

"Right, as you were, let's put some distance between us and the other ships before they can double the island,"

Pulling the tiller to his chest, he guided the *Griffon* due south, towards the safety of Danish waters. Looking back, Beowulf, Hudda and Bjalki saw the dragon headed prow of the dracca approach the tip of Hesselo.

"Come on… come on," Hudda murmured as he watched the ship approach the shallows.

Suddenly the dracca shuddered as its keel grounded firmly on the sandbank, bringing it to a complete stop. They just had the added satisfaction of seeing the lookout falling from the top of the mast before they passed beyond the promontory and the ship was lost from view.

"Serves him right," Hudda laughed. "He should have looked where he was going. If he had been my lookout, I would have thrown him overboard too!"

Within the hour the wind returned and the crew were able to ship their oars as the sail was hoisted again. The men fell to stretching and flexing weary shoulder and back muscles as Tiny moved amongst them with ale, bread and cheese. The smaller ships had dropped too far behind after their detour around Hesselo and had given up the chase entirely when they had found that their leader had not reappeared. Hudda, Bjalki and Beowulf gathered together on the steering platform as the *Griffon* entered the safety of Danish controlled waters.

"If I have another son I am going to call him Hudda!" Bjalki exclaimed clapping the big ship master on the shoulder.

"If I have another son, I am going to call him Hesselo," Hudda joked, laughing aloud.

A cry carried down to them from above and they all peered upwards.

"Land ahead!"

"For the gods' sake come down and have some ale, Ratty," Hudda called, shaking his head.

"I forgot you were up there!"

3

Beowulf stood at the prow as the *Griffon* approached the island of Sjaelland. The name meant the Spirit Land and it was the heart of the kingdom of the Danes. A fine spray was thrown into the air around him as the bows rose and fell in the swell, covering his clothes and hair in a delicate mist of water. As they neared the entrance to the bay, now clearly visible, the island seemed to reach out on either side of them. Beowulf had a vision of the tiny *Griffon* being slowly swallowed by an enormous whale as the land on either side seemed to shepherd them inexorably down to the gap in the cliffs which marked the entrance to the sound.

He watched as a small vessel detached itself from the point, snaking towards them as the ship master tacked against the force of the wind. Hudda ordered the sails lowered and stowed, slowing the *Griffon* to a halt as the Danish ship drew level. Beowulf picked his way aft and joined Hudda and Bjalki on the steering platform. Although only seven winters old he was still nominally the leader of the embassy to the Danish king by virtue of his birth. With practised strokes the Danish crew brought their craft alongside the wallowing hull of the Waegmunding ship. A tall Dane hailed them from the steering platform as it came up.

"Welcome to Dane Land, what is your business?"

"I will answer for us." Beowulf instructed as Bjalki sucked in a breath to call a reply.

"My name is Beowulf. I am the son of the Waegmunding ealdorman, Ecgtheow. I have been entrusted by my lord to deliver fine gifts to King Hrothgar as a mark of his high regard, and as a token of his continuing friendship."

"You are welcome Beowulf, as are your companions." The reeve replied. "I know of your father and I know of the high esteem in which my lord, King Hrothgar, holds him. If you will allow me to board your vessel I will guide you to a berth and arrange for your onward passage."

Beowulf watched as the Danish ship master leaned into the steer board and brought his ship alongside for the brief moment needed to enable the Danish reeve to jump deftly aboard.

"Once more, I welcome you to Dane Land!" he smiled. "My name is Harald. I am the reeve of this port."

The man before them was dressed quite plainly for a man of his importance, with the higher quality materials used for his clothing being the only indication of his superior status. He had a friendly, engaging, manner which, added to his weather worn features, told of a life lived around work and the sea. Beowulf could tell that both Hudda and Bjalki had taken an immediate liking to the man. It was obvious why he had been chosen for his role.

"Did you have a good trip?" Harald was asking. Hudda smiled.

"I have not enjoyed myself so much for a long time, Harald. Not for a long time."

BEOWULF WAS AMAZED to see the size of the bay which opened up before them. From seaward the harbour looked small, but once the *Griffon* passed through the entrance the bay opened up before them on either side into a vast sheltered anchorage stretching off into the distance. Hundreds of ships and boats of all types and sizes bobbed gently at anchor. Dozens of boats moved about the bay, their oars rising and falling rhythmically as they went about their errands. From high above came the cries of gulls, while smoke rose lazily into the warm summer air from the many settlements which lined the shore.

The size and might of the Danish kingdom were obvious to any foreigner in this place and Beowulf could not fail to be impressed. To his surprise Harald indicated that Hudda should take the *Griffon* into a tributary which entered the bay to their left. Passing through a small channel marked by woven buoys, Hudda brought the *Griffon* into a further inner harbour before swinging the ship south.

"Take your ship down to Hroars Kilde," Harald said to Hudda. "I will arrange for a hall to be provided for your men tonight where they can rest and prepare themselves."

"Just another hour's rowing and you will be up to your eyes in Danish hospitality," Hudda called to a shipload of relaxed, smiling faces.

Hroars Kilde fjord consisted of a number of small bays, each one separated from the next by choke points where the land on both sides came closely together. Added to the many islands, the fjord would present a formidable obstacle to any attacking force thought Beowulf.

"Has the harbour ever been attacked, Harald?" Beowulf asked the Dane.

"Attacked, yes, but never carried," the ship reeve replied. "Only a fool would risk his ships in such a fine defensive position." The Dane smiled at him. "Why, are you thinking of attacking us Beowulf?"

"Of course," he replied. "My father told me to always observe how best I should attack or defend land which is unfamiliar to me."

Harald threw back his head and laughed.

"That is why your father is a great lord and warrior, Beowulf, and he gives you wise council. You can never be over prepared for any event which may befall you."

"IF YOU WILL WAIT with the ship I will arrange your accommodation," Harald called out as he leapt onto the landing bay.

The *Griffon* was secured to stout posts at stem and stern as Harold spoke with another Dane. From the quality of his clothing he was obviously a man of some importance in the settlement.

"The Port Reeve, come to fix us up himself. Now that's what I call hospitality!" Ucca declared with a smirk.

"They are trying to find a place downwind, for your sorry arse!" Tiny called out to jeers from the rest of the crew. Beowulf smiled as the men began to relax.

A lot had happened since they had awoken on Anholt that morning. The long chase and then what seemed like the inevitability of fighting, Beowulf realised, had been the most exciting events to have happened to him in his life so far, even more than the fight with the eagle. He recognised for the first time why the wolf and bear, fierce though they were, were forced to eke out their lives in woods and desolate places. Man really was the most dangerous of the gods' crea-

43

tures. One thing had puzzled him though. When it seemed that the vikings must overhaul the *Griffon*, the charm which he hung around his neck had felt almost too hot to bear against his skin, almost as if it were warning him of danger. He had had the charm made from the piece of Hrani's staff which he had been given that night after he had taken the chicks. Encased in silver, the charm never left his person, and Beowulf was convinced of its magical properties. He rubbed it between his thumb and forefinger absent-mindedly as he thought. Although it was of no value, he would not be parted with it for anything.

The man approached them, smiling.

"Welcome, my name is Sweyn. I have the honour to serve my lord, King Hrothgar as his reeve for the port of Hroars Kilde."

"My name is Beowulf Ecgtheowson," Beowulf replied. "I am charged by my father with the pleasurable duty to deliver to his friend, King Hrothgar, these gifts as a sign of his respect and affection."

Flanked by Hudda and Bjalki, Beowulf hoped that he had discharged his duty with a confidence which did not yet come naturally to him.

"I will arrange for your belongings to be transported to the hall, it is only a short distance, and a guard will be placed on your ship," Sweyn added helpfully.

SWEYN RETURNED to the hall late the following afternoon. Fully refreshed by the hospitality offered by the Danes the previous evening the warriors had spent the morning preparing for the meeting with King Hrothgar. Mail shirts had been polished with sand until they shone, leather oiled, weapons honed. Each warrior wore a highly polished helm. Intricately chased dragons of gleaming silver straddled the crests. Boars guarded the eyes, while interlaced serpents wove their intricate patterns on cheek pieces. Each warrior had been supplied with a blue cloak by Ecgtheow while Beowulf was to wear a red cloak on which eagles, stitched with gold thread, soared and dove. At each man's neck a warrior ring shone gold.

Horses had been provided by the Danes while a small cart awaited the gifts. Mounting the steeds, the Waegmundings followed Sweyn along the road which led away from the hall and further into Hrothgar's realm. The crowds moved respectfully aside at their approach, their eyes downcast. Above, swifts and swallows tail chased each other through the hazy blue skies of full summer. Beowulf rode abreast of Sweyn as the troop journeyed.

"We have only a short distance to travel until we reach the hall of the father of the Shieldings." Sweyn said cheerfully. "Is this your first journey to our land, Beowulf?"

"It is," Beowulf replied. "You are a populous race."

Sweyn laughed.

"It can seem like that sometimes but this is good land and it can support many farmers. Many farmers can feed many people who all pay taxes, and taxes make a kingdom strong Beowulf. Taxes pay for warriors and warriors keep the people safe. It is a simple but effective system don't you think?"

For the first time Beowulf realised that the forests and lakes of his homeland were poor by comparison. When he became ealdorman he would find better land he decided. Cresting a slight rise a large settlement came into view huddled beneath its mantle of wood smoke.

"Hleidra," Sweyn announced proudly.

THE HALL of the king sat atop a steep hill which arose abruptly from the gently undulating land which surrounded it. Passing through the gateway in the surrounding palisade, Beowulf and his companions were shown to a smaller hall which lay off to the right.

"You will await your audience with the king here, Beowulf," Sweyn smiled. "Thralls will of course be at your disposal but if you have any further desires please let Voislav here know and he will attend to them."

The slaves appeared, leading their horses away to the stables as Sweyn made his way to the main hall to report their arrival. A stocky, dark haired thrall approached them and bowed low.

"Welcome to Hleidra, lord."

Voislav indicated that the troop should enter the hall. The hall was a replica of the one in which they had spent the previous night, benches and tables lined the side walls, while a low fire smouldered in the central hearth. Motes of dust swirled in the shafts of light which entered the hall from the open shutters at the far end.

"I have kept the fire low on account of the hot weather," Voislav added, "but I can make it up if you would rather food be cooked in your presence?"

"That will not be necessary Voislav, I think that if the king wishes us harm we are already in his power," Beowulf replied.

The men removed their cloaks and weapons and sat at the benches while ale, mead and food were brought in for them. Beowulf watched the thrall with interest. He had clearly not been born into the lowly position in which he now found himself.

"Join us, Voislav," Beowulf said. "We would like a tale to pass the time while we wait and you look like you have a tale to tell."

Although the steward was a thrall he possessed an aura of self confidence which was unusual in those of low birth. Darker than the Waegmundings in both hair colour and skin tone and of a shorter height, Voislav was heavily muscled and his forearms bore the tell-tale scars typical of a warrior. Wary at first that he was being mocked, Voislav quickly relaxed as he realised that the warriors were genuinely interested in sharing their food and ale with him and hearing his tale, if not as equals, at least with respect.

"It is true that I was not born to the life of a thrall," Voislav began. "I too was a warrior of my people."

"Who were your people?" asked Bjalki.

Orme joined in the questioning. "Aye, you look like you have travelled some distance to end up here Voislav, what is your story?"

Voislav explained how he had been a warrior of the Obrzanie, a part of the Polans tribe which lived in the great forest to the East. He had been part of a peace emissary sent by their king to the neighbouring Pomorzanie but they had been betrayed. Overcome one night in their hall, they had little chance to defend themselves and had been sold to slavery in the West.

"My life here is not so bad," he added. "I have food and responsibilities, but I still pray daily to Perun, god of Thunder, that I will regain my freedom when the fates decide."

THE REEVE RETURNED as the sun dipped towards the western horizon in a splash of scarlet. Gathering up their arms and gifts, the Waegmundings followed Sweyn up the path to the hall of King Hrothgar. As was the custom everywhere in the north, they deposited their weapons with a retainer at the entrance to the hall. Ale, boastful warriors and sharp steel were a dangerous mix, but luckily one of the ingredients was relatively easy to control. Beowulf entered the hall, followed by Bjalki, and then the other Waegmunding warriors in columns two abreast. He was conscious of hundreds of pairs of eyes following his progress up the length of the hall to where King Hrothgar sat on a raised dais at the far end. As he approached, Beowulf studied the first king that he had met. Hrothgar sat on a golden chair raised above the level of his surroundings. He wore a white tunic and breeches, edged in red and gold, while a matching cloak hung about his upper body, secured by a massive gold brooch. To emphasise his authority Hrothgar wore a richly jewelled sword suspended from a baldric, while a matching seax hung from an ornate golden belt. Flanking the king stood two of the largest warriors that Beowulf had ever seen, resplendent in shining mail shirts and helms, each one fully armed with swords and spears, their gaze fixed directly on him.

Beowulf came to a halt twenty paces before the king as custom dictated and fell to one knee.

"Rise up, Beowulf," Hrothgar commanded. "It is with great pleasure that I welcome you to the home of the Danish folk."

"I have journeyed to your land at the request of my father, Ecgtheow, tasked to deliver these gifts humbly to you as a mark of my father's respect and gratitude for the friendship you have always shown to him and the Waegmundings. He hopes that you will receive these unworthy tokens of his esteem and bestow your favour on his only son."

The gifts were brought forward and laid at the feet of Hrothgar.

"I am happy to accept these gifts on behalf of the Shield-ings and thank you for them. In return I hope that you will accept these trinkets in return."

Rising, the king approached the assembled warriors. Hrothgar removed the Seax from his belt and handed it to Beowulf.

"Receive this gift with my affection, Beowulf, along with my friendship. You do your office well and it gladdens my heart to see my friend Ecgtheow has been favoured by the gods with such a son."

Hrothgar motioned to a retainer and further gifts were bestowed on Bjalki and the other Waegmundings before they were shown to a place of honour near the top table, to the accompaniment of loud cries and the banging of tables by the assembled Danish warriors.

"Well done, Beowulf," Bjalki said happily as they took their places at the benches. "Now bring on the ale!"

His official duties completed Beowulf had the opportunity to study his surroundings. The hall was by far the largest building that he had ever been inside. Benches lined the walls in the usual fashion but the roof of the hall towered above them, becoming lost in the smoke which collected from the many cooking fires which snaked their way along its centre. Every available wall space was covered by richly embroi-dered hangings, each one depicting an episode of the history of the Danish folk, the Shieldings, or a tale of the gods. Behind the king stood Hrothgar's personal flag, a white hart on a red background, its worn condition testament to the many successful campaigns waged by the king. Suddenly the warriors at the far end of the hall, nearest the doors, rose to their feet, as a tall figure entered the hall attended by maid servants.

"That must be Wealhtheow, Hrothgar's Cwen," Bjalki muttered quietly as they rose with the others.

Smiling, Wealhtheow calmly walked the length of the hall and took her seat at the king's side. Once she had taken her place, the Shielding warriors sat and resumed their talk. Serving women moved amongst them bearing great platters of pork and beef cut from the spitted animals turning slowly over the hearth. Others were tasked with ensuring that the ale flowed freely or freshly baked bread was to hand. Beowulf saw the Cwen look their way and lean over to the king, obviously enquiring their identity, and was gratified to see the Cwen smile and incline her head to him. Once the meal was completed a skald took his place in the centre of the hall.

"FRESWÆL!" he cried, *"FRESWÆL!"*

The Danes in the hall stopped their conversations and, turning to the Skald, again cried and beat the tables in appreciation. Orme leant across.

"They like this one," he smiled, "Frisian Slaughter, sounds good!"

The tale told of a young Danish noble called Hnaef who was visiting his sister Hildeburgh in Frisland where she was married to the Frisian king, Finn. Unfortunately both Danes and Frisians contained rival parties of Jutes within their numbers which led to bloodshed, including the death of Hnaef. Although King Finn tried to recompense the Danes for their losses, the feud continued under the leadership of a warrior named Hengest, and the Danish party killed Finn and took Hildeburgh back to Denmark. More table banging accompanied the end of the tale.

"That was complicated, good though!" Orme called over with a beery grin.

. . .

As THE EVENING wore on and the entertainment became bawdier Beowulf saw that Wealtheow had left her place at the king's side and was moving amongst the warriors, noting the pride in the eyes of those whom the Cwen chose to honour by her attention, and the obvious affection in which she was held by those in the hall.

She smiled as she reached his table. "Welcome to the land of the Shieldings Beowulf."

"The honour is mine, Lady." Beowulf replied, inclining his head in respect.

"The king wishes to ride with you tomorrow morning. He would like to get to know his old friend's son better before he returns to the land of the Waegmundings."

"I would like that very much," Beowulf replied happily.

The Cwen leaned forward and lowered her voice. "I suggest that you are ready at dawn, Beowulf. The king does like to spring nasty surprises on people."

"You ARE READY, EXCELLENT!" Hrothgar exclaimed from horseback.

"I can't abide a man who wastes half his life in bed."

The sun had barely risen above the eastern hills, casting long shadows on the party as they waited for the thralls to bring out the horses for Beowulf and Bjalki. The horses arrived and the pair mounted and joined the king and his companions. Forewarned by Wealtheow, they had drunk moderately the night before and had risen before dawn to prepare for the king's arrival. Voislav had appeared out of the dark to make sure that they were adequately fed and had no other needs. Beowulf was amused to see that the Cwen had obviously not warned all of the others of the early start, several of whom looked as though they had come straight from the hall.

"Right, we're off!" Hrothgar suddenly cried.

Digging in his heels he cantered through the gatehouse and along the road which led up to the heath. Scattering any early risers before them, the group thundered after the king. Patches of early morning mist still clung on in the hollows and small valleys as the riders made their way across a heath-land dotted with yellow broom. Pipits and woodlarks rose into the air as they passed and swallows swooped low, plucking insects from the warm morning air. High above a hawk hung motionless in the still air, searching the ground below for mice and voles. It promised to be a glorious summer day.

"Beowulf, join me," Hrothgar called back over his shoulder as the pace slowed and the riders fanned out into a widely spaced skirmish line.

"What do we hunt, lord?" Beowulf asked as he drew alongside.

"Ah, nought but mountain mist today, but at least we get a good ride in the morning sun out of it. I have seen enough of the inside of smoky halls for a while. Some of the country folk have been complaining to their thegns that they have seen two trolls up on the heath. They tell me, and I come up to hunt them down if I can find them. It's what kings, ealdormen and thegns do Beowulf, protect their people, remember that."

"I will lord," he replied as the king took a long pull of ale. He belched and turned to the boy.

"How is Ecgtheow?"

"In good health, lord." Beowulf answered proudly.

"And your mother?"

"Very well, lord. Did you know them both?"

"I know your father very well, as you know. He lived with us for two years. We fought together in more than one shield wall, that's an experience which forms a special bond between men. Once we were in a hard fight with the Hetware, outnumbered as usual in those days," he recalled with a smile, "and a Hetware warrior managed to hook an axe over the top of my shield and pull it down. I could see the joy in the eyes of the warrior opposite me as he began to thrust his seax at my face. He knew I was dead meat and he could already hear the skalds singing his praises in the hall as the killer of Hrothgar, that shielding bastard!" he laughed.

"But the blow never came. A sword came over my right shoulder and split his head like a rotten apple. I recognised the blade. No doubt you will wear it one day. Your father saved my life Beowulf and still he thinks that he owes me gifts for a few years food and shelter!" Hrothgar smiled as he turned his gaze on Beowulf. "The truth is that I was able to turn the situation which your father created with the Wuffings to my advantage. Well," he chuckled, "to both of our advantages actually. It's what the Romans and Greeks call politics Beowulf. We call it being canny up here in the North, but it amounts to the same thing. Every situation can be turned to your advantage if you think long enough about it. Take the fight between your father's warriors and the Wuffings for example. He acted properly of course, another nation starts to encroach on your land so you go and kill them. It's the way the world works. If the Geats had moved quickly to support your father he wouldn't have had to seek a refuge with us, but they were wary of upsetting the Swedes so they hesitated. The Wuffings have always been close to the Swedes and your grandfather, King Hrethel, didn't fancy a Swedish army appearing in his lands while he was down south with his forces supporting the Waegmundings. The Swedes are a powerful nation, always on the lookout for an opportunity to expand their territory, so it suits us here in Dane land to have the Waegmundings and the Wuffings between us and them." Hrothgar shifted in the saddle as they crested a small rise.

"We, on the other hand," he continued. "We see our old enemies the Engles and Jutes leaving their lands, good lands, and moving south into Britannia. We want those lands to become part of greater Dane land but we have to move fast because further south, the Saxons and the Frisians are also moving into Britannia and the Salian Franks are expanding into their lands from the South. I want the new border between the Frankish empire and greater Dane land to be as far south as possible, so, in order to stabilise my rear what do I do? I arrange for a shipload of treasure to be paid as compensation to the Wuffings, far greater than the value of their loss. They are flattered and agree to marry their princess, the lovely Wealhtheow, to me to seal the deal. This gives me not only a wise and beautiful new Cwen but it also increases my influence with the Wuffings and lessens their attachments to the Swedes." He turned and winked at Beowulf. "This is where you come in to the story."

"I now let it be known by King Hrethel in Geatland that I would be willing to release my good friend Ecgtheow from his oath to me in return for the hand of his daughter, Sigrid, your mother, another shipload of treasure and my friendship. Are you with me Beowulf?"

"Yes, lord."

"Explain to me who benefits from the new arrangements."

"The Wuffingas gain treasure, influence at the Danish court and a powerful new ally. The Waegmundings are now linked by blood to the Geat royal household and have strong links to the Danes through my father's personal relationship with you, lord. The Geats gain treasure, secure their southern border, placate the Wuffings and extend their overlordship of the Waegmundings."

"So who benefits the most then?" Hrothgar asked.

"We do, lord." Beowulf replied. "You have formed a buffer of friendly nations between yourself and the Swedes, allowing you to expand your territory to the west and south."

Hrothgar nodded gravely.

"So who loses?"

"The Swedes, lord."

Hrothgar glanced at Beowulf. "You said *we do* when I asked you who benefited. Who was the other beneficiary?" he asked, puzzled.

"I gained the most, lord. I was born of the marriage between my father and mother."

Hrothgar and Beowulf looked at each other and laughed.

"You have promise, Beowulf, you really do! If there is anything that I can do for you, let me know, I can see that I will need to keep on good terms with you if my scheming is to bear fruit in the future!"

A smile crept across Beowulf's features. "Actually, lord," he said, "there was one thing…"

THE FOLLOWING morning the Waegmunding party left Hleidra for home. As a mark of the esteem in which they were held, King Hrothgar accompanied them on the road back to the harbour at Hroars Kilde.

"Take a last look at my hall Beowulf, next time you come it will have been replaced. I am having it torn down next spring and a mighty new hall built in its place. It will be called Heorot, The Hart, after my personal emblem. It's going to be the wonder of the north Beowulf. You must make sure that you and your father visit me once it is completed."

They rode on in silence for a while, the boy and the king both comfortable in each other's company. Bjalki looked on in admiration. Beowulf had changed almost beyond recognition on this trip. At ease amongst kings and warriors he had started to display the qualities of self confidence and leadership which he would need to lead men in battle later in life.

He exchanged a look with Voislav who rode beside him. The man still had an amusing look of shock on his face at the events of the last few hours. He had been greeting the returning riders from the troll hunt when Hrothgar had brusquely walked up to him and demanded to know who his most capable replacement was. He had nervously indicated a man, his mind racing as he tried to think of any wrongdoing he may have done to upset the king.

"Right, Alf, congratulations you are the new head man. Voislav you have the rest of the day to teach him his duties, as of sundown you are a free man."

With that the king had turned his back and retired to his hall leaving Voislav open mouthed and the party of Waegmundings laughing uncontrollably. Voislav had been given permission to join the party as they made their way to the harbour. Beowulf had provided him finer clothing and enough silver to enable him to return to his homeland, brushing aside Voislav's offer of fealty.

"You have unfinished business at home, Voislav, a man must take revenge or it will eat his at his soul, besides I am too young as yet to support my own hearth troop."

Stopping only to gather Hudda and the crew of the *Griffon* the party made its way to the dockside.

"I have a gift for your father. I would be grateful if you

would see it delivered safely for me Beowulf," the king announced as they approached the boats.

"It has no name as yet. Perhaps 'Skull Splitter' would be appropriate!" he laughed.

Before them was the finest ship that any of the Waegmundings had seen. Eighty feet in length, the ship was more than the combined height of four men in the beam, with rowing positions provided for nearly thirty rowers. The side strakes were painted alternate red and blue while from the spar hung a sail of red and gold. A gilt weather vane sat proudly atop the mast, while its crew sat expectantly at their positions awaiting orders.

"This is a gift fit for a king!" Beowulf exclaimed. "You do my family great honour, lord."

"The pleasure is mine Beowulf, another ship will accompany you to return the crew, I want those back I am afraid!" he joked.

A commotion further along the quay drew their attention away from the ship.

"Unferth! Where in Hel's name have you been?" Hrothgar cried.

Hel, the goddess of the underworld was a fitting comparison to the figure which Beowulf saw pacing towards them. The man seemed to radiate hostility like a fire radiated heat.

"My apologies lord," he said as he neared them. "I am afraid that I must report to you that your ship master has damaged one of your best ships."

"How so?" Hrothgar enquired.

"He ran her aground passing too close to Hesselo. Luckily I had two other ships with me or we may not have made it back at all, and then I would have completely missed our honoured guests here," he replied, flicking a mocking glance at the assembled Waegmundings.

"Beowulf, this is my nephew, Unferth," Hrothgar indicated with a frown.

"We shall have to swap stories over our ale another time Beowulf, perhaps sometime after your balls drop would be nice. I was so much looking forward to hearing tales of Geatland, all those trees and lakes, elks, beaver that sort of thing. Still it's a loss I shall just have to try and live with."

Hrothgar reddened at the insults which were aimed at his guests.

"You must forgive my brother's son, he has noble blood but no manners."

"On the contrary lord, his manners are clear to all I think," Beowulf replied, acidly.

Shooting a look of contempt at Beowulf, Unferth asked Hrothgar for permission to leave.

"Please do," he replied, "and send the ship master to me, I wish to question him."

"Oh did I not say?" Unferth replied. "I am afraid that I had him hung for incompetence."

The king glowered as his nephew sauntered away from the dockside. Beowulf tried to lessen Hrothgar's embarrassment by hurrying his men aboard the ships.

Taking station on the *Griffon*, the small flotilla dipped their oars into Hroars Kilde fjord and began to draw away.

"Be careful of trolls, lord!" Beowulf called from the steering platform with a wave.

"Trolls!" Hrothgar cried with a laugh.

"What are trolls going to do to me? Tear the doors off Heorot and murder all my warriors?"

4

————

Their breath misted in the cold morning air as they waited for Beowulf's mother, Sigrid, to pass around the mead. They were keen to be on their way and the skies, full and dark, promised a tempestuous day ahead. Cupping his hands around the horn of warmed mead, Beowulf tried to lock away in his memory every feature of his mother for it may be years before they met again. He looked on with pride as he watched her move amongst the riders, handing up drink and making friendly comments to the warriors who were to accompany Ecgtheow and himself to Gefrin, the hall of the Geat king perched high upon Miklaborg, the great rock fortress of the Geatish folk.

He knew that she was as upset at their parting as he was himself, but that she would not let that emotion embarrass herself amongst the men. As the daughter of the king he would have expected no less. With a smile and a dip of her head to Ecgtheow, her husband and lord, Sigrid stood back as the men drained their horns and, spurring their mounts, urged the horses away from the hall towards the nearby road. Just before they entered the shelter of the forest, Beowulf could not resist a last glance back over his shoulder at the hall in which he had spent his whole life so far, but she had gone.

"We shall need to make good time today if we are to make Geatwic by sundown. Let's hope that this rain holds off for a while, my days of sleeping rough are hopefully behind me!" Ecgtheow declared after a while. Throwing his young son a smile he continued. "I haven't said how proud of you I am for your conduct in DaneLand. I should have, I apologise. When you are busy telling folk what to do all day you some-times forget that they might appreciate some recognition of their efforts. A kind word will sometimes work better than a whole day's cajoling, Beowulf."

Since he had returned from King Hrothgar Beowulf had noticed that his father had taken far more interest in him. He had no doubt that it was largely due to the report on his conduct there which he had been given on his return by Bjalki. He had noticed his father and Bjalki deep in conversa-tion outside the hall a week or so after their return. Ecgtheow had invited his thegns and their families to the hall to cele-brate Haerfestmonath, the successful gathering in of the year's crops. It was a time of still, warm days, plentiful food and drink and crowds of high spirited people. It had always been Beowulf's favourite time of the year.

The folk in the local village had dressed up the last sheaf to be gathered and had made a man and woman of them. Crowned by garlands of Mistletoe for luck, they had been paraded through the settlement, stopping at each home for refreshments, before presiding over the evening's merriment. At Ecgtheow's hall the men had shown their proficiency with a bow by shooting at apples suspended from a tree and other martial feats, while the younger members and some of the women bobbed for apples in one of the barrels. Nobody had been surprised when Hild had won again, although they were all too polite to point out that it may have been due to her having the teeth of a stallion.

Beowulf had noticed that his father had taken the opportunity while everyone was occupied of taking Bjalki to one side. Sat on the wood pile, a horn of ale in one hand and a loaf baked from the new season's barley in the other, Beowulf remembered thinking to himself that he had never seen his father so happy or relaxed. From the glances cast in his direction it was clear to Beowulf that they had been discussing him and he was relieved when Bjalki had thrown a reassuring wink in his direction. Of course the magnificent ship that King Hrothgar had sent his father, now officially named *Sea Eagle*, would have helped lighten Ecgtheow's mood, as would the many other priceless gifts they had brought back from the Danish court. Tonight Ecgtheow would distribute the gifts amongst his thegns as a true ring giver should, and the night would be passed in ale, meat and storytelling, reaffirming the bonds between them.

"Bjalki would have reached Alfhelm's hall by now and they will be making preparations to receive us, I hope!"

Bjalki had been sent on ahead the day before to make arrangements for the party's accommodation on the journey.

"He is a good man, more than a hearth warrior to me, a good friend," Ecgtheow continued.

"And he speaks very highly of you, Beowulf. I trust his judgement. You handled yourself with honour amongst the Danes, well done."

"I enjoy Bjalki's company, he has been a good mentor for me," Beowulf responded.

"It is important that you learn to judge a man's qualities Beowulf, and your relationship with Bjalki pleases me. I also heard about your conversation with Unferth. I knew him as a child when I was with the Danes and he was a little arse then.

It does not surprise me that he has grown into a big arse!"
Ecgtheow chuckled.

Squinting up at the sky Ecgtheow pulled his cloak up
around his neck and draped it securely around his upper legs.
Turning his head he called back down the column of riders.

"Svip! Keep that bird dry unless you want to be appointed
the new horse shit shoveller when we get back!"

Looking back, past the grinning faces of the warriors,
Beowulf saw Svip adjust the cover which shielded the young
eagle from the worst of the weather. Ecgtheow squinted up at
the leaden sky. "Here it comes!"

Looking up, Beowulf watched as thick, dark, clouds
rolled in from the west. Gusts of wind shook the tops of the
trees as, hunched up in their cloaks and helms the party of
warriors picked their way steadily north.

THE WEATHER IMPROVED the next day as they resumed their
journey to Miklaborg. It had been a weary and rain sodden
party which had reached the hall of Alfhelm the previous
evening but their spirits had risen as their clothes had dried
and their bodies had warmed themselves once more around
Alfhelm's roaring hearth. Ecgtheow and Alfhelm were both
ealdormen in the Geat kingdom, having fought together in
many engagements. Their obvious trust and affection for each
other had been shared by many of the hearth warriors, as old
friendships were rekindled and news passed between them. It
had been an enjoyable evening. Beowulf glanced again at the
gold brooch which now fixed his cloak at his right shoulder.
A parting gift from Alfhelm, it bore the image of a one eyed
man above which flew two ravens. Ecgtheow noticed him
looking and smiled.

"A fitting gift for one Woden born, make sure that you live up to it. Fostering can make or break a young man."

They followed the river north all day with just the occasional hail from a passing boat to break their journey. Later in the afternoon small farms began to appear in the landscape and ceorls began to be seen as they went about their duties. The numbers slowly increased until, suddenly, as they rounded a knoll, the fortress of Miklaborg rose before them. With their goal in sight and the promise of a fire and hot food before them, the party unconsciously increased their pace.

The fortress was entered via a raised causeway from the settlement which hugged the northern shore at the juncture of two rivers. To reach it the party had to ride along the southern bank until they reached a bridge which spanned the river further downstream, giving Beowulf an opportunity to study the fortress from close quarters as they passed. The main island of Miklaborg rose from midstream, gently at first, its lower levels a tangle of rushes and sedges sprinkled with purple moor grass. Abruptly the ground rose almost vertically to a wide plateau. At the highest point, safely ensconced behind its protective palisade, lay Gefrin, the hall of King Hrethel. High above the hall a white boar, the emblem of the king, curled and snapped in the fresh breeze. Another low island lay off to the right of Miklaborg, again a mass of rushes and willow, but unused by man, the home of birds and otters. To the left of Miklaborg, and connected to it by a high causeway lay a smaller island.

"That is home to the temple of the gods. A few volva live there, but it is not a place I would choose to spend any more time than necessary," Ecgtheow explained as he followed Beowulf's gaze. "The gods are best left untroubled in my experience," he continued, "unless you are really desperate!"

Despite its steepness, the island which contained the

temple, unlike the main island on which Gefrin had been constructed, was crowned by a crowd of ash trees through which Beowulf thought that he could just make out the outline of a building. Indistinct shapes moved slowly to and fro in the shadows amongst the branches of the trees. The whole area contained by the trees seemed to wallow beneath an atmosphere which was both heavy and mysterious. Silently agreeing with his father's assessment of the place, Beowulf moved on with a shudder.

Crossing the bridge with a clatter of hooves the party came upon the first of the guards. Beowulf noticed the man on guard motion to another who was taking shelter from the freshening wind in a small building nestled to one side of the northern entrance to the bridge. Even if the guard did not recognise them by sight, their clothes and bearing would have marked them out as men of importance. Beowulf noticed the more senior of the two narrow his eyes as he emerged into the light, trying to recognise the visitors.

"Ealdorman Ecgtheow, you are welcome lord. It is good to see you again!" he greeted them.

"Thank you, Binni," Ecgtheow replied, "and how is life treating you? I trust you have not been upsetting any of our Swedish friends lately?"

Beowulf noticed the guard's eyes shine with pride.

"Not since they chopped my sword arm off, lord!" he laughed, holding out the stump of his right arm.

"Nonsense, a one armed Geat is more than a match for any two Swedes!" Ecgtheow countered as they passed the smiling guards. Binni laughed happily and waved the riders through.

"Always try to remember their names, Beowulf." Ecgtheow explained once they had passed out of earshot. "That man was once a great fighter but now he spends his days in a hut next to a bridge collecting tolls from merchants and farmers. Let them know that you remember them and they keep their self respect. A man is nothing without his sense of honour."

The crowds parted respectfully as they made their way through the settlement to the causeway which led to the fastness of Miklaborg. Beowulf was glad that they were mounted as they made their way through the glutinous mud which comprised the main thoroughfare. The heavy rains of the previous day had clearly overwhelmed many of the pits located at the rear of the buildings to accommodate human waste, the contents from which were now seeping between the buildings to mix with those deposits left by swine and horses during the course of the day. Reaching the end of the causeway they were again greeted by smiling guards while, ahead, Beowulf could see a small group of people waiting to welcome them. Clearly running the main road along the length of the river opposite before reaching the crossing was not accidental he reflected. Set in midstream, high above the surrounding area, Miklaborg was an ideal defensive location and, placed as it was where the river split into two as it made its way from the great inland Sea of Vanern to the coast, an ideal place to collect tribute.

Led by Ecgtheow and Beowulf, the company advanced slowly across the causeway towards the waiting group.

"Watch your backs boys and don't bend over to pick anything up, whatever the value, not while we have country boys in Gefrin," the leading man growled.

The heavily muscled man was dressed in the finest clothes, while a sword of the exquisite workmanship hung from a belt heavily decorated with gold and silver embellishments. His face was framed by the fairest, shoulder length hair and neatly trimmed beard. He was clearly someone of great importance and for a moment Beowulf was reminded of his meeting with Unferth on the quayside in Dane land. He hoped that this was not to be a repeat of that uncomfortable meeting, not in the first moments of his fostering. Beowulf watched anxiously as his father replied to the insult.

"If I leave my horse in your care, promise me that you will be gentle with him. It will be his first time taking the part of the mare. Unless of course," Ecgtheow smiled coldly, "he will be taking the part of the stallion? He's not used to the customs of fortress dwellers."

Beowulf cringed as the warrior's eyes widened at the insult before his face inexplicably creased into a smile.

"What if I just run you through and have done with it kinsman!" he bellowed.

"What if you just help me off this horse and fill me with ale, lord!" Ecgtheow replied with a laugh.

Jumping from his horse, Ecgtheow and the man embraced before Beowulf's startled eyes.

"What a bloody great idea, and don't call me lord. All day I get lord this and lord that, if you can't call me by my name, kinsman will do."

"Beowulf!" his father declared. "Meet your uncle, Hygelac."

The pair began the long climb up towards Gefrin, laughing easily together before Beowulf's astonished eyes.

"Come on Beowulf," Ecgtheow called out.

"*This* is Beowulf!" Hygelac asked in mock astonishment. "You have changed so much since I last saw you."

"That would be because you have never seen him, you arse. What, a two day journey to see your sister and her family is too much trouble for the great Hygelac is it?"

"Oh I would have come but you know me and long horse rides. I get a sore arse after a couple of hours."

"That is what I told my horse!" Ecgtheow laughed.

Hygelac laughed again. "The gods know that I have missed you, Ecgtheow. What's your news…?"

LED BY HYGELAC AND ECGTHEOW, the party ascended the steep pathway to the hall. Above them loomed Gefrin, its lime washed walls shining white in the weak autumn sun. Richly decorated woodwork studded the gable end of the hall. Red and gold dragons lay intertwined throughout the woodwork while a giant serpent encompassed the entire hall, representing the Midgard serpent which encircled middle earth. The message was clear to all. Here, within these walls, lay the world of the Geat people.

Handing their weapons to the steward at the door the party entered the hall. The familiar sights and smells of the hall greeted Beowulf. Rich tapestries hung at the bench lined walls where the hearth warriors of King Hrethel rose in greeting of Hygelac ætheling. Massive posts of oak lined the centre of the hall, richly decorated in gold, leading the eye unerringly to the far end of the hall where King Hrethel sat in splendour.

"We have visitors, father," Hygelac announced as he led the warriors through the hall.

King Hrethel sat, flanked by two fully armed Geat warriors, in a shaft of light which cut diagonally down from the southern side of the hall. At his feet lay two, iron grey, wolfhounds. Approaching the dais, Hygelac bowed respectfully to his father before moving to one side.

"Our kinsmen father, the Ealdorman Ecgtheow," he indicated, "and Sigrid's son, Beowulf."

Ecgtheow knelt before his king and inclined his head in respect.

"My king, I humbly present you with this tribute," he said, indicating that the gifts be brought forward and set before the king.

"These are fine gifts and we thank you for them," Hrethel responded happily.

Beowulf stepped forward and knelt beside his father.

"May I also honour you with a gift, lord?" he announced to Hrethel's surprise. At this Svip made his way forward from the group and, kneeling, displayed the hooded young eagle to the king.

Hrethel gasped in delight. "This is a fine gift, grandson!" the king exclaimed. "I accept it with joy." He indicated that Svip come forward and stand at his side. Addressing Ecgtheow's party the king spoke.

"Rest and avail yourselves of the pleasures of my hall, we will speak more when you are refreshed from your journey."

Thanking him they made their way to the places assigned them on the benches.

BEOWULF AWOKE in the hall as the light of the following dawn reddened the plaster high in the eves. Rising quietly, he made his way to the door and, as silently as he could, made his way out into the cold dawn air. Acknowledging the smiles from the Geat guards at the entrance, Beowulf made his way to the southern side of the plateau. Climbing the wooden steps to the walkway which circled the enclosing palisade, Beowulf breathed in deeply, trying to rid his lungs of the smoky atmosphere of the hall. Wrapped tightly in his cloak, he surveyed the scene below. The sun was just creeping over the hills to the east, illuminating the clouds with a pink glow. Below, the valley remained in gloom, the trees surrounded by skirts of yellow leaves which grew ever higher with each gust of wind. On the road beside the river the first early risers were beginning to go about the business of the day.

"Up early?" a voice broke into his thoughts.

Turning, Beowulf was surprised to see the figure of the king approaching him along the walkway.

"Your father told me that you took my eagle from the nest and had to fight off the mother to do it," he smiled.

"You're either brave or mad and I can use both sorts in the family. I have thought about your fostering and I am going to send you to live at Hygelac's hall. I told him last night, so when you return to the hall you are to join his retainers straight away. Your father took his leave and returned to his lands earlier this morning. Use your time well with Hygelac. He is a fine son to me and a good warrior who can teach you a lot. You have promise Beowulf. Apply yourself to your duties and you will become a credit to our family." Hrethel smiled. "Go now," he continued, placing an affectionate hand on Beowulf's shoulder, "you are expected."

HYGELAC SNAPPED awake and instinctively reached above the bed to the place where he kept his weapons. It was the early hours, long before the wolf would chase the horses back into the eastern sky to herald the beginning of the new day and someone, a man, was moving around in the hall. Gripping his sword firmly he swung himself noiselessly from the bed and moved slowly and cautiously to the door. Closing his eyes he listened intensely to the tiny sounds which were emanating from his hearth side. His senses heightened, he was sure that it was a single intruder. He let out the faintest sigh of relief. Hall burnings were a common form of attack in the northern lands but this was something different. Flinging open the door Hygelac heft his sword and began to advance on the intruder, the man violating his family home, when he stopped, his arm dropping slowly back to his side as he realised the identity of the man sat before him.

Awestruck and terrified the Geat ætheling moved towards the dying flames and knelt in supplication.

"Forgive me, lord. I would not have raised a weapon had I known that it was you!"

The man motioned for Hygelac to join him and, throwing back his wolf skin hood regarded him with his one remaining eye.

"You have been entrusted with the care of one who is of interest to me," the one eyed man began. "I would like you to ensure that he grows to become the greatest warrior in the north. In return I can offer you reputation and riches." He paused and fixed the ætheling with his penetrating stare. "Do we have a deal?"

A smile played across Hygelac's features as he began to realise the opportunity which was presenting itself to him. A god needed his help and was willing to bargain. He decided to grasp the opportunity with both hands.

"I want to be king."

BEOWULF IMMEDIATELY FELT at home in Hygelac's hall, Skara. Nestled at the head of a fjord on the north-west coast of Geatland, the place had none of the splendour of Gefrin and was all the better for it, he thought. Hygd, Hygelac's wife fussed over her nephew on his arrival, showing him to his bed space.

"This is where Heardred slept as a boy, it will be good to see it occupied again."

Heardred, she explained was their son, now twenty winters old.

"He was fostered with the Engles when he was about the age you are now and has been raiding with them in the South since he came of age. He did come home one summer a few years ago, but life here is too quiet for a young man. I expect that you will feel the same in a few years," she sighed.

"And this is Astrid," she added with a smile as a girl of about Beowulf's age entered the hall.

Astrid was almost as tall as Beowulf, slim and fair. She was dressed simply in a knee length dress, gathered at the waist by a simple leather belt. Only the gold bracteate, a small medallion featuring a stylised image of Woden accompanied by two ravens which hung from her neck, indicated her rank as the daughter of an ætheling.

"You are back earlier than I expected father, and now Beowulf thinks that his cousin is a milk maid!" she complained with mock annoyance.

"Even if you were a milk maid, you would still light up the room every time you entered, as well you know," Hygelac responded with a smile.

Beowulf enjoyed Astrid's open, easy, manner and felt confident that they would become good friends.

"Right! Now the introductions are over with," Hygelac declared suddenly. "Let's get to work on the boy. We need men for the future or we will have no future. Off with those clothes, there is no place for finery on a farm."

Beowulf removed his fine clothing, conscious of the amused smiles of the watching Hygd and Astrid, and was aghast when Hygelac scooped them up and deposited them on the fire.

"Here these will do," he said, tossing some rough work clothes in Beowulf's direction.

Hygelac watched as Beowulf quickly pulled on the work clothes.

"I have seen more meat on a dog's bone," he sighed, shaking his head in mock disappointment. "Come on," he cried out, "let's see what we can do about that."

Hastily tying his shoes, Beowulf, followed him through the door. Hygelac was stood waiting before a pile of cut timber.

"Here you go, that's a tree trunk, that's an axe and that's firewood. I am sure you can work it out, a bright boy like you. Let's see how tough those hands are."

That night Beowulf could barely eat as the skin peeled away from his blistered hands and the muscles of his shoulders burned.

"Here, put these on in the morning," Hygelac smiled, handing Beowulf a new set of clothing. Beowulf took them from him, the weight of them causing him to look up in surprise. "They are my own design," Hygelac declared proudly. "They have an inner lining which is filled with sand. I want you to wear them every day. They will build your strength up in no time. Also," he added, "I had Astrid make this up for you."

Reaching behind him he produced a small leather ball. Catching it, Beowulf was no longer surprised to find that the ball was heavy.

"There is just enough give in that to develop a strong grip. I want to see you squeezing that at every free moment, until it becomes second nature. This time next year you'll have a grip like Thunor himself!" he laughed.

BEOWULF'S first winter passed with Hygelac, Hygd and Astrid.

At the Yule gift giving, to Beowulf's delight, Hygelac presented him with a smaller version of a warrior's mail byrnie.

"Arms up," he grunted. "Hurry up, this is heavy!"

Feeling the weight of a mail shirt on his shoulders for the first time made Beowulf inordinately proud.

"Right let's see if you have full movement then."

Beowulf jumped up and down and moved his arms in circular motions.

"Perfect," Hygelac declared. "Now I don't want…"

"To see me without it on," Beowulf finished the sentence for him as laughter rang around the hall.

Slowly the winter released its icy grip on the land. The small river which fed into the fjord shook off its covering of ice. Patches of green began to show themselves on the hills and the days grew slowly longer and warmer. Seemingly overnight the cherry tree which stood outside the hall began to burst forth with delicate white blooms. Soon the swifts and swallows would return. One morning Hygelac called to Beowulf to follow him down to the fjord.

"Right strip off, we are going for a swim," he announced.

Beowulf did as he had been instructed.

"I thought you said we?" he questioned, when he noticed that Hygelac had not undressed.

Ignoring his comment, Hygelac continued.

"You see that small island, the one with the cormorants? Well, we are going to see who can swim there the fastest, but I will be wearing my clothing and byrnie, ready?"

Laughing the pair splashed into the shallows before plunging head first into the waters. He had never been a natural swimmer, as soon as he stopped moving he seemed to sink, but Beowulf struck out for the island followed closely by Hygelac. To his amazement Hygelac soon passed him and struck off into the distance, despite being weighed down by clothing and a knee length mail shirt. Reaching the island Beowulf found Hygelac stretched out on the rocks, drying his sodden clothing in the warm spring sunshine.

"That was amazing!" he spluttered as he pulled himself from the sea.

"No, that was nothing Beowulf. That was just strength and practice. The amazing thing is you will be doing it yourself by this summer's end. I want you to practice every evening until you can beat me and then I want you to practice some more."

Once Beowulf turned nine winters Hygelac decided that the time had come to introduce weapons training to the boy. Although he still possessed the smaller seax which had been gifted to him by King Hrothgar, Beowulf was still not tall enough to handle a full size sword and shield, despite the increase in strength which had been achieved by him under his care. An oak sword and shield were made for him, both of which were inlaid with granite.

"If you can handle these effortlessly the real thing will be easy," Hygelac explained.

Soon Beowulf was encouraged to travel with his sword and shield everywhere. His days were filled with swimming, hunting, weapons training and sailing. Every activity Hygelac introduced to his nephew was designed with one thing in mind; to produce the strongest and most accomplished warrior in the Geat kingdom.

Beowulf's twelfth summer passed and the familiar rituals of autumn were played out once again in the land of the Geats. Haerfestmonath came and went. At Blotmonath the surplus animals were slaughtered and dried or salted for use in the coming months. As the days grew ever shorter, minds began to turn to the great festival of Yule which was fast approaching.

"Here, take those old rags off and put these on." Hygelac said to Beowulf one day. "Let's see how fast you really are."

"Faster than you, lord!" he replied with a smile.

"Oh, I don't doubt that you are. That's why you won't be racing me," he laughed.

Stepping outside Beowulf saw a two riders waiting for them. The older of the two was clearly one of Hygelac's brothers although he could not know which one. He had inherited the same muscular build and colouring and was if anything even more distinguished looking than Hygelac. Swinging down from his horse the man approached Beowulf with a friendly smile.

"Kinsman, I am pleased to meet you at last," he declared, reaching out to embrace him. Holding Beowulf by the shoulders he continued. "My brother tells me you can outpace the wind. That is something I would like to see! But forgive me we have yet to be introduced. I am Herebeald, your eldest uncle and that poor young man is Eofer, my foster son."

Herebeald indicated the young man on the horse who looked to Beowulf to be a few years older than him, maybe fourteen winters, he thought to himself. The youth smiled down at Beowulf and nodded.

"He fancies himself a fast runner, does our English friend, what do you say that we match him against someone who can 'outpace the wind' if one can be found. What do you say are you up for it?"

Beowulf shot Eofer a look of surprise. He had had no idea that Engles were being fostered amongst the Geats.

"Where to uncle?" Beowulf replied.

"Excellent!" Herebeald exclaimed with a grin. I feel a wager coming on little brother."

EOFER DISMOUNTED and removed his cloak and outer garments until he stood clad only in trousers and shoes and commenced a series of stretches, loosening his muscles. Beowulf, dressed identically, sipped at a cup of mead which Astrid had brought out to refresh their guests, while her father and uncle discussed the route to be taken. Beowulf noticed that Astrid had lost her usual confidence around Eofer and was looking coyly at the floor.

"Right then, lads, you see that promontory?" Hygelac indicated a point several miles distant.

"We are going to ride over there and prepare some food for a pair of hungry runners. There is a road which leads directly to the summit, but there are also other routes which are shorter but more difficult. There are no rules, the first one to reach us is the winner, got that?"

The pair nodded their acceptance.

"Well, why are you still here then?" Herebeald put in. "Lost your nerve?"

With a glance at each other, Beowulf and Eofer dashed out of the yard and onto the road which led north. Each wary of the others reputation, they both settled into a steady pace for the first mile, as each of them sought to conserve their energy for the latter stages. Although neither of them had visited the promontory before they were both astute enough to realise that it had not been chosen at random. They had both noticed the brothers' smiles while they were discussing the route to be taken and, knowing them as well as they did, they knew that there would be more to the race than a straightforward dash up the road.

After a while the gradient of the track began to increase subtly, and the surface became rougher and more pock-marked. Eofer began to draw slowly away from Beowulf. Despite his great strength, Beowulf found that the steady gradient suited Eofer far more. A head taller than Beowulf and less heavily built, Eofer increased his pace until a clear, and increasing, gap opened up between them. He knew that he would need to find a shorter route, and quickly, if he was to overtake his opponent. A smaller path opened up to the left of the main road and Beowulf quickly decided that this was perhaps his only chance of winning the race. Turning onto the track, he plunged into the enveloping gloom of the forest.

Slick with mud from the autumn rains, the path soon became little more than a track through the trees which crowded in on him. Yellow leaves lay thickly scattered about the floor of the forest, here and there building into thick banks where they had been swept by the autumn gales. Settling into a steady rhythm, his breath pluming in the cool air, Beowulf could see that he was now making good progress towards his goal, glimpsed occasionally through the canopy.

He suddenly became aware of something irritating the skin of his chest. Grasping the talisman hanging at his neck, the sliver of Hrani's staff, it suddenly felt hot to the touch. Was this another warning of danger he thought to himself, like the time on the *Griffon*?

The smell of woodsmoke came to him as he neared a small clearing. Rising from their fireside, Beowulf saw two men collect spears and walk slowly over to block his path.

"What have we here?" the taller of the two inquired as he took up position to one side of the path.

His companion stood to the other side of the path, their

spears crossed, blocking Beowulf's way ahead. Irritated but alert Beowulf drew up several paces from the men.

"A half naked boy running through the forest, not a sight you see every day, eh Hucca, where are you off to boy?" he inquired.

Incensed at the lack of respect shown to him and desperate to continue the race, Beowulf snapped.

"Get out of my way wolfs head and address me as lord or I will see to it that you hang like all common thieves before the day's end!"

"There's no need to be so unfriendly, '*lord*', we were just passing the time of day. That is a lovely knife at your side though. Can I have a look at it?"

Beowulf had kept his seax, 'Hrothgar's gift', on his belt for the race. Even in well ordered lands like those ruled by Hygelac wolfs heads, robbers, haunted the roads. Besides, all free men carried arms as a mark of their status. The spears had been lowered now and pointed menacingly at Beowulf's chest, supporting their demand. Beowulf instinctively knew that he had to move fast and take control of the situation.

In a flash he darted inside the spears, drawing the seax from its sheath and across the face of the smaller man. With a scream of pain he dropped his spear as his hands moved up to his lacerated face. Barging him aside Beowulf just had time to register the look of surprise and shock on the face of his companion as he reversed the seax in his hand and plunged it deep into his spine. The outlaw fell immediately as all use of his lower body left him. Turning, Hrothgar's Gift tore through muscles and tendons as he stooped and hamstrung the shorter man, leaving him writhing on the forest floor, unable to stand. Picking up one of the spears he used it to flick their weapons out of reach before depositing them together a short distance away.

"What are you going to do with us?" the taller one sobbed.

Beowulf kicked the man hard in the face, feeling his nose crumple under the blow. The man screamed in pain as blood poured down his shattered features.

"What are you going to do with us, *lord!*" Beowulf hissed. Unable to find anything more suitable Beowulf removed the reins from the horses which were hobbled near the camp fire.

"What are you doing, lord?" the man moaned as Beowulf returned to them.

"I promised you that I would see you hang before the day was out and I always keep my promises."

Tightening the hide rein around the terrified man's neck, Beowulf tossed the loose end over a low branch and pulled down with all his weight. The man rose, kicking and squirming, into the air until with a final twitch he became still. Securing the rein to the branch he left the robber hanging there, as his terrified companion looked on. Unable to stand, the man began to drag himself towards the pile of weapons which Beowulf had collected.

"Where do you think that you are going?" he spat, as he looped the other rein around his neck and dragged the man back to the tree. "There's room for two on that branch and I am sure that you wouldn't want your old friend to travel to meet Hel alone, not after all the good times I am sure you two must have shared."

"Lord, we have treasure. I can show you where it is if you will spare me," Hucca croaked as Beowulf looped the hide over the branch.

"You have treasure hidden!" Beowulf feigned interest.

Given a glimpse of hope the man responded eagerly.

"Yes, lord we have it not far from here. It can all be yours if you will just let me go with one horse. I promise never to return to these lands."

Beowulf gazed into the distance as if contemplating the offer.

"No, I have enough treasure," he suddenly announced. "My honour is my treasure. I can carry it around with me even if I appear to be a half naked boy."

Beowulf saw the last light of hope leave Hucca's eyes as he pulled down again on the hide.

Dedicating the corpses to Woden, the god of the hanged, Beowulf led the horses away from the now unseeing, grotesque faces of their former masters.

~

"Here he comes!"

They rose as one as Herebeald called out from his place beside the fire. The heavily carved side of pork stood testament to the fact that they had not waited for him before they began their meal. Smiling broadly, Eofer sat next to Herebeald, his chin glistening as he tore strips from the large piece of pork he held in one hand, while he gripped a horn of ale in the other.

"Where did you pick up two horses?" Hygelac inquired.

"I met two wolfs heads in the forest."

"And these outlaws gave you their horses and weapons?"

Herebeald, suddenly aware of the dangerous situation Beowulf had found himself in shot a concerned look at Hygelac.

"They made no move to stop me, lord." Beowulf responded.

"Not after I had hung them."

5

The horses thundered along the track, great clods of dirty snow flying in their wake. The sky was darkening quickly now, turning from a hard, icy blue, to a leaden black. Already the first stars were visible, promising a night of exceptional cold ahead for those unfortunate enough not to have gained the shelter of a fire warmed hall by nightfall. The sun had fallen to rest on the western edge of middle earth, throwing great shadows across the land where the ice crystals sparkled and shone amongst the great drifts of snow.

It was three days before Yule and Hygelac and Beowulf were on their way to Gefrin at the invitation of the king to celebrate the turning of the year. Hygelac would overnight at the halls of two of his thegns, both of which lay on the route south for just this purpose, before they all journeyed on to the festivities. The shortness of daylight added an extra day to their journey at this time of the year. As they neared the hall they reined in, immediately becoming enveloped in an equine scented mist which rose from the flanks of their mounts in the cold air. They allowed the tired horses to pick their way around the worst patches of icy ground. Tired horses, ice and a deepening gloom were potentially a lethal combination and it did not pay to test the will of the gods too far. Beowulf decided that now would be a good time to question Hygelac on a subject on which he had pondered since the meeting with Eofer the previous year. With the term of his fosterage due to end the following summer such opportunities to be alone with his foster father may become increasingly rare.

"Lord, why are we placing such importance on developing good relations with the Engles. We have a good friend in King Hrothgar of the Danes, are we not risking this by courting his enemies?"

Hygelac rode in silence for a short while.

"It's a good question Beowulf," he answered.

"I am pleased that you think on such matters. I can turn any boy into a warrior, but a thoughtful warrior is a rarer beast. Since my Grandfather's time," he continued, "it has sometimes seemed that the whole of the North is on the move. Roman power in the South has waned, opening up new opportunities for conquest and settlement. The softness of the land and climate in the South is only matched by the softness of the inhabitants. I was there as a young man and Heardred is there now making a reputation for himself with the Engles. It is true that Hrothgar has been a good friend to the Geats, but always remember that he does not do this for our good. At the moment it suits him for us to cover his back while he expands his kingdom as far south as he can into those soft southern lands. Perhaps the next Danish king might prefer to marry a Swede and divide the lands of the Geats and the Wuffings between their kingdoms. We are like a man between two bears, hoping not to get mauled. Our links with the Engles gives us an ally on Hrothgar's southern border which reminds him to treat us with respect. The English are carving a new kingdom in Britannia, Anglia they call it in their tongue. I think that the day is not so far off when the whole kingdom of the Engles will have transferred itself to the other side of the German sea. I sometimes think that our future would be better there also."

Hygelac was interrupted by the sight of lights moving on the road ahead. Soon riders came into view, several of which carried torches to light the way.

"We are there." Hygelac announced with a smile.

THE GROUP of men stood drinking, awaiting the arrival of their king. It was the longest night of the year and it seemed like an age since the red orb of the sun had dipped below the horizon the previous day. Gathered in the king's private quarters at the rear of the royal hall, Gefrin, were some of the most notable subjects of the king. As the king's grandson and fosterling to the royal ætheling Hygelac, Beowulf had been invited to take part in the ceremony to be enacted by the volva, the priestess, designed to pay homage to the gods and usher in the New Year. Dressed for war the assembled warriors made for a magnificent sight and Beowulf hoped that he did not look too out of place. As a minor, he had yet to be granted the right to wear full armour and bear arms, although he owned a mail byrnie and was now fully proficient with all the weapons he saw in the room. In fact, freed from the weight of his padded clothing and mail his now powerful torso moved with a grace and vigour uncommon even amongst his peers.

Hygelac's preoccupation with his companions had given Beowulf the first opportunity since he arrived at the hall the previous day to study the royal party. Some of the group he knew of course from previous meetings. He had been greeted affectionately by Alfhelm of Geatwic, while Hygelac's thegns Hromund and Ulfgar had been splendid hosts on their journey south. Naturally Hygelac was in good spirits and clearly popular with all in the hall, he smiled to himself. His older brother, Herebeald, Beowulf had met a few weeks back of course when he had raced the Angle, Eofer. He clearly had an especially close relationship with Hygelac. Both men were naturally outgoing, fond of each other and popular amongst the others, unlike, it would seem, his third uncle, Hythcyn. Stood to one side of the hall he was speaking to a group of the king's thegns. Beowulf could see from their demeanour that they were finding the conversation more one of duty than pleasure. Hythcyn had arrived at the hall later than most and although he had been well greeted by his brothers, Beowulf could not help but notice that none of the warmth of their own reunion had been evident. He had been accompanied by his foster son Breca. About his own age, Breca was from the Bronding people near Lake Vanern to the North. Vain and boastful, Beowulf had taken an almost instant dislike to him. It would seem that Hythcyn and Breca had been well matched when King Hrethel had decided the pairings for each of the fosterlings.

Suddenly the door to the main hall opened. The conversations trailed away as those present turned to face the king.

"All here? Good, pass me some ale will you Beowulf. I would rather face a dozen hairy Swedes than cross that bridge!" he laughed.

Smiles spread on the assembled faces as, taking the proffered ale, he continued.

"Herebeald, Hygelac, Good Yule! And to you Hythcyn and my lords."

Beowulf noticed the brief flicker of disappointment on Hythcyn's face as he reacted to the king's obvious lack of favour before he regained his composure, and was shocked to see a look of pure loathing cross the ætheling's face as he looked towards his unsuspecting brothers. Sensing that he was being watched Hythcyn suddenly turned his gaze onto Beowulf. Caught unawares, a cold chill seemed to run down Beowulf's spine as it became obvious that his uncle had correctly guessed his thoughts. A thin smile formed on his lips as, holding his gaze firmly on Beowulf, he inclined his head slightly to whisper something in the ear of Breca. Flicking a look in his direction Breca nodded sternly before looking away. Unaware, the king had moved on to embrace his favoured sons before addressing those present.

"It is time for those of you who will accompany me to cross to the Temple. This year as we are all present, I will be accompanied by my sons and their kinsman Beowulf." He grinned mischievously. "My lords will have to forgive me if they have to miss the ceremony this year as space over there is limited, as you know."

Ironic smiles greeted this announcement from the assembled lords and Beowulf got the impression that they would not feel that they would be missing out at all. With a final draining of their drinking horns, the chosen party opened the rear doors to the hall and stepped through them into the all embracing darkness.

Ahead, Beowulf could make out the shadowy outline of the ornate gateway which guarded the causeway leading to the temple complex. Beyond, slightly darker against the night sky, arose the faint outline of the temple itself rising high into the midwinter gloom. As his eyes became accustomed to the dark, Beowulf began to make out more details of the gateway which lay in their path. Stout wooden doors were flanked by thick, ornate, door posts which rose and converged above the entrance in a pair of intertwined bird heads.

"They are 'Thought' and 'Memory', Woden's ravens." Hygelac whispered. "They keep the Wanderer informed of all that happens on middle earth."

Beowulf nodded nervously. He was confident now amongst the lords and warriors of the hall, in fact he had become a popular and respected member of the Geat nobility, but the gods demanded respect and it was clear to him that even his Grandfather and Uncles were uneasy in their presence. A small light appeared between the boards of the gate, faintly at first, but quickly growing in intensity as the bearer of the flame approached, followed by the sounds of a heavy locking bar being removed. With a groan the doors were opened inward to reveal the torch bearer.

Before the royal party stood a woman of about sixteen winters. Her delicate face was framed by a hood made of cat skin, while a cloak of the same material fell from her shoulders to the ground. Beneath this she wore a delicate shift which, illuminated by the brand which she held aloft, clung seductively to her body. She was the most beautiful woman that Beowulf had ever, and, he was sure in that moment, would ever, see.

Turning, the woman led the group back across the causeway which led to the temple. Enclosed on both sides by high walls, the causeway was illustrated by carvings depicting tales of the gods. Beowulf recognised the tale of Thunor grappling with the world serpent and Woden hanging on the world tree, pierced by a spear. With a pang of nostalgia he noticed Tiwaz with his hand in the mouth of the wolf, Fenrir, as it was bound with the magic fetter made by the dwarves. His mother, Sigrid, had worn a golden bracteate depicting the scene and it was one of Beowulf's earliest memories of her. As they approached the end of the causeway, Beowulf saw that the way ahead appeared to be blocked by the largest Yew tree he had ever seen. More than three spear lengths in width, its gnarled, knotted trunk twisted and turned as its silhouette climbed and melted into the charcoal-like blackness above.

Their guide suddenly extinguished the brand which had guided them across the causeway. The ensuing darkness revealed a pale light which emanated from the trunk of the yew. At its base, great age had caused the trunk of the tree to split forming a passageway through which men could pass into the temple beyond. Standing to one side their guide indicated that the royal party should enter. Led by King Hrethel, they passed through the passageway to emerge into a well lit courtyard. At the centre stood an ornately carved table upon which rested a large bronze cauldron. The courtyard was enclosed by a series of heavily carved arches while Beowulf noticed that a roofed gallery circled above. Further back, to the rear of the courtyard, a larger arch contained three huge, indistinct forms.

An older woman, dressed identically to their previous guide, handed the men a horn of drink as they entered. Following the example of his companions, Beowulf raised the horn to his mouth and began to drink the bitter tasting liquid, continuing until none remained. Immediately he began to feel the effects of the strange drink. A warm, almost hot, sensation spread throughout his body, his lips became numb, and his hands and feet began to tingle. Although fully awake, Beowulf felt as if he had not just lost control of his mind and body, but that his every thought and movement was now decided by another. Dimly he became aware of a circle of women appearing from the shadows of the gallery. All were naked but for the upper half of a goat skull which crowned their heads. The women began to sing softly as several cats, dogs and goats and a naked man were led into the courtyard.

Nooses were placed around the necks of the animals and, one after another, they were hoisted, choking, up into the canopy where crows immediately alighted on the corpses, feeding on the still warm eyes.

Obviously under the influence of seith, powerful magic, the man seemed unaware of his fate. Beowulf watched as a noose was placed around his neck by the volva, the seeress, and the man was pulled upright until his feet barely touched the ground. At last he seemed to become dimly aware of his situation as a look of alarm came to his face. Clad only in a cloak of cat skin and the skull of a ram, the volva took up a spear from the table. Holding the spear aloft, she turned towards the shadowy figures at the rear of the courtyard.

"Woden, Allfather. Accept this sacrifice we make in your honour. Bring forth the Sun for this New Year, that it may warm our blood and nourish our crops. Keep our royal family strong that they may protect the Geat people from their enemies."

Turning back, she thrust the spear into the side of the man as he was finally hauled off of his feet and into the branches of the tree. The bronze bowl was collected and held towards the corpse as it swung lazily in the light breeze, blood from the wound in its side running down the shaft of the spear until it fell, spattering the bowl and the volva beneath. Returning the cauldron to its place on the table she beckoned the royal party forward. Following their example, Beowulf approached the table and placed one hand on a large golden ring which was mounted upon it and the other on the shoulder of Hythcyn to his left. Following the lead given by the volva they repeated their vows to protect the Geat people and honour the gods during the coming year.

Dipping a small wand of yew wood into the bowl she proceeded to flick blood from the sacrifice onto them while her companions approached and, dipping small bunches of holly, ivy and mistletoe into the blood, proceeded to move about the temple, anointing the surfaces. Turning back, Beowulf saw the first faint lightening of the sky to the east as the pre dawn cast its orange glow. Soon the sky became flecked with red and orange clouds as the dawn of the New Year approached. As the sun broke cover from the confines of the Earth it illuminated the perfect image of a goat's neck and head on one of the main branches of the yew. Perfect in every detail, the rising sun shone directly through the eye of the goat, its beam falling directly onto the rear part of the compound. To his surprise Beowulf saw that the large shadowy figures of the previous night were no longer there, the sunlight illuminating a pair of large doors which led into the temple complex. Intrigued, but unsure whether it was acceptable to speak during the ceremonies, Beowulf decided to wait until they had left the temple complex before asking any questions.

Thankfully a perceptible lightening of the mood amongst his companions seemed to indicate to him that the end was near, a feeling reinforced by the reappearance of the woman who had guided them the night before. Retracing their steps they emerged from the yew tree into the full glare of the now fully risen midwinter sun. Beowulf caught his breath as every curve of her body was outlined by the light streaming through her fine clothing. Her face, a perfect oval, was framed by the darkest hair he had ever seen while her eyes shone deepest brown. A smattering of freckles only added to her beauty as, now smiling, she led them back across the causeway. Removing the locking bar, she stood to one side and bowed her head as the king led them back towards Gefrin. Plucking up courage Beowulf decided to ask the woman about the figures before she disappeared back into the temple. Trying to sound far more confident than he felt, he smiled.

"Who were the three giant figures I saw in the shadows during the ceremony? I was surprised when they were gone with the coming of the dawn."

A look of shock crossed the woman's face as she realised what he had said.

"You saw them!" she gasped. He was about to ask her name when he was cut short.

"Beowulf!"

He turned to see Herebeald indicate that he follow them. Turning back he was just in time to see the doors to the causeway slowly draw together. Gratifyingly, the woman's gaze remained fixed on him until the doors finally closed with a soft thud. Rejoining his kinsmen he was surprised by his Uncle's stern look.

"Don't even think about it, you saw what went on over there, you'd get less burnt sticking it in the fire!"

With a sigh and a smile Herebeald relaxed.

"Come on Yule starts here, we have a day of eating, drinking and games ahead of us."

Placing a friendly arm around him, his eldest uncle led the way back to the hall.

REFRESHED and relieved to have completed their religious duties, the royal party made their way from Gefrin across the town for the Yule games. The games were held at every midwinter and midsummer in a meadow, across the bridge on the southern side of the river. Thralls had been preparing the ground since long before dawn and by midday when the games traditionally began the familiar smells of mead, ale and roasting meats drifted tantalisingly across the clearing. Nearing the royal enclosure Beowulf was hailed by the king.

"How are your skating skills, Beowulf?"

"I can skate of course lord, but it is not my strongest sport if I am honest," he replied.

"That's a shame because you have been entered in the skating race. Apparently Breca, Hythcyn's foster, has issued you a challenge. I suggest that you go and get some practise. It wouldn't do for one of the family to lose to a Bronding now, would it?" The king smiled as he leaned closer. "Hygelac was a good skater when he was younger," he suggested with a wink.

Beowulf sought out his foster father amongst the good natured crowd.

"Ah, there you are, my champion skater!"

Turning, Beowulf saw Hygelac and Herebeald making their way over.

"Best we go and find you some skates if the family honour is in peril!" he laughed.

To one side of the meadow a temporary market place had been set up for the duration of the games. A ramshackle collection of stalls, tents and wagons had sprung up overnight as traders, ale and food sellers jostled for business. Several men, guarded by lord less warriors, were in the process of offering odds on the prospects of the participants in various races which were to be held that afternoon. Soothsayers hovered around these like so many crows around a corpse, offering to guide the choices of those who were undecided.

"Can I be of service to you lord?" offered one of the stall-holders as they approached, "I have a wagon full of the best goods you will find for sale today, and if you cannot see what you desire I can get it for you quicker than anyone else here."

Short and portly, Beowulf noticed that the man was

dressed in finer clothing than the majority of the sellers. While his face was not unfriendly his eyes already seemed to be calculating how much profit he could take from them if he could persuade them to visit his wagon.

"I want the finest skates at the fair for my foster son, do you have them?"

"Skates are my speciality!" the man exclaimed. "You won't see a finer pair today, lord."

"You'd better hope that I don't. Do you see that spitted pig over there?" he indicated with his head. "That could be you."

Approaching the wagon the man called to his companion.

"Bring out our finest skates for our young lord here!"

Indicating that Beowulf should sit, the seller continued.

"Let's see what size you will need, lord."

Beowulf sat and raised his foot. The seller blanched and his mouth opened involuntarily.

"Your feet are in proportion to the rest of your body, lord," he said recovering. "Perhaps the runners from the wagon would be suitable?"

There was an uncomfortable pause as Hygelac and Herebeald looked at each other before they both roared with laughter.

"I assume that we can prepare the spit then?" Hygelac grinned.

"Not at all, lord," the seller replied. "I will take some measurements and personally make the finest pair of skates here today. When does the race start?"

"The first skaters are already on the ice."

The seller's face fell again, before he rose to the challenge.

"I will personally deliver them to you in good time."

"WHERE ARE YOUR SKATES, BEOWULF?" Hythcyn asked. "I understood that you were in the race this afternoon?"

The royal brothers and their retainers were sipping ale and watching the participants of the forthcoming race warming up out on the frozen river. Beowulf noticed that several seemed far more proficient on the ice than he, not least Breca, who seemed to revel in his skating ability. For the first time since coming north, he worried that he would be bested in a trial of strength or skill.

"I needed to have some made for me uncle. The traders only seemed to have child sizes for sale. Maybe that's why Breca had no trouble finding a pair."

Hythcyn snorted at the reply.

"Perhaps you would care to place a wager on your victory today then, if you are so confident?"

"Come now, brother," Hygelac interrupted. "You know that Beowulf has no means of his own until he reaches manhood next summer, I will share a wager with you if you want."

"I will be happy to take your money also if you wish, but you are quite wrong. Beowulf wears a fine seax at his belt does he not? I would be willing to have a sword made to match it for our kinsman should he win today. What do you say Beowulf?"

All other conversations had ceased as those in earshot turned to follow the duel of words between the two.

"That was a personal gift to Beowulf from King Hrothgar as you well know Hythcyn. You have enough wealth without taking the only thing of value our kinsman owns." Hygelac growled.

Those nearby sensed the air of tension which had crept into the conversation.

"Nonsense, Uncle," Beowulf interrupted. "If I remember rightly you taught me that a man's wealth is measured in his good reputation not the accumulation of possessions."

Unstrapping 'King's Gift' he held it out towards Hythcyn.

"I would be honoured if you would accept this unworthy gift, uncle," Beowulf declared.

A murmur of appreciation rippled around the room at Beowulf's extravagant gesture. For a moment Hythcyn stared at Beowulf as if in recognition of a worthy opponent before, with a slight inclination of his head, he left the tent.

"That was well done kinsman," Herebeald said, placing a friendly hand on Beowulf's shoulder. "Unfortunately Hythcyn is somewhat less than noble. It gives me no pleasure to say it, but I fear that you are making an enemy of my brother. You would do well to keep your wits about you during the race this afternoon."

Ulfgar, Hygelac's thegn, approached the group.

"There is a short fat man outside holding a pair of enormous skates, lord. Shall I send him away?"

"What, and miss Hythcyn's face when Beowulf humiliates his precious Bronding?" Hygelac responded with a laugh. "Come on Beowulf you've got work to do!"

An old familiar voice broke in on him. "Good luck, lord!" Beowulf turned and was surprised to see the beaming face of Svip, a now fully grown eagle on his wrist.

"Svip!" he exclaimed. "I wondered where you had got to. I assumed that you were at the king's hunting lodge upriver."

"I am usually, but the king wanted Thunderbolt here to give a display later. She is a fine bird, the best I have trained, and I have trained a few that's for sure. It makes my heart sing to be seen with such a bird and I know that the king feels the same way. You certainly know how to please the king, lord."

"Thunderbolt here was only part of the gift Svip. You know full well that your knowledge and training created the fine hunter that we have here."

Beowulf stood and admired the bird for a moment. It truly was a king amongst birds with a powerful brown torso flecked with golden highlights. Yellow, curved talons the size of small knives gripped Svip's thick leather gloved hand while above, a powerful hooked beak emerged from the leather hood which enclosed the bird's head.

"She is beautiful, that was a good day's work I did all those years ago, eh?"

"It was lord, it was," Svip agreed, glancing away as a wildly gesticulating Hygelac caught his eye.

"I think that you are needed, lord," he added, nodding towards where the others had gathered to await the race. "Good luck!" Smiling, Beowulf took up his skates and turned to rejoin the royal party.

"Come on Beowulf, everybody else is waiting for the off!"

Beowulf just had time to briefly practise on the ice and warm his muscles in preparation before the competitors were called to the starting position by the king. To his relief the trader appeared to have been as good as his word and the skates were a perfect fit and beautifully finished. Beowulf was filled with a new feeling of confidence and was looking forward now to the contest. Spectators had gathered on both banks of the frozen river to watch the contest, their breath misting and hanging in the still midwinter air. The sun was beginning to dip now on the horizon and the cold of the northern winter was tightening its grip on the land. The race was to be the penultimate event of the day, only Thunderbolt's display was to come, ensuring that the day's festivities finished on a suitably exciting note.

"The race will consist of three circuits of the islands of Miklaborg and Goat Island," the king began. "There are no rules and may the best man win. Off you go then!"

It took a second or two for the racers to realise that the king had declared the race begun, then, accompanied by a roar from the crowd, the skaters burst forth from their positions. At first the course took them away from the fairground, towards the main river which led north to Lake Vanern. Soon they had all settled into a steady rhythm, cautiously shadowing each other, increasing speed only when one of their number lengthened his stride in an attempt to open up a clear gap between himself and the others.

Beowulf was happy to settle into the pack for now as he became accustomed to his new skates. Occasionally he skated ahead of the others, noting with satisfaction how most of the other competitors found it increasingly difficult to keep in contact with him. The one exception was Breca. He was clearly a very accomplished skater, swift and skilful, and it was becoming clear to both the participants and the watching crowd that the winner was most likely to come from one of these two. Slowly Beowulf and Breca began to put some distance between them and the chasing pack until, by the beginning of the third and last lap, the gap between the pair and the others had grown to the distance of a good spear throw. As they rounded the eastern tip of Miklaborg for the last time Beowulf was slightly ahead of Breca. The river passage here was little more than a narrow channel and ahead the willow lined shore of Goat Island loomed before them. Dimly, Beowulf became aware of a burning sensation on his chest.

With a sudden movement Breca came up behind Beowulf

and grabbed the back of his clothing. Taken unawares, Beowulf had no time to react as Breca changed direction and hurtled towards a large willow which stood half in and half out of the frozen channel. Recovering from his surprise, Beowulf tried to reach behind and grapple with Breca but he kept his body just out of reach. Just as he began to despair and prepare himself for the bone crushing impact of the tree he felt the grip loosen as a black shape fell from above onto the head of the Bronding.

Crying out in alarm, Breca released his grip on Beowulf as the crow beat about his head and shoulders with its wings. Just in time Beowulf was able to drop to the ice and slide, feet first, into the trunk of the tree. Looking back he saw the crow leave Breca and rise, cawing, to the temple which loomed above them. As he squinted up at the building Beowulf saw the crow alight on the arm of the woman who had been their guide to the temple that morning. Smiling briefly, she turned and was swallowed up once more amongst the buildings.

The swish of skates brought his mind rushing back to the race. The tussle between them had allowed the following pack to overhaul them and now both Beowulf and Breca stood little chance of victory. With a weary smile at Beowulf, Breca set off in pursuit of the others. Rising to his feet Beowulf found that one of the bone blades of his skates had been broken cleanly in two by the impact with the tree. His race over, he tossed the skates onto the shore and made his way across the island on foot, emerging just in time to see the end of the race on the far bank. All that was left for him to do was to sling his skates around his neck and make his way unsteadily across the ice to the waiting group. To his joy he found that Breca had come in second place, a son of one of the minor thegns emerging with the honour of winning the race.

"Did the skate break? I'll spit that trader!"

Hygelac pushed his way through the crowd.

"No uncle, the skates were fine, in fact they were far better than that. They were the finest skates that I have had the pleasure to own. I would be grateful if one of your men would have the man repair them and pass on my thanks to him. Let's just say that I had a bit of an accident with a tree. If you will excuse me I have a duty to perform."

Beowulf made his way across the royal enclosure seeking out Hythcyn, whom he found berating Breca. Unbuckling 'King's Gift' he held out the seax.

"Congratulations lord, she is a fine knife, now rightfully yours."

Looking up Hythcyn at first looked confused until he remembered the wager.

"Don't be stupid boy, Breca didn't win, he came second and second place is nowhere."

He shot a withering glance at Breca who was sitting, shamefaced, at a bench.

"With respect lord," Beowulf continued, "I believe that the wager was on my victory and I never completed the course, so the seax is rightfully yours."

Realising that he was honour bound to accept, Hythcyn reluctantly took the knife and tossed it to Breca.

"As you seem to value the seax so little perhaps we can have a return contest between them to determine final ownership brother?"

Turning Beowulf saw that Hygelac had followed him on his errand.

"May I suggest a swimming race between them on midsummers day?"

Hythcyn appeared to brighten up immediately.

"Agreed, brother, that will give our young kinsman here time to practice, although I would be surprised if an ox like that will get very far!"

"Yes, he hasn't swum much, but he does try hard. I'll tell you what," he added as an apparent afterthought, "let's make it more interesting and have them both fully clothed and wearing mail."

THE KING LED his people back across the bridge to the settlement on the northern shore. On his arm sat 'Thunderbolt' whom they had all just seen swooping and diving for their benefit. One particular display had proven to be the highlight of the day's entertainment. Svip had released the bird which had then slowly circled the meadow, all the while gaining height. In no time the expectant crowd were craning their necks and shielding their eyes against the bright midwinter sun as they attempted to keep the eagle in view. Suddenly Svip gave a series of short, sharp, whistles and the crowd gasped as Thunderbolt tucked in her wings and plummeted earthwards. At his signal a waiting thrall released a grouse from a cage to one side of the clearing. Hemmed in by the crowds the bird had taken the most obvious route to safety, straight across the meadow, unaware of the eagle hurtling towards it. At the last moment the bird seemed to sense the danger and tried to take avoiding action but it was too late. Thunderbolt, legs and claws extended, hit the grouse in an explosion of feathers. Landing with its prey, Thunderbolt had folded its wings around the doomed bird as it fed. It was a suitable end to the events of the day and the watching Geats had erupted into wild clapping and cheering as their proud king looked on.

With bellies full of food and ale provided by their king and a full day's entertainment to brighten the dark midwinter day, the Geat people were thankful to have such a benevolent and noble king. In the thirty years he had ruled them, the Geats had not known invasion or defeat. Harvests had been good and the people had prospered under the protection of the gods. The more thoughtful of his subjects might have reflected on his great age, he was surely over sixty winters by now, and looked to the royal brothers who followed him. Even here it seemed to them that the Geats were blessed. To have three fine sons survive into adulthood must be the work of the gods. As the sun dipped on midwinters day the Geats hurried back to their own celebrations, safely locked inside their homes or those of their friends. Yule time was always a time for friends and families to gather together for feasting and drinking as the short, cold, days left little time for outside work. Tonight would see Woden ride throughout the lands of the north on his 'Wild Hunt', accompanied by dead riders on spectral horses, giant hounds baying at their heels. Yes, it was time to hurry home and stoke up the yule log.

Regaining Gefrin the party removed their weapons and entered the hall. The familiar smells and sights of the hall were welcome after a day spent in the cold winter air. A long hearth blazed away along the centre of the hall, spitted joints of meat crackling in the heat as the juices burst forth and dripped, sizzling, onto the fire below. This meat was not intended for the warriors and nobles on this night. Midwinter day held one more duty for them before they could retire.

Clearing the hall of all others the king assembled his closest family and hearth companions. Looking around himself Beowulf realised with pride that he was now a fully accepted member of the company. This summer his fostering would finally end and he would endure the rituals which would confirm his status as a man and warrior of the Waeg-mundings. Here surrounded by his Grandfather, King Hrethel, his Uncles Hygelac, Herebeald and, yes, even Hythcyn, and warriors like Alfhelm, Hromund and Ulfgar, Beowulf felt proud of his progress under Hygelac's guidance. One day, perhaps soon, he would most likely stand in a shield wall shoulder to shoulder with some of these men as he fought for honour and reputation. He longed for that day to come.

"Knives and spears only. Nothing else." Hrethel ordered when the others had left. The hall steward appeared with an armful of boar spears. Thicker than regular spears, boar spears needed to be strong enough to withstand the powerful thrashings of a wounded boar without breaking.

"Keep your wits about you Beowulf, I have seen this bastard and he is huge and meaner than Hygd at full moon," Hygelac smiled.

"Seriously," he continued, "I know that we have hunted boar together but this one is trapped and frightened and as heavy as a man. We have too much time and effort invested in you to see you lying on the hall floor trying to stuff your guts back inside your belly. Watch those tusks!"

The dogs began to grow agitated as they caught the scent of the approaching boar, whining and growling as they paced the floor. There were three of them, grey coated and utterly fearless, and Beowulf looked forward to the day when he had his own 'Wolfhounds' scavenging in his hall.

Shouting a warning, the steward and his helpers threw open the hall doors and the boar burst in. As the door slammed shut to its rear, it stood taking in its new surround-ings. The beast had poor eyesight but Beowulf could see its snout testing the air as it sought out signs of danger. Immediately the dogs raced in to attack. Two of them hung back and circled the boar as the biggest dog went straight in regardless of the danger from the blade-like tusks. The speed of the attack had obviously taken the boar by surprise and the dog was rewarded for its courage as it managed to lock its jaws around the boar's throat. The boar kicked and thrashed wildly as it sought to escape, while the dog hung on grimly.

Both of the other dogs now attacked, one from each side, and it looked to Beowulf as if the contest was to be far briefer than they had expected. Suddenly the first dog lost its grip on the boar's throat. With a toss of its head the boar sent the dog spinning through the air, landing heavily on its back. In an instant the boar seized its chance and, with an upward flick of its head the tusks opened up the belly of the dog before it had time to recover. Ignoring the attacks of the other dogs the boar trampled on the writhing form, battering it into a bloody mess.

Raising its head from the carcass it stood, legs planted and dripping blood and gore, ready for the next attack. A length of the dog's intestines had been speared and hung bloodily from one of the boar's tusks. As the dogs backed away the men spread out and advanced on the boar, spears held ready to ward off any sudden attack. Sensing the new danger the boar looked around for an escape route. With an explosion of energy the animal suddenly made for the small gap which had opened up between Beowulf and Herebeald as they moved either side of a bench. With lightning reflexes Herebeald swung his spear to his right and transfixed the boar against one of the hall pillars. Leaning against his spear he sought to keep the wildly thrashing beast pinned as the others scrambled to his aid. Writhing, squealing and kicking, the boar began to work loose from the spear as Herebeald desperately pushed against it with all his weight. Beowulf was the first to reach the struggle but as he lunged with his spear the boar broke loose, sending it spinning from his grasp. Enraged, the boar made straight for the near defenceless Herebeald as he desperately drew his knife.

Beowulf instinctively threw himself onto the back of the boar as it charged past. Grabbing the tusks with both hands he twisted the swine's head to one side. As they fell together, Beowulf managed to wrap his legs around the boar's waist and tighten his arms around the upper body, frantically fighting to keep a grip on the murderous tusks. Closing his eyes and concentrating on holding on to the screaming, thrashing, mass of the animal, he was only dimly aware of the arrival of the others as they sought to lash the flailing legs of the boar together. One of the dogs clamped its jaws around the boar's throat and Beowulf felt its struggles begin to lessen as it seemed to realise that its end was near. Opening his eyes Beowulf saw that he was now surrounded by the rest of the group. A hand took his shoulder.

"You can let him go now, kinsman."

He looked up into the grinning face of the king.

"You are destined to be a great warrior or soon to be dead. Try to make it the first for my daughter's sake."

While the dog still held the boar by the throat, the assembled warriors knelt and placed their right hand onto its still heaving torso. Dedicating its life to Tiwaz, the warrior god, they each reconfirmed their vows to each other as warriors and asked the god to protect the Geats in the coming year. Drawing his knife from his belt, Hrethel felt for the rear of the skull before pushing the blade in up to the hilt. The boar jerked before, with a final judder, it stilled. As the carcass was carried away to be butchered and cooked for them, Herebeald passed Beowulf, thumping his chest, looking him straight in the eye and nodding sternly.

Beowulf was filled with pride at the gesture from a man he admired and whose life he had probably saved. One day, perhaps soon, Herebeald would be king and Beowulf would be one of his most trusted warriors.

Neither man could know that Herebeald had just spent his last Yule on Middle earth.

6

Slowly the days grew longer as the winter released its grip on the land. The sound of running water returned to the brook behind Hygelac's hall and the sun rose a little higher in the sky each day, searching out the remnants of the winter's snow. Stag moss began to reappear, its antler like shapes one of the first signs of spring, soon the ground would be covered in sweeps of blue borage. Warblers and finches busied themselves tidying old nests and building new ones for the coming brood. Children studied the sky searching for the return of the swifts and swallows or stopped to listen for the call of the cuckoo.

This was to be an important year at Skara, Hygelac's hall. Astrid's betrothal to Herebeald's foster son Eofer, the Engle, had been formalised during the winter and preparations were being made to provide the daughter of a Geat ætheling with an appropriate dowry. Hygelac and Hygd had been busy collecting items of rarity and value for many months. Hygelac had taken the opportunity at the midwinter fair to scour the traders' wares looking for unusual items. He had returned with a collection of exotica to the delight of both women. Gold and silver coins bearing strange lines and dots jostled with those bearing the heads of Romans and Greeks.

A small silver bowl, finely engraved with a scene of a naked youth vaulting the horns of a large bull particularly caught Hygelac's eye.

"We will have to incorporate that in our warrior initiation!" he had joked to Beowulf, for it was the year that he finally took the tests of manhood and would be fully accepted into the warrior elite. The prize find of the day however was a green pot made from something which the trader called jade. Delicately carved around the side of the pot were depictions of giant, large eared, creatures with tusks which appeared to be the size of an enormous bull. As beautiful and eye catching as the pot undoubtedly was, the real treasure was contained within. Small, brown, wrinkled seeds called pepper. When ground they produced a powder which could be added to food, improving the taste of just about any meat or fish. Hygelac and Beowulf had been allowed by the seller to try a tiny amount on a piece of smoked fish to seal the deal, and soon after Hygelac was the proud owner of a pot of pepper. Ever since he had been trying to persuade Hygd to keep a little of the pepper for their own use but she was unmoved. Locked away within her personal chest the items bought for the dowry were not to be touched. One more thing needed to be added to the dowry before the day came and that was definitely Hygelac's area of responsibility. It was the custom of a bride to take an item of war gear to present to her first born son on his coming of age as a gift from her family.

Hygelac had decided that the gift of a small seax would be the ideal.

"Eofer's family will no doubt have a full size sword already set aside for the boy, a shield is too big to keep hidden for fifteen winters and he'll soon grow out a mail shirt," he reasoned. "Besides, that seax of Beowulf's, King's Gift, was beautiful and made short work of those two wolf heads. You can come with me Beowulf, we need to order you a couple of things for your coming of age. We will take the ship around to Geatwic. Alfhelm will be pleased to see us."

They set off at first light the following morning. A thrall had been sent ahead the previous evening to instruct Hygelac's ship master, Harald, to make sure the ship was ready for sea. They rode for a time in silence as the sun cleared the southern hills, warming their backs. Seals lay sunning themselves on the offshore skerries, inland the rhythmic hammering of a woodpecker echoed amongst the trees. Hygelac was the first to break the spell. "This will be a hard year for Hygd you know, Beowulf, losing both Astrid and then you within a few months of each other will tear the life out of the hall. It was bad enough when Heardred left for foster but at least then we expected to see him again one day, and of course she still had Astrid to care for. When a daughter is married abroad there is a good chance that they will never see their mother again. It is hard on both of them," he paused as the horse ambled on. "What I am trying to say is if Hygd seems a bit irritable over the next few months try to under-stand that it is not anything you have done. On the contrary we are both as proud of the man you have become under our care as we would be if you were our own. You will be busy when you are a warrior, but try and get back to see Hygd once in a while. I know she would want that."

"Of course I will uncle, you have my word, I could not have asked for a finer upbringing, in a more loving hall."

"I know you will son, I know you will," he replied, before adding with a frown "and if you see Heardred on your travels, tell him that if he doesn't come home one day and see his mother I will break every bone in his body!"

EMERGING from the tree line the path dropped down to the boathouse below. Beowulf recognised the familiar sights common to every shipyard he had visited from Geatland to Dane Land. Piles of timber lay drying on racks while shipwrights, ankle deep in wood shavings, worked with adze and saw, shaping timbers into new planks, beams or ribs. Safely away from the wood a smith worked his trade, stripped to the waist against the heat of the furnace, hammering out iron nails and fittings before quenching them in a cloud of steam and adding them to the ever growing pile. It was a good place to be.

As they neared the boathouse Harald appeared from behind a hull wiping his hands on a rag. Seeing Hygelac and Beowulf he smiled broadly and approached them.

"All is ready, lord. I was just helping to caulk one of the boats while I waited for you to arrive. I can't stand being idle, and there is always something to do in a shipyard."

Dismounting, the pair handed their reins to a waiting thrall. Stretching, Hygelac took a deep breath and smiled.

"Ah, the smells of a shipyard, wood, pitch, damp, sweat, shit. It's all coming back to me."

"Honest smells, lord!" Harald declared still smiling. "The smell of men at their work."

"That must be why you spend so much time at sea then, I can't say that I blame you!" Beowulf chuckled.

"Well, it might help to recruit a crew," Harald agreed, tapping the side of his nose, "but don't tell them that. Come on over to the hard, I have some refreshments all ready for you."

CLEARING THE HARBOUR, the ship made its way steadily south-west until it finally emerged into the open sea. Once clear of the land a steady breeze from the North whipped the sea into a herd of wild, white flecked horses. Shipping the oars, Harold ordered the sail to be hoist aloft.

"This will speed our journey lord," he called over. "We couldn't have asked for better weather. I will keep inshore though, amongst the skerries, it looks a bit choppy over there."

Looking over to where he had indicated Beowulf could see that further out, in the open sea, the waves were rolling and crashing, spindrift flying in long tendrils. Even in early spring these waters were often stormy and many vessels had come to grief amongst the rocky islands and shorelines of Geatland. Beowulf watched as Harald braced himself against the steering oar, eyes darting left and right checking the way ahead was clear of obstacles and was reminded of the journey all those years ago on his father's ship with Hudda and his crew. At the time, he remembered, he thought that he was off on a great adventure, Beowulf the eagle fighter with men to command. Looking back he was a little embarrassed at how naive he had been on that trip. He now realised the desperation which had led Hudda to gamble his lord's ship and the life of his only son by taking the vessel through a gap which was barely wide enough. Vastly more experienced now in the ways of warriors, he recognised the moment when Bjalki and his men had donned their war gear, intending to sell their lives as dearly as possible in his defence and felt humbled. Quiet now, he took himself off to the bows for the remainder of the voyage where he could be alone with his thoughts as he watched the coastline pass slowly off to larboard, the antics of gannets, cormorants and gulls the only distraction.

Rounding the headland, Hygelac's ship, *Swan*, entered the

wide estuary of the Geat River. At its head lay the great trading centre of Geatwic, their destination. Soon they were pulling alongside the wharf which belonged to the ealdorman of Geatwic, Alfhelm. Recognising the flag which flew at the masthead the port Reeve came down to the shore and personally oversaw the docking, while a man was sent to inform Alfhelm of their arrival. Soon the dockside resounded to his booming voice as the dockside workers scrambled aside to clear his path.

"Ætheling, Beowulf, you have no idea how good it is to see you two. I have been stiff with boredom since Yule, stuck here dealing with the problems of grasping traders. If one of them has a rat in his bilge they all want one," he laughed. "Come on up to the hall, I feel a good feast coming on, I'll see if I can rustle up some entertainment for the evening. Mind you," he winked, "you should have sent word that you were coming. I don't think that I can arrange boar wrestling at such short notice!"

Laughing, they all mounted and made their way across town to the hall. Beowulf liked Alfhelm, he liked him a lot.

Rising late the next morning they all made their way back through the town to the quarter frequented by the craftsmen and artisans. A plain breakfast of cheese, bread and ale had done much to settle their stomachs from the overindulgences of the previous evening. The highlight of the entertainment had come in the form of a madman who accompanied various popular songs with an act which consisted of a series of extravagant leaps and farts. Both Hygelac and Beowulf had almost caused themselves physical damage with the amount of, no doubt drink stimulated, laughter that had ensued. Now Alfhelm was leading them through the back alleys of Geatwic on their way to see the smith he had recommended. It said much for the abilities of the man that he felt able to walk through these parts of the town unescorted.

"This is the place I was telling you about," he said at length.

Alfhelm had stopped outside a nondescript hut much like any of the others in the town.

"It may not look much," he whispered, "but Eadgar is a smith and jewel maker to rival Wayland himself."

Pushing open the door they entered a work area, beyond which lay the living quarters of Eadgar and his family. To Beowulf's surprise he found himself in a large, clean, well-ordered space. Seeing them enter, a large man, obviously Eadgar's bodyguard rose to his feet and approached. Smiling he greeted them.

"Welcome, lord... sorry, lords," he corrected himself, noticing the obvious rank of Alfhelm's companions.

"And how is Cola today, not working too hard I trust?"

"Work is for thralls, lord!" he grinned, revealing a line of rotten teeth.

"What happened to your teeth man, they look like you have been chewing dung!" Hygelac exclaimed.

"Too much mead, lord!" Cola beamed with unseemly pride.

Hearing the conversation outside a tall, slim man emerged from the rear quarters. Tufts of red hair stuck out at various unrelated angles lending a slightly comic air to his appearance.

"Lord Alfhelm!" he exclaimed with obvious warmth. "Your item should be ready in a few days. I will have one of the boys deliver it as soon as it is ready."

"There is no great hurry. I have brought Lord Hygelac and his foster son Beowulf to see you. They intend to commission a seax as part of a dowry and I recommended your work to them."

"Ætheling, you honour my house with your visit. Of course you can have complete confidence in my work. I pride myself in only producing the finest pieces. And you Lord Beowulf, you are welcome of course, although I don't think that I can produce a boar to wrestle at such short notice!"

Beowulf and Hygelac shot each other a look of surprise as Alfhelm grimaced and rubbed his nose.

"I sometimes stop by for a drink with Eadgar and it may have slipped out. Sorry lord."

"I wish that I had been there," chipped in the genial Cola, "it sounds just my sort of thing!"

Hygelac sighed. He knew Alfhelm well, and knew the most likely type of man who he would choose to call upon when he felt the need to 'stop by' anyplace. He may as well be the one to set the ball rolling.

"Did someone mention drink?"

BEOWULF TOOK the opportunity to examine some of Eadgar's work while the others sat at their ale. To his surprise Cola appeared at his side.

"Can I help you lord? I have worked with Eadgar for many years and can show you some of the best examples of his work that he has to hand."

"Cola, I thought that you would be interested in the drinking."

"Oh, there will plenty of time left for drinking, lord, especially when Lord Alfhelm pays us a call," he smiled. "Besides I take almost as much pride in the work produced by my kinsman as he does himself."

Seeing Beowulf's surprise he continued.

"Eadgar is married to my sister, Edith, she is out the back with the bairns, come and meet them."

Cola led the way through the door and into the main hall. Ducking beneath the lintel they entered a wide cross passage, the door at the rear leading out onto a small wattle enclosed area. To the right twin doors opened onto smaller rooms.

"The buttery and the pantry, lord. The buttery for the butts, of ale, and the pantry to store food," he explained. A wall of vertical oak planks formed the interior walls of the hall, screening the main room from the outside. From the interior came the unmistakable sounds of children at play. Knocking on the wall Cola ducked through the opening and entered the main room of the hall, calling out;

"We have a visitor, sister!"

Stepping over the sole plate, the ground beam which formed part of the frame of the house, Beowulf ducked through into the hall. In many ways it was similar to the halls which he was used to but in a smaller form. A fire glowed and crackled in a single hearth at the centre of the room. Along each side were benches, above which hung tapestries of the gods and scenes of wildlife. At the rear of the hall a further door led into the solar, the family's private sleeping area, while off to one side a curtained off bunk had clearly been set aside for Cola's use. On one of the benches tussled two children, their faces obscured under a tangle of red hair. The woman bent over the cooking pot was, Beowulf decided, unexpectedly attractive, considering the dishevelled appearance of her husband. Slightly lighter coloured hair fell in gentle sweeps below her shoulders, perfectly complementing the paleness of her skin. Looking up Beowulf watched in amusement as her face changed suddenly from a welcoming smile to one of horror as she took in the details of the young nobleman standing before her.

"You are welcome, lord," she managed as, recovering her poise, she whipped up her headgear and tucked her hair inside. "You must forgive my brother he has the manners of a thrall," she said, shooting Cola a chastising look.

"As you can see lord, Edith shares our family's good looks." Cola smiled, once again revealing a crowd of rotten teeth.

"This is young Beowulf. I am just showing him some of Eadgar's work. Eadgar is outside with Alfhelm and Hygelac."

"There is an ætheling in my home and you don't think that I might need to know?" she replied, once again horror struck. She rounded on the children.

"You two! Get off there and smarten yourselves up in case your uncle decides to invite them to stay for the night or something. Who knows, maybe King Hrethel is in the neighbourhood and fancies dropping in for some bread and cheese?"

The children's mass of hair was swept back by their mother, revealing two smiling copies of their parents. Scrambling from the bench they rushed to their clothes chests.

"Take a seat lord, I'll get the pieces."

Cola disappeared into the solar and emerged with a small chest. Smiling, Edith handed him a cup of ale.

"This is just a few bits and pieces of course, work in progress, that sort of thing, but it will give you an idea of Eadgar's skill."

Opening the chest Beowulf saw that it was divided into several individual compartments. Strips of beaten gold lay inside one of them while another contained small pieces of red stone. Gently picking one up, he held it up to the light.

"I have seen these on the Royal helm, just above the eyes.

They reflect the light in different ways. Over one eye they are lighter than the other."

"That effect is produced by backing the small gold cells which hold the stones, garnets they are called, with specially prepared gold foil so that they reflect the light in different ways. You will have seen the same effect on sword pommels of course. It produces such beautiful results. I can look at them all day."

Beowulf looked at Cola and realised that he had underestimated the man. Beneath the mead swilling, sword swinging image he presented to the world lay a far more thoughtful, and, he realised, interesting man than his first impressions had led him to believe. Removing the upper trays Cola revealed an item wrapped in oiled cloth. Gently lifting it out of the chest he carefully uncovered it. Inside nestled a small seax of no more than a hand's length. A handle of alternating light and dark bands of bone was topped by delicate work of gold with inlaid garnet. At the base of the handle rested a pair of pyramidal gold clips. Decorated with raised, swirling, beads of gold filigree, Beowulf thought that they contrasted magnificently with the dark background of the horn handle. The blade of the seax had been made of plain, highly polished steel, devoid of any of the swirling patterns Beowulf was more familiar with from the larger seax and swords produced through pattern welding. However along the top of the blade Eadgar had worked an inscription in gold runes. Beowulf had been taught to read the runic alphabet as one of the accomplishments expected of the son of an ealdorman. Along the upper half of the blade he read, *Alfhelm mec ah*, Alfhelm owns me. Turning the blade carefully over revealed, *Eadgar mec agrof,* Eadgar made me.

"The runes were added by inlaying gold wire and carefully grinding and polishing them flat." Cola explained, reverently.

"This is breathtaking work Cola," Beowulf murmured before carefully wrapping the seax and replacing it in the chest.

"How would you like to show me around the other workshops in the area?"

WITH A SMILE and a nod Hygelac waved Beowulf away before he had even half finished informing him where they were going. Beowulf recognised the signs of a good impromptu drinking session now and this seemed to have all the makings of a lengthy affair. Closing the door to the courtyard behind them the pair set off.

"What would you like to see first, lord? We make just about everything a warrior could need in these few lanes."

"I will need a good byrnie soon," Beowulf replied. "Take me to a mail workshop."

Picking their way through the alley Beowulf was unsurprised to see that Cola seemed to be known to everyone and universally popular.

"Those were not Geatish names you had back there. Where are you from?"

"We are Engles, lord. We have lived here for fifteen years or so now. The bairns were born here so maybe they are Geats?"

"That's an unusual path to take, most of your people seem to be heading south and west to Britannia, how did you end up here?"

"We *were* in Britannia before we came here, lord. There was a big battle between ourselves and the British which we lost. It looked at the time that our power had been broken and many Engles left for Gaul or home, although many stayed in the eastern part of the island."

"You were in this battle?"

"I was there lord, but I was only seven or eight winters old, not much more than a bairn really. I did fight at the end though, killed my first men there when they broke through to the camp. My father must have been killed in the fighting because I never saw him again and my mother had died a few years before. Eadgar had been a friend of my father's and he took us in. Edith was already fourteen or fifteen so they ended up marrying." Catching Beowulf's expression at this Cola added. "There was never any pressure from him and he was always honourable towards her. Although there is a good difference in age, it was a love match. Eadgar is a good man who saved us from an uncertain fate. I would happily kill or die for him. I am proud to call him kinsman." Stepping to one side Cola pushed open a wide oak gate. "Here we are," he announced, "the best mail smith in the North."

Beowulf and Cola entered a large courtyard. To one side stood several braziers each with its attendant boy, ready to pump the bellows when needed. Several men worked at anvils and benches, each apparently responsible for a different stage in the manufacturing process.

"Cola!" a voice hailed from the shadows. "Go away I am out of mead!"

A figure emerged from the lean-to structure containing the main furnace. Stripped to the waist but for a leather apron, the man wiped sweat from his brow as he approached.

"I was hoping that you could explain how a shirt of mail is made to our Lord Beowulf, Ulf," Cola responded.

Noticing Beowulf for the first time Ulf apologised. "Of course, it would be my pleasure, lord."

Ulf led them around the courtyard as he explained each process. Small strips of iron were heated and drawn through a series of holes, decreasing in size until the required diameter wire was obtained. This was then reheated and wrapped around a rod of steel to create rings of the correct diameter. The rings were then cold chiselled along the top edge, removing them from the rod. Each link was then forced through a conical tube which forced them to overlap, the ends of which were either flattened to take a small rivet or heat welded forming a continuous chain.

"From that simple, basic, design we can make mail in just about any shape or size depending on the customer's requirement," he explained.

"We also make splint armour over here," he continued, "for lower leg and forearm protection, which is much simpler but very effective when flexibility is not so important, and occasionally we produce suits of lamellar armour." He glanced across to the young Waegmunding. "Are you familiar with it lord? We happen to have a lamellar shirt here for repair if you would care to see it."

Leading them into the main building, Ulf indicated a mail shirt of a design which was unknown to Beowulf. Consisting of small metal plates sewn together by leather thonging arranged around the body in horizontal hoops, it certainly looked impressive.

"How effective is this, Ulf?" Beowulf asked.

"Well I am perhaps not the best person to ask, nobody tries to hack me to pieces as a rule. I am told that it is very good against arrows and generally very effective. I think that the main reason that you don't see more of it is that it is less convenient. Not only does the use of so much leather require more maintenance as it can rot, it is more difficult than ring mail to store on a journey or campaign and more difficult to slip on in a hurry. Generally I would say that the fact that very few warriors, whatever their status, choose to wear it speaks for itself. It does shine up beautifully though if you want to impress."

The rest of the afternoon was spent touring the various workshops. Shield makers, sword smiths and spear makers were all visited. Beowulf thought that perhaps the best was kept until last as Cola introduced him to the owner of a helmet workshop. He marvelled at the variety of plates and decoration available to the warrior, each piece enabling him to personalise this most visible and necessary piece of personal protection.

Arriving back at Eadgar's hall they found that Hygelac and Alfhelm had already returned to his hall. One of Alfhelm's hearth warriors had ridden to accompany Beowulf, leading a spare mount. Beowulf thanked Cola for providing him with one of the most enjoyable afternoons he had spent. Riding back to the hall he made a mental note to remember Cola when he assembled his own hearth troop. The big Angle might look unusual he smiled, but he enjoyed his company immensely and he was sure that he could be trained into a fine warrior in no time at all.

They left early next morning, their horses seemingly enjoying the clear air and empty streets of the town. Arriving at the wharf they found Harald and his crew, forewarned of their plans, waiting patiently for them. Bidding a fond farewell to Alfhelm, they boarded the *Swan* and settled their belongings safely beneath the steering platform. Soon the ship was in midstream, coasting swiftly away from the town, propelled by the ebb tide and the slow easy strokes of the oarsmen. Within the hour they had rounded the cape and struck out north for home.

Beowulf had enjoyed his time in Geatwic and realised

that in some ways it was to be an end to one part of his life and the beginning of another. He had taken a keen interest in the weapons and armour he had seen. In a short time he would own items just like them and would be taking his place amongst the Waegmunding warriors, once more back at the home of his family. It seemed strange to be going home after so long. He could barely remember his real parents now. In many ways he would feel a stranger there.

A rogue wave slapped against the side of the hull sending a spray of salty water across the after part of the ship. Jolted from his thoughts he glanced at Hygelac, in many ways a father to him now. Gripping the strakes of the ship he had taken the full impact of the wave. A glance at the crew revealed that they had seen it too. Most of them were looking at the deck, clearly trying to suppress a smile.

Glancing up, Hygelac gave Beowulf a pained expression as, inhaling deeply he fought to control the contents of his stomach.

"Remind me not to visit Alfhelm too often Beowulf," he groaned.

7

"Right once again. And this time give me a chance!" Hygelac exclaimed, "I am not as young as I was."

They had been practising with spears, one on one, for most of the morning and Hygelac was beginning to tire. Although the spear tips had been bound tightly in cloth both men wore full protection to their upper bodies, mail shirts over a padded jerkin and full faced grim helms on their heads. Droplets hung, glistening, from the base of each face plate as their breath condensed on the cold iron and they were constantly blinking away the drops of sweat which ran, stinging, into their eyes. Hygelac moved forward to attack, feinting to the left before flicking the tip of the spear up and to the right, going straight for Beowulf's heart and a 'kill'. Twisting inside the thrust, Beowulf calmly brought his spear across his body, deflecting the strike harmlessly up and to the side while his left arm swept the base of his spear in an upward arc, clattering into the right side of Hygelac's helm and knocking the man to one side.

"Shit, Beowulf that hurt!"

"Sorry uncle."

"No, don't be sorry lad," he gasped. "The truth is there is nothing more I can teach you. All you need is experience in the field and I can't give that to you here. Practise your moves for the initiation next month and my work will be done."

Hygelac eased his helm off and stood rubbing his right ear before removing the leather cap from his head and wringing out the sweat.

"Come on, that will do for now, let's have a break."

Tossing his gear to a waiting thrall, Hygelac made his way to the grass bank at the rear of the paddock. Beowulf joined him as Astrid brought out a basket of food and a jug of ale.

"You are a treasure," Hygelac grinned as she approached. "Come and sit with us for a while girl, we shan't have many more opportunities."

Astrid placed the basket on the floor and sat on the grass facing them. It was difficult to believe that in a short while she would be a married woman with a household and thralls of her own. It only seemed like yesterday that Beowulf had spent most of the day with his cousin exploring the surrounding woods or swimming off the beach. This time next month he would be a Waegmunding warrior and they would both be far away from here. Although he was excited at the prospect he could not help but feel more than a little sorry to leave his life here behind. He could only imagine the doubts and fears which were going through Astrid's mind as she took the great step into adult life. Still, he thought as he looked at her, she was, like him, the grandchild of the Geat king and this was the path intended for her by due of her birth and she certainly seemed happy enough at the match.

Beowulf and Eofer had become good friends during his time as foster to Herebeald and he was looking forward to visiting them in their new hall amongst the English. He would arrive unannounced accompanied by his hearth troop of grizzled warriors. Perhaps Cola would be with him, he hoped so. He liked the big Angle. In fact he seemed to like all of the Engles he met. Beowulf's thoughts were suddenly interrupted as a nut bounced off of his forehead.

"You are not listening are you, you big ox!"

His eyes refocused on the smiling face of Astrid as Hygelac laughed.

"Good shot!"

"I was saying how I hope you will both come to visit me when I am the mistress of the hall but perhaps it's not such a good idea after all. It wouldn't do for Eofer's family to see that my cousin sits there staring gormlessly into the distance while people are speaking to him!"

Hygelac sat back, watching as his daughter and nephew traded good-natured insults and the occasional piece of well aimed bread or cheese. Smiling contentedly he congratulated himself and Hygd on producing such well balanced, happy adults. Although they couldn't be expected to realise, caught up in the excitement of youth, their leaving would just as surely mark the passing of a stage in the lives of the couple. The hall had echoed to the screams, cries and laughter of children for twenty winters and Hygelac realised for the first time that old age beckoned them. He smiled broadly at the memory of Heardred dashing through the yard, throwing a huge slab of honeycomb in Hygd's direction, and calling out, "Here I have got some honey for us," before disappearing, hotly pursued by a swarm of angry bees and diving full length into the fjord. And the time when Astrid had gone missing and one of the thralls had found her hanging from the branch of a tree by the back of her dress, too proud to call for help. His pride when Beowulf had emerged from the forest leading the horses he had taken from the wolf heads. Life would certainly be quieter in the future he sighed. Unless of course, he thought, brightening, there is a good war.

IT WAS three days later that two sails appeared on the horizon. Hygelac and Beowulf changed into their best clothes and, mounting two white horses, they rode to the headland to welcome the new arrivals. By the time they arrived the hulls were clearly in view. Obviously Eofer had brought a friend to collect his new bride they assumed. As the ships came nearer a great cheer went up from the leading vessel.

"Your eyes are younger than mine Beowulf. Can you see what's going on out there?"

Shielding his eyes from the sun, he craned forward in the saddle to get a better view.

"One of them is oar walking, uncle, from the look of his clothing I would expect it is their lord."

Oar walking demanded the greatest poise and balance, one slip on the wet blade or the slightest movement by the oarsman could send the man tumbling into the sea. Weighed down by weapons and a mail byrnie like this man, Beowulf thought, he would find himself lying on the bottom of the sound before he even realised that he had fallen. A great cheer went up as the man completed the run before leaping into the bow and standing, blond hair streaming, balanced precariously on the stem post.

"This one's a bit of a show off, just what we need Beowulf, an Angle for you to cut down to size. What does he look like?"

Beowulf blinked hard to clear his eyes and stared hard at the figure.

"He looks like," he paused and turned, smiling to Hygelac.

"He looks like you a younger version of you, uncle."

CLATTERING BACK into the yard they dismounted, throwing the reins to the waiting thrall.

"Heardred's back!" he exclaimed to the waiting women.

Beowulf could see Hygd struggling to control her emotions in front of the thralls while, less affected, Astrid smiled and hugged her mother. She had only seen Heardred once as an adult, and that only briefly, so, if she had been honest she was disappointed that the ship had not contained Eofer.

Sensing this, Beowulf added with a wink. "There are two ships cousin, don't lose heart yet."

The women set about preparing the hall as, remounting, Hygelac and Beowulf rode down to the beach. With a scrunch the two ships were driven onto the sand, crewmen tumbling from their sides to make the vessels fast to the mooring posts. Dismounting, Hygelac walked forward to greet his son as, leaping from the bow of the ship into the shallows he splashed up the beach. Grinning widely, they embraced, each slapping the other's back before taking a pace backwards.

"Where on middle earth have you been boy? Your mother has been worried sick!" Hygelac exclaimed.

"I am fine thank you father, thank you for asking," Heardred smiled in reply, before they both roared with laughter. With his arm around Heardred's shoulder, Hygelac turned to a grinning Eofer.

"Welcome back, son. A man can never have too many

kinsmen of your quality. I will send word to my brother that you have arrived, and tell him to bring plenty of ale."

Looking across to the crewmen he called out, "I *am* right. Engles *do* drink ale?"

A chorus of cheers interspersed with several good natured comments seemed to confirm that they did.

"And this must be the cousin I have heard so much about. If only some of it is true I shall have to watch my back!" Heardred beamed.

"If I am behind you kinsman you would have no reason to fear Hel herself!" Beowulf replied.

"Then it seems that I have heard correctly. We can help each other forge new kingdoms in the South. We can be the three powerful kings of Anglia!"

"When you three have finished carving up Britannia between you, I think that the women would like to see you." Hygelac observed. Leaving the horses to find their own way back, the party trudged, noisily, up the path which led to the hall.

Herebeald arrived with his hearth troop the following afternoon, along with his wife Hild and several wagons of food and ale, much to Hygd's relief. The ships crews had erected awnings amidships for sleeping but all day they wandered around the area consuming all available food and drink. Eventually a large party of them were sent out to hunt in the surrounding forest, more in the hope that it would help to prolong the supply of ale than in the expectation that they would provide any meat for the table. Much to everyone's surprise and delight they returned two days later carrying the carcasses of two deer and a small boar between them.

That afternoon the preparations for the formal betrothal feast began. Tables and benches were brought out from the hall for the most important guests, while the Anglian crews either brought up their own sea chests to use or made do with the grassy bank near the paddock. Thralls prepared the fire pits in the courtyard, above which were fixed the spitted deer and boar. Barrels of ale and mead were stacked near the hall, as far away as possible from the crews on the bank, in the hope that the long walk would help to prolong the supply. By late afternoon the aroma of roasting meat hung over the area, heightening the sense of anticipation.

As the pale spring sun dipped below the headland, Astrid finally emerged from the hall. Accompanied by Hygelac, she wore a simple dress of white, on which gold thread had been delicately woven. Gold and silver thread had also been woven into her hair which hung loose down to her waist. Soon she would no longer be a maiden and she would wear her hair bound up and covered as was decent amongst women of quality, but for now, as the setting sun reflected off the thread, she seemed to shine and sparkle like a goddess. Hygd and Hild sat together beaming, as a murmur of appreciation swept the assembled warriors. Following a mercifully short speech by Hygelac and an acceptance from Eofer the betrothal was formalised under Thunor's hammer and by the exchange of gifts.

The last act of the ceremony involved the ritual opening of the first cask of ale by the host. Raised on a frame the height of two men, the cask sat with its stopper facing the gathering crowd. As the men gathered beneath the frame and raised their cups in anticipation, Hygelac raised his spear and prised away the wooden bung. Accompanied by a deafening cheer the ale burst forth in a golden cascade, showering those below who, more in hope than expectation, jostled cups in their outstretched arms, hoping to catch a drop of the first ale of the evening. Beowulf and Heardred stood together, laughing, as the scrum at the base of the ale stream grew more and more riotous until, just at the point that they felt the first fight of the evening couldn't be far off, the stream subsided to a trickle before stopping all together. Good humour instantly restored, the group made off in search of a fresh supply. Hygelac passed them on his way to join Hygd and Hild who had now taken their places alongside Herebeald.

"Two down, one to go!" he grinned as he passed them, reaching out to tousle Beowulf's hair affectionately.

BEOWULF ROSE EARLY next morning and, collecting his clothes, picked his way over the sleeping bodies which littered the floor of the hall. He quickly dressed in the cross passage before stepping through the door into the main court-yard. Screwing up his eyes against the glare of the early morning sun he surveyed the debris left from the night before. Already thralls were moving amongst the scattered bodies attempting to clear up the worst of the evidence of the excesses of the previous evening. Over by the paddock, a line of sleeping warriors lay haphazardly against the grass bank while others just appeared to have slept where they fell. Crows moved amongst the scattered food, one of which was busily picking the choicest pieces from a splash of vomit. He smiled at the efforts of the thralls as they attempted to noise-lessly fill in the pits they had dug the day before to act as a latrine for the guests.

"I don't know why they are bothering with that," came a voice from behind him. "As soon as the boys start waking up they will need to dig a new one to take the next lot after last night."

Turning, Beowulf saw that he had missed Heardred sitting

beneath the eaves, cup in hand, his eyes closed but clearly enjoying the warmth of the early morning sun on his face.

"You rise early too kinsman, I see,"

"Not if I can help it," he croaked, "I haven't turned in yet, it looks as though I may have missed my chance."

Beowulf crossed the courtyard and lowered himself down beside him.

"Here grab yourself a cup."

Beowulf picked up one of the cups from the floor, shook out something from the bottom and held it out. Gingerly sipping the ale he tried to hide the involuntary shiver his body made in protest.

"That's why you should never go to sleep the same night," Heardred observed without opening his eyes. "As soon as you stop drinking you feel like shit."

They sat in silence for a while sipping ale. Beowulf found that the more he drank the better he felt until, after a while, he felt his customary energy levels returning.

"Did you see my mother?" Heardred shook his head and smiled again. "She got like that last time I came home. You won't see her today until at least midday, and then she will go around trying to pretend that she is fine and she just has a cold or something. She does it every time."

"Will you be there for my initiation?" Beowulf asked. Heardred opened his eyes for the first time and looked straight at him.

"Yes, kinsman, there is no place that I would rather be."

Draining his cup he tossed it at one of the crows picking at a deer bone, "Fancy a swim?"

BEOWULF SLUNG a fresh barrel of ale on his shoulder while Heardred gathered a collection of bread, warm meats and cheese and proceeded to wrap them tightly in a large square of leather he had produced from somewhere.

"Oiled seal skin," he explained. "Double wrap anything you want to keep dry and bind it tightly with seal skin thonging. You don't spend weeks at sea without picking up a few helpful tricks."

They walked together down to the beach through a tunnel of fresh green leaves dotted with white and pink blooms as the full effects of spring lay on the land. Birds darted to and fro, their beaks stuffed with worms and insects, as they attempted to satiate the demands of their first brood of the year. Passing the ships drawn up on the strand they smiled at the sounds of the slumbering crew within. Beowulf had to suppress a sudden desire to bang on the side of the ship and call out the alarm just to see the resulting chaos. Heardred was pleased to see that the man on guard was fully awake and armed as they cleared the bows. The man smiled as he recognised them.

"Rannulf, what did you do to deserve this duty?"

"Oh, you know me lord. I would much rather stand here freezing my balls off than sleep and miss the beauty of a Geatish dawn."

"Here, I have brought you some warm food."

Tossing the package to the delighted guard Heardred noticed a barrel of ale tucked discreetly amongst the bushes.

"That must have rolled down the hill during the night. I'll make sure it gets back lord."

"You do that Rannulf. I suggest you make sure that it is empty first, not everyone is as strong as Beowulf here," he replied, indicating the barrel balanced on his shoulder. As they walked on he continued with his advice. "Little things like your lord remembering you are standing alone and bored on a chilly beach with an empty belly mean a lot to a man. Loyalty cuts both ways kinsman."

Reaching the point opposite the island, Beowulf swung the barrel down to the sand and worked his shoulder and arm, rubbing vigorously to restore the feeling in his fingertips. Stripping off their clothes they made their way to the water's edge. Beowulf had tied a cord around the barrel, allowing him to tow it across while Heardred now gripped the food package securely in his teeth.

"There's only one way to get into a freezing sea and that's straight in!" he called as the pair launched themselves into the sound with a mighty splash.

Held back by the weight and drag of the barrel, Beowulf arrived at the island just behind his cousin. Hauling themselves up onto the rocks they picked their way carefully over the loose scree and up onto a platform of rock worn smooth by the action of the tides. Carefully selecting a south facing position sheltered from the wind, they sat down and let the sun dry and warm their bodies before unpacking the food and tapping the casket of ale. Beowulf sensed that Heardred had asked him here for a reason and decided to wait for his cousin to reveal it to him in his own time. Suddenly Heardred grew serious.

"I understand that you have made a bit of an enemy of our uncle. Saving Herebeald's life with your boar wrestling act wouldn't have helped much either. You don't need me to remind you that should anything happen to Herebeald, Hythcyn would be next in line to the throne. If that ever happens, either seek me out or go to the Swedes and ask for protection."

"The Swedes!" Beowulf exclaimed in shock. "I don't think that the situation is that bad."

"No, you are wrong, Beowulf. From what folk tell me you are in some danger. You could have been seriously hurt at the Yule skating race, or worse. I know Hythcyn from when I was a boy, there's something sinister lurking in his very being. He used to scare the life out of me when I was a child, even in a roomful of people. You humiliated him with that seax business and he won't forget or forgive. Remember this conversation if the time should ever come."

Shocked at the apparent depth of Hythcyn's animosity towards him Beowulf pondered on the advice.

"Why the Swedes, I have met King Hrothgar of the Danes, he gave sanctuary to my father and surely the English would protect me?"

"What makes you think that you are so important? You are just a minor member of the ruling family of a minor power. If 'King' Hythcyn requested your head be delivered to him as a Yule gift, do you not think that he would get his wish? Kings and rulers are far more interested in the balance of power between themselves than the fate of Beowulf or Heardred. We are just pieces in their games, never forget that. You would be more useful alive to the Swedes, if only as a potential replacement for Hythcyn."

Chastened, Beowulf sat in silence for a while.

"Tell me about this Anglia. Have you been there? Would I be any safer there?"

Heardred thought for a while.

"I have been there twice. The English have a great trading port at a place they call Gippeswic. It is a land of oak forests, wide rivers, rolling hills and fens. It is a rich land and one day soon I think the Engles will no longer call it the new lands because they will all be living there. Arthur can't live forever and when he dies the British will start to fight each other again."

"Who is this Arthur?" Beowulf asked. "I heard Eofer talking about him."

"Who is Arthur? My father has neglected your education Beowulf! Arthur is the British warlord. Before the Romans came, Britannia used to be made up of a dozen or so different kingdoms all constantly at war with one another, just like everywhere else in the northern lands," he laughed. "Of course as soon as the Romans left they started up again. For a long time they did the same as all the old Roman lands. They hired people like you and me to do their fighting for them, expecting us to do as we were told, take our pay and go back home. But why would you leave when there is a better land, full of lazy people, just waiting for new masters. So about fifty or sixty winters ago the Jutes rebelled under a leader called Hengest."

"I know of Hengest," Beowulf interrupted. "I heard a tale involving his fight at Finnsburg in Frisia when I was in Hrothgar's hall."

"Yes, I have heard that one too, a messy business. Anyway, naturally they defeated the British host sent against them and ended up being ceded a kingdom called Cent if they promised to be good. I haven't been, but I hear that it is fabulously wealthy. It lies in the part of Britannia nearest to Franc Land so it controls the trade for the whole island."

"Why would the British leaders let the Jutes stay in such a strong position, they are helping to destroy themselves surely?"

"Because satisfying their greed is more important to them. Their leaders are men without honour Beowulf. They have no regard for their own people whom they see as just objects to work, pay taxes, and keep them in the comfort to which they feel entitled. If those people are British or Jutes, Saxons, Engles, Geats even, so long as they get to amass more and more riches they would fill the land with people from any nation. There was a great battle on a hill, Badon they called it, about the time you must have been born. Arthur led the British to a great victory there and pursued the English back east. They could have broken our power forever but at the moment of victory the British leaders reverted, once again, to their own rivalries. Once Arthur dies, the island will fall to us, it's as clear night follows day, even I think to them."

They sat in silence for a while, draining their cups.

"I would like to try my sword one day in Anglia, perhaps we can go together kinsman?"

"You won't be going anywhere until you have passed the initiation next month and become a warrior. If you become even half the warrior that I think you could become, Hythcyn will see you as a dangerous rival, not just an annoying young relative. That would be a dangerous development so remember our words here today."

Stretching, he motioned towards the barrel which lay at Beowulf's feet.

"Was that the last of the ale?"

Assured that it was, Heardred rose and retraced his steps back down to the water.

"Come on, let's get back," he called over his shoulder, "I need some hot food."

Unencumbered by the barrel and package and aided by the incoming tide the return journey to the mainland was quickly completed. To their surprise their clothes remained on the beach where they had left them several hours before.

"The boys must be feeling really rough today to miss that one!" Heardred observed.

Approaching the ships they could see the crews were now up and about. A few were dunking their heads in buckets of seawater to revive themselves and some of the hardier ones were leaping into the sound from the sides of the ships. From the greetings they received from the crew members, Beowulf was sure that the events of the previous evening had done Anglo-Geat relations no harm at all. Arriving back at the hall they saw Hygelac over by the paddock talking with Eofer.

"Thanks for the invitation, boys, after all I don't like to swim do I," he called over.

"You shouldn't lie in bed all day then father. Where is mother?"

"I am standing ten paces away, so can you please stop shouting son," came a frail sounding voice from behind.

Turning they saw Hygd sipping from a small cup, clearly trying to summon up the energy to take charge of the clearing up efforts of the thralls.

"Did you enjoy your evening?"

"I did, thank you Beowulf, as did everybody else by the looks of the yard." Heardred gently nudged Beowulf before inquiring with a sparkle in his eye.

"How do you feel mother, you look a little pale this morning?"

"I am perfectly fine thank you," she responded, "I just seem to have picked up a bit of a cold last night."

SUPPLIES for the journey had been loaded earlier that morning, the crew remaining with the precious cargo. With a final hug and kiss for her parents, the bride was passed up into the waiting ship, into the care of her beaming crew. Beowulf, Hygelac and Heardred put their shoulders to the bows and heaved the ship out into the sound. At the command the oars slipped out in unison from along the wales and began to gently beat the water. Pulling slowly into mid channel the craft slid gently out to sea leaving the small group of family and friends gathered on the beach peering at the slowly diminishing shape, trying to catch a last glimpse of the girl they had known all her life, before the ship was swept beyond the point and became lost from view. Already Beowulf felt a sense of loss as his childhood friend began her new, adult, life in a foreign land.

Subdued, he walked back up to the hall with Heardred, silent and reflective. Looking back he saw that Hygelac and Hygd were the last to leave the strand, walking silently, arm in arm, in their wake. For the first time Beowulf saw the pair as he now realised that they had begun to see themselves, growing old. As excited as he felt for himself and Astrid, both now on the cusp of the great adventure of adulthood, he felt a pang of sympathy for the couple who had shown him such care and affection during his time there. He wondered if his own parents were beginning to look as old, and realised that they must be. Would he even recognise them when he met them again?

8

Two days later, a long, low, shape slid silently into the bay. Indistinct at first in the pre dawn gloom it slowly formed into the shape of a dragon ship, the beast topping the prow standing out as a solid block against the slowly lightening sky. Half an hour earlier one of Heardred's crew, the fastest runner, had returned from his position on the headland confirming that the ship was on its way, a shipload of men intent on robbery, killing and enslavement. Instead, forewarned, their intended victims stood, shoulder to shoulder, in battle array. Despite all their planning, and though they did not yet know it, they rowed stealthily to their deaths.

The gods had smiled on Hygelac and his family. One of his thegns, Gunnar, had left the celebrations early to return to his hall. His wife was unwell and had not been able to travel. Hygelac had insisted that he should return home once the formalities of the betrothal had been performed and he had been entertained at the top table. Sent on his way early, he had almost reached his hall on the island of Marstrand when he met one of his hearth warriors on the road. The man had been sent to advise him that a ship's company of armed men had been seen, apparently hiding, in one of the bays on the western side of the island by his shepherd. The man had hastened to the hall and advised the remaining warriors of his discovery. They had accompanied the shepherd to the place and, after observing them, unseen, from the cliffs, they had come to the conclusion that it was most likely that they were lying in wait, ready to attack and rob the returning ship containing Eofer, Astrid and of course, the valuable dowry.

Hurrying back to the hall Gunnar had quickly thrown together a scratch crew to man his largest warship. Although consisting largely of fishermen, waterfront carpenters and shipwrights, stiffened by the majority of his hearth warriors, Gunnar had lined the wales with every available shield to give the impression that the vessel contained dozens of seasoned warriors and sent her out to intercept the English ship with instructions that they hail them, advise them of their fears, and escort them over the horizon. It would be almost suicidal to attack two fully armed crews with one ship. They would simply double up on you and attack from both sides at the same time. Outnumbered already, they would then have to divide their crew into two to defend both sides. Against seasoned fighters it would be unlikely that even the toughest crew would last long against those odds and besides, this crew was after relatively easy plunder not a full scale war, so Gunnar had every confidence that his ruse would succeed. Too weak in manpower to offer battle himself, Gunnar had been forced to organise a defence of his hall and the nearby town. He had however correctly guessed that, thwarted in their original plan, the pirates may well decide to attack the hall of Hygelac. A rich target at any time, the hall would also contain many gifts sent by Eofer's family to their new kins-men, making it an even more tempting target, and had sent one of his warriors, Orme, to warn his lord.

That day Hygelac had sent word to all free men who owed him allegiance to assemble, fully armed, at the hall by nightfall. Heardred had taken his ship into the river which entered the sound at its furthermost end and carefully concealed it, not wishing to betray their presence. That evening, guards were posted along both sides of the bay with orders to return with news as soon as they were sure that a ship was approaching.

Hygelac presided at Beowulf's first council of war that evening as he disposed of his warriors and decided on the tactics to be used. It was decided to let the pirates come ashore, dawn was the most likely time they would attack, and Hygelac, with his hearth warriors and the local levy would block the top of the pathway which led to the hall. Once they had passed by their position at the foot of the path, Heardred and his men would silently ghost from cover and block their retreat. Bowmen were hidden near the landing stage to kill any men remaining with the ship as guards before Heardred took up position. Two remaining bowmen were placed on the higher ground to both sides of the track with orders to pick off any of the enemy who were foolish enough to leave their sides unguarded once the fighting began.

"Beowulf you will take position in the second rank, behind me, If I should fall, step up, you know what to do."

Beowulf had expected to be placed in the second rank, but the disappointment must still have shown on his face.

"You don't even have your own arms yet, they'll be plenty of fights in the future for you if you remember all our work together over the last seven years," Hygelac consoled him.

Heardred winked encouragingly at him from across the table.

"Right, let's eat and make ready. Gods willing, we dance in the morning."

ONCE WORD HAD ARRIVED that the vikings were near, the men formed into a wall of shields and spears, three men deep, at the top of the incline. Hygelac walked slowly along the lines giving encouragement and advice to the freemen who formed the bulk of his force.

"Remember our training and all will be well, lads." He began. "Keep your shields locked and spears to the front. Remember you are covering the man on your left and your right hand man will cover you. Tofi, Ealhstan, Wulf and Thurgar are on the ends of the lines so no one will be outflanked. Keep your discipline like we practised at the muster and we will make a great slaughter here today."

Beowulf noticed the nervous smiles of the men as Hygelac spoke.

"What? Did you think that the muster was just so that you could eat and drink me out of hall and home?" Hygelac gasped, a look of mock surprise on his face.

Nervous laughter ran along the ranks as Hygelac continued.

"Don't show these bastards any mercy, for you would receive none from them. Nobody asked them to come here and try and kill us and carry our wives and children off to the slave markets of the South. There will be no taking prisoners today, kill them all as a lesson to others of their kind. Geat women and children will never be slaves while their men still breathe. What do you say lads?"

A look of grim determination had overtaken the earlier nervousness of the freemen.

"Kill them all!" they hissed.

THE SHIP GLIDED NOISELESSLY to the beach. Armed men began to lower themselves carefully from the sides of the wale, hanging for a moment before dropping as quietly as possible into the shallows. Unslinging the shields from their backs they assembled on the beach before their leader took up position at their head and they began to move towards the path which led up to the hall.

Still out of sight of them at the top of the hill, Beowulf found that his hands had begun to sweat, despite the cool of the morning. Resting his spear against his shoulder for a moment he wiped them against his breeches before resuming his position. All their eyes were fixed on the point on the path where the first of the raiders would emerge around the bend. Beowulf suddenly found that he really needed to piss. There was no time now. How ridiculous would he look if he went now where he stood and the enemy emerged into view? Then again if he didn't, he might lose control of his bladder during the fighting and people would think that he was a coward. It was a chance he would have to take he finally decided. The world seemed to hold its breath as the sun finally cleared the hills to the east. He saw Hygelac in front of him smile as it did so. His plan was working splendidly. Now the bastards would have to fight uphill with the glare of the morning sun directly in their faces. He made a mental note to sacrifice to Woden, Allfather, after the battle.

Beowulf felt a sudden burning sensation against his chest as the tips of spears showed briefly above a bush before the first men rounded the corner and hove into view. He saw them hesitate, shocked and confused, as they realised that they were facing fully alert defenders arrayed in an ideal defensive position. He recognised the moment that their courage deserted them, draining away like ale from an upturned cup, as their minds raced and sought a way out of the trap which had been set for them, before they mentally rallied and came on as they all knew that they would. Fanning out quickly, the raiders arrayed themselves in a shield wall, two deep, facing them. Stepping forward, Hygelac raised a spear and cried out.

"I dedicate the fallen here today to Woden, the Allfather, may he choose wisely from the slain." With a grunt of effort Hygelac drew back his arm and launched the missile away over the heads of the enemy.

With a roar they charged up the path, struggling to keep a boars head formation against the steep gradient, hoping to smash their way through the front ranks of the defenders and into the less experienced fighters in the rear. If that happened it was likely that they would break and run. It was the raiders' only chance and they all knew it, so they came on screaming and shouting and clashing their weapons against their shields hoping to intimidate them. As they grew nearer Beowulf half sensed the arrows begin to fly in and take those men on the flanks of the boar snout.

At the last instant Hygelac screamed *"Now!"* above the din. In a well practised move the front rank of the Geats took a pace forward and braced. Moments later the opposing shields met with a resounding crash which knocked both attackers and defenders back briefly, before they regained their footing and clashed again. Placing his shield boss between the bodies of Hygelac and the man to his right, Beowulf braced himself and pushed forward. A spear glided past his cheek and there was a cry behind him as it found a victim among the tightly packed bodies. Using the enemy spear as a guide he slid his own spear along the shaft seeking out its owner and was exultant as he felt the tip enter soft tissue and continue on into the man.

Suddenly the enemy wall seemed to falter and give way. Caught unawares, Beowulf almost fell as the pressure to the front suddenly lessened, but the man to his right grabbed him under the arm and hauled him upright. Ahead of him Hygelac and the other hearth warriors had dropped their spears, drawn their swords, and were forcing their way inside the enemy ranks, slashing and stabbing in a frenzy of killing. Drawing his own sword, Beowulf followed. Stepping inside the crumbling enemy line he sent his shield boss crashing into the side of the man beside him before following up with a sword thrust to the man's undefended left side. He felt the momentary resistance of his byrnie before the links gave and the blade slid smoothly into him. Beowulf barged into him again, helping to free his blade, before moving forward in search of a new victim. Those coming behind him would finish the man off with their spears.

Another warrior appeared before him wearing a full face grim helm. Before him he held a bloodied shield in which a small hand axe stood embedded. Both men roared as they drew back their arms, ready to impale the other. Suddenly his opponent darted to one side, parrying Beowulf's blow with his shield, before stepping back inside in one swift, fluid movement. Taken by surprise by his opponent's speed, Beowulf waited in horror for the blade to slice through his byrnie and into his belly. To his shock the man threw his arms around him, pinning his arms at his side.

"I had you there kinsman, you need to work on your speed!"

To his relief Beowulf recognised the voice of Heardred. He realised now why the enemy line had given way so suddenly. Attacked from behind by Heardred and his men they had instinctively formed into small groups as they desperately attempted to defend themselves from attacks from both directions. The Geats now swarmed around the dwindling groups, overwhelming them by sheer force of numbers. Even the freemen of the levy surged forward, sensing the battle all but won, and eager to wet their spears in the blood of their enemies while the chance still remained. They could already picture themselves returning home, blooded spear blade in hand, to the admiration of their families and neighbours. In fact the crush had become so great that Beowulf and Heardred found it difficult to re-enter the fight, which in truth, was now drawing to its bloody conclusion. One group of raiders had managed to fight their way to the side of the path. They stood, shoulder to shoulder, their backs against its sheer rock wall. In a strong position they had survived the slaughter of their comrades and now stood surrounded by increasing numbers of excited spear men as they gathered for the final kill.

Reaching up with his sword hand, one of the pirates grasped his helm by the nasal and, removing it, let it drop with a clatter to the ground. Shaking the sweat drenched hair from his face he called out,

"I have no need to ask who the Lord Hygelac is among you for I saw him clearly in the place of honour in the shield wall. I challenge him now to fight me, man to man. I ask nothing for myself, just the lives of my men and my son, you can kill me win or lose."

Hygelac pushed his way to the front of the spear men.

"Dead men can't make bargains. You will all die within the hour. The only choice open to you is whether you choose to die with a sword in your hand or on the end of a rope. You chose your fate when you decided to attack my daughter on the high seas." Shaking with anger now, he spat. "You would plan to take turns with my daughter before throwing her over the side and you ask me for your son's life so he can avenge you?"

Incandescent now Hygelac reached out and grabbed a spear from the man closest to him. Slamming it up and into the leader's head just behind his chin it emerged an instant later through the top of his head. Beowulf just had time to see the look of surprise enter the viking's face before he fell to the ground. As if released from their indecision by the act, the remainder of the Geats swarmed forward and cut down the remaining pirates, stabbing and hacking at the bodies as they satiated their bloodlust.

Once the killing was over thralls brought casks of ale down to the men as they began to strip the bodies of anything of value. Beowulf smiled as Hygelac approached him, and was about to offer his congratulations on the victory when he realised that something was amiss. Hygelac's face still looked like thunder as he strode past him.

"Come with me!" he snapped.

Following him to a quiet spot away from the others, Beowulf was shocked when he turned on him and grabbed him by his mail shirt.

"What happened there?" he demanded. "Don't you ever lose concentration in a fight again! One mistake and you are a dead man there are no second chances in this game. Orme had to drop his shield to hold you up, you idiot, leaving himself defenceless." Seeing Beowulf's shocked face he paused as he attempted to regain control of himself. "If you fall down in a shield wall, you never get up again. You are on your face or hands and knees in a crush of bodies. You won't even see the spear or sword which kills you." Calming now, Hygelac sighed wearily. "Remember our lessons Beowulf.

You have had years of the best training that I can give you, but you need to concentrate and not rely on brute strength. I have more riding on your performance in battle than you know," he added cryptically, and Beowulf saw in the ætheling's eyes that he had instantly regretted the last sentence. "A skilled man can kill a bear," he sighed, "what makes you think that you are any different?"

Visibly drained now as the battle fever left him, Hygelac turned and walked away.

"I am sorry uncle, I will go and thank Orme for saving my life," he called after him.

Hygelac shook his head sadly as he retreated. "You can't Beowulf, he's dead."

A PYRE WAS MADE on the headland for the raiders' bodies as the thralls cleared up the worst of the blood and body parts from the battleground. Hygd had overseen the provision of fresh food and drink in the courtyard, outside the hall. Wearily, the men made their way back up the path, some comparing wounds, a few mourning lost friends. The cost of the victory had been thankfully very light. Of the warriors only Gunnar's man, Orme, had been killed, although a few had gained new injuries to add to old scars. Five of the levy had paid for their loyalty with their lives and their bodies were washed and prepared by the thralls in preparation for their return to their families. Crestfallen, Beowulf sat on the bank by the paddock draining horn after horn of ale. A man had given his life to save his and now he felt unable to join in the celebrations.

"I would hate to see your face when we lose!"

A voice broke, unwelcome, into his thoughts. Looking up

he saw the smiling face of Heardred approach, a horn in each hand. Handing one to Beowulf he lowered himself to the ground beside him.

"I would rather be alone if you don't mind," Beowulf murmured, his gaze still on the crowd. As much as he liked Heardred, he was too ashamed to face him.

"Don't be an arse, cousin!" Heardred chided him. "There was a fight, somebody got killed. It's what generally happens, didn't you know?"

"It was my fault. He dropped his shield to save me as I fell and got killed for his deed."

"Who told you that?"

"Your father," Beowulf mumbled.

"He might have told you that Orme is dead, but I saw him die and he was carrying his shield then. He was fighting their leader, the one who issued the challenge to my father at the end, and he met his match. Orme died well, sword in hand fighting for his lord. He'll be feasting in Woden's hall as we speak, instead of sitting here looking at somebody feeling sorry for still being alive. Come on, father has asked us to go and look in their ship and see what riches we can uncover. We can look for something appropriate to send to Gunnar as wergild, for losing a good warrior."

They rose and, ale in hand, made their way across the courtyard stopping only to pick up some bread and meat. Descending the path to the beach, Beowulf was shocked to discover how his feelings for the place had changed. Before today he thought that he had known the place well. He had been back and forth to the beach for the last seven years, he had even played among its crags and bushes with Astrid when they were younger, but now, having fought there, he found that he really hadn't taken any notice of the place at all. He had never really realised that the pathway turned sharply a hundred paces from the top and that the rising sun would then shine directly into the eyes of any attacking force. Looking closely, he realised that the path had been designed that way for just that purpose for an older, easier, route had been blocked by boulders at some time in the past. Other details caught his eye. Choke points had been created at several points and the path had been kept deliberately narrow he now realised, both measures designed to prevent an attacking force from fully deploying an effective shield wall. The bodies of the vikings lay in a heap to one side of the path, awaiting transport later in the day to the pyre. The Geat dead had already been carried, with reverence, back up to the hall along with any valuable items carried on the raider's person. Separate piles of helms, mail, weapons, gold and silver were awaiting disposal as Hygelac saw fit later that day.

Reaching the beach they saw the ship, bow on to the beach, its dragon head awaiting the return of its now dead crew. Nearby lay the arrow perforated bodies of the two men left to guard the ship. Beowulf noticed deep, gaping, cuts to their throats where they had been finished off.

"We were on them before they realised that they had been hit," Heardred explained proudly. "We couldn't have them shouting out and warning the others."

Gripping the wale they swung themselves aboard, knives at the ready. The ship had already been given a cursory check to make sure that there were no more crew hiding aboard, but it still paid to be prepared. It felt strange, picking among the belongings of men who had, until that morning, lived and sweated at these benches. Scattered about them lay a collection of inferior quality weapons. Obviously, Beowulf thought, a man would take his best weapons and armour with him to battle. Searching the individual sea chests was more profitable. Anything of value was tossed into the area of the mast and soon a sizeable pile of coins, amber and hack silver had grown there. Moving aft they finally came to the steering platform. Here they knew the leader of the crew would keep his hoard, and they looked at each other in anticipation before removing the wooden covering.

"I feel like a child at the Yule gift giving," Heardred smiled as he began to draw the cover to one side.

Beowulf just caught the glint of metal from within the well. Before he even had time to think he had kicked the hatch cover out of Heardred's hands and shoved his cousin roughly to one side. A cry came from within the well as the top half of a sword stabbed upwards, inches away from Heardred's chest, before coming to rest, pinned between the hull and the hatch cover. Recovering quickly they leapt back and drew their swords.

"You can come out here and die with a sword in your hand or we can go and get a bowman to shoot you like a rat in a barrel," Heardred snarled.

With a rasp the hatch cover slid forward and fell to the deck. Rising from the well, the last crew member stood, squinting in the sunlight. Grimacing with pain, the man stood facing them. His undershirt and mail were covered in a great circle of blood, from the centre of which the flights of an arrow rose and fell in time with his laboured breathing. The man clearly had little time left to live, but was obviously intent on fighting to the last.

"Shit, another guard!" Heardred exclaimed. "I should have checked with the bowmen how many they had picked off." Shooting Beowulf a glance he continued. "The best of us can make mistakes, eh? You saved my life kinsman."

Turning back to the wounded man he hissed. "I have just about had enough of you lot today." Stepping forward, Heardred knocked the sword contemptuously aside with his own before running him through. He gasped and fell to his knees before Heardred removed the back of his head with a backward stroke. "And stay dead. Try and kill me you bastard!" he growled.

Dragging the body roughly to one side, they peered cautiously inside. A large chest lay at the bottom. Slipping down into the well Beowulf pulled back the lid to reveal a storehouse of precious goods. Gold and silver arm rings lay among purses of coins and finger rings. Amber and jet necklaces shimmered in the light while, to the side of the chest, several finely worked swords and helms shone brightly. Grinning, they looked at each other.

"That should cheer the old man up!"

Hygelac spent the next week visiting the families of the men who had been slain in the battle to protect his hall. Accompanied by Heardred and Beowulf, he spoke to the wives, and especially, sons of the men, telling them how well their men had died and paying them wergild for their loss. Beowulf noticed that Hygelac paid them far more than they were due under the king's law. Older sons were confirmed as heirs to their father's estate and offered the chance to train as warriors within Hygelac's household. Hygelac had insisted that Beowulf accompany him on the visits as the final part of his education.

"It is important that you see this side of war, Beowulf, it's not all shiny war gear and heroic tales. Remember these people when you are a lord. Even the humblest spear man can be a hero in the eyes of his family."

Before he had dismissed the levy he had distributed the wealth found on the battlefield among them. Most of them had gone home wealthy men, a good day's work considering a large number of them had not got closer than two spear lengths of the enemy, Beowulf thought to himself.

"That does not matter," Heardred had replied when he asked him about it.

"Numbers are important. In any battle only the men at the front, the full time warriors, really do the fighting, unless you are really in the shit and about to die!" he laughed. "Imagine what those bastards felt when they rounded the corner and saw the skyline packed with shields and spears. The men of the levy are worth every piece of silver they receive kinsman."

Beowulf remembered the effect it had had on them, their indecision, as they sensed for the first time that they were about to die, and knew his cousin had spoken the truth. He would never underestimate or begrudge the men of the levy their due again he decided. On their return to the hall at Skara, Hygelac had the pirates' ship cleaned, repainted and refitted. The old dragon head from the stem had been removed and burned with the bodies of the crew the previous week. Heardred and his crew sailed Hygelac around to the harbour of his thegn, Gunnar, on Marstrand, where he presented the ship, complete with the hoard contained beneath the steering platform to him as reward for his actions in safeguarding his daughter and family, and as wergild for the loss of Orme. Beowulf stayed at Skara as he made final preparations for his initiation the following week. Within a day of their return, Beowulf left Hygelac's hall. He would not return.

9

It was the week before the midsummer celebrations and the land lay sweltering under a perfect cobalt sky. It had grown hot several days before and now the fine grey dust from the road hung in the air, coating the riders and their mounts in a gritty powder. Thankfully, Beowulf reflected, Hygelac had sent word ahead to his thegns, Hromund and Ulfgar, that they would be breaking the journey at their halls in the coming days.

It had been an emotional parting at Skara the previous day. Hygd had wished Beowulf farewell and he had promised to visit her as often as possible, but they both knew that the realities of a warrior's life could lead him far and wide, leaving little opportunity for casual visits. Although the journey could have been completed at this time of year with just one overnight stop, indeed it had been done with no stop at all in times of emergency, Hygelac had decided to set a slow pace, hoping to lay the effects of the dust as much as possible. Besides, the weather was glorious, and there was no need to hurry.

A deer emerged from the tree line ahead and stood,

frozen, watching them approach, its markings blending in perfectly with the sun dappled roadway, before disappearing back into the gloom. Above the river which ran alongside them a kingfisher perched, motionless, before darting into the depths. The road here allowed them to ride three abreast which helped to reduce the problems created by the dust. It was no fun, Beowulf decided, bringing up the rear on a day like this.

Suddenly a grey shape flashed across the road not fifty paces ahead. For a moment the three riders looked at each other in shock before Heardred found his tongue.

"Wolf!"

Spurring on their mounts they crashed into the forest in its wake. Beowulf could not understand why his horse was so much slower and unwieldy than the others until he remembered that the pack horse was still attached to the saddle of his mount. Quickly drawing the knife from his belt he reached down and cut the cord tying them together. Freed of its load his horse bounded forward after its companions. He could see the others up ahead, crashing through the undergrowth, spears in hand, searching for the wolf. He reined in his horse and listened. He thought he could hear a faint noise, although in truth it was difficult to hear very much with the amount of noise the others were making up ahead. He concentrated hard. There it was again, a soft whistling sound coming from somewhere very close. He slowly lowered his gaze, searching intently in the shadows and bracken for the source. A slight movement caught his eye twenty paces to his left. There, in the shade of a fallen tree, lay the immobile form of the deer, the wolf's jaws clamped tightly around its throat. Paralysed with fear the deer lay motionless, its faint breathing making the soft whistling noise which had revealed it to Beowulf. The wolf lay with its ears down, its body pressed flat to the forest floor as it attempted to remain hidden from the riders. It realised that if it killed the deer the resulting struggle would alert the men, and so they both remained still, a moment frozen in time.

In one fluid movement Beowulf twisted his body to the left and launched his spear. It flew true, and, a heartbeat later, sank deeply into the flank of the wolf. With a yelp of pain it tried to rise and make its escape but it sank back to the forest floor. Twisting its head it tried to bite at the spear protruding from its side. Slipping from the saddle Beowulf walked slowly over to the mortally wounded animal. It turned and growled at him as he approached, its lips curled back revealing a line of yellowing, razor like teeth. Kicking him in the head, Beowulf reached out and grabbed the spear shaft. Treading on the wolf's neck, he pushed firmly down on the shaft, twisting it as he did so. The wolf shuddered and grew still. Looking up he noticed that the deer still lay, frozen in terror, beside them. Nudging it with his boot he spoke, "Go on friend, it's your lucky day. I don't fancy venison tonight." Still the deer lay there, its big eyes wide with fright. Raising his voice a little, Beowulf gave the deer a harder kick. "Go on, last chance or you are in the pot!" With a sudden jolt the animal seemed to realise that it was free. Scrambling to its feet it darted off into the trees and was soon lost from view. Beowulf retrieved his spear and, stooping, swung the wolf's carcass across his shoulders before returning to his horse. Even dead the wolf made his mount skittish, but a handful of oats and few soft words from him soon calmed it as he slung the wolf's body over the mount and climbed up behind it. Following the trail of broken branches and trampled bracken, he retraced their steps back to the road. He reattached the pack horse and waited patiently for the return of Hygelac and Heardred. After a while he heard the unmistakable sounds of them forcing their way back through the forest.

"There you are we thought that we had lost you!" Hygelac exclaimed. "We should have stayed with you. The bastard is miles away by now." Beowulf smiled triumphantly at the pair. "This must be a different one then uncle."

THEY REACHED Miklaborg two days later. Accompanied now by Hromund and Ulfgar, they rode through the town before crossing to the island. Leaving their mounts at the stables they climbed the familiar steps to Gefrin to report their arrival to the king.

Two days of festivities followed. Horse fights, as ever, proved popular with the nobility, large sums exchanging hands in a short space of time. Beowulf watched in amusement as the two nearest villages competed in the annual game of Sol. Named in honour of the midsummer sun, the men and boys of each village competed to carry a pig bladder stuffed with hair, by any means they could, to a destination in the opposing village. This year the opposing mobs had to hit the communal barn in which the villagers stored their hay for the winter in order to win. The previous summer, he remembered, the aim had been to carry the bladder physically across the river which lay approximately midway between the two places. In the resulting scramble several men had drowned, so the new change in destination was probably a good idea he mused. As usual the unmarried maidens of the nearby settlements had congregated in groups near the area set aside for dancing and, as usual, they had largely had to dance with one another as the young men took advantage of the free ale provided by their king. What was different this year, at least as far as Beowulf was concerned, was the fact that he was banned from participating in any of the festivities. Tomorrow they were to stage the swimming race between himself and Breca, agreed upon at the midwinter festival, after which would come the ceremony which would mark the passing of his childhood and the beginning of his adult life. To his disappointment he had not been asked to attend the midsummer ceremony at the temple on the Hill of Goats that morning. He had been expecting to go and was hoping to meet the young woman again who had escorted them across the causeway, but King Hrethel had not chosen him again this time.

"You are looking pensive, Beowulf. With good cause I hope."

Beowulf turned and greeted his uncle.

"Hythcyn, I was just wondering how to spend all my winnings from the race."

Hythcyn pursed his lips and slowly sucked in his breath.

"Still sharp I see. I should be careful if I were you, you may cut yourself badly. I should not worry about that too much if I were you, while you have been fighting vikings and wolves, Breca here has been practising his swimming. He's really rather good you know."

Beowulf glanced at Breca who stood nearby. He smiled back and inclined his head in confirmation.

"Until tomorrow then, oh and just one other thing," Hythcyn smiled. "Boys don't call adults by their first names, even boar wrestling boys. If members of the royal family start to let standards slip, where will it all end?" Turning on his heel, he made his way to the royal enclosure.

"Tell me you didn't annoy him for once." An arm was thrown around his shoulder and the figure of Heardred appeared beside him. "Go on cousin, just this once."

THEY ASSEMBLED on the field opposite the Hill of Goats early the next morning. Thralls had been readying the site since before dawn, preparing food and drink for the spectators, noble and commoner alike. The swimming race had generated a great deal of interest at all levels of

Geat society in the months following the announcement and now the moment had come. Beowulf and Breca were both fully dressed and wearing mail shirts, as agreed between Hygelac and Hythcyn. Both participants had taken a light breakfast and now stood waiting for the king to give them permission to proceed. The race was to take place in the North river, which ran from Miklaborg to the sea, a distance of about six miles. If there was no clear winner by that stage, and most people thought it unlikely, the swimmers were to continue in the open sea as far as the small rocky isle of Riso, a further five miles or so. The king and several nobles were to lead the way in the king's favourite ship. Already the sun had burned off the early morning mist from the riverside and it promised to be another hot summer day, heightening the holiday atmosphere among the waiting crowd. Once the king's ship was in position the pair entered the water.

"Have my seax ready for me when I get back Hythcyn!" Beowulf called as he lowered himself into the shallows.

Hythcyn flushed with anger as Heardred at his side shook his head and grimaced. Supremely confident this time, Beowulf was sure the day was to be his.

A loud note from a horn sounded on King Hrethel's ship, followed by a roar from the crowd lining both banks, signalled the start of the race. Beowulf and Breca looked at each other and grinned.

"Let's go!"

They may have been rivals and potential enemies but both recognised the other as a worthy opponent. Striking out from the shore, they both headed for midchannel where the current would help to sweep them downstream, and the chances of becoming entangled in reeds and banks of shingle were lessened. If Hygelac had sought to gain an advantage from suggesting that the swimmers compete in mail, it was not apparent to Beowulf, as Breca matched him stroke for stroke. Settling into a steady rhythm, the pair swam westwards towards the sea, and, hopefully victory. Ahead of them the passengers were clearly enjoying their river trip. The crew were able to row at a reasonably slow pace for once as they kept a constant distance between the ship and the swimmers, while the rest of the party appeared to be more interested in the supplies of food and ale on board than the contest taking place in their wake.

After about two hours of swimming it became obvious to Beowulf that the end of the river was near. The banks slowly drew wider apart, while the water clearly began to taste brackish. To his disappointment, Breca was still abreast of him. Obviously Hythcyn had taken the opportunity to train Breca intensively once the ice had thawed in the spring, and, if he was honest with himself, he had to admit that he was surprised and impressed with the level of ability shown by the Bronding. The figure of King Hrethel appeared suddenly at the stern of the ship. Cupping his hands to his mouth he bellowed.

"Congratulations boys you have reached the sea. It looks as if we are going to have to carry on to Riso if we are going to separate you. Follow the ship and we will lead the way. Good luck!"

Within minutes the waters became choppy as the swimmers left the calm waters of the river. Beowulf was accustomed to swimming in the open sea, even in mail and clothing, thanks to years of training by Hygelac. He steadily increased the pace until, slowly at first, but with increasing certainty, he began to draw away from Breca. Clearly, he thought, this was why Hygelac had shrewdly suggested that they both wear mail for the contest. Swimming in the calm waters of a river and in the sea were two very different things. During what he estimated must be the second hour at sea, Beowulf noticed that a crew member had been sent to the top of the mast where he peered aft. He smiled to himself. The race was as good as won if they could not see Breca from the deck of the ship. The island was near now, its rocky outline growing on the horizon every time that the swell carried him high enough to see beyond the ship. A sudden realisation struck him that Breca could be in trouble. He found to his surprise that he was worried for his safety. Despite the incident at the midwinter skating race and his attachment to Hythcyn, he found that he could not help but like the young Bronding. He was pleased that another ship had joined them as they reached the sea. Each competitor would have help close to hand should they need it. A good swimmer was stripped and ready to enter the water at a moment's notice on each ship. A cramp or any other problem out here and, weighed down by clothing and mail, they would be on the bottom in no time.

Beowulf started as he felt something brush, disconcertingly, against his leg. Deciding to ignore it, he struck out again. The island seemed so close now and victory was clearly to be his.

He jumped as whatever it was returned and bit at his mail shirt, tugging him, momentarily, beneath the surface. Breaking the surface he spluttered and coughed as he fought to clear the sea water from his mouth and nose before whatever it was attacked him again. He was dimly aware of the splash as his would-be rescuer leapt from the stern of the ship. Before the man could reach him Beowulf saw a long, snake like, object, rise from the depths and, again take his mail shirt in its powerful jaws. Again the creature headed for the depths, dragging Beowulf with it. Luckily he had seen it approach this time and had been able to take a deep breath. Opening his eyes he peered into the murk, trying to make out his opponent. To his consternation he saw that he was surrounded by a writhing mass of conger eels, each one of which appeared to be the length of a man or more. Razor sharp teeth flashed in their gaping jaws as they whirled about him. Reaching behind him he felt for the knife which he always carried. Fumbling with the sheath he managed to drag the blade forward. Desperately, he stabbed at the head of the eel. Blood misted the water as his knife slid home. Wounded, the eel let go of him and retreated. Other eels took its place, squirming amongst themselves to gain a purchase on his shirt. He began to panic as his lungs screamed for air, his defensive actions becoming more and more unfocused as he began to lose consciousness. Pulled in several directions at the same time, he began to accept that he would not survive. A particularly savage tug pulled his byrnie up and over his body, the rings scraping, painfully, across his face. His mind began to act strangely. The faces of his friends and relatives came to him, smiling and happy. He began to feel warm, calm and serene.

With a sudden roar, they were gone. Warm air surrounded him and he was being roughly slapped around the face. Somebody was holding him around the chest and striking him with the other hand. He wanted to strike back but found that he was unable to do anything but spew up great quantities of foul tasting water. A wooden wall rose above him and he felt a hook catch in the collar of his jerkin. Eager hands reached over and dragged him bodily over the wale before lowering him gently to the deck. Face down he continued to retch until his body ached. Finally, after a few minutes, he began to regain his composure. Wiping the warm water from his face he turned onto his back and lay, propped on his elbows, staring up at the crowd of bodies which had gathered around him. His grandfather, the king, knelt beside him, a concerned look on his face. Beowulf grinned, hoping to reassure him that he had recovered.

"Shit, that was fun!" he gasped, trying to lighten the atmosphere. "Has the sea level dropped?"

Relieved that he was well enough to joke, they all visibly relaxed.

"It appears that you owe your life to, I am sorry, what was your name?"

"Finn, lord."

Beowulf looked to the man. He stood in the middle of a puddle of seawater created by his dripping body, his eyes lowered in deference.

"Thank you, Finn, you will be well rewarded."

Bowing, Finn, returned to the stern of the ship. With a jolt, Beowulf suddenly remembered the race. Scrambling to his feet he raced to the ship's side. One hundred feet away, just drawing level with his ship, Breca was slowly over-hauling them. Without thinking he climbed onto the wale and launched himself back into the sea. Breaking the surface he struck out for the island which he could see barely half a mile away. After his enforced break and without the added weight of his mail byrnie, Beowulf easily outpaced his opponent and was waiting on the beach to help him as he came ashore a short time later. Breca lay on his back, breathing deeply, as the hot sun dried their bodies. Turning to Beowulf he demanded.

"Why were you on the ship? So much for Geat honour! And where is your mail shirt?"

Looking down Beowulf was shocked. "I don't know!" he stuttered, confused, before the memories of the struggle came back to him.

"It was pulled off me by sea monsters!" he added.

Realising how ridiculous he sounded his face broke into a grin. As the royal party made their way up the beach from the moored ship they were surprised to find both swimmers lying on their backs, helpless with laughter.

As they ate their food on the beach Beowulf noticed Finn sat on a rock, eating alone.

"Who is he?" he asked one of the others.

"Oh, just some fisherman we hired from the village by the river mouth. We didn't expect the race to get this far and we only found out that none of the party were good swimmers until it was too late."

He filled two cups of ale from the barrel and made his way across the beach. Seeing Beowulf approach, Finn stood up and bowed his head.

"There's no need for that Finn," he called, smiling. "I owe you my life."

Handing one of the cups over, he searched for a flat rock and sat down.

"Sit down man, and tell me what happened out there."

Nervously Finn sat opposite him. He was clearly unnerved being in the company of nobility and Beowulf smiled, he hoped reassuringly, at him.

"You were attacked by congers, lord, they like pretty things, you know shiny things, and that mail shirt of yours must have dazzled them. Once I got it off you though they chased after it and left us alone. They are real monsters some of them, they make a good stew though if you can catch one. That's how we snare them, we attach large fish scales to the lines and that draws them in."

Noticing Beowulf's puzzled expression he explained further.

"We thread them on the line and they move in the current, reflecting the light. It must look like lots of lights to them down there in the dark."

"Tell me a bit about yourself Finn, have you always been a fisherman?"

"My family had hopes that I would become a warrior. I was always the best in the village at anything like running, throwing, that sort of thing."

"And swimming!" Beowulf added.

"And swimming, lord," he conceded with a smile.

"What happened?"

"My father just disappeared one day. He sailed out with my uncle, his brother, one day and we never saw either of them again. That was three years ago now. There was only my mother and me left so I had to take up fishing and forget all about becoming a warrior."

"I am glad that you said that," Beowulf said delightedly, "I think that I can help."

THE SHIP ARRIVED BACK at Miklaborg late in the afternoon. Finn had swum ashore as they rowed past his village, a purse of silver tied around his neck. Added to Beowulf's promise of a place within his hearth troop, once he had been trained by King Hrethel's warriors, it had truly been a life changing day for the man, Beowulf reflected. To his disappointment, he had

had to agree that the fight with the eels had cost him the race. Although he was certain that he would have won quite comfortably had it not been for their intervention, and he had still reached the island first, clearly the loss of his mail byrnie had disqualified him, not to mention the fact that he had also 'rested' on the king's ship for a time. There was clearly some disappointment within the expectant crowd as King Hrethel announced the result but Beowulf suspected that much of that was due to the, clearly delighted, reactions of the bet takers who had set themselves up near the beer stalls. As the ship nudged alongside the landing stage Beowulf noticed the royal brothers Herebeald, Hythcyn and Hygelac waiting for the party to step ashore. Led by the king they descended the boarding ramp. Hygelac looked searchingly at Beowulf, "What happened?"

BEOWULF SPENT the rest of the day at the smaller hall at the lower end of Miklaborg. Warriors had been arriving all day to witness his initiation into their order, all of which had been ushered directly into the king's main hall, Gefrin. From the amount of noise which was coming from the hall, and the number of horses which he had witnessed collected, both on the island and the nearby mainland, he estimated that there were fifty or sixty witnesses assembled with perhaps more to come. To his relief Heardred had been appointed as the initiates friend. As someone who had undergone the ritual only a few years before his help and advice would be invaluable.

"Right get those old rags off!" Heardred announced. "It is time that you prepared."

Beowulf removed his clothes while Heardred went to the large chest which had been deposited in the hall on their arrival. The chest was one of the most beautiful things that he had seen. Made in the shape of a boar, dozens of smaller boars had been chased out of its solid gold surface. These had been highlighted in black niello, the whole then highly polished. Along the ridge of the boar's back ran a line of real boar bristles. Removing the head of the boar, Heardred reached inside and carefully took out an ornately wrapped bundle. Reverently undoing the binding, he removed, much to Beowulf's surprise, a thick, quite crudely made, leather belt. Completely unadorned or decorated in any way, it was completed by a heavy buckle and plain strap end.

"Put this on cousin."

Beowulf could tell from the emotion in his voice that the belt held great significance for the order.

"It is said to be the belt worn by the first king of the Geats, Woden himself!"

Returning to the boar chest he reached back into its interior. Carefully he withdrew an ornate helm and held it admiringly. Beowulf recognised it immediately for it reminded him of one of earliest memories he associated with his father. Unlike a normal helm intended to withstand the rigours of warfare, this was more ornate and a symbol of his order. The main part of the helm was large and splayed at the base, more bowl like and totally unlike the close fitting ones he was used to. Attached to the front was a large, square, ornate plate. Curling upwards from this, two stylised eagle heads rose to meet, face to face, at the top, the whole forming a complete circle. Beowulf had seen the design repeated above the eyes on regular helms and now realised that they identified initiates of the warrior cult to each other. Placing the helm on his head he waited patiently while Heardred adjusted the fitting before fastening it securely. Two wrist bands made of raven's feathers completed his attire. Taking a step back, Heardred gazed approvingly at him.

"You'll do, let's go."

Heardred called out and the doors to the hall swung inward. Standing before him were two warriors, both fully dressed for war, complete with full faced grim helm, spears and shields. Beowulf felt a surge of pride. Not only would he be permitted to dress like them in a short while, but, more importantly, he would be accepted as their equal. The warriors turned and, clashing their spears against the rims of their shields, led them up the hill towards Gefrin. They rose up the familiar steps towards the heavy doors above, thrown into relief by the flaming torches fixed at their sides. The night air was warm against his bare skin while a faint glow to the West told him that the sun had just barely set. Reaching the top of the stairs they paused before entering the hall. He was handed a golden chalice and told to drink. Beowulf recalled the taste, it was the same liquid that he had been given to drink at the temple at Yule. A hood was placed over his head and pulled lightly closed, completely enveloping him in darkness. Again he felt the numbness spread throughout his body as the effects of the strange liquid took effect. He heard the doors to the hall swing open and drank in the familiar, comforting, smells of Gefrin. Heardred took his arm and led him inside. Although unable to see and disorientated by the effects of the drink, he sensed that he was among a large group of men.

"Remember the things of which we spoke Beowulf. Do everything which is asked of you unquestioningly. Remember that every man here has endured the same ritual so you nothing to fear. Good luck, kinsman."

Heardred brought Beowulf to a halt and with a last, encouraging, squeeze of his arm retreated away.

He was aware of the soft whimpering of a child. The sound grew as the child was obviously being led towards him. His hands were held out and closed around the child, which he now estimated to be a boy of about four winters. An arm took his and led them both to one side of the hall. The boy was suddenly wrenched, screaming, from his grip and his cries abruptly stopped. Beowulf was led roughly back to the centre of the hall and the hood was torn from his head. Before he could focus his eyes a hand slapped him, hard, around the face two or three times and a voice screamed at him, "Why are you here, you worthless dog!" Facing him was the snarling face of a wolf. Thrusting a snout into his face the wolf repeated the question. *"Why are you here you worthless dog!"* Pushing him backwards it thrust out a giant paw containing a bloody pink and white ball. To his horror Beowulf realised that he was being handed the heart of the child. "Eat this!" he was instructed. Unhesitatingly he took the still warm heart from the wolf and bit into it, tearing off a piece and, fighting against the overwhelming desire to retch, bolted it down whole. The wolf snatched back the heart and threw it to one side.

His eyes began to become accustomed to the light. To his relief he could see now that he was faced by a wolf warrior and not a supernatural being. Wolf warriors lived in groups in the remote places of Geatland. Shunning comforts, they were men who lived only for war, supporting themselves in times of peace by hunting and raiding other lands. Flicking his eyes beyond the wolf warrior he saw that they were in the middle of a ring of braziers, the glow and flames from which prevented him from seeing into the shadows beyond. The glint of reflected metal however revealed that he was in the middle of a large number of armed men.

Men like Hygelac, Heardred, Alfhelm and maybe even his father he realised.

He had seen the dancing warrior design on their battle helms and remembered Heardred's last words to him. They had all once stood on this very spot and undergone the same ritual.

There was nothing to be afraid of!

Confidence flowed back into him and he felt nothing but scorn for the pathetic attempts of someone who needed to dress as a wolf to try and intimidate him. He realised that there would be no bloody corpse of a child nearby either.

Another trick!

An arm appeared from behind him holding out two spears. He took them and prepared to dance. He was looking forward to it now. He had practised the moves of the warrior dance many times with Hygelac and felt confident and relaxed. The wolf warrior took up his spears and held them, crossed, in front of him, mirroring Beowulf. From the darkness came the slow, rhythmic sound of spears being dashed against shields. Turning and twisting, the wolf warrior and Beowulf began to move in time to the beat. Slowly the beating of spears on shields increased in tempo as, leaping and stabbing, the dancers also increased their pace until, with a final flourish the wolf warrior's spear appeared to pass through Beowulf and he fell to the floor. As he had been taught he lay, deathly still, on the floor of the hall. This was the moment of his rebirth as a man and a warrior, in many ways the most important moment of his life. As he lay there he felt a waxen object placed over him. He knew that this was the hide of a sow boar, the symbolic mother of his rebirth as a warrior. Strong hands reached under and, gripping him under the arms, pulled him back into the light. Standing, he now saw that King Hrethel was seated on his high seat at the end of the hall. The way was lined now by warriors in full war gear. Accompanied by the beating of the spears on shields he approached the king. Rising, the king advanced to meet him.

"Beowulf, accept these gifts from your king. You have proven yourself to be a man and a warrior fit to wear them in actions and character over these last years. We are happy to accept you into our company."

"I accept your gifts gladly lord and swear fealty to you and the Geat People," he replied.

Smiling now, Hrethel held out a shield and a spear, the symbols of a free man. Beowulf noted with pride that the shield carried the design of a man wrestling a boar painted onto its leather covering, flanked by gold eagles, both images recalling important events in his life. Hygelac stepped forward. Smiling, he placed a hand on his shoulder and turned him around. There, before him, stood his father, Ecgtheow, for the first time in nearly eight years.

"I return your son to you, Ecgtheow," Hygelac's voice carried from behind him, "a man."

"I thank you, Hygelac," he replied, "for the honour which you have shown us."

Loud cries and stamping announced that the ceremony was completed as the warriors moved forward to congratulate him.

Beowulf smiled as he looked once more on the face of his father.

Clothes were produced and he made his way to the benches occupied by the Waegmungs for the first time. To his delight he found both Bjalki and Hudda waiting for him there. He had known that Bjalki had been an initiate because he had often seen him wearing his helm and remembered the plates with the dancing warriors above his brow, but Hudda had been a surprise.

"I fought on land when I was younger," he explained, "but I got a taste for the sea. Mind you, not as much as you did this morning I hear!" he joked.

Ecgtheow produced a fine grim helm for his son complete, Beowulf noted with satisfaction, with plates depicting the dancing warriors above the eye pieces. Hygelac came across and presented a fine seax to him.

"Cola told me how much you liked the one which Eadgar had made for Alfhelm so I commissioned one for you as a parting gift," he explained.

Beowulf admired the blade, complete with the maker's inscription. Turning it over Beowulf smiled in pleasure as he read the runic inscription,

'Beowulf mec ah'

It was the beginning of a riotous night. It seemed to Beowulf that the hall was filled with every warrior he could have wished to see. Even Hythcyn seemed in good spirits, while Herebeald was his usual popular self. Hygelac and Ecgtheow spent a large part of the evening together, no doubt, Beowulf reflected, discussing the events of his fostering. He hoped that he had always acted with honour, he was sure that he had.

10

They left the next day. Beowulf was overjoyed to discover that his father had travelled to the initiation aboard his ship, the *Sea Eagle*. It was the same ship in which he had returned from Dane Land all those years ago and it brought happy memories flooding back to him. The crew were mostly the same men who had carried him to see King Hrothgar, Hudda of course, but also the ever jovial Ucca and the large bulk of 'Tiny', who stood beaming as they welcomed him aboard.

"Still here I see. How's the new ship?" he asked.

"Not so new now lord," Ucca replied, "but she is a fine vessel make no mistake, she glides through the water like an eel."

Beowulf grimaced. Perhaps it had not been the best choice of comparisons to make after the events of yesterday.

"Where's Ratty? Don't tell me he hung up his oar?"

It was Ucca's turn to look uncomfortable.

"In a manner of speaking he did, lord. He was lost overboard a few years back. Hudda turned the ship around and made a search for him but he had just disappeared. It's almost

171

impossible to see somebody's head in a stormy sea," he sighed. "Still, that's the way it goes eh, lord?" he added with a shrug. "When the norns decide to snip your life thread you have to accept it."

Slipping the moorings, the *Sea Eagle* was allowed to drift into mid channel before the oars were dipped and, with gentle strokes, she moved casually downstream towards the open sea. Beowulf shielded his eyes and searched the top of the Isle of Goats, hoping to catch one last glimpse of the mysterious woman from the temple, but if she was watching she was being discreet, for he saw no sign of her. Perhaps he was being foolish, he reasoned. Just because he had spoken to her once and she had intervened, saving him, at the midwinter skate race, didn't necessarily mean that she held any feelings for him. She was after all a priestess of sorts, and forbidden to enter into any relationship with a man. Perhaps Herebeald was right, he should forget all about her, as difficult as that might be. Relaxing against the steering platform alongside his father, his mind went back to the previous day. He had swum these very waters with Breca. He had been a boy then, and now he was a man and a full initiate into the warrior brotherhood. Suddenly the race seemed like it had taken place in another life time, which in a way he reflected, it had.

THE JOURNEY SOUTH had taken most of the day. They had stayed overnight at Hudda's hall before moving on the next morning, back to the hall of his father. Orme, another of his father's warriors who had accompanied him to Dane Land had brought horses to the coast, and, making good time on the hot, dusty roads, they had made the hall before nightfall. In truth the reunion with his mother had been an awkward affair.

She was, as he remembered her, quite an unemotional woman. The daughter of a king, she had been raised to be dutiful and controlled. Beowulf never felt that she didn't love him, but after the warmth of Hygelac and Hygd, his parents' hall seemed a far more subdued place. Of course, he realised, there had been no other children to upset the calm and order of the place. He had got into more than his fair share of scrapes with Astrid, he recalled with a smile, perhaps if his mother had had to run a more chaotic household she might have become a different person.

He was to travel to Geatwic with his father in six weeks, once the harvest had been safely collected. Alfhelm had invited the leading nobles in the land to a great hunt which was to take place in the forests to the east of the settlement. No doubt influenced by Alfhelm's famous hospitality, it seemed that most had accepted including Herebeald, Hygelac, Heardred and, to most peoples surprise, Hythcyn. Perhaps he was making more of an effort to be sociable, Beowulf hoped so. He found that the friction which had developed between them upset him, although he could not be completely sure why.

The late summer passed slowly for Beowulf. He spent most of his time riding around his father's lands, reminding himself of their extent. One day he found himself in the vicinity of the eagle's nest he had raided all those years ago. Curiosity drew him back to the tree where he had fought for his life against the enraged birds. It seemed smaller than it did in his memory and at first he wondered if he was at the right place. Moving his horse to one side he craned his neck and peered upwards, through the canopy. At the very top of the tree rested the vast pile of debris which constituted the eyrie. He was tempted to climb up and explore the nest again but decided against it. The branches had given way under his weight as a child and it was best not to test the patience of the gods a second time he decided. Leaving the nest site he rode slowly over to the site of Hranis' camp. Dismounting, he poked around in the soil with his toe. Of course any signs of the camp fire were long gone, but he felt strangely compelled to investigate the area. He was about to come away when he noticed old, weathered, markings on the tree which stood there. It was the tree which Hrani had slept against that night he remembered. Brushing away the lichen which had grown there he discovered runes carved into the trunk of the tree. Although he could read most runes these were unknown to him and he decided that they must be a form of magic. Unnerved he quickly remounted and rode away.

Summer passed slowly into autumn. The long period of hot weather which had gripped Geatland that year ended in a violent storm the likes of which nobody could remember. The ceorls and thralls cowered as Thunor unleashed his mighty lightning bolts, lighting up the night, as his chariot rumbled noisily through the sky. Hail the size of eggs crashed into the parched soil, heralding a downpour the scale and power of which threatened to destroy the year's entire crop. The next morning even Ecgtheow, Beowulf and the house warriors had stripped off their finery and helped in the fields, hoping to save as much of the crop as possible. A feeling of unease crept into the people, high and low born. Wise women muttered that the storm was a warning from Thunor that a great evil was about to take place. Placing little faith in the ramblings of the local cunning women, Ecgtheow, accompanied by Beowulf, had visited the temple in nearby Skansen and, after making an offering, asked the gods directly. The priest had cast the rune sticks several times, becoming more and more concerned each time, Beowulf noticed. In the end he had confirmed that a great evil was about to change their lives. Troubled, they had ridden back to the hall in silence.

One day, soon after, Ecgtheow had called Beowulf, Bjalki and Orme over to the paddock. Four stools had been placed in a circle, in the midst of which had been placed a barrel of ale and four cups. Smiling at their arrival, Ecgtheow had motioned that they sit and handed each man a cup.

"We are going to sit here and drink this barrel dry," he began, "and during the time it takes us we are going to discuss what to do about these bad portents. With the exception of Hudda who is at sea, you three are my most trusted advisers here and I want you all to speak freely because I would value your advice," he said. "Should we stay here and not travel to the hunt at Geatwic next week?"

Beowulf looked about him, waiting for one of the others to speak. Although he now outranked them he was obviously far less experienced in most things and was interested in their thoughts.

"I think that it would be wise for either Orme or Beowulf to stay behind with the men to guard the hall," Bjalki put in. "Both of them have been in a fight and know how to command warriors."

"What if I stayed?" Ecgtheow suggested.

"You would lose honour, lord. You cannot be seen to hide from ghosts and demons."

"Then why should I?" Beowulf gasped.

"You would be protecting your mother, lord," Bjalki replied.

Orme suggested that it was obvious that Bjalki was the best suited to stay behind and soon the conversation started to become heated.

"I have heard enough," Ecgtheow finally said with a smile. "As I thought, nobody thinks that they should stay behind and, you know what, I think that you are all right. If the Ragnarok is to take place soon it matters little where we are when it happens. If we die with a boar spear in our hand we will soon be fighting at Woden's side and he will need all the help he can get. If it's not the end of Middle earth we would look cowardly if any of us stayed behind. We will all still go."

MOUNTING their horses they waved a cheerful farewell to the party of people which had gathered to see them off. Urging his mount on Beowulf had fallen in beside his father. Leaving the courtyard they pointed the horses' heads north, rounded the bend, and disappeared from sight amidst the trees. The beginning of their journey brought back poignant memories for Beowulf. Of the original party which had accompanied him on his journey to King Hrethel's hall, and ultimately his fostering with Hygelac, only Svip was missing. He had been a nervous boy then, maybe a little fearful for the future. Now, he reflected, he could not be mistaken for anything other than a high class warrior. Resplendent in highly polished mail, his gold adorned shield hung from his saddle alongside his silver inlaid spear. A leather bag containing his grim helm hung by his knee, while at his side the finely decorated hilt of a sword, a gift from his mother, protruded from a red scabbard which hung suspended from a matching baldric, the whole contrasting finely with his silver mail shirt.

They made their way north, the horses picking their way amongst the debris which still littered the road from the storm the previous week. Parties of men were just beginning to clear the road after the festivities of Haerfestmonath. It was one of Ecgtheow's responsibilities as ealdorman to ensure that the roads were always passable, and although it was assumed by most of the population that this was done for their benefit, in truth it ensured the speedy deployment of the armies in an emergency. The harvest had been forced on them early this year as they struggled to gather the crops damaged in the storm and Ecgtheow had decided to hold the festival at the same time to try and lighten the general mood. Although people had tried to rise to the occasion it had to be admitted, he thought, that it had only been a partial success. It seemed that the sense of imminent disaster had taken a hold of the entire population.

They rode north for most of the day until, around mid afternoon, Ecgtheow turned off of the main road and took a path which led them eastwards, deeper and deeper into the forest. The sheer number of closely packed trees seemed to have prevented the worst of the storm's fury from penetrating here and the way ahead was generally passable, if slow.

"We should be there soon," Ecgtheow suddenly announced. "If I remember correctly, the hunting lodge is just beyond this lake."

There was a noticeable increase in the pace set, Beowulf noted, as thoughts turned instinctively to hot food and warm ale, not to mention an evening of entertainment provided by Alfhelm. Soon the smell of woodsmoke came to them on the breeze along with, they were quite sure, the smell of roasting meat. Casting smiles at each other, the riders joyfully approached the end of a hard day in the saddle. Entering the clearing they came upon a sight guaranteed to warm the heart of any weary traveller. Suspended above a series of fire pits the carcasses of several animals turned slowly on spits, the flames below flaring and spitting as hot fat dripped from above. Men stood in groups drinking from large horns or tearing flesh from hunks of meat, their beards glistening from the juices. Heads turned their way as the guests looked to identify the new arrivals. Beowulf was pleased to see so many of his friends and relatives. Dismounting they handed their reins to a waiting groom, before taking the proffered horn of ale from one of the thralls.

Alfhelm strode, smiling, towards them. "Welcome to my humble hunting lodge! It is good to see you again Ecgtheow. And you Beowulf, I shall have to keep an eye on the ale supplies!" Noticing Ecgtheow's raised eyebrow he continued mischievously, "What, didn't he mention the last time he was at my hall, it was only a few months ago. He drank his uncle Hygelac under the table!"

"I seem to recall the evening rather differently, Alfhelm." Beowulf replied, grinning. He noticed that Bjalki and Orme seemed to be enjoying his discomfort immensely. "Shall we eat, it's been a long day," he suggested, quickly changing the subject.

"Of course, of course. I have to go and arrange the entertainment for the evening. You have already seen him I am afraid, Beowulf," Alfhelm apologised. "That night was a sort of trial run to see if he was funny enough. Don't let on, I want it to be a surprise."

"Oh, I think it will be, Alfhelm," he laughed. "You need have no worries there!"

As expected the evening passed in a riotous fashion as copious amounts of meat and ale were consumed. Herebeald was the star of the evening as he tried to emulate the farting act. Most of the watchers agreed he was doing very well until he abruptly froze and his expression suddenly changed to one of shock and horror. The audience had laughed themselves hoarse as the unfortunate ætheling had clutched the seat of his breeches and retreated slowly and unsteadily around the back of the lodge. Beowulf was pleased to see that Hythcyn was making the effort to mix freely. Although he was not the easiest of people to get along with, he was still his uncle and he genuinely hoped that they could repair their relationship. The official entertainment of the evening was brought to a close by a scop who gave a tremendous performance of the tale of 'Sigurd, Dragon Slayer', which held the guests enthralled from beginning to end, a performance which made him considerably richer judging by the number of purses which were hurled his way by the appreciative audience. Beowulf spent most of the evening in the company of Heardred, his cousin.

"What has got into Hythcyn tonight?" They were both sitting on a bench, their backs to a table, sipping from their horns.

"Maybe he has decided that he wants to join the rest of us and have a good time for once. It must be lonely always being on the edge of things."

"No," Heardred muttered. "He is up to something. I have never seen him this happy before. Watch your back tomorrow kinsman, the snake is planning something and you are not his favourite person."

BEOWULF EMERGED from the lodge early the next morning. The fires had been fed and the thralls were moving about preparing the food and drink for breakfast. Other early risers were moving about the camp, food and drink clutched in their hands. He made his way over to a line of bushes and, unfastening his breeches, closed his eyes in relaxation as he emptied his bladder.

"That's a fine new seax you have there."

Opening his eyes he saw that Hythcyn had joined him.

"You have as fine a seax as any uncle."

"I do. Maybe we can think of a way for you to regain it?"

"I would rather that you kept it, Hythcyn, it was a gift, and as you say I have a fine replacement." Finishing, he adjusted his clothing and turned to leave.

"Good hunting today!" Hythcyn called, airily.

Heardred was right, Beowulf decided to his disappointment, *he hasn't changed and he is up to something.*

They rode east, following the river, into the heart of the forest. The wide, grassy riverbank dozed in the warmth of an early autumn day. Birds picked at berries and squirrels scurried, busily gathering the abundant acorns in preparation for the hard months ahead. The head of an otter rose, momentarily, from the surface of the river before dipping back beneath the surface. The hard work of rearing young over for another year, it seemed as if the wildlife of the forest was racing to put nature's abundance to good use while there was still time. The wilting leaves and shorter days were unmistakable signs of the winter to come for man and beast alike.

Alfhelm rode in the place of honour at the head of the column. Although he was outranked by the æthelings they had insisted that he lead them in thanks for the splendid hospitality he had shown them. It was late morning before they reached the area in which the hunt was to take place. Dismounting they collected their weapons. Each man carried a boar spear and a bow. The boar spear was shorter and thicker than a normal fighting spear. Strong and aggressive, a boar at bay was a fearsome adversary and a broken spear could prove fatal. The bow was for use against fleeing prey, hopefully deer Beowulf thought. A hunk of venison was always welcome after a day in the field. Withies had been placed every twenty-five paces, marking the starting position for each of the hunters. A draw had taken place before they left the lodge, each man having been allocated a number which corresponded to a matching number on each withy. Experience had taught them that this was the fairest way to allot places for the hunt. Ale, weapons and ego's never were easy bed-fellows. Beowulf had been drawn between Heardred and his uncle, Herebeald. To the far side of Herebeald, Hythcyn stood, flexing his bow.

"I am glad that Herebeald is between you and Hythcyn," Heardred had muttered to Beowulf as he had passed him on the way to his starting position. "Stay alert, cousin," he said patting his arm.

A horn announced the start of the hunt and the hunters moved into the forest. At first Beowulf could still see the others to his left and right as they moved stealthily forward. Half a mile ahead they had been warned that the cover became much denser. Beaters were working their way from the other side of this, driving the animals out of cover and directly towards them. He could faintly hear the cries of the men and the beating of their staffs as they moved closer to them. The forest cover grew denser as they moved deeper into its embrace. Where shafts of light had clearly illuminated the forest floor only a few moments ago, now, Beowulf found, his neighbours grew less and less distinct until they were finally completely lost from view.

Suddenly a fox emerged from the bushes and skidded to a halt twenty paces in front of him. Beowulf raised his bow and took aim as the animal stared straight at him. For a moment he hesitated, before slowly lowering his bow. He wouldn't kill merely for pleasure, he decided, only for the table. The fox seized its chance and raced by him, disappearing in an instant. With a clatter, several doves rose from the branches of the trees ahead. Just as they reached the top of the canopy an arrow transfixed one of them and it fell, lifeless, to the ground. Smaller animals continued to dart from cover as the beaters approached but nothing, he sighed, that he would look forward to eating.

With an almighty *crash* a large deer tore through the bushes immediately ahead. Surprised by him, it hesitated, before darting forward again. Beowulf raised his bow and sighted, but he was too late. With a bone-jarring smash the deer collided with his chest, knocking him backwards. He landed, hard, on the forest floor, his bow spinning from his grasp. A moment later the deer crashed down beside him. Beowulf reached down to draw the seax from his belt as the deer struggled to regain its footing. Panicking, the deer lashed out, its hooves pounding against him. Abandoning any thoughts of finishing off the deer with his seax, Beowulf curled up and buried his head in his arms. He lay, prone, for what seemed like an eternity as the strong hooves pummelled his arms and body before he realised with a shocking sudden-ness that the pounding had stopped. Slowly uncurling himself he glanced up, just in time to see the panic stricken deer bolt back into the trees. Beowulf lay still for a moment before slowly raising his hand to his face. Nervously his fingers felt his face and skull for any signs of damage. He had taken a beating, but the images of flaps of bloody flesh hanging from his shattered skull remained, thankfully, in his imagination. His mail had protected his body, but still he was bruised and shaken.

Heardred crashed through the trees to his right, a look of concern etched on his face. "I am fine," he smiled, "just a bit of bruising." Holding up his arm, he waited for Heardred to help him to his feet. To his surprise he merely glanced down at him as he crashed on, spear point first, to Beowulf's left. Alarmed now Beowulf scrambled to his feet. Picking up his own spear he raced after him. He was aware now of cries coming from ahead as he raced to catch up. He saw Heardred stop suddenly, dropping his spear. He tensed, gripping his spear tighter, as he neared his cousin. Sliding to a halt he crouched and scanned the bushes ahead for any signs of threat. At first he didn't notice the figures at his feet. Slowly he became aware that Heardred was staring not into the forest but downwards, his face a mask of horror. Slowly he lowered his gaze. Before him Hythcyn sat cradling the lifeless form of his brother, Herebeald, an arrow protruding from his head. He was only dimly aware of the cries of others as, one by one, they arrived at the scene. Slumped on a decayed trunk, he retched.

The body was carried back to the waiting horses, the other hunters following on in a silent daze. Some of them no doubt began to think of the implications of Herebeald's death. Whether Hythcyn had meant to kill his brother or not, and he had certainly acted convincingly grief stricken, he was likely to become the heir to the kingdom. King Hrethel was not a young man. In fact he was far from being a young man. Heardred fell in beside Beowulf, "We need to talk," he whispered. "Behave normally until the funeral, while I make some plans."

Herebeald's body was tied to his horse and led back to the lodge. There it was transferred to a wagon for the journey to Miklaborg. Leaving immediately the members of the hunting party formed an escort for the body for the sad journey. Ecgtheow and Orme left the party at the edge of the forest, riding south to break the news to Beowulf's mother of her brother's death. Travelling through the night they came to the fortress late the next day. Crossing the bridge into the town, they wearily made their way to the island. A silent crowd gathered as word of their arrival spread. Crossing to the fortress they drew up in the lower courtyard. King Hrethel appeared at the entrance to the hall above, having been informed of the sombre procession by his guards. Concern etched on his features, he descended the steps, his eyes scanning the waiting warriors, obviously trying to see who was missing.

"Herebeald?" he pleaded.

Hythcyn stepped uncertainly forward.

"He's dead, father."

Beowulf watched as the old man grimaced before visibly fighting to retain his composure.

"How did he die?" he finally whispered.

Everyone looked at Hythcyn waiting for him to answer, but none came. Finally Hygelac, shooting a look of scorn at Hythcyn, answered for him.

"He was killed by an arrow during the hunt, father."

"Bring me the killer, I wish to kill him myself," the king replied his voice now steady and emotionless.

Falling to his knees Hythcyn began to plead for his life.

"I killed him accidentally father. I saw a deer. I swear it!"

Hrethel looked at his son, uncomprehendingly, before the truth of the words struck him.

"You killed your own brother?" Covering his face with his hands he turned and retraced his steps, unsteadily, to Gefrin.

The body was carried to the hall, where it was laid out in a position of honour. The king retreated to his private quarters and would admit no visitors. Since the death of his Cwen more than a decade before he had become more withdrawn, Beowulf was told. Most of the time, he was still the perfect king, jovial, good natured and a generous ring giver, but he was prone to periods of melancholy which he seemed increasingly unable to shake off. The death of Herebeald at the hands of his brother seemed to have finally broken him.

Hygelac left, characteristically assuming the unenviable task of informing Hild that she was now a widow. He would escort her and Hygd back to Miklaborg for the funeral which was due to take place in three days. Orme arrived the next day, informing Beowulf that his parents would overnight with Alfhelm, before travelling on to the funeral.

The following days were amongst the hardest that Beowulf would ever spend. Days and nights were spent sharing the hall with Herebeald's body, clearly on display, as people arrived to pay their respects and await the funeral. Even drinking seemed to hold no appeal to the warriors who increasingly crowded the hall. Hythcyn sat alone with his thoughts, even more the outcast than usual. On the island below Miklaborg, Herebeald's hearth warriors were busy erecting a funeral pyre for their lord.

The day of the funeral arrived just as the good weather broke. Winds gusted, worrying the tree tops while a fine, chilling, drizzle swept in waves across the clearing. Towards sunset Herebeald's body was carried to the pyre and placed upon it. The body was covered by a shield. A spear was laid alongside. Herebeald's sword, mail and helm would be laid at his side when his ashes were finally buried. Warriors, dressed in their finest war gear ringed the pyre, their eyes downcast. Silently King Hrethel stepped forward and took two flaming brands from a warrior. He handed one to Hild and they both approached the pile. Without a word they both thrust their brands deep into the base of the wood. Soaked in oils and fats the wood caught fire immediately, flames hungrily licking the sides. Soon the pyre was a roaring mass of flame. Herebeald's body became more and more indistinct until, with a sudden roar, the flames finally hid it from view. As the sun dipped below the western horizon King Hrethel turned away. Without looking at the assembled nobility the old king made his way wordlessly back up to his hall. Many of those present suspected that he would never leave it alive again.

Strangely, thought Beowulf, given the fact that Herebeald lay, consumed by flames, only yards away, the finality of the act and the departure of the king had had the effect of lifting the spirits of those who remained. The general mood seemed to lighten almost immediately, despite the best efforts of the weather, as those remaining sought out friends and relatives.

"Ale, kinsman?" Turning he was pleased to see the smiling face of Hygelac, a cup held in his outstretched hand. "Let's go and liven them all up, it is what he would have wanted."

To his surprise, Beowulf had an enjoyable night in Gefrin. As everybody drank and feasted they retold tales of Herebeald's life, each one seemingly bawdier and funnier than the last. Beowulf was grateful that his last memory of his uncle had been his imitation of the leaping, farting fool, the night before the hunt. He would never be able to think of him now without a smile. Maybe that is what was so important about reputation he pondered. To leave good memories in others really was a form of immortality. Sadly, to the disappointment of all, King Hrethel refused to leave his private rooms, despite the pleas of his sons, Hild and his daughter. Beowulf was pleased to see that his mother also seemed to have recovered. As she sat with Hygd and Hild she seemed happier and more relaxed than he thought he had ever seen her. At the other side of the hall Ecgtheow stood with Hygelac in animated conversation, while Bjalki and Orme seemed to be having some success in persuading two of the serving girls to accompany them outside.

"When I go I want you to do this for me, Cousin." An arm draped itself around his shoulder, closely followed by a beery, smiling face.

"When you go I will be following along soon after, kinsman," he replied. "We shall have to hold our wake in Woden's hall!"

"Herebeald will be there, won't he? I never thought of that. He didn't die in battle, although he *had* been in a few."

Heardred half belched, his finger prodding Beowulf in the chest. Clasping his head, affectionately, to his chest, Beowulf asked Heardred.

"Who's the Lord of the Hunt?"

"Woden."

"Where did Herebeald die, spear in hand?"

"Ah!" Heardred slurred, waving a finger and grinning like a fool. He grabbed Beowulf's shoulder and swung himself to face him, his mouth close to his ear. "Don't look, but we are being watched by a very cunning wolf. I will come to your father's hall within the week and we will decide where we are going. This is not over yet, kinsman, trust me."

Letting go, Heardred grabbed Beowulf by the head and planted a kiss on his forehead before he moved away with a wave. Smiling at the retreating form of his cousin he crossed the hall on the pretext of refilling his cup, surreptitiously checking the sides of the hall. Finally he saw the cause of Heardred's warning. There, in the darker recesses of the hall sat Hythcyn and a number of other shadowy figures. Most were unfamiliar to him but, looking as hard as he dare without drawing attention to himself, he saw to his shock and disappointment that Alfhelm was among them.

11

Beowulf had waited impatiently at home for the best part of a week. They had left Gefrin the day after the funeral, breaking the journey, as usual, at the hall of Alfhelm in Geatwic. Suspiciously, Alfhelm had not been able to accompany them but had sent word ahead that they intended to stay. Late one afternoon the sound of horses approaching from the coast road came to Beowulf as he practised sword-play with Orme in the courtyard. Halting, they replaced the weapons in their scabbards and walked over to the gate, wiping the sweat from their brows as they did so, arriving just as Heardred and Hudda reined in their mounts. Dismounting, Heardred slapped the neck of the horse before embracing his cousin.

"I expected you sooner, kinsman." Beowulf chastised him. "Come inside and tell us your news. Come, Hudda."

A thrall hurried over and took the horses from them as the group made their way over to the hall.

"My father is visiting one of his thegns but he will be back soon," he continued. "Let me show you some Waeg-munding hospitality while we wait."

Ecgtheow returned shortly after. Entering the courtyard he noticed the saddled mounts and hastened inside.

"Heardred, Hudda, this is a pleasant surprise I hope."

"It is good to see you lord," Heardred replied. "My father sends his warmest regards to both yourself and his sister."

Throwing his cloak to one side, Ecgtheow sat on a bench and proceeded to lever off his riding boots.

"How is the king?" he asked, looking up.

"As far as we know there is no change. He still refuses to leave his rooms. Worryingly it seems that Alfhelm has taken to caring for him, and as you know it appears that he has chosen to ally himself with Hythcyn."

Ecgtheow pulled a face. "What are your father's thoughts on this?"

"He thinks that the king's life is in great danger and asks that you join forces with his own to restore the king's liberty to him. He has made preparations for the mustering of his levy and has been in contact with Hild. She has promised her support. Herebeald's old hearth companions are of course with us. With the help of the Waegmundings we should easily overwhelm them."

A new voice interrupted their deliberations.

"What of my other brother, Hythcyn?"

Sigrid, Beowulf's mother, stood framed in the doorway.

"Am I to be privy to the plans which are likely to lead to the death of one or both of my father and brother? Or maybe it will be my husband and son? Who knows what the gods have planned for you." Turning on her heel she walked out into the courtyard. There was an uncomfortable silence before Ecgtheow sighed and continued. "She's right of course. I will speak with her later and try to allay her fears."

Beowulf was reminded of the tale of Hengest and Finn which he had heard all those years ago in the hall of King

Hrothgar of the Danes. The fighting which had broken out there had left the Cwen with a dead husband, brother and son. Unable to take direct, physical action, the lot of a woman in these power struggles was not to be envied, he reflected.

"Of course we are with you, the ties of blood and obligation are as strong as any here on middle earth. Return to your father in the morning and give him the news. Take Beowulf with you. He can help to co-ordinate our plans. Orme, you go along too."

"Yes, lord," he nodded curtly.

"Well," Ecgtheow sighed, "it seems that the days of peace and plenty have come to an end. Let us hope that we can restore them quickly by striking fast and hard before anything else dreadful happens."

They all nodded in agreement. Rising, Ecgtheow started to move towards the door. As he passed through he paused and turned back to them, grinning widely.

"Why all the long faces, this is why we are all warriors! I could understand it if you were facing a day of work in the fields tomorrow. Imagine being shackled to a plough, staring at an ox's arse all day."

They smiled thinly, the mood still reflective.

"That reminds me, Orme," Bjalki smiled wickedly as he attempted to help his lord lift their spirits. "Are you going to see that girl you went with at Gefrin again?"

They spent the night in good humour. Now that plans were being made they all felt as if a weight had been lifted from their shoulders. All the waiting and uncertainty of the previous weeks were about to be ended as they marshalled their forces and marched to relieve the king. Even Sigrid had seemed happier when she had joined them later. Ecgtheow had decided that he would council banishment as a punishment for Hythcyn and Alfhelm and this had no doubt helped her to accept the situation. After all they were primarily concerned with the welfare of the king, her father, and there was only a suspicion that Herebeald's death had been anything but a tragic accident. His head filled with plans, Beowulf found it difficult to sleep that night. Eventually he fell into a fitful sleep, thoughts of leading men into battle against his king's enemies filling his head.

HE AWOKE WITH A START. His small wooden charm, the gift of Hrani all those years ago, had never failed to warn him of danger and now it felt hot against his skin. Outside a horse snickered, followed by another. Closing his eyes he listened intently, slowly turning his head first one way and then the other, straining to hear anything untoward. Slowly he slipped from his bed and padded, as stealthily as possible, over to Heardred. He shook him gently by the shoulder and put his finger to his lips, warning his cousin to be quiet. Seeing Beowulf's expression, he was instantly fully alert and reaching for his weapons. Beowulf moved on to his parents' private quarters. He tensed as the door squeaked open. Reaching in, he laid his hand gently on his father's shoulder.

"Father," he breathed. "There are men outside."

Quickly dressing and arming they moved to the door. There were six of them, five of whom were seasoned warriors, dressed and armed for battle, plus Beowulf who, despite his youth had already killed, both alone and in a shield wall. Looking around the group Ecgtheow smiled.

"Whatever awaits us out there I want you all to know that it fills me with pride to lead such a group of men. I ask that you follow my lead, however difficult it may seem. It is better to live to fight another day than throw your life away need-lessly. If we are to prevail we must not be wiped out piece-meal. Our day will come. Do you understand?"

Grimly they nodded.

Ecgtheow looked directly at his son and repeated the question. "Beowulf, do you understand?"

He hesitated before replying. "Yes, lord."

Opening the door they stepped through, into the weak dawn light.

They gathered in a group outside the hall door, Ecgtheow to the fore. Sat astride a horse Hythcyn smiled triumphantly at the tiny band of warriors facing him. To his side sat Alfhelm looking suitably uncomfortable, Beowulf noticed. Arranged to left and right of them were, Beowulf quickly calculated, twin ranks of ten warriors, two ranks deep. Glancing about him, he counted another twenty or so to both sides of the hall, with others no doubt out of sight behind the hall. Beyond Hythcyn and Alfhelm more riders held the reins of the warriors' mounts, so that made, Beowulf estimated, possibly upward of a hundred warriors facing them with the further possibility of more nearby. He understood now his father's address before they had left the hall. They were of course impossible odds.

"Hythcyn, you should have sent word. I would have laid-in more supplies to entertain so many guests."

"Ever the wit," Hythcyn replied. "I know where your son gets it from now."

Beowulf felt a chill as Hythcyn turned his gaze on him. For a moment he considered the odds of reaching him and cutting him down, but quickly discounted it. One of the warriors would take him down before he got half way and even if, by some miracle, he did reach him, Hythcyn was an experienced warrior with height advantage. He would open his skull in an instant.

"I am afraid that I have some bad news for my sister, is she available?"

"Of course I am."

Beowulf tensed as his mother walked from the hall and over to her brother.

"You show me honour, brother, to ride through the night on my account. Let me guess. Our father was taken suddenly ill and died? Our father slipped and fell to his death while inspecting the guard perhaps?"

Hythcyn pulled a wry smile.

"You should not joke about such things sister. Our father appears to have choked on his food. Nobody really knows for sure since he insisted on eating alone, as you know."

Beowulf watched as his mother took a deep breath and visibly fought to control her emotions. To his surprise he saw only sadness in his mother's eyes as she looked at Hythcyn. The man was a monster who had almost certainly killed her brother and father and now stood before her husband and son with an armed force, but clearly she felt only pity for him. Not for the first time, Beowulf was thankful that he saw people as either friends or enemies as most men did. She continued in a strong, unemotional, voice.

"Then I have another funeral to prepare for, please go now."

"There is no need. That has already been taken care of. The body was," he hesitated, "there is no easy way to put this, corrupting very quickly, so we felt that people would rather remember him as he was in life. It was all done with the honour due to a king of the Geats. A burial mound is being prepared for him as we speak. He was accompanied on his journey by his eagle and your old falconer, Svip was it? Whatever his name was, he also travelled with his king to help with the bird in the afterlife. Maybe you would like to visit next spring, when the weather is better?"

After an uncomfortable pause in which she stared coldly at Hythcyn, Sigrid replied. "As you say then, next spring would be fine, goodbye." Turning she swept past the group at the door and disappeared into the hall.

Ecgtheow spoke. "You have delivered your message, Hythcyn. I believe the lady of the hall told you to leave. We will follow on by ship, since it seems accommodation in Geatwic is now unavailable," he said glancing at Alfhelm.

"Follow on, why? Oh of course, do forgive me I was so busy talking of family matters that I forget to tell you my other news. *I* am your king now. My Bronding friends here," he waved a hand, "insisted."

Simultaneously the hands of Ecgtheow and the others automatically went to their sword hilts.

"Unwise," Hythcyn smiled, "expected, but still unwise."

To the left and right of Hythcyn, Bronding warriors raised drawn bows.

"Ecgtheow, you are not a fool. I am offering you favour and advancement. Place your hands in mine and become my man. Others have chosen wisely and stand to benefit from it why not you? Other nations are enriching themselves on the carcass of Rome's Empire and we sit here gathering our harvests and sitting in our halls listening to the tales of the past. Let us make some new tales for future generations of Geats to marvel at on a long winter's evening. Put down the plough and become a hero with me!"

Ecgtheow regarded Hythcyn before responding.

"I will need to speak with my companions."

"Of course, they are a fine group of men. All would be welcome in the new order."

Ecgtheow turned, as the group gathered around him.

"Speak freely you may not get another chance."

"That was a good speech. We *have* sat on our arses too long while lesser people reap the spoils in the south. I can't say that I am not tempted, lord," Bjalki offered, "but you know you have my oath, I follow where you lead."

"Anybody else? Now is the time."

"I cannot answer, lord, until I know what has happened to my father and mother," Heardred put in.

"No, of course, I shall make it a condition that they are safe."

"A condition?" Beowulf bridled. "A condition of what, father?"

"We have no choice but to accept that he is king for now. The alternative is that we all die in the next few minutes, including your mother, Beowulf, and where will that get us? He will still be king and there will be none left to oppose him. Remember that an oath taken under duress is not binding. We bide our time for now and live to fight another day. Does anybody else have anything to add?" His eyes flicked from face to face. "No? We all agree then? Beowulf?" He looked around the group. One by one they all nodded grimly. "Let's get it over with as quickly as possible then," he sighed.

Turning back, Ecgtheow addressed Hythcyn.

"What of Hygelac?"

"Naturally we visited my brother first of course. Æthelings still outrank ealdormen in my kingdom, even those married to my sister. He has taken the oath. What did you decide, life or death?"

Walking forward, Ecgtheow knelt in front of Hythcyn's horse and, clasping his hands together, held them outstretched in front of him. Smiling, the king dismounted and placed his hands around them.

"On my oath I swear to serve you and do as you command, as Woden is my witness."

"And I accept your oath with joy!" Hythcyn replied.

Ecgtheow rose and they embraced. One by one they went forward and took the oath of loyalty under the watchful eyes of the Bronding warriors, whose notched arrows still guarded against any attack on the king.

"I will not swear until I have seen that my father still lives."

Heardred had approached Hythcyn but remained on his feet. The Bronding bowmen tensed, guarding against a sudden strike.

"I assure you that your father lives. It's disappointing that you distrust me, but no matter. You can take the oath later. After all," he sneered, "you are not very important are you?"

"I think that he will regret saying that one day," Hudda murmured from the rear of the group.

"Right, that concludes our business here today. A good morning's work, and all before breakfast," Hythcyn declared. He raised a hand and a warrior walked forward holding the reins of two horses. "Beowulf and Heardred, your king requests that you accompany him for a short time, just until things settle down a bit. Regime changes can be messy things and I would like to keep you two safely near me for a while. After all, you are the kingdom's future. I would hate to think that any harm would befall you."

With no choice but to comply, they both mounted. All around them the Bronding warriors were doing likewise and organising themselves into a column. They had left the hall armed only with their shields and swords in their hurry to face the attackers, and a thrall now ran from the hall bearing their spears.

"No, no spears," Hythcyn called.

Shocked Beowulf turned to him. "But they are the mark of a free man!"

"Yes," the king replied. "I believe that they are."

12

The journey north had been an uncomfortable experience for Beowulf and Heardred. Immediately upon leaving Ecgtheow's hall they had been separated. Beowulf, his oath given to Hythcyn, rode at the front of the column alongside the king and Ealdorman Alfhelm, while Heardred found himself isolated in the rear, surrounded by grizzled Bronding veterans.

They moved slowly north, through a landscape which was rapidly changing from the lush greens of summer to a blaze of yellows, reds and russets. Each breath of wind produced a flurry of leaves which turned and danced as they spun lazily to the roadway. Great banks of them had begun to gather in hollows and ditches, while others blew softly in waves across the path. Most mornings now men awoke to a land whitened by frost as the coming winter began to gather them into its icy embrace.

If the journey had been fraught, then the evening spent at the hall in Geatwic had been more so. Alfhelm had tried his best to be a good host, something which Beowulf had to admit, came naturally to the man, but the forced humour and stilted conversation had been uncomfortable for all of those present. It had clearly been a relief for all when they bade farewell to Alfhelm the next morning and continued on their journey to Miklaborg.

Their arrival at the fortress that evening had been an uncertain time for Beowulf and Heardred, but despite their fears that they were to be locked away or quartered in the stables, to their surprise they were accommodated amongst the warriors in Gefrin itself. As the northern winter tightened its grip on the land, the cousins were forced to spend more and more time with the king. Heardred, accompanied by several of Hythcyn's hearth warriors, had been allowed to travel north to visit his parents soon after their arrival and on his return he had kept his word and given his oath to a beaming Hythcyn.

Much to his confusion, Beowulf found that he preferred the sense of purpose which now infused the inhabitants of Gefrin. Gone were the days of drift and sloth, as warriors grew fat and lethargic on a diet of lazy days and nights feasting and drinking as they relived tales of past glories. Beowulf and Heardred found themselves, to their disquiet, excited to be included in the plans of the king for the coming year. Alfhelm arrived before Yule and was appointed by Hythcyn as leader of a raiding expedition in the spring aimed at either the Heatho-Reams to the north or the Jutes on the other side of the Kattegat. The raids promised excitement, riches and the chance for young warriors to make a reputation. The contrast with the old order of his grandfather could not have been greater.

Yule came and with it Hygelac and Ecgtheow. Both were escorted to the celebration by warriors of known loyalty to the new king, despite their oaths of allegiance. Despite his best efforts, the king presided over a sullen and lacklustre Yule at his hall.

Beowulf alone had accompanied Hythcyn and Alfhelm to the dawn ceremony at the temple on the Hill of Goats. Heardred's delay in pledging his allegiance had obviously elevated Beowulf to the status of favoured nephew, and although he was astute enough to realise that Hythcyn was using him to undermine any opposition to his rule, Beowulf could not but feel attracted by his new position of importance.

The group collected in the pre dawn darkness awaiting the familiar footsteps to approach from the temple. Beowulf could not help casting his mind back to the only previous time that he had stood on this spot. Exactly one year ago he had stood with his grandfather, King Hrethel and Herebeald as they waited to be admitted to the temple complex. Now both men were dead, he was no longer a boy and the Geat nation was flooded with Bronding warriors.

His mind came back to the present as he heard the bolts securing the double doors being pulled back. Creaking on their iron hinges the doors were drawn inward. Eagerly his eyes searched the gloom, trying to see if the same woman was to be their guide. At first Beowulf was disappointed as, backlit by the flaming brands which had been placed along the causeway to light their way, the woman had the fuller figure of a more mature woman. As she stood to one side, allowing them admittance, he was shocked to see that it was in fact her after all.

Led by Hythcyn they made their way across the causeway to the temple. Ducking inside the Yew tree, they emerged once more inside the temple complex. Ahead of them stood the familiar table with the oath ring, gleaming in the reflected light of the torches, upon it. Once more they awaited the rising of the midwinter sun. Again Beowulf marvelled at the appearance of the goat's head from the branch of the tree as the sun emerged from the confines of the eastern hills to shine, ruby like, in the eye of the beast. The sacrifices to the gods were made and oaths renewed before they began to make their way back to Gefrin.

On the journey over, Alfhelm had taken the rear position in deference to Beowulf's position as kinsman to the king. Determined to try to talk to the priestess, Beowulf nodded him through. After a moment's confusion, Alfhelm's face broke into a smile as he recognised Beowulf's reason for the switch.

Dropping into step beside her he cleared his throat and introduced himself.

"I am Beowulf. I just wanted to thank you for sending the crow to save me during the skating race last year."

"I know who you are. You seem to forget that I am a volva. I know more about you than you know yourself."

"Do you ever leave the temple?"

"No."

"Can I visit you?"

"No!" she gasped, shocked at the suggestion.

They walked on as Beowulf's mind frantically cast about for something else to say. The doors at the end of the causeway were already close and he could not wait another year for an opportunity to talk to her again. He felt light headed at her closeness, her scent filling him with desire.

"Can I ask you one more question?" he ventured.

"My name is no concern of yours," she answered with a weary sigh.

Regaining the doors he turned and, to her shock, took her hand.

"Why did the gods not come from the temple to witness the ceremony this year?"

DESPITE HIS MISGIVINGS, the afternoon games and entertainments proved to be a great success for King Hythcyn. Despite the fact that King Hrethel had seemed very popular with the Geatish people, Beowulf was surprised by the speed with which he seemed to have been forgotten by the vast majority of the population. As Alfhelm, more familiar than the majority of them in day to day dealings with the common folk had explained. "Give them a day off work and free food and ale and they will be happy to call your dog, King Dog!"

The atmosphere was rather more strained in the king's enclosure. Beowulf and Heardred had naturally spent the afternoon in the company of their fathers. For Beowulf it was the first opportunity to speak to Ecgtheow since the morning of the oath giving outside his father's hall. Although it was only a few months before, he was surprised to have feelings bordering on disloyalty towards Hythcyn as he discussed the situation in the kingdom. Hythcyn had made a conscious effort it seemed to leave the four of them in privacy, realising perhaps that if he did not trust them at some stage he could not expect them ever to accept him as king.

"I hear that you are becoming accepted as part of his inner circle," Ecgtheow said. "That's good, the more he trusts you the easier it will be when the time comes. He seems to think that he can kill the king and heir to the throne, his own father and brother, and carry on as if nothing has happened."

"Yes, you are doing well, Beowulf," Hygelac added. "Better than some who seem to be letting pride stand in their way." He clapped Heardred on the shoulder. "The longer this goes on the harder it will be for us to avenge our kinsmen. At the moment memories are bright and wounds are fresh. The longer we leave it the more likely it is that he will be able to buy his way into acceptance. You saw the people today. Only a few of us have a code of honour. The rest of them are always available for the right price. Sometimes even the most surprising people set a price on their honour," he muttered glancing over at Alfhelm.

The others nodded in agreement.

"Beowulf, never think that we don't realise that you find the thought of serving under him attractive. We were all young once and yearned for a chance to prove ourselves on the battlefield. Well, you will get your chance soon to fight alongside us against the monster that my brother has become. Each time that he gives you some responsibility or shows you favour, think of the picture of Herebeald with an arrow through his head or your grandfather, the man who embraced you and gave you the shield and spear of a warrior, 'choking' on his food."

"My son does not need reminding which side he is on kinsman," Ecgtheow reproached him. "You yourself helped to teach him the responsibilities of manhood."

Hygelac sighed. "I know, I am sorry, but I have been told how he has targeted you Beowulf. We have plenty of men inside Gefrin still. Remember that. You are still surrounded by friends, even though you do not know who they are. Anyway," he concluded, glancing about them, "I think that we had better try and mix a bit with the others. We would not want anybody to think that we are plotting or anything!"

The rest of the day passed uneventfully. The evening was spent in the hall. Alfhelm provided a range of novelty acts which helped, in addition to copious amounts of ale and mead, to let them all to forget for a short while the events of the previous few months. The next morning Beowulf and Heardred bid their fathers farewell and returned to the hall.

SLOWLY THE WINTER released its grip on the land. The days lengthened allowing the warriors to spend more time in preparation for the coming campaign.

It had been decided that the Jutes were to be attacked in early summer. Many of their warriors would have left to go raiding in the South leaving them vulnerable. The Geat army would occupy Jute Land for the summer and return with their spoils after the first harvest.

The harbours and shipyards along the Geatish coast had been busy since the first signs of a thaw, preparing the fleet for the attack. Repairs had been carried out to older ships and new vessels built to replace those deemed to be too far gone to handle the amount of booty which all confidently expected. Vessels patrolled off the coast, preventing any word escaping of the plans. It would be unfortunate to say the least to find the Jute army arrayed on the beach as they approached.

Beowulf had been sent south to inform his father of the plans and had spent an enjoyable few days with his family. Although he still felt part of the conspiracy against the king, he had been so busy lately helping to prepare the raiding force that he had almost forgotten of its existence. To be home again and exposed to the machinations of the conspirators felt strangely odd. To his disquiet, he found that as the time between the present and the events leading to the accession of Hythcyn grew, so the importance of gaining revenge for the deaths of his grandfather and uncle seemed to become less important. He was enjoying the responsibility given to him by the king. He had helped to train warriors and had spent some weeks at the coast organising the invasion fleet. Hythcyn was everything a good ring giver should be to Beowulf, generous and vigorous in the defence of the kingdom, and he felt torn between the two camps. After all, he pondered, nobody had actually seen either of the men die and Hythcyn may actually have been innocent.

He returned to Gefrin more confused than ever over his divided loyalties.

Spring was now in its full glory. The fruit trees, apple, cherry and pear, were in full bloom in the orchards outside the village. Everywhere Elm, Oak and Maple shook off the winter's gloom and burst forth with new green shoots. The fields and forests echoed to the call of the cuckoo while overhead, cranes returned from their winter roosts over the southern sea. In the world of men, excitement mounted as the time drew near for the great adventure against the Jutes to begin. Beowulf was in the courtyard below Gefrin one morning when he noticed the king approach.

"Kinsman," Hythcyn smiled. "How are our preparations coming along?"

"Well, lord. Everything will be ready in good time."

"Of course it will, I know your qualities. I have one small task which I need to entrust to someone reliable before we leave. Maybe it would interest you?"

Beowulf began to decline the offer. After all he was far too busy with the preparations for the campaign to be distracted now, until his eyes were drawn beyond the king to the top of the staircase which led to Gefrin. There, dressed in men's riding clothes, stood the woman from the temple.

Hythcyn laughed as Beowulf's mouth involuntarily opened and closed like a freshly landed trout.

"Alfhelm suggested that you might be the one to ask. It seems that he was right," he chuckled. "She needs to travel to see the Bronding volva for some reason apparently, and what with many of their warriors at the coast ready to join us in the Jute campaign I would feel better if she had an escort. She asked for you by name when I suggested it. I take it you'll go?"

THEY HEADED NORTH, following the Geat River which led directly to the Bronding border. Beowulf had refused the offer of any companions or thralls to serve them on their journey. He had waited over a year for this opportunity and he was determined to make the most of it. A pack horse had been loaded with gifts for the Bronding king, Hrothulf, alongside various mysterious packages which had been supplied by the temple on the Hill of Goats. "Kaija," the woman announced suddenly after they had ridden for some distance.

Beowulf glanced across, "Kaija?"

"My name is Kaija," she replied with a smile, her eyes remaining fixed to the road.

"That's an unusual name, where are you from? I have never seen a woman who looks as you do."

"See if you can guess," she replied lightly, turning her face in his direction.

Once again Beowulf was captivated by her beauty. It was the first time he had seen her in full daylight and if anything she looked even lovelier than he remembered. For the first time, he noticed the high cheek bones and slightly narrowed eyes of the people who inhabited the far north.

"You are a Finn!" he exclaimed. "You are the first of your people that I have met. Are they all as beautiful as you?"

"Without exception," she smiled happily. "Beowulf," she continued softly, "you must understand that there is no possibility of any physical relationship developing between us. I am the property of the gods. I asked for you to accompany me on this trip because I have several questions to ask you, that is all."

"Ask away," he chirped happily. They all started off saying that, he knew, but they did not really mean it. His cousin Heardred had told him so, and he knew all about women.

"All in good time," she replied before digging her heels into the flanks of her mare and, with a whoop of joy, racing off along the meadow. Taken unawares, Beowulf was left floundering in her wake as he tried to cajole the pack horse, reluctantly, out of its torpor.

He caught up with her at the outskirts of a small settlement. Ahead, scattered alongside the road, stood a few huts surrounded by the small fields from which the people eked out a living. To one side lay a pen containing several cows, the only objects of any value which Beowulf could see in the place. As he approached he could see Kaija's horse, its head lowered, contentedly munching the fine grass which grew alongside the road.

A small crowd had gathered at the pen, silently watching something inside. One of them became aware of him as he approached, and she immediately dropped to her knee and lowered her head in deference. Others noticed her actions and were quick to follow suit, allowing Beowulf his first glimpse inside the pen.

One of the animals was clearly sick and had been penned off from the others. Frothing at the mouth, its flanks were streaked in a lather of white foam. Alongside the animal Kaija stooped, slowly running her hands over its flanks.

A man stood to one side of the pen, clearly the owner of the beast. Torn between concern for his valuable cow and anxiety at being so close to Kaija, the man stood wringing his hat nervously in his hands. Seeing Beowulf alight from his mount he too dropped to his knees.

Motioning everyone to stand, Beowulf rested his arms on the top bar of the fence and watched Kaija as she worked her hands quickly and methodically over the body of the cow. Straightening up, she noticed him for the first time.

"Beowulf, good, you are here at last. Pass me that bag from the pack horse, the one with the yellow binding, if you would?"

The crowd parted silently before him. Untying the pack from its companions, he remembered the valuables which were packed alongside.

"What is your name boy?" he questioned one of the onlookers.

A boy of about ten winters shuffled forward, his red hair hung forward, half covering his eyes, while a smattering of freckles lay haphazardly about the bridge of his nose.

"Henrik, lord," he replied with a cheeky grin.

"Well, Henrik, If you can take care of our horses for a while I'll see if I can find a reward for you. What do you say?"

"Well," he paused, "could my sister Hanna help, lord? She is good with horses too!"

A tall, slim, girl of eight or nine winters pushed her way through the crowd, her smiling face framed by long hair the colour of wet straw. Beowulf laughed at their impudence.

"I think that I can find two rewards today, if only to

compensate your parents for the hard time you two must give them."

The crowd laughed and visibly relaxed at the exchange. Handing Henrik the reins he strode over to the pen.

Kaija flashed him a warm smile.

"When you have finished charming the local children this cow has about an hour to live unless I can save it."

Taking the bag Kaija undid the fastenings and, reaching inside, removed a small green bowl. Walking over to the sick cow, she removed a small pouch from the bag and half filled the bowl with a bright yellow powder. She breathed deeply and murmured an incantation over the powder as the crowd looked on in awe. Passing her hand across the bowl, the crowd gasped as a small flame flickered. Suddenly a bright, intense, flame glowed in the bowl before, as quickly as it had appeared, it diminished and was swallowed by a cloud of thick yellow smoke. Moving swiftly to the head of the cow, Kaija gently stroked its muzzle, calming it as it breathed in the pungent mixture. She turned to the wide eyed farmer.

"Hold this here while I continue." She ordered.

Hesitant, but too afraid of Kaija's powers to disobey, the man dropped his cap and did as instructed.

Moving her hands swiftly down the side of the cow, she stopped at its clearly distended stomach. Bunching her fingers together into a ball she moved them methodically, as if searching for the correct spot. As she began to work her fingers in a circular motion a thin trickle of blood suddenly began to escape from the body of the animal.

The cow swayed and shuddered slightly as the terrified farmer sobbed against her muzzle.

A woman in the crowd let out a short involuntary scream as Kaija's hand appeared to pass deep inside its flank. Slowly she worked her arm deeper inside as the watching crowd clung to each other in terror and staggered backwards.

Beowulf watched, amazed, as Kaija withdrew her hand and wiped the side of the beast with her clean hand. Apart from a small bloodstained patch on the cows hide, there was no sign of any entry wound on the beast, although Beowulf had clearly seen her hand and arm enter deep inside it.

Some of the women in the watching crowd sobbed, with emotion, fear or both. Kaija straightened up and calmly took the bowl from the pale faced farmer.

He immediately retreated to the fence and stood with his neighbours. Kaija placed her hand over the muzzle and murmured softly. The cow stood, transfixed, as she removed a short knife from her tunic. With a flash, she made a mark with the blade on the cow's forehead. A small trickle of blood ran down towards the muzzle, leaving a dark brown stain in its wake.

The cow seemed to slowly become aware of its surroundings, as if it were waking from a deep sleep. Lowing softly, it nuzzled Kaija and, with a final shake of its head, it began to feed on the hay which was strewn around the pen.

It was all too much for the farmer who began to sob unashamedly with relief.

As if released from a spell, the villagers suddenly fell to animated chatter. The farmer approached Kaija and, falling to his knees, whispered his thanks. Smiling, she laid her hand on his head and spoke a brief incantation. Gathering up her bag she strode across the pen to Beowulf.

"Shall we go?"

LEAVING THE VILLAGE BEHIND, they tracked the river north westwards. Kaija had refused any payment from the farmer for her services, although some of the village women had pressed them to take some fresh bread and cheese which she had gratefully accepted.

"I love cheese," she shrugged in reply to Beowulf's questioning look.

Henrik and Hanna had agreed to settle on a small piece of hack silver for their brief services, their attempts at bargaining being cut abruptly short when Beowulf had explained that Kaija could always turn them into worms instead and he could save his silver.

"You are wondering why I refused payment for my services at the village," she questioned, breaking into his thoughts.

"How did you know?"

"I see many things. Warrior's minds are among the easiest to read. They are usually very simple creatures, given to simple needs. War, food, ale, women. Not necessarily in that order of course." She shrugged again, nonchalantly. "Warriors and merchants."

"Merchants?"

"Merchants are almost without exception grasping creatures who would sell their soul for a profit. And you know the funny thing is," she continued, "although they don't realise it, that is just what most of them *are* doing. They are people who know the price of all things but the value of none. The gods have no need for their gold and silver, they value qualities like courage, honour and honesty far higher, qualities which they find in people regardless of whether they live in a splendid hall or a swine herder's ramshackle hut. But you are different Beowulf, which is why I asked for the opportunity to spend some time alone with you. In answer to your question, I took no payment because they had nothing that I needed. They were poor people. That cow represented the single most valuable thing that the family owned. Without it they would have been very likely to be reliant on the help of their neighbours to survive the next winter. Even then, they would quite possibly have to sell one or both of the children into thraldom to ensure their survival. Of course that is not something that the son of an ealdorman would realise. Luckily for them the cow was not possessed by spirits or elf shot, that would have been more difficult. One of its stomachs, they have four you know..."

"They do?" he interrupted in astonishment.

"One of its stomachs," she continued patiently, "was twisted on itself. Painful but easily curable if you know how."

"But I saw you put your hand inside the cow and leave no mark," he replied with awe.

"Of course, I am a volva," she answered, adding brightly. "This looks like a nice place. We'll make camp here."

They hobbled their horses and cleared the chosen patch of ground of stones and twigs. "You start a fire and I will go and catch us a few fish."

Kaija made her way to the river's edge and stripped off her breeches before wading in. Bending forward she lowered her hands into the clear, gushing, water. "You are supposed to be making a fire, the forest is that way!" she indicated with her head.

He realised that he was staring at her, open mouthed. Embarrassed, Beowulf turned and went to gather fuel for the fire. When he returned she was already dressed again. Beside her lay two beautiful brown trout, already washed and gutted and ready for cooking.

"Don't tell me, they jumped onto the bank for you, and offered up their bellies," he smiled as he arranged the wood.

Soon the smell of roasting fish drifted around the camp site. The sun dipped as the day drew to a close. Soon it hung directly at the foot of the valley, its soft light casting lengthening shadows along the meadow. His belly full of warm fish, fresh bread and cheese, Beowulf sighed contentedly as he sipped at the ale Hythcyn had provided for the journey. They had eaten in silence, both of them savouring the sights and smells of the countryside, each seemingly reluctant to break the spell.

Slowly the shadows grew longer until, almost unnoticed, they blended into the full darkness of night. Beowulf removed the weapons and valuables from the horses and placed them at the foot of his sleeping area. He took the remaining food supplies and hauled them into the higher branches of a nearby tree as he had been taught as a boy many years ago. Kaija watched him from her position by the fire. She sat, hugging her legs, knees drawn up to her chin, as he made the area secure.

"I don't think that anyone would be mad enough to attack a fully armed warrior and a volva," she smiled as he returned, "and if a bear happens along I will ask him to leave us alone. I have a gift with animals."

She rose and went to her mare, returning to the fireside with a thick, grey, hooded cloak. Wrapping herself against the evening chill she stared into the flickering flames.

"Tell me what you think that you saw at the temple. You told me that you saw giant figures the first time you came and then asked me why they had not returned the second time."

Beowulf thought for a moment.

"Well, exactly that. The first time that I attended the midwinter ceremony and my grandfather was king, three giant figures watched the sacrifices from the shadows at the rear of the complex. Once the ceremony was complete I looked for them again but they were gone. They seemed to have come and gone into the temple by those big doors at the rear. This last year when I attended with King Hythcyn I looked for them again but they never appeared at any time. Who were they?"

She regarded him for a moment, the flames from the fire dancing in her dark eyes. "Let me examine you," she said softly.

Beowulf smiled happily and settled back. *This is how it starts. Heardred really does know everything about women!*

Unfolding herself from the cloak she crossed to his side of the fire. Kneeling behind him she began to gently part his hair as if searching for something.

"I have a thrall to rid me of lice!" he joked.

Completely ignoring his attempt at humour she carried on searching his scalp. As attracted as he was to Kaija, he had to admit to himself that he found her a little unnerving at times.

"Turn your head!" she suddenly exclaimed.

Pushing his head down towards the fire to catch the light, she spread a patch of his hair roughly apart with her fingers.

"You have one!" she exclaimed in triumph.

"A head?" he replied, confused.

Kaija returned to her place opposite and sat staring excitedly him.

"I have what?"

"Tell me, have you ever met a lone traveller? He often wears a wide brimmed hat and carries a staff."

"You mean Hrani," he replied, still confused. "I shared his camp fire when I was a child. I had just taken two eagle chicks from an eyrie. One of them seemed to have been injured but Hrani ran his hands over it and it seemed to regain its strength. I made a gift of a chick to him for his help and took the other chick home to my father."

Kaija threw back her head and laughed, hugging herself with delight. When she looked back her face shone with excitement.

"My, dear, dear, dumb oaf Beowulf," she smiled. "Does your description of Hrani remind you of anyone you may have heard tales about? I'll take you through it, slowly. You are a warrior after all," she teased him. "A lone traveller wearing a wide brimmed hat and carrying a staff appears mysteriously nearby when you need a fire for the night. He takes an injured eagle from you and revives it with his touch. Tell me, what did Hrani give you in exchange for the gift of this chick?"

Beowulf felt inside his shirt and pulled out the sliver of Hrani's staff on its thonging.

"This is a piece of his staff. He said that it would help to keep me from danger. It feels hot against my skin if any threat is nearby."

Kaija pressed her hands to her face and groaned.

"Beowulf, you fool! Hrani is one of the names which Woden uses. I found his rune, Ansuz, the mark of the traveller, on your head where he had marked you. Those 'giants' at the temple are the statues of Woden, Thunor and Tiwaz. The spirits of the gods occupy the statues during the ceremony to witness our devotion."

"Then why did they not choose to appear this Yule?" he asked.

"It can only mean one thing. The gods disapprove of our new king. There will be a price to pay for the treachery of the last few months. You have been marked out as a favourite of Woden, but he is a fickle god and he can just as quickly turn on you if you anger or disappoint him in any way. You have the potential for greatness, but the year ahead will be a difficult one for the Geats. Choose your path with care."

THE FOLLOWING day they resumed their journey. Their immediate destination the Geat border town of Edet, an easy morning's ride ahead.

Apparently the small settlement where Kaija had saved the cow was called Little Edet, and stood midway between Miklaborg and Big Edet.

"They are very unimaginative with their choice of settlement names out here," Kaija had observed.

It had become a running joke as they threaded their way alongside the Geat River that morning.

"Look that must be Stone Edet!" Beowulf had laughed, pointing at a large rock in midstream. By the end of their journey they had passed Tree Edet, Rapids Edet and a shepherd's shelter which was elevated to the grand title of Tiny Edet.

As the sun rose and burned off the morning mist they slowly made their way north through a landscape of water meadows, dotted with small, affluent, farms. Soon they came to the series of rapids and waterfalls which marked the boundary of the settlement of Edet itself. The traffic on the road increased as they grew nearer to the town. Goods moved along the roads bound for the market, passing wagons loaded with goods from the North, pelts and skins, timber and antler.

The town of Edet sat at the southern end of the great lake of Vanern. The River Geat had its source here, running through the town before continuing its journey south to the coast, passing Miklaborg and Geatwic on the way. The town had grown here to control this northsouth trade, ensuring a steady flow of duties to fill the treasury of the Geatish king. It was a wealthy and important town.

Passing through the town only served to remind Beowulf

of how much he disliked them, however. The rutted earth roads were dusty in summer and a quagmire in winter. Human and animal waste added to the glutinous mixture, the smell of which hung about the town like a thick woollen cloak. Townsfolk, farmers from the hinterland and traders from far and wide all added to the throng, incidentally adding the smell of, largely unwashed, humanity to the mix. It was a potent mixture and Beowulf was happy to leave it behind them as they crested the small rise to their destination for the day. Ahead of them lay the hall of the ealdorman of Edet, Wulfgar.

Beowulf had met him briefly several times at Gefrin and had enjoyed his company, so it was with more than the pleasure of leaving the town behind them that he approached the warriors guarding the entrance to the compound.

"Good day to you, lord," the taller of the two guards greeted him, "can I be of assistance?"

It was doubtful that the guard had ever seen Beowulf, but his clothing, weapons and bearing clearly marked him out as one of the Geat elite.

"I would be grateful if you could inform Ealdorman Wulfgar that Beowulf and a lady companion request his hospitality for the night as we pass through on the king's business."

"If you will follow me lord, I will lead you to the hall personally."

They dismounted and led their horses through the large, open courtyard which lay before the hall. The sounds of metal clashing on metal filled the air as a dozen warriors practised their sword craft in the open. To the side sat other warriors awaiting their turn. Beowulf noticed several of them smile and nudge their comrades as they obviously made a comment about Kaija.

They reached the steps which led to the hall doors.

Thralls appeared to take the horses.

"What is your name?" Beowulf asked the guard who had accompanied them.

"Ulf, lord."

"Ulf, I am holding you personally responsible for my horses and the goods they carry. I bear gifts from King Hythcyn to King Hrothulf of the Brondings, while the lady Kaija carries valuable goods pertaining to her craft."

Ulf flicked a questioning look at Kaija.

"She is a volva."

Beowulf saw a look of alarm flicker across Ulf's features.

"So I would also explain to your companions in the court-yard that they were not only lucky that I was in a good mood today when they made comments about her and decided against gutting one of them for their lack of respect, but that the Lady here could shrink a certain part of them so that they would need to squat with the girls when they needed to take a piss." He leaned in closer to emphasise his words. "Again, she is in good mood today, although she could decide to do something far worse. You know how unpredictable women can be."

Kaija inclined her head and smiled sweetly at Ulf.

"Of course, lord," he stammered, "I will see to everything."

A steward appeared from the hall.

"Lord Beowulf to see the ealdorman." Ulf hastily informed him.

Smiling, the steward indicated that they follow him to the hall.

"So how are things in Miklaborg?"

They had just finished the evening meal and Kaija had made her excuses and left the men drinking. There had been an almost audible sigh of relief from the inhabitants of the hall when Kaija had announced her intention to retire to the quarters which had been made available to her. To be fair to them, he got the impression that Kaija was as uncomfortable in the presence of so many men as they were with her, so he was also a little relieved when she chose to depart early.

Beowulf was experienced enough now to recognise that Wulfgar was being careful not to indicate any opinions he may have on the succession of Hythcyn before he knew where Beowulf stood on the matter. Beowulf could readily understand his caution. He would know that both his father and foster father were likely to be opposed to the new regime, but here was Beowulf on an important errand for Hythcyn, apparently a trusted servant of the king.

Beowulf glanced up and replied. "Busy. The fleet will set sail in a few weeks. The kingdom is alive with marching men."

"I envy them. I have to watch the border, although with so many Bronding warriors already in Geatland some people are saying that we are occupied already."

Beowulf could see that he was being closely watched by Wulfgar and his thegns for any clues to his allegiance by his reaction to this statement. He decided to bring the matter into the open.

"Speak freely, Wulfgar. Do you think that Hythcyn is our rightful king?"

Taken by surprise by the bluntness of his question, Wulfgar's mouth opened and closed as he searched in vain for an answer. Beowulf fought back a smile as he surveyed the shocked faces around the table.

"I understand your reluctance to answer so I will help you out if I can. You wonder if Hythcyn killed Herebeald intentionally and then killed my grandfather to get the throne. Anyone who says they don't harbour these thoughts is a liar. From what I have seen of you Wulfgar I know you to have honour and I am confident that you would surround yourself with men of similar calibre," he said, looking carefully at those around him.

"The truth is I don't know. The first to arrive at the body of Herebeald was my cousin Heardred and I was moments behind him. We found Hythcyn cradling his brother in his arms, apparently very upset. He said that he had loosed at a deer, and a deer had just run into me, knocking me over, so it *is* possible." Beowulf took a sip of ale before continuing. "Who can say how King Hrethel died, he was apparently alone. All I can say of my uncle is that he is a very clever man. This war with the Jutes is just the thing to unite the country behind him. After years of inactivity, our warriors are at last going to get the chance to wet their swords and earn a reputation. We will all have to see how things progress, but Kaija has warned me that we are in for a torrid year so be on your guard."

Wulfgar scanned the faces of his men and gave them a small nod before answering. "Thank you for your honesty, Beowulf, I know that I speak for all of us when I say that we appreciate your words. We sometimes feel that we are forgotten up here. As long as the taxes are collected and sent south regularly, nobody thinks to let us know what is going on. The first we knew of our great new Bronding alliance was when Alfhelm rode through with one hundred of their warriors one morning. As you say, who knows the truth of the events of the past six months, but I share the view of your volva, I don't think that this wheel has turned full circle yet."

They left Wulfgar's hall early the next morning. It was a further fifty miles to the hall of King Hrothulf and they wanted to complete the journey that day. Beowulf was keen to return to the coast. The thought of the fleet sailing to Jute land without him was almost too much to bear and, nephew of the king or not, he doubted that they would delay starting a war until he was ready.

Bidding farewell to his host, Beowulf was pleased to see that none of the warriors in the courtyard looked in their direction as they made their way slowly past.

Leaving the town behind, they again followed the river north, towards its source. Rapids and waterfalls roared and crashed alongside them as they headed towards the twin peaks of the Troll's Hat.

Rising from the plain, the hills appeared to be one from a distance. As it drew nearer, the road seemed to disappear into the side of the hill, but, rounding a bend, they found themselves entering a steep sided gorge. Sheer grey rock rose on either side of the road as they wend their way slowly towards the Bronding border. Ravens soared above them and the guttural bugling of an elk resounded around the canyon. Wulfgar had invited Beowulf back to hunt Elk up on the plateau his ale-sodden mind recalled hazily, something about having a fine hunting lodge up there.

He must remember to take him up on his offer one day he decided.

Emerging from the hills, the road skirted the southern shore of Lake Vanern before resuming its northerly path.

Four or five miles on from the Troll's Hat, Beowulf and Kaija reined in their mounts on the bank of a small river.

A tall, carved, brightly coloured stone lay beside the road, informing travellers that the river marked the border between the kingdoms of the Geats and Brondings.

Nearby, beavers scurried along the banks, their massive home of logs and branches clearly visible upstream, while away to their left the vast expanse of the Vanern stretched as far as the eye could see.

Urging on their mounts they splashed into the river and entered Bronding territory.

13

T he horses cantered up to the top of the small rise. If his calculations were correct he should be able to see the Bronding capital, Skovde, in the distance once they reached the crest.

The road was less well travelled than the one which had lead them from Miklaborg to Edet and was consequently of poorer quality, but Beowulf was pleased that they had still made good time since leaving Wulfgar's hall that morning. At this rate they could expect to reach the town in the late afternoon.

Although he was looking forward to meeting the Bronding king and sampling their hospitality, he found that he was already reminiscing about the evening he and Kaija had spent alone beside the Geat River. They had been able to act as two ordinary people that night. While he had enjoyed the opportunity to lay aside the part of the boisterous, feasting, drinking warrior for an evening, he had begun to realise how much this trip must mean to Kaija.

While he was organising invasion fleets, hunting and generally living his life to the full, she had spent years of her life cut off from the rest of humanity, surrounded by statues of the gods and daily ritual.

It was no wonder that she had galloped off that first morning. Just the act of moving faster than a walking pace must have been a great freedom for her. The reactions of the warriors to her at Wulfgar's hall, and even the fear of the folk at Little Edet, would have made it clear to her that she lived outside of normal society, even if she had not experienced it before. She must have noticed the relief in the hall when she left, how must that feel to a young woman?

"How long have you been at the temple?" he asked.

"Since I was a small child, why?"

"What do you do all day, don't you get bored?"

"The ways of the volva are not for others to know, or seek to know!" she snapped.

"I just wondered…" he started to say before she turned her face to him.

In place of the relaxed, happy, face of a young woman, Beowulf was shocked to see her face was as hard as iron. He shuddered as her dark eyes bored into him.

"Don't wonder about anything! I am not like any other women you have met. I have dedicated my life to the gods and I only came on this journey because I suspected that they had taken an interest in you. Now that I have found out the truth of that I could return to the Hill of Goats. There never was any other reason to take this trip for me. As for those men at Edet, they were just pathetic little boys who think that owning a sword and a shield makes them powerful. I could have crushed them with a look if I had thought it worth the trouble."

Shaken by the intensity of her words, Beowulf rode on in silence. Reaching the crest of the hill they curbed their mounts and stared across the treetops to the distant smudge on the horizon which was Skovde.

"Now *that's* trouble," he muttered.

~

EVEN FROM THIS distance the pall of smoke which lay over the town was obvious. Scanning the horizon, Beowulf could just make out smaller, fainter, columns of smoke rising lazily into the warm summer air.

"Wuffingas?" Kaija suggested.

Beowulf shook his head.

"I wish that it was. Those smaller fires lead off to the north-east. It can only be the Swedes."

They stared at the scene for a few moments.

"Shit!"

"We have to get back to Edet. They won't move again today…" he twisted his body and squinted up at the sky. "Late afternoon…" he pondered aloud. "No, they will enjoy the spoils of a captured town for the rest of the night. Let's hope that they have a good time. That will slow them up tomorrow. That's not to say that they won't send out mounted columns to check the route ahead tonight though, best we get moving."

He paused and looked at the pack horse standing patiently behind him. He thought about burying the gifts that it carried in its packs and setting the horse free but decided against it. It would slow them down a bit, but not as much as making a detour to bury the valuable objects he decided. Besides if any Swedish patrols happened upon an abandoned horse they would guess that they had been spotted.

With a last glance back at the burning town, they turned and galloped back down the road.

By early evening they had regained Lake Vanern. The road improved and they began to make good time as they rode on into the gathering dusk, and soon they were back at the river which marked the border of Geatland.

They halted and allowed the horses to drink and rest awhile before they covered the last few miles to Wulfgar's hall. Beowulf jumped down from his mount and stretched his legs as the horses drank softly beside him. Looking about him he began to automatically study the lie of the land. He had not spent a life amongst warriors, much less seven years of fosterage with one of the greatest of the Geatish fighters, without having learned the art of reading a landscape.

"What are you doing?" Kaija interrupted his thoughts.

"Thinking," he replied distantly.

"A thinking warrior," she replied brightly. "Who would have thought that I would live long enough to meet one of those!"

After her outburst outside Skovde they had been concentrating on getting news of the Swedish invasion back to Edet as quickly as possible and there had been no opportunity for conversation above the clatter of hooves. Now it seemed she had reverted back to the fun, pleasant, companion of the previous few days. He knew which one he preferred, but it would take him a long time to forget her words and the scornful look on her face as she spoke them.

Remounting, he urged his horse on into the river, splashing noisily back into Geat territory.

NIGHT HAD FALLEN when they wearily approached the hall. The men on guard were surprised to see them return so soon and, noticing their fatigued condition, shot each other a questioning glance. Something was clearly wrong, very wrong.

Beowulf was greeted on the steps of the hall by the same steward as before.

He cut short his cheerful greeting.

"Take me to the ealdorman, right away!"

Leaping the steps two at a time Beowulf handed the surprised steward his sword as he hastened inside.

He paced outside the doors to the inner hall impatiently as he waited for permission to enter. He had considered just entering, unannounced, but he had decided that Wulfgar deserved to be shown the respect he was due. Besides, a few moments would make no difference in the events which seemed to be about to unfold.

The steward reappeared and hastened Beowulf into the hall.

"Beowulf, what brings you back so soon? Wolf heads?"

Wulfgar had risen from the table and approached him with a look of concern.

"The Swedes have invaded the lands of the Brondings, they are sacking King Hrothulf's hall as we speak. I would guess that you can expect unwelcome guests here very soon."

Wulfgar frowned. "How long do you think we have?"

"I am pretty sure that they will spend the night in Skovde and move this way in the morning. We were fifteen to twenty miles away when we saw what was happening and we turned straight about and raced back. You know as well as I do," he continued, "they could have mounted elements here, what, tomorrow afternoon?"

"There's plenty of time for you to get some food and rest then, come and join us while we decide what to do. And bring that scary woman in here," he smiled. "We may need the help of the gods before the next few days are over!"

"Bjorn!" he called out to one of the men waiting attentively at the benches.

"Send your best two messengers to the king at Miklaborg. Tell them to report that we expect a Swedish army to attack us here sometime tomorrow and that I will make plans to defend the town unless I receive orders to the contrary."

"Yes, lord," Bjorn replied as he rose and made his way to the door.

"Oh, and Bjorn."

The man stopped and turned back. "Lord?"

"Make sure that they leave straight away and that they take different routes. The enemy may have infiltrated the obvious route to stop any messengers getting through."

"Yes, lord."

Bjorn hurried out of the door, pausing only to grab his sword from the steward.

"Or one of them might ride straight into a bloody great tree in the dark!" another of the seated warriors added with a grin.

"Aye, or that!" Wulfgar conceded, joining in the laughter.

Beowulf's spirits rose for the first time since he had spotted the Swedish force. They were in a strong defensive position and the spirit amongst the clearly well led warriors remained high.

"Are you staying for the dance, Beowulf?"

"More than that," he replied. "I have an idea to win us more time."

BEOWULF BOLTED down a quick meal and then attempted to get some sleep. Tomorrow promised to be a busy day, and, coming straight after today's long ride, he needed both his body and mind to feel refreshed on the morrow.

Of course that only made sleep harder to come. His mind went over his plans for the defence again and again, until, just as he despaired of sleeping at all he must have finally slipped into unconsciousness.

He must have slept deeply because he was suddenly awoken by the pale light of the dawn as it crept slowly along the rafters, high above. Instantly awake, he swung his legs from the bench and vigorously rubbed his face to clear his thoughts.

Rising, he made his way to the table and poured a cup of ale from the beaker.

"Thank the gods that you're awake!" someone called from the far end of the hall.

Concerned that he may have missed the arrival of the Swedes or some other dire event, Beowulf looked for the source of the voice in alarm. Wulfgar was striding down the hall, a half eaten joint of chicken in his hand. He grinned, wiping the grease from his beard with the back of his hand.

"You grunted so loudly all night we had to post a guard on you in case somebody mistook you for a boar and ran you through!"

The hall filled with laughter as a score or more warriors stood, grinning, at him. Obviously, he thought, the word had gone out in the night to the local thegns to assemble at the hall with their men. Their speed at complying with the summons and obvious high spirits bode well for the day he thought to himself.

"Here, have some chicken, it's just come up."

Wulfgar snatched up half of a chicken from the table as he passed and tossed it to Beowulf.

"Your men are in good spirits I see, they do you credit."

"My men are in good spirits because up until an hour or so ago they thought that they were going to be sitting in their halls all summer while every other Geat old enough to wield a sword would be off hunting Jutes. They are warriors, Beowulf, just like you and I. If they had wanted to sit around scratching their arses all day they could have become merchants or farmers."

Beowulf tore off a mouthful of chicken and pointed the carcass at the ealdorman.

"What did you decide about my plan?"

Wulfgar sighed. "I know where you mean of course. It's a good plan, but I haven't enough warriors to give you as many as you asked for. I will have too few left for the main shield wall as it is. If no help arrives from the South very soon we will be overrun within moments of any serious fighting breaking out."

Beowulf contemplated the reply for a moment before making a suggestion. "How about the men in the town?"

"What about the men in the town? They are not warriors. They will run before the Swedes even reach you."

"Maybe not if you can spare me... a hundred warriors?"

Wulfgar bit his lip as he thought through Beowulf's plan.

Beowulf pushed harder.

"You are writing these men off. I intend to survive this and return most, if not all, of the men to the main position before you need to fight there. That is the whole point of my plan, to delay them until our reinforcements arrive."

Wulfgar blew out his cheeks and exhaled loudly.

"I can let you have seventy. You'll have to make up the numbers with townsmen and the like. I wish that I could do more but I need to keep enough men back to present a solid shield wall to the enemy at our main line of defence or it will be all over before it starts. I will let you have half of my men and add a few from each of the companies which my thegns have brought in. If I give you Bjorn and Ulf the men will rally to them naturally during the fight. They are both good men, you can rely on them and you already know them by sight. Bjorn you will remember from last night and Ulf you threatened with emasculation last time you came so I am told, so he should do as he is told straight away!" he grinned.

They gripped each other by the shoulders.

"Good luck, Beowulf. Don't leave it too long to get out of there once the wall begins to break. Get yourself back to the main line in one piece."

Beowulf shrugged. "Either we feast a great victory in your hall tonight or we feast with Woden in Valhall."

Snatching up a few items of food, Beowulf collected his sword from the steward and left the hall. Outside, the chill light of early morning was creeping slowly along the buildings and streets in the town below, bathing them in a, soft, pink glow. Below him a group of warriors had gathered, their upturned faces eagerly awaiting his instructions. Beowulf smiled, he had always liked this time of the day and now he was to lead experienced warriors into battle for the first time. Despite the fact that they must all know that they would be heavily outnumbered, they all seemed in good spirits, fully armed and ready for war.

He stood and addressed them from the steps.

"Good morning lads!" he called brightly.

A low murmur came in reply.

Never mind, press on!

"Every single one of you standing here has been personally chosen by their lord for a vital task. I have a plan to delay the enemy long enough for the rest of Ealdorman Wulfgar's thegns and warriors to arrive and deploy in our main defensive position. The longer we can hold out, the stronger our defence will become. Riders were sent to the king last evening so we can hope to see more troops arriving from the South sometime today. Today is the day you have all been longing for, a day to make reputations and wet your sword in the blood of a Swede. They thought that all of our warriors were away so they felt brave enough to mount a surprise attack on us. Let us surprise them and make them rue the day they crept out of the east like so many wolves to prey on our defenceless women and children."

Won over, the men cheered as Beowulf descended the steps.

That's better!

"Bjorn, Ulf, divide the men into three groups. I want them to round up men of fighting age from the town. If they protest tell them that it is *their* women and children we are trying to protect. If they still protest, hang them, understood?"

"Yes, lord!" they smiled, obviously looking forward to dragging comfortable townsfolk from their beds.

"Tell them to take a weapon and horse if they own them, otherwise one will be provided by the ealdorman. I will take twenty men with me and go to the dock area. There are some things that I particularly need there. I will meet you all in one hour at the stone which marks the Bronding border, understood?"

"Yes, lord," they replied in unison.

A small voice came from behind him.

"I am returning to the Hill of Goats."

Beowulf turned and saw Kaija standing on the steps.

"Of course, I will arrange for an escort for you," he replied.

"There is no need. I think I know the way. Besides the road is likely to be swarming with warriors heading this way,

I doubt that even a 'defenceless woman' would be in any danger today." She smiled.

Beowulf blushed as he realised that she had been present during his speech to the warriors. He could think of several descriptions for Kaija but none of them included the word defenceless he had to admit to himself.

To his shock she kissed him lightly on the cheek as she made her way down the steps.

"Take care. You may have the favour of Woden, but remember that he can tire of people very easily. If he decides you no longer amuse him he can just as easily destroy you."

She stroked his face affectionately and made her way over to the stables.

Composing himself he turned to organise his men.

To his embarrassment he found that every man in the courtyard had stopped whatever they were doing, as if frozen in mid action, and were staring at him open mouthed. They had all heard about the volva who had accompanied him but the show of affection had shocked and frightened them in equal measure.

"All right, it's all over," he snapped, striding over to his horse amid a buzz of comments from the men, "we have uninvited guests to prepare a welcome for."

THEY PASSED through the slumbering town and took the road north to the dock area.

The river was unnavigable at Edet due to the falls and rapids which were located just south of the town. Goods from the north had to be unloaded from the boats as they reached the southern end of the lake and transported by road past these obstacles before they could resume their journey south.

Dogs barked as they approached the tumble of shacks, warehouses and boathouses which comprised the dock area.

A watchman appeared from a roadside hut.

Seeing them approaching from the town he turned his head slightly and said something to an unseen companion inside.

"Good morning, lord. How can I help you?"

"How many men do you have here?" Beowulf asked.

"In the whole area, there is usually…" he blew out his cheeks as he thought, "about sixty or so, lord, twenty full time dock workers with their families plus another twenty carters to take the goods past the falls and ten to fifteen boat crews. I can't be too exact, boats come and go and the lads don't always make it back from the town's evening entertainments, if you know what I mean."

"Right, show my men where they all sleep, your companion in there can help me with something else."

They all dismounted and secured their horses. Turning, Beowulf saw that the watchman had edged nervously towards the doorway.

"Well, call him out, we are in a hurry!"

"I am alone lord," the watchman stammered nervously, "I can show you anything you need to know in the dock area. I have lived here for years. I know it like the back of my hand."

He started to lead them towards the buildings. Drawing his sword, Beowulf opened the door and ducked into the gloom. At first the room appeared empty but a slight movement in the farthest, darkest, corner made him tense and raise his sword.

"Come out," he ordered.

Slowly, wide eyed with fear, a girl of about six winters edged out from behind a pile of baskets. Her red hair hung, matted with grime and grease, to her shoulders, framing her pale terrified face. Her frail body was covered by a roughly made dress of old sacking from which stick-like arms and legs hung, grotesquely. Deep blue and yellow bruises covered the parts of the girl's body which were visible.

Beowulf gasped. He tried to smile and reassure the girl but his shock at her condition was such that he was not sure that he was managing to conceal it from her.

"Come to me girl, you are safe now."

He held open the rough wooden door and waited for the girl to step outside before following her through.

A low growl erupted from amongst the waiting warriors as they saw the condition of the tiny girl.

The watchman blanched when he saw her. "She is my sister's child, lord. She just keeps me company, that's all," he offered pathetically as he felt the hostile gaze of the men turn on him.

"Well your sister will be relieved to learn that I will be looking after her from now on," Beowulf replied.

"Now get going and round up all the able bodied men here. *Go!*"

His men pushed the watchman roughly ahead of them as he led them towards the collection of rough shacks which held the dockworkers. He turned back to the clearly terrified girl.

"I am Beowulf, what is your name?" he asked gently.

He went on one knee, aware that his towering height would intimidate her.

"Ursula," she whispered.

"Ursula, the bear," he smiled.

"Well, Ursula, you don't look much like a bear at the moment, we'll have to see what we can do about that. When was the last time that you ate?"

"Yesterday morning, lord. I had some bread and pottage."

"You won't grow fat on soup and mouldy bread will you, let's see what we can find for you."

He stood and made his way to his horse. Opening one of the bags slung from the saddle, he rummaged inside and produced a piece of chicken he had brought from the hall. Ursula's eyes widened at the sight of it, and, hunger overcoming any fear or shyness, she stepped smartly forward and took the food from his outstretched hand.

As she ate the food Beowulf gently began to question her.

"So the man is your uncle?" he started.

She shook her head, "No, he won me in a game," she replied as she tore off great gobbets of chicken.

"What happened to your mother and father?"

"They were too poor to feed us all so they had to sell me to thraldom."

Beowulf thought as she ate. The last thing he needed at this moment was another responsibility but he couldn't leave the girl here to suffer the gods knew what at the hands of this watchman. A voice at the back of his mind reminded him of the two children at Little Edet. Kaija had said then that if she had not saved the family cow, poverty would most likely force the farmer to sell those two children to thraldom, slavery, just to ensure that they survived. He tried to remember their names but, to his shame, he found that he could not, even though he had only spoken to them a few days ago. He resolved that he would take a greater interest in the lives of his people if he survived this day.

"Stay here, Ursula, I have work to do. I will be back soon."

Beowulf strode down the dusty track which led to the dockside. Keeping to the centre of the track he managed to avoid the worst of the dust which collected in the pits and crevices created by countless wagon loads of goods as they journeyed south, past the falls.

He smiled to himself, despite his now sour mood, as he became aware of the commotion up ahead. A dozen or so men were standing in a group alongside several of his men. Women and children moved at the edges of the group, remonstrating with the warriors, who, in time honoured tradition, completely ignored their pleas.

Further along the ramshackle terrace several more of his men were emerging from the shacks, pushing sleepy, dishevelled men before them.

Once they were all gathered together by the loading bay, Beowulf addressed them.

"Men! Your king requires your services to defend our land from a Swedish invasion. Sometime today we expect a Swedish force to arrive here. Some of you may have served before, while others of you will have seen the effects that an army has on the land it attacks. Help is on its way from the South, but we need to hold them here until it arrives. Send your families to Edet and come with us and fight to protect them."

There was a shocked silence as the men, many still half asleep, absorbed his words.

Suddenly the silence was broken as a long, rasping, fart tore the air.

"I am not a Geat, what do I care?" The culprit, a large black bearded man, responded insolently.

The others, some smirking, looked to each other as they waited to see Beowulf's reaction.

Staring at the man Beowulf calmly spoke.

"Bjorn, I believe we have our first volunteer."

"Yes, lord, I believe we do," he grinned.

Pushing his way into the centre of the crowd, Bjorn

approached the black bearded man. Surrounded by his friends, the man drew himself up to his considerable height and puffed up his chest. He was about to snarl a challenge to Bjorn when his head shot upwards. Unseen, Bjorn had gripped the hilt of his sword and powered the pommel straight up, into the chin of the troublemaker. The others jumped back in shock as the man slumped at their feet. Quickly Bjorn reversed his blade and brought the pommel smashing down two or three more times into the man's disintegrating face.

Women screamed and ushered their children away as two more of Bjorn's men pushed their way through and dragged the man out from the crowd. His hands clasped over his broken face, the first indication that the man had of his fate was when the noose was slipped, roughly, around his neck. His cry of alarm was cut short as the rope was hauled up over one of the beam ends of a boat house.

The rest of the crowd looked on in shocked horror as the two warriors pulled him, kicking and squirming, up into the air. His hands grasped at the rope around his neck, revealing for the first time the full horror of his broken face to those below.

"Make it quick, we haven't got all day," Beowulf ordered.

Immediately another warrior stepped forward and hung briefly onto his legs, tightening the rope and choking the life out of him, before jumping back to avoid the inevitable results as the man's bladder and bowels loosened.

"Make your choice quickly men, are you accompanying us or him today?"

Without a word they moved quickly to his side.

"Good choice. Now, how many carters do we have here?"

Several fingers were raised, hesitantly, from among the group.

"Right shackle your horses to them and I want you to remove the thatch from the boathouse roofs. Fill every wagon but one with it, as much as you can, and bring it up to the river which marks the Bronding Border. The remaining wagon I want filled with barrels of pitch. Got that?"

They all nodded in confirmation.

"If I don't see it within the hour I will come and find out why, do I make myself clear?"

"Yes, lord." They quickly replied.

"The rest of you, if you own a horse take it now and meet me at the river. If not follow on as quickly as you can on foot. Horses will be provided later for your use by the ealdorman. Weapons are already on their way but take any of your own that you have."

He turned to go before stopping and turning back to the group.

"Oh, I almost forgot. Should any of you get lost and find themselves heading south instead of north there are warriors between here and the town with orders to help you on your way."

He looked at the body swinging slowly at the end of the rope and could see from the men's expressions that his warning had been clearly understood.

"Right, Bjorn. I am going straight up there. Leave a handful of men here to speed things up. Tell one of the women to look after the girl until I return, and take care of the watchman."

"Yes, lord," he replied as, grim faced, he unhooked another length of rope from his saddle. "Right away."

~

APPROACHING the river site Beowulf was pleased to see a large group of armed men awaiting him. Others were making their way, on foot and horseback, in groups from the town. A cheer rang out as he approached with his men. Reining in, he dismounted and addressed them with a smile.

"Have you all eaten?"

Most, he found, had managed to grab a paltry breakfast of bread or cheese before they had left for the rendezvous, nothing more.

"Men will be here soon from the ealdorman's hall to prepare meat and ale for us. We will make a start and take a short break when it is ready."

Grins and light-hearted comments greeted Beowulf's announcement.

"Right you all know who is on the way. We are going to hold them here as long as possible to enable the main army to get into position to our rear. The longer we can last out, the more chance we have of taking the day and protecting our lands and families. Horses are being collected and brought out to us to enable us to retreat in good order when I decide that our position is becoming untenable. If I fall, first Bjorn here…" Bjorn took a step forward and donned his helm so that they could see what he would look like, "or Ulf," he indicated to his other side, "will take command and responsibility for ordering the withdrawal. This is not a last stand, fight to the death. If we do our duty here today we will deliver a great victory for our king and people and live to tell the tale!"

Men cheered his speech, although Beowulf couldn't help noticing that the contents had met with less enthusiasm than the one about the meat and ale.

"Ulf, take a party of men and go back fifty yards or so and have them cut and shape, let's see, how many…" He paused, looking from the tree line to the edge of Lake Vanern. He estimated that the distance was about one hundred yards.

Two rows, approximately two yards apart

"Have them cut and shape one hundred stakes, each six feet long. And get them back here as quickly as you can."

"Yes, lord."

Ulf scampered off calling out to a score of men to follow him as he went.

"Bjorn. Organise a party of men to begin dismantling that beaver dam up there."

He pointed upstream to where the large dam sat astride the river.

"Just remove material from the top for now and leave it in piles alongside this bank of the river. I don't want the dam to break before I am ready, is that clear?"

"Yes, lord."

Beowulf turned and scanned the men for signs of bows.

"Where are the bowmen?"

He was pleased to see that they had come as a company. They would all be familiar with each other and used to working unsupervised. A man stepped forward smartly and introduced himself.

"My name is Harald, lord. I lead these men."

He had the ruddy complexion of a man used to hunting and living an outdoor life. Beowulf could tell immediately from his demeanour that he was a man he could rely on.

"You see those wagons approaching us from the docks, Harold?"

They turned as one to look in the direction he indicated.

"They are loaded with straw and pitch. I want you to spread the straw on the forest floor just inside the tree line on this side if the burn. Take half of the pitch barrels and place them amongst it, but try to keep them hidden. They are my surprise present for the Swedes," he smiled.

They cast each other a questioning glance.

"Make sure that you do it well, that's where you will be when the attack comes, so your lives will depend on it. And make sure that you have plenty of fire arrows to hand for when I give the word."

They all smiled as his plan become clear to them.

Soon Ulf returned with a wagon loaded with sharpened stakes.

"The river bank slopes gently here so I want the stakes driven in paired rows, ten feet back from the river itself. When that is done, start to make a low wall out of the trees and branches from the beaver dam which is piled up behind you. When the lower layer is complete we will dismantle the rest of the dam and build up the wall. That will release all of the water which has built up behind the dam and flood the plain. Hopefully it should be nice and muddy by the time our visitors arrive."

"Lord, can I take a few spear men back to the dam with us?"

Confused, Beowulf turned towards one of Bjorn's men.

"It's the beavers, lord," he continued, shamefaced, "they don't like us dismantling their dam and are trying to bite us!"

The group of men with Beowulf burst into laughter as he added, defensively.

"They have got bloody great teeth, and their tails can give you a nasty whack, lord!"

Between laughs, Beowulf managed to gasp. "You're not helping yourself, I wouldn't say any more if I were you!"

Finally, realising how absurd he sounded, the man grinned sheepishly before volunteering. "Perhaps they are Swedish beavers, lord!"

"Perhaps they are," Beowulf laughed. "Of course, take a few spear men for protection," he continued, "we don't want our numbers decimated by an attack by Swedish beaver berserker before the battle even starts!"

Wiping the tears from his eyes, Beowulf walked back to see how close the food was to being ready. So far he was pleased with the way the preparations were going, just a few more hours and he would be as ready as he would ever be.

∼

"RIDERS!"

Everyone stopped work and peered northwards, along the lake.

"All right, we knew they were coming," Beowulf called out. "Back to work, there is no time to waste."

Beowulf walked calmly to the edge of the burn and looked up the road which led to the heart of the Bronding kingdom. Men would look to him to see how he reacted and it was important that he controlled the excitement and nervousness which had gripped him on hearing the warning.

"Over there lord," the man indicated, "just beyond those trees."

Seconds later a group of warriors rode into full view, the sun glinting off of their polished mail and spearheads. Beowulf watched as they drew to a halt, fanning out as they all jostled for a view of the unexpected opposition which had appeared before them, blocking their route.

"Scouts," Beowulf muttered to himself. "Any second now, three... two... one... off he goes!"

A rider detached himself from the group and raced back along the road which led to Skovde, dust billowing in his wake. The rest of the group trotted forward and drew up a long bow shot distant.

Bjorn and Ulf had made their way to his side, ready to receive orders, as soon as the alarm had been given.

"Bjorn. Tell the men to remove the rest of the beaver dam and make these barriers up to chest height."

"Yes, lord!" Bjorn mounted and rode away to the dam.

"Ulf, count off every second man and tell him to go and get some food and drink. They won't be here for a good while yet and there is no point in going hungry for the sake of half a dozen scouts. They can change places in a while."

As Ulf left, Beowulf thought through his plans one last time in case he had forgotten anything. As he did a cry went up as the waters were released from the beaver dam. A rush of dirty, debris strewn, water swept down towards the lake. Channelled to its right by the Geat fence, it swept over the opposite bank and spread out, covering the ground in a branch and stone laden, glutinous mess.

Quickly the remaining branches and trunks from the dam were added to the fence, bringing it up to chest height.

Surveying the scene before him Beowulf was pleased that he had not built their fence right on the river bank as he had originally thought to do. The power of the water released from the dam was impressive and it could easily have damaged or even washed away a barrier built too close to the watercourse. Success or failure, indeed life or death, could hinge on one silly oversight he thought to himself.

With the fence complete and the opposite river bank flooded and strewn with debris, Beowulf called his leading men to him. A table had been prepared for them on which had been placed spit roast meats, bread, cheese and ale. They all helped themselves to the food and drink as he went over his plan one last time so that all understood exactly what was expected of them.

"Harald, how did you get on with the straw and pitch?"

"There was plenty, lord It is at least ankle deep in there, deeper still on the more obvious routes through the trees. I half sunk the barrels of pitch to make them less noticeable."

Beowulf nodded in satisfaction.

"I am going to split your company into two equal parts and place them on the wings. I need to guard against flanking moves, we are going to be heavily outnumbered and we need your men to close that option off to them. Choose your best man to lead the other group and remember to listen for the call to retreat. You will be the furthest away and it's likely to get very unhealthy, very quickly, once they get through."

"Oh, don't worry lord," he smiled. "You won't be going far without us!"

"I will station some horsemen behind you to back you up if you come under pressure."

"Thank you, lord."

"Bjorn, Ulf, I will take the centre of the line and you two position yourselves midway between my position and the ends of our line. I have had a look and the river bank has no obvious weak points so we should be fine that far apart. Any questions so far? Feel free to say anything. You are my most trusted men."

"We need a reserve." Bjorn stated. "As we are, if one small part of the line gives we are finished. Most of the men out there are carters and blacksmiths. If they start to see Swedish warriors behind them they will drop their weapons and run. Once a shield wall breaks there is no retrieving it, none of us will reach the main lines, lord."

Beowulf clenched his teeth. How could he forget something so obvious? He cursed himself for showing his inexperience, after all the thought he had given the battle.

"Of course you are right, well done. You know the men better than me. Choose someone dependable to form a flying reserve of six to eight mounted men with orders to reinforce our line at any place it looks likely to break."

One of the warriors left the wall and approached them.

He waited, respectfully, until they turned his way.

"Yes?"

"They are here, lord."

14

"Time to arm I think. Happy hunting!"

They all grinned and wished each other good luck as they trotted to the rear.

Beowulf removed his finely decorated shirt and donned a quilted under shirt as a thrall stood by, ready to help him into his mail byrnie. Removing it from its leather case he held it by the shoulders as it tumbled earthwards, unravelling to its full length. Beowulf smiled as the thrall's shoulders sagged, involuntarily, under the weight of the shirt. Bending forward from the waist he raised his arms and wriggled his head and arms into the shirt before standing up and letting the links fall over his torso with a satisfying metallic swish. The thrall held up the two pieces of his leather battle coat. Seeing the piece Beowulf was reminded of the trip to the workshop which he had made with the Angle, Cola, that day in Geatwic. He had watched, fascinated, as the workers had cut and trimmed the hides into shape and then boiled the pieces in oils to fix the heavily muscled design. Although Beowulf's battle coat was of a plain design, it had been boiled in wax mixed with ox blood. It now shone with a deep, dark, red, shedding water as well as any duck. Trimmed at the neck and shoulders with fine gold linen, the colours had been carefully chosen by his grandfather, King Hrethel to complement the shield he had received after the initiation ceremony. Beowulf held the front piece in place as the thrall offered up the rear, joining them together at the shoulder with finely wrought gold and garnet clasps. As the man tightened the leather thonging which laced the sides of the coat together, Beowulf twisted and turned his body ensuring that it was comfortable and afforded him full movement. With a small smile he recalled a comment from long ago which Hygelac had made the first time that he had tried one on,

Once you are up to your eyeballs in big hairy Swedes it's a bit late to discover that your battle shirt is chaffing your neck!

Arm guards were laced to Beowulf's forearms. Backed by padding, these strips of metal plating protected his forearms from overhead sword strikes. Similarly constructed greaves were fastened to his lower legs to guard against a low thrust, beneath the shield wall. His belt was fixed by means of the large, ornate, buckle. A mass of writhing, golden worms, they glittered as the sun reflected from their surfaces. His seax already hung from the belt and he withdrew it and admired at the blade. It was beautiful workmanship and a gift worthy of his foster father. He wondered how far away his old seax 'King's Gift' was now that it was owned by King Hythcyn, very close by he hoped, flicking a hopeful glance towards the South. He held his sword and scabbard as the thrall passed the strap of the baldric over his shoulder for him to fasten. After one last roll of his shoulders he mounted his horse.

The thrall offered up his shield and he slipped his hand into the boss, gripping the handle tightly.

Gently urging his horse forward with his knees, Beowulf

took his *framea*, his thrusting spear, from the thrall and made his way slowly towards the gap in the wall which had been left for them.

Fully armed now save for their helms, Bjorn and Ulf joined him as the horses passed through the shield wall and splashed down into the river. He concentrated on keeping his balance as the horse picked its way among the debris strewn watercourse. A tumble here would not only be humiliating but the bad omen would very likely cause a collapse of the, already uncertain, morale of his men.

He was pleased to note that the river, even in its lowered state, was at least knee high to the tallest man. It would break the inertia of any charge before they reached their position and his spirits rose.

His horse climbed out of the river and began to wend its way across the far bank. Beowulf looked up for the first time at his foes.

Arranged before him, stretching in an unbroken line from the tree line to Lake Vanern, there appeared a sold wall of gleaming metal.

The Swedish leaders sat, awaiting them, midway between the armies.

"The one on the left is Ohthere. Next to him is his brother Onela, they are King Ongentheow's sons, æthelings." Bjorn murmured as they approached.

The royal brothers looked magnificent in highly polished scale armour, the sunlight danced and flashed upon them as they moved, reminding Beowulf of the pike he used to fish for in the lake near Hygelac's hall. It all seemed so long ago now.

Just behind them sat a large powerful warrior in more regular chain mail. His hair had been tied back revealing a heavily scarred face while from his chin hung a long, plaited, beard. Beowulf saw the warrior lean forward slightly and quietly speak to the brothers.

Without looking around he saw that Ohthere gave a slight nod of acknowledgement. So, this is not an equal partnership, Beowulf thought to himself, locking the memory away for possible future use as he reached the fiend.

"Beowulf Ecgtheowson! Are the Geat grown ups busy today, or have they gone sailing?"

"My lords, Ohthere, Onela, how good of you to come. I must apologise for the mess," Beowulf indicated the branch strewn mud with his hand. "You should have let us know that you were coming. We could have tidied the place up a bit."

Ohthere smiled.

"And miss the chance to loot a defenceless kingdom? That would have been a pity."

"My king is a very few miles from here, hastening forth to crush you. You still have time to turn back if you hurry."

"We were told your king is dead, apparently he was killed by his own son, what's his name…?"

"Hythcyn, lord," the warrior behind them announced with a malicious grin, "the one who murdered his brother."

"Hythcyn, he's your uncle I believe Beowulf. I should watch your back if I were you."

The ætheling's companion smiled menacingly behind them.

"Your Troll looks even uglier when he smiles, Ohthere, should he be out in the daytime?"

Everyone knew that Trolls were turned to stone by the rays of the sun and the Swedish brothers both looked down at their mounts as they tried to suppress a smile.

Behind them the warrior's eyes narrowed in hatred.

"Look, I don't want to have to kill you Beowulf. The truth is I am rather taken by your courage. Join us and we will help you get rid of this murdering king. Who knows this time next month there could be a King Beowulf ruling Geatish lands. What do you say?"

Beowulf paused before answering.

"You know, I was just admiring that armour of yours and wondering if it would fit me, but I decided that it was too small. I shall have it repaired after it is taken from your broken body and give it to my son one day. He can use it for play," he smiled, "before he grows out of it."

Ohthere gave a wry smile and started to turn his mount.

"You see Beowulf, you already have more honour than that man you call king. A pity I would have liked to feast with you. I am afraid we shall have to wait until we meet again in valhall. You will be there very soon, save a place for me."

Onela inclined his head and turned to follow his brother.

"What is your name, Troll?" Beowulf asked the grizzled warrior as he turned to follow the æthelings.

"Beowulf's killer," he replied, shooting Beowulf a look of scorn.

Beowulf, Bjorn and Ulf turned their mounts about and made their way slowly back to the Geat shield wall.

"Do you always choose the biggest, ugliest bastard, to pick on, lord?" Ulf chipped in as they rode.

Beowulf chuckled as they regained the burn: "Always."

AS THEY RODE BACK through the line it was closed behind them by more trunks and branches. Beowulf, Bjorn and Ulf dismounted and handed their reins to a waiting thrall who handed each of the men their battle helms in return. Donning his helm, Beowulf rested his shield and framea against himself and tied the strap beneath his chin. Turning, he acknowledged the good wishes of Bjorn and Ulf as they loped off to take up their positions. Beowulf made his way to the place of honour in the battle line, in the centre of the front line, and peered out at the Swedish force.

He could clearly see the Swedes being formed into the traditional swine head formation, readying themselves for their first assault.

Good, nothing too adventurous and heading straight at our strongest point. The mud and river will blunt their attack and then we will cut them down as they try to scramble up the bank.

"Has everybody got a throwing spear?" he shouted.

A roar and the clatter of spear shafts on shield rims told him that they had.

"Give them a volley just before they reach the river. We want their bodies to impede those behind and they can't do that if they are swept away."

A deep roar came from the Swedes as the first attack moved off from its starting position and began to make its way across the opposing meadow. Led by one huge warrior, others filed in on either side with every step he took towards them. In no time, it seemed to the watching Beowulf, the warrior stood at the tip of a large arrowhead pointed directly at him. When the man was fifty paces from him Beowulf drew back his arm and launched the first spear at the approaching horde.

"I dedicate the dead to Woden, Allfather," he called as the dart sailed deep into the Swedish ranks.

Immediately the air was filled with scores of spears, all converging on the swine head. The enemy held their shields, interlocked, the length of the formation, while those on the inside held theirs to cover the heads of those in the front. It was an effective tactic and most of the Geat spears either glanced off or fell in the mud. Had they kept their formation they could very well have crossed the river relatively intact, but the battle fury was upon them and their discipline could no longer contain it. Told that they faced a collection of smiths and wagon drivers their pride drove them to abandon the safety of their shield wall and come on at a rush.

Leaping into the river they began to frantically wade across. Sensing the disarray amongst them, Beowulf abandoned his earlier plan and screamed.

"Spears. Now!"

Pulling another spear from where it had been stacked just behind the line, he hurled it with all his might at the leading warrior.

Just as he thought he must skewer the man, he must have sensed, rather than seen, the missile. Twisting his body sharply, the spear brushed his mail as it flew past to embed itself deeply in the man behind.

Cursing, Beowulf had time to collect and throw one more spear before the first of the enemy rose, dripping, from the river onto the Geat bank.

"Framea!" he cried.

Immediately the Geat shield wall bristled with hundreds of heavy thrusting spears.

As they stood upright, the Swedish warriors unleashed a volley of francisca throwing axes at the Geat line. Instinctively most ducked behind their shields as the axes thudded harmlessly into them, but screams of pain here and there along the line told where a few had been too slow to take cover.

Beowulf braced himself and thrust forward, blindly, with his framea against the foe who he knew would arrive at any moment.

With a crash, their shields met.

Despite his size he was driven momentarily back by the sheer force of the attack. Putting his shoulder to his shield he drove forward with all his might. The man behind him threw his own shield against his back and added his weight to the drive forward.

Beowulf felt the pressure increase as more and more of the enemy struggled across the river and added their weight to the push. Desperately he stabbed his framea through the small gap between the shields, repeatedly twisting and turning the blade, trying to find a soft body part to drive it into. An unseen hand grabbed the spear and tried to wrest it from his grasp. Panicking, he pushed and pulled the shaft until it he felt it free again, and withdrew it. Glancing down he noticed that the spearhead was slick with blood. Elated, he thrust it through the gap again and again. This time he felt the slight loss of momentum as the blade slid in and out of a body. Frantically he stabbed at the same spot and slowly he felt the pressure begin to ease on his shield.

With a final thrust he pushed the framea deeply into the enemy, letting go and drawing his sword in one movement.

Stepping into the gap left by the falling man, he slashed to left and right forcing his way deep into the enemy formation. He was dimly aware of his men following, fanning out in his wake, as the Swedes began to break and run.

Now he was at the tip of a swine head of his own, pushing the remaining Swedes back into the river.

One giant warrior tried to rally the others but, just as it looked like he might be successful, an *angon*, a light throwing spear flew out from the Geat line above and took him in the neck. Beowulf watched as a look of shock, then disbelief, crossed the warrior's face. He fell slowly to his knees before pitching forward into the river.

The enemy warriors, seeing their champion fall, finally turned and ran back towards their own lines.

Yelling madly, a few of the less disciplined Geats hurdled the fence and began to chase after the fleeing Swedes. Desperately Beowulf tried to stop them from their headlong charge, but in their excitement most either didn't hear, or chose not to hear, his orders.

Beowulf stood on the bank watching as the backs of a score or so of his force chased down the retreating attackers, waiting for the inevitable.

Suddenly one of the Swedes cast a glance back over his shoulder.

Flinging his arms out wide he shouted for his nearest companions to halt. Rallying, they rushed at their pursuers, swords and spears raised.

Suddenly facing a fight with warriors, the Geats slid to a halt in panic. Some made feeble attempts to defend themselves but most were butchered either as they turned to flee or tried to beg for mercy.

In moments the men had been reduced to a pathetic pile of blood stained bodies.

Their courage restored by the easy victory, the Swedish warriors jeered and called on the Geat force to come down and fight them in the open like men.

Aware of the sullen atmosphere which had descended on his force, Beowulf considered crossing the river and offering to fight a man in single combat, but decided against it. These were just ordinary warriors in front of him. They were not under the same obligations of honour which bound men like Ohthere and Onela. If they decided to overwhelm and kill the enemy leader it would be a disaster for the Geats.

Sadly he turned his back on the taunting Swedes and, slipping and sliding on the sodden, blood soaked grass, he made his way back to the shield wall.

Beowulf was furious, those idiots had turned a victory into a defeat. It was time for another speech. He handed his helm to the warrior beside him and smiled at those around him. "Good work, lads, we held the first attack by their best warriors with ease. Keep that up and we'll all have a tale with which to thrill our grandchildren when we are old and grey."

They all visibly brightened at the praise from their leader.

"Who was the first one through the wall with me?" he asked.

"I was, lord."

Beowulf looked into the grinning face of a youth of about sixteen winters. Although young, he was heavily muscled with huge hands stained brown with pitch.

"Don't tell me, you work at the docks. What is your name?"

"Gunnar, lord. I am a sailor."

"Did you finish that big bastard off for me, Gunnar the sailor?"

Gunnar held up a blood stained framea in reply. Nodding, Beowulf clapped him on the shoulder in thanks.

"Remove this fence for me will you, I am going to ride out there in a short while."

Beowulf was pleased to see that Bjorn had organised a party of thralls to pass along the line with barrels of ale. Fighting makes for a raging thirst. Besides, men always fought better with a plentiful supply of ale at hand.

Calling for his horse, he mounted and, passing through the gap his men had made in the fence, crossed to the opposite bank of the river. Men stopped their conversations and turned to look as he slowly rode along the bank.

When he was sure that he had their attention he began.

"I am afraid we have disappointed the enemy."

He paused to let the statement sink in, noting their puzzled faces, before continuing.

"They thought that you were a collection of weaklings, led by a wispy bearded youth, who would flee at the first sign of an attack by their warriors. And it's true!" he shouted. They looked at each other in confusion before he continued.

"I *have* been advised not to go out on a windy day," he laughed, tugging at his beard.

Nervous laughter rang out from the Geatish formation.

"We just gave the Swedes a bloody nose and sent them running back in confusion."

A roar arose from the Geat line.

"And we will do it again, next time!" he continued to more cheering.

"Because they are about to find out that although some of you are only warriors for this day, the heart of a warrior beats in every Geat breast be he a farmer or dock worker, smith or sailor." He pointed up to the grinning face of Gunnar above him.

"But," he cried as they cheered.

"*But!*" he cried louder.

"We will only defeat them if we keep our discipline."

"Those men out there," he pointed over to the scattered, blood stained, bundles lying in the meadow.

"Those men lost their discipline for a moment and it cost them their lives. Look at them now."

He paused for emphasis.

"If we lose our discipline that will be all of us."

He paused again as the silent ranks stared across at the sad remains.

"Stay behind the fence. That is why we spent so long building it, it will protect you. We are not here to destroy a

Swedish army, we cannot. We are too few. We will delay them long enough for our forces to gather in our rear and then we will join them. My dearest wish is that we reach our people having not lost one more Geat life. They will be back soon for another try."

He turned his horse to face them and raised his shield and spear aloft.

"Send them to Hel!"

He recrossed the river and climbed the bank to a chorus of loud cheers and the clatter of spears on shields.

Alighting from his horse he took his helm back from Gunnar and raised a horn of ale, draining it as he awaited the next attack.

BEOWULF SENT Gunnar to ask Bjorn, Ulf and Harald to meet him at the rear.

"Good speech, lord, let's hope that they all remember it next time." Ulf called out as he approached the group.

"Yes, things like that are unnecessary, but they can be a good example to the others. There is nothing like seeing twenty of your mates getting chopped to pieces to make you stop and think. Could have been a good thing." Bjorn added.

"What is done is done," Beowulf declared. "What do you think they will try next?"

Bjorn scratched at his beard as he thought.

"If it were me, I would attack on a broad front. Hit us with several boar snouts at the same time and overwhelm us with their whole force. What were they thinking with that piddling little attack?"

"I agree," said Beowulf. "They clearly underestimated us first time and they won't let that happen again. We have looked at their force from close up now and it's not an invasion army, it's a large raiding force. King Ongentheow is not present, it's being led by his sons Ohthere and Onela. They have even got a grizzled old warrior as a minder, no doubt supplied by their father. They were not expecting a big fight. From what Ohthere was saying it sounded like they had got wind of our Jute expedition and they must have assumed that it would have sailed by now. They thought that they could sweep down for some easy rape and pillage and be home before the harvest."

"Which means," Harald added, "that they don't want to get bogged down in static fights."

"Or take unnecessary casualties," Beowulf added.

"If we can hold them here for one more attack I think that there is a chance that they will call it a day and go home, especially now that I have sowed some seeds of doubt in their minds that our fleet may not have sailed yet. One more thing, I have been up and down that bank on foot and horseback now and it gets as slippery as a bride on her wedding night. Get some men down into the river and have them scoop as much water onto the bank as they can. Tell them to use their helms if they have to. The slipperier and muddier we can make it the better. I have sent half of the men out to find a long branch or small tree trunk which can be sharpened and used against horses, just in case. Right let's get back, grab what food you want, I'll have the thralls distribute what is left amongst the men. One last push then."

"One last push!" they echoed.

Satisfied that he had done all that he could, Beowulf strode back to his place at the centre of the wall.

After the failure of the initial attack, the Swedish force had hesitated.

Beowulf hoped that there was dissension amongst their

leaders about which was the best course of action to take. Their men, although repulsed, would have reported back on the size and make up of the Geat force which faced them and it would be obvious that they were a scratch force, stiffened by a few warriors.

He smiled as he imagined the arguments raging in their camp.

Clearly the Geats were expecting to be relieved by a larger, more powerful, force.

By remaining here any longer than was necessary they risked being ambushed and annihilated if the Geat royal army did make an appearance.

Would they make another attempt or not?

He would soon know, he decided, as he gazed on the Swedish line.

15

As the sun began to sink in the West it became increasingly obvious that the more belligerent members of the enemy had won the argument.

The arrival of several boats from the North had possibly tipped the balance in their favour he reflected. As soon as they appeared around the headland, their long oars flashing in the sunlight as they dipped in and out of the water, Beowulf, indeed every watching Geat, knew that they were not to win the day after all.

As soon as the boats could be loaded with warriors they would work their way along the coast and discharge their lethal cargo in the Geat rear.

Either they had to withdraw before that happened or they would be fighting a battle on two fronts which they knew they could not win.

Beowulf cast a glance up at the sky as his men sullenly watched the Swedes boarding the boats. There was no chance of night coming in time to save them from being outflanked he decided, especially at the height of summer.

He glanced back at the boats. They had completed

loading and were making their way into deeper water before making the turn for the short trip down the beach.

"How many were there, Gunnar?"

"Four boats, ten warriors in each boat, plus the crews at six oars a side, I make that ninety-two, lord."

"Really? I make that eighty-eight." Beowulf replied.

"That's because you forgot to count the four helmsmen, lord," Gunnar answered with a smile.

Beowulf laughed as he realised that Gunnar was right, before giving him an appreciating look. Bravery, strength and intelligence were rare in a man, especially when found allied to such a good nature.

"Seek me out when this is all over, I can use you. At the moment I need to talk to the men again."

Turning on his heels, he called for his horse.

He decided not to risk the now water drenched slope down to the river and turned his mount parallel with the rear of the line. The men turned to him. He could see the look of fear in many of their faces as he passed. Already some of them were casting longing glances to the rear. It would only take a few to break and the wall would collapse. Once that happened even seasoned warriors lost all reason and ran, panic stricken, throwing away their weapons in their haste to be away from the place of slaughter.

"It seems that we are not to throw back the Swedish horde after all," he began with a smile.

Some of the men tried to return the smile with difficulty, while others lowered their gaze and shuffled, nervously, with their feet.

"We were never intended to, that was never our task here. We have delayed them for most of a day by our presence and fighting ability. All that time our forces have been building up to our rear. Soon we will go to join them as I promised.

Horses are being brought up from the rear as I speak, enough to enable each and every one of us to retire to the main position as I promised you earlier. I will make you one more promise today. I give you my word that I will be the last man alive from our force to leave this place. We have one more battle to fight. May the gods hold their hands over you all."

A few, half hearted, cheers rang out but they quickly trailed away.

Terrified men find it difficult to cheer.

He rode up to Harald's position at the tree line.

"I cheered, lord!" he greeted him, mischievously.

"I know. It was quiet enough to hear you all the way down there," he laughed.

"How much of the pitch do you have left?"

"Half a dozen barrels, lord."

"Get some men to empty them onto the fence. I want to fire it to cover our escape."

"Yes, lord."

Beowulf made his way slowly down to the group of bowmen he had positioned next to the lake. Behind him a wagon bumped and rolled as Harald distributed the remaining barrels of pitch amongst the defenders.

He glanced over at the Swedish boats. They had completed their move into deeper water and were beginning to turn their tall, curved, prows parallel to the beach. Beowulf watched as the nearside bank of oarsmen backed oars in a welter of flying spray, helping to turn the head of the boat his way in moments.

For a moment he studied the steersman high at the rear. His mind went back to the journeys he had made on his father's and Hygelac's ships. He smiled as a picture of Hudda came into his mind. Stood squarely, laughing at a comment from Bjalki, his weight leaning on the steer board tiller as the wind whipped spray across his features. It was a moment frozen in time from his first journey to Dane Land all those years ago he realised. If he survived this day, and the Jute expedition of course, he resolved to seek Hudda out and join his crew aboard the old *Griffon* for a few weeks.

He inhaled deeply, savouring the smells of the land, the warm earth and dry grasses beneath his feet mingled with the occasional sweet smell of pine resin which wafted over from the tree line. It really was a beautiful day.

The heat of the day had started to abate with the setting sun. The shadows of the trees over to his right had begun to creep slowly over the meadow. Swallows and martens skimmed over the surface of the lake now that the cool of the evening had brought out the insects on which they fed. He marvelled at their speed and grace as they soared and dove at incredible speeds to within a whisker of death, turning this way and that in search of food.

This would be a nice spot to roast a boar he thought if it was not for the fact that there were hundreds of armed men who wanted to kill him a hundred yards away.

"Lord?"

A voice broke his reverie.

He looked down, in response, from the back of his horse. Below him stood one of the men he recognised from the group they had collected earlier.

The man dipped his head in respect, clearly nervous at approaching a lord uninvited.

"Begging your pardon lord, but I am one of the men that joined you from the dockyard, a sailor actually."

"I remember you," Beowulf responded. "Speak freely, you have nothing to fear."

An image of the black bearded man hanging, his face a

horror, came to Beowulf. It was little wonder that the man was afraid to approach him he realised.

"It's just that I had an idea, I am sure that you have already thought of it lord, but the others insisted that I tell you."

Beowulf realised that he must seem terrifying to the man. A mounted lord dressed for war was intended to intimidate, and this man had already witnessed the consequences of a word said out of place to someone of his authority.

Beowulf swung himself down from his mount and stood beside the man, whose expression changed instantly to one of fear.

"Unless you say that you are a Swedish spy you are completely safe I assure you. I value the opinions of all my men, whatever their rank." He smiled, trying to reassure the man.

The man, obviously still not completely at ease, stammered. "It's just that we were watching the pitch being spread over the barrier. Wood burns very well soaked in pitch, as you know lord. Boats are made of wood. We thought that those bowmen might be able to cause all sorts of trouble for those boats heading our way if they used fire arrows on them. As I said, I am a sailor, and I know how frightened sailors are of fire."

Beowulf grinned and clapped the man delightedly on the shoulder.

They still had a chance.

BEOWULF WALKED his horse back to his position at the centre of the Geat line where he handed it to the waiting thrall.

One of the remaining barrels of pitch had been deposited

with the bowmen, and they had been busy preparing the arrows when he left them. He had left further instructions for their most accurate man to aim at whoever was steering the enemy boat. If they kill or injure the steersman they would cause chaos on the boat.

Regaining his place at the front of the line he jammed his battle helm back onto his head and fastened the chin strap.

Come on you bastards, let's get this over with.

As if in reply, a line of mounted warriors emerged from behind the trees on the Swedish left and trotted casually along the front of their battle line.

Beowulf's spirits leapt. It seemed as if they were going to do exactly as he had anticipated.

The mounted warriors turned to face the Geat position and stared, impassively, down the meadow at them.

The reason for their inactivity soon became clear as three riders left the cover of the trees and took up position at their head. Two of them sat astride magnificent white horses while the third horse, which took up position just to their rear shone a gleaming, deep, black. Beowulf hardly needed the confirmation provided by the ripples of light reflected from the scale armour to know that the three riders were Ohthere, Onela and the mystery troll. He had to admit that they looked magnificent in full face 'Grimhelm' and scale armour. Purple cloaks added to their sense of grandeur, a nice Roman touch Beowulf decided. As expected the troll wore a heavy set of armour which, although clearly of the highest quality, even from this distance he decided, looked as though the wearer had been chewed and spat out by an outraged dragon. Both it and its owner had clearly seen a lot of action together, he must be sure to keep an eye out for him when the fun starts.

Ohthere raised his shield and spear high in the air and shouted something unintelligible in the distance.

He was answered by a mighty roar from the Swedish host and, as one, they moved forwards, towards the waiting Geat line.

Beowulf risked a glance over to the lake to check on the progress of the boats just as an arrow fell with a barely discernible splash into the water ten yards ahead of the leading one. A ranging shot he thought to himself, good they are nearly there. Switching his gaze back to the front he noticed that the Swedes had already covered the first quarter of the distance which had separated the two forces at the beginning of their march.

"Make ready with the stakes, but don't use them until the horses are on this side of the bank. It's important that they are taken by surprise."

He cast a quick glance to the rear. Some of the horses were being brought up but not nearly enough. Still he could not leave the line now, the men would think that he was running away and would probably overtake him before he could even begin to explain. He would have to trust those whose duty it was to do their job.

He did manage to notice that the supply wagon had deposited a large pile of arrows fifty yards back from the line though, so at least that part of his plan was ready.

A sudden swoosh from his left brought his head snapping back. He looked up just in time to see a score of arrows reach the top of their trajectory. Dipping their points, they fell, quickly gathering speed, to land in a tight cluster around the steering deck of the leading Swedish boat. A loud cheer left the mouths of the watching Geats as the steersman fell backwards and slipped out of sight. Beowulf forced himself to tear his eyes away from the minor victory and concentrate on the force of warriors approaching them.

Any moment now he expected Ohthere to lead the

mounted warriors in a charge at their positions and he couldn't afford to be distracted, however much he wanted to watch the private battle on his left.

A cry from away to his right forced him to look that way.

Smoke began to billow from the tree line where Harald and his men were positioned. As he strained to hear, he began to make out the whoosh of arrows coming from that direction. In the corner of his vision he could just make out the mounted warriors of the reserve force cantering over to aid their comrades. Flames began to lick at the base of the trees as the straw and pitch began to catch and burn fiercely. At this time of the year the thatch had been tinder dry, ideal for the purpose to which they had put it. Screams and the sound of fighting came from the flank as some of the Swedish force broke through into the Geat positions.

Obviously, Beowulf thought, a force had been sent through the woods to outflank them and strike in co-ordination with the main attack.

A cry went up on the left. Returning his gaze to the front he saw that the mounted Swedes had hesitated and were looking to left and right themselves, observing the impact that their flanking attacks were having.

Beowulf took advantage of the Swedish indecision to risk a glance back towards the lake. To his joy he saw that the leading boat was ablaze. A large fire had taken hold in the area of the mast, just where any sailcloth and other flammable materials would be stored. The boat had swung out of line, its prow now resting on the wale of the boat which had tried to overtake it, the crew from which were now frantically trying to push it away with their spears. A cloud of arrows and fire arrows continued to fall on the stricken ships and crews.

In a panic, Beowulf realised that Ohthere must launch his mounted attack at any second.

He would realise the effect these setbacks on the flanks would have on his watching warriors and would need to close with the Geats as quickly as possible, before their morale became affected.

"They are about to attack look to your front!"

Almost simultaneously he saw Ohthere kick in his heels and charge.

With a cry his mounted companions followed suit while behind them the Swedish line roared and broke into a run.

BEOWULF BREATHED DEEPLY as the mounted warriors thundered towards the line. All now depended on the discipline of his men. If they could face down this mass of muscle and metal and follow his instructions they would likely live to tell the tale. Break now and they were all lost.

"Steady boys."

Ahead of him the leading horses leapt into the river with a mighty splash.

To his right a horse stumbled as it crashed into a fallen tree trunk, part of the old beaver dam, throwing its rider head first into the near bank, snapping his neck like a dry twig.

The first horses were now across the river and beginning to scramble up onto the bank. Many of their front legs were flailing about uselessly as they attempted to gain a foothold on the slippery bank.

"Release. Now!"

A volley of spears flew from the Geat line and clattered into the Swedish shields.

"Again," he screamed. "Aim for the horses, not the men. *The horses!*"

Another volley of spears flew the few yards down into the

enemy. This time the results were far more spectacular. Many of the horses were caught just as they began to scramble out of the water. Beowulf saw at least a dozen spears find their mark, burying themselves deeply inside the chests and exposed flanks of the animals. Terrified and driven mad with pain they fell, kicking and screaming back into the river or onto the Geat bank, trapping and crushing their hapless riders.

The survivors came on, screaming their war cries.

As one, the Geat line suddenly sprouted a hundred or more sharpened stakes as they were pushed through the gaps in the fence and into the faces and chests of the attackers. The horses reared as they caught their full force. Although they had not been driven with enough force to penetrate deeply inside them, many of the riders were thrown, landing heavily amongst the dead from the previous attack. The rearing horses exposed their soft bellies to the Geat fighters and several were disembowelled, their steaming entrails spilling out to mix with the blood and mud on the sloping bank of the river.

"Careful, lord!"

Beowulf felt Gunnar's hand on his arm as a flaming brand was thrust into the wood of the barrier next to his right leg.

Immediately the wood began to smoke as the fire took hold deep inside its pitch soaked interior. He stepped back to the front and peered through the rapidly thickening smoke at the enemy. Several were attempting to negotiate the turmoil of broken and bloody bodies, man and horse, which lay strewn the length of the bank. Injured men lay crying for aid while several horses lay on their backs or sides, their flailing legs threatening to dash the brains from any who ventured too close.

A face suddenly rose up in front of him. Taken unawares he tried to bring his framea to bear but he knew that he would be too late. He just had time to duck his head and throw it forward into the blow. A heartbeat later the sword struck his helm with a force which thrust his head down onto his chest. Staggering, Beowulf was vaguely aware of being pulled violently backwards, landing with a crash on the ground.

As his vision began to clear he realised that he was lying on his back, surrounded by fighting men. Several stood protectively over him as he struggled to regain his feet.

He rolled out from the back of the melee and stood unsteadily for a moment before, drawing his sword, he threw himself back into the fighting at the barrier.

He snatched up his framea from where it lay amongst the feet of the struggling warriors, its distinctive red and white shaft contrasting sharply with the muddied grass of the bank. Raising it above his head he thrust forward repeatedly over the heads of his men at the Swedish warriors.

Several were using their own framea to hold back the Geat defenders while others used the blades of their francisca throwing axes in an attempt to hook away the material from the barrier.

Unable to get close enough to really make much difference to the fighting due to the press of bodies and rising flames, Beowulf cast about for something which would be more effective. His eyes alighted on a stack of unused throwing spears. Dropping his framea he raced over and grabbed several of the missiles.

"Get down!" he yelled as he prepared to launch the first of them at the attackers.

Recognising his voice they ducked back out of harms way.

Beowulf quickly aimed at one of the enemy warriors who, bent forward, was intent on dismantling the defences. The Swedish warrior behind him attempted to lower his shield to deflect the angon but he was too late. The spear pierced the shoulder of the man and passed deep into his body. The Swede slumped and slid out of sight, behind the wall. Other defenders snatched up the remaining angon and launched them at the men in the break.

Unable to withstand the onslaught, they slowly retreated behind the cover of their shields.

Spotting the wagon nearby which had been used to deliver the pitch he called some men to him.

"We need to get this wagon in that gap as fast as possible, come on."

Throwing their shoulders behind it they pushed the wagon, yoke first, into the gap in the fence. Already soaked in pitch from its earlier duties it burst immediately into flame.

Quickly scanning the rest of the line, Beowulf could see that the barrier was now well ablaze along its complete length.

Thick black smoke billowed into the warm summer air, while orange flames licked high above the matted tangle of branches and trunks. Beaten back by the heat and smoke, the Geats were beginning to look to him, anxiously awaiting the order to retire.

He turned to the rear and cupped his hands against the noise of the fire and battle.

"Bring the horses forward," he cried, beckoning them with his arm.

On seeing his signal the men quickly brought the horses up to the front line.

"Let's go boys, two to a horse. We have only got to go five miles or so. Well done everybody!"

Immediately scores of men abandoned the inferno which the barrier had become and streamed back across the clearing.

Leaping eagerly onto the horses they spurred them back along the road which led to Edet.

"Bowmen," he called. "To me."

The group headed by Harald mounted up and crossed the field with some difficulty as the retreating Geat forces cut across their path, but they finally arrived, looking triumphant.

"It was carnage in the woods," Harald called as he got nearer. "We must have roasted dozens of them!"

"The barrels exploded in the heat and covered lots of them in burning pitch," one of the younger bowmen added quietly. "It was horrible, lord."

Beowulf looked at the man and could see that he had been crying.

"They were screaming that it wouldn't come off and even their own mates were killing them to save them from any more agony."

Beowulf could see that the man was badly shaken.

"Pick one of the other men up and give him a lift to the rear," he said quietly.

"You have done your duty, today, thank you."

The bowman nodded his thanks and, turning his horse, made his way slowly to the rear. As they watched him go he casually tossed his bow aside.

Beowulf sighed as he watched the man go. He suddenly felt exhausted. He realised that his head was throbbing painfully where he had been struck earlier and he had to fight back an overwhelming feeling of nausea. It was as if the exchange with the bowman had drained him of all his energy and he had to force himself, mentally, back to the matter at hand which was he knew, survival.

He looked around. All faces were turned to him awaiting their instructions. Whatever his personal situation he knew that he was responsible for these men's lives. Forcing a smile he addressed them. "Some people are just not made for this, that's why we have warriors. He was a brave man. He stood and did his duty until I relieved him. Don't think any less of him."

They murmured their agreement.

"Right!" he snapped, suddenly regaining his old energy.

"If we can survive the next few minutes we will have a tale fit to tell the king."

"If he comes," a voice muttered in the rear.

Beowulf shot the group a sharp look but decided that there was no time to discipline anyone.

"We remain mounted and hang back a short bow shot from the barrier. Anyone who forces their way through gets an arrow for their trouble." He cast a quick glance around the group of faces before him. "When I say go, we go, fast. Let's give the men as long as we can to get back to Wulfgar's forces. Spread out and keep one eye on me. Let's go."

They waited on their horses, strung out in a long line, arrows notched and ready to loose but no horde of enemy warriors appeared.

To Beowulf's relief a steady breeze had sprung up at their backs, driving the smoke and flames directly into the faces of the attacking Swedes. A few mounted warriors had splashed through the shallows to be greeted by a rain of arrows from Beowulf and his men.

They had done no harm. The experienced warriors had easily deflected them with their shields. One of them had actually raised a small cheer from his companions when he plucked one from the air with his hand.

Clearly the horsemen had returned and reported to their masters that the Geats had retired. With no enemy to defeat and the daylight drawing rapidly to a close, Ohthere obviously felt that the flaming barrier could serve him as an equally effective defence against the sudden arrival of King Hythcyn's army as it had the departing Geats.

Sure now that all of his force must be safe, Beowulf ordered Harald and the bowmen to retire.

Beowulf sat alone and surveyed the battlefield. It had been his plan and he had commanded the forces in action for the first time. They had achieved their goal, and more, with light casualties. It remained to be seen whether the Swedes would continue with their raid in the morning or retire. The army would be in a perfect defensive position by now and the Swedes risked annihilation if they persisted. To his surprise he found that he wanted them to live to fight another day. He had enjoyed meeting the Swedish æthelings, Ohthere and Onela, and hoped that they would meet again in more peaceful circumstances.

Wheeling his horse, Beowulf fulfilled the promise which he had made to his men.

He was the last Geat to leave the field of battle alive.

16
_____

$\mathbf{B}$ eowulf tracked back along the road which led to the hill
known as the Troll's Hat.

Ahead of him the evening sun formed a hazy ball of
orange light as it hung, suspended, just above the trees. High
above, thin, wispy, clouds streaked the evening sky, their
lower surfaces painted shades of scarlet and pink by the
setting sun.

He watched as the first bats circled the air, twisting and
turning as they gathered in the first of the evening's catch. His
tired mind wandered back to one evening long ago when he
had still been a child in Hygelac's hall.

Hygelac's daughter, Astrid, had suddenly screamed from
the pantry and he had raced to investigate, ready to protect
her from harm. He had flung open the door to find the room
in darkness and no sign of Astrid. Quickly grabbing a brand
from the cross passage wall he had entered the room to find
his cousin crouched in the corner with her knees drawn up
and her hands covering her head, sobbing that there was an
elf or sprite in the room with her.

It was only a small room but he had checked the corners

and any potential hiding places but found nothing. Then he too felt the presence of the spirit as it beat about his head, attacking him from every direction. Steeling himself he had raised the brand and looked for his other-world opponent. He smiled now at the memory, as the light had revealed not some malevolent being but a tiny bat which must have entered the room through the small open shutter at the rear and was unable to find its way back out.

He had crouched down and tried to explain what it was to the terrified girl, but to his amusement it had only had the effect of increasing her state of terror.

As he had crouched protectively at her side, he had watched, amazed, as the bat tried to find its way out of the room. It did not seem to be able to see the wind hole which was clearly visible to him by the light of the brand, but flew backwards and forwards at great speed between the walls, turning sharply just as it had seemed to him that it must fly straight into the wall. Eventually it had shot through the opening and was swallowed up by the darkness.

Reassuring Astrid that it had gone, they had sat there for a moment while she recovered.

He remembered how he had sat there, marvelling at the actions of the bat. Clearly it had not seen the open wind hole which was so obvious to him in the light so it must be blind, or nearly so. But the whole time it had been there it had never landed once and had fluttered around the small room, the small dark room, he recalled, at great speed without touching either them or the walls even once, so it couldn't be blind. It had confused him then, and he had ever since watched the antics of bats with a sense of wonder.

A group of mounted warriors blocked the road up ahead, Beowulf quickly counted six of them. All were dressed in good quality mail and helm and carried raised spears, and he was pleased to see that they all wore the dark cloak of Wulfgar's hearth warriors.

He noticed that they all sported impressive beards. These were obviously some of the ealdorman's finest and most experienced men, and he felt a flicker of pride when he realised that they must have been sent to accompany him to their lord.

"Welcome back, lord," they grinned as he reined in his mount, "congratulations on your victory! Bjorn and Ulf are already with the ealdorman and he has asked Harald and me to accompany you to him while the rest of the boys keep an eye on the road."

"Another Harald!" Beowulf laughed. "Is everyone in this part of the kingdom called Harald?"

"I'm not, lord, my name is Thorfinn," the first man chirped happily, "Thorfinn Haraldson."

BEOWULF KNEW that Wulfgar would be keen to hear his report on the events at the border and, he admitted to himself, he was keen to boast of their achievement. There was a very good chance that the king was there by now, maybe even his father, Hygelac and Heardred, and the thought of basking in their congratulations restored the energy to his exhausted mind and body.

Ahead lay the sheer wall of the Troll's Hat, its creamy white face rising majestically from the dark green forest at its base. The road curved gently to the North here as it left the meadow lands and entered the dark forest which lay between the mountain and the lake, a mile or so to their right. It would make a fine defensive position Beowulf thought to himself as they rode its length, if it were not for the fact that there was an even finer position up ahead.

It was still light when the three riders slowed their horses to a canter as they approached the mouth of the gorge which led down to the town of Edet and the valley of the Geat River. They had ridden at speed since they had left the other warriors at the meadow and Beowulf had not had the opportunity to speak to Thorfinn and Harald. They had been friendly and clearly pleased to see him but there was something about their demeanour which, as he had time to reflect on their encounter, he had found troubling. There was clearly something which was causing them concern.

Two guards at the head of the gorge raised their spears in recognition as they passed before they slowed to a trot and approached the Geat camp. Looking around him Beowulf was surprised to see so few men gathered together. There should have been plenty of time for Wulfgar's thegns to have arrived with their men by now which, added to the army from the South, should have provided them with an overwhelming force considering the size of the Swedish incursion.

Wulfgar must have split his forces for some reason he decided. He wasn't sure that he agreed with the tactics until he remembered that there was a peninsula which continued for several miles out into Lake Vanern in a direct line from the end of the Troll's Gorge. Obviously Wulfgar had stationed the rest of his forces in this neck of land, ready to fall on the rear of the unsuspecting Swedes. Beowulf smiled at the plan. The Swedes would see a paltry force and attack immediately. While they were heavily engaged the rest of the Geat army would arrive, trapping them between the sheer walls of the gorge and the twin Geat shield walls.

It would seem that the king of the Swedes, Ongentheow,

was about to lose his sons to either Woden's feast hall or ignominious captivity.

He hoped it was the later. He would like the opportunity to feast and hunt with the brothers while their ransom was decided.

They dismounted as they neared the tent which marked the position of Wulfgar and his thegns. He had noticed, with pride, how men had stopped their preparations for the battle to come and grinned as he passed them. He recognised several of them from the fighting at the river and made sure to smile and nod at them in recognition. He had never forgotten the lesson which his father, Ecgtheow, had taught him all those years ago when he had taken the trouble to recognise the one armed veteran, Binni, at the bridge which led to Miklaborg, and the man's obvious delight. It had been a lesson which had served him well.

The guards at the entrance to the tent smiled at Beowulf and his companions as they approached, leaning to one side to pull the tent flap open for them with a swish. Ducking inside Beowulf quickly scanned the room.

The space was lit by several lamps on iron stands which cast a yellow glow over the interior. Otherwise it was bare save for one long table at the far end which held a selection of meats, cheeses, bread and of course ale. He suddenly realised how long it had been since he had eaten or drank anything.

To his disappointment none of his relatives were present, but Wulfgar was to one side, talking earnestly to Bjorn. Glancing up on hearing the tent flap opening he gave him a tired smile. "Welcome back Beowulf, I was just hearing about the 'Battle of Beaver Lake'," he smiled. "It sounded like a lot of fun, congratulations. I must admit that I was a bit sceptical at first, but to be honest if we had concentrated our forces there we may well have been better off than we are now."

"And how *are* we now, lord?" Beowulf replied cautiously. "Where are the rest of the men?"

Wulfgar grimaced. "It looks at the moment as though this is it."

Beowulf looked at him in shock.

There were barely enough men outside to form a shield wall which would stretch across the gorge, much less allow for a defence in any depth.

"How many men have come from the South?" he questioned.

"None, if you don't count my thegn, Wulf, who holds lands around Little Edet. It seems that we have either been abandoned to our fate or the messengers that I sent the other night never got through."

"If that is the case," Beowulf replied, "nobody in Miklaborg even knows that there is a Swedish invasion!"

His heart sank as he realised the full significance of the situation they found themselves in.

He quickly came to a decision.

"We must retreat lord. I am sure that Bjorn has informed you of the strength of the Swedish forces. Although this is not a full scale invasion it *is* a well equipped, highly experienced, raiding force. We cannot hope to hold them here with the number of men that I just saw outside."

Wulfgar sighed and put his arm around Beowulf's shoulder.

"Come and share my ale, drink as much as you can," he smiled, "I would rather you drank it than a Swede."

Wulfgar poured a horn of ale and handed it to Beowulf.

"When is the last time you ate? Grab some food while you can."

Beowulf crammed a thick slice of pork into some bread

and tore hungrily at it while he waited for Wulfgar to continue.

"You are right of course, I should retire before them. As you say they are a raiding force and they will not want to push far into Geat territory now that we are aware they are here, especially now that you have told them that the army has not sailed for Jute Land yet. They must have intercepted the first rider which I sent to Miklaborg, the one which went the direct route down the Geat Valley, or reinforcements would have arrived by now. They wouldn't have got the second one. There is no way that they could know the back ways like him, he is a local, the son of a woodsman, so I am sure that he will get through, but it looks as though he may have been too late to save us."

"Kaija!"

Beowulf suddenly remembered his volva companion. She had taken the same route south.

"Don't worry about her, she will be fine. Any Swedish warriors would leave a holy woman alone. They worship the same gods as us after all. Even if they did try anything I have a feeling that they would soon regret it!" he smiled.

Beowulf remembered her reaction to his comment on the road to the Bronding capital at Skovde and knew Wulfgar was right. It was more likely that they were in a lot more danger than she could possibly be.

"No, I have to stay here and defend the town and border lands. These are my lands and my people, what sort of lord would I be if I ran off and left them to their fate at the first sign of trouble? Besides you forget, I sent a message to my king that I would defend this position unless he told me otherwise, and I have received no word from him as you know. But..." he continued. "You made no such commitment and I want you to leave."

Beowulf looked at him in shock.

"You want me to run away while you all fight and die here. I cannot!"

"Listen to me, Beowulf," Wulfgar replied, lowering his voice so that only he could hear him.

"Every man who remains here will die. You have seen these Swedes, they are tough bastards. They know the quality of the men who were with you at the border and you humiliated them. If it were not for that they may have been content with sacking the Bronding lands and gone back home for a celebratory feast, but now they cannot do that with honour. I fear they must come on, whatever the risk, and kill as many of us as they can before retiring. You did your duty, and you did it well. The kingdom cannot afford to throw away the lives of young warriors of your abilities in a futile defence of a shit hole like Edet. Towns are easy to rebuild, warriors like you are rare. What could I say to Ecgtheow and Hygelac when they finally pitch up at valhall and ask me why I squandered all the training and hopes that they had invested in you over many years? You have done your duty and you must go south."

Beowulf pursed his lips as he thought deeply on Wulfgar's words.

He understood the truth of them but could not bring himself to act on them.

"I'll organise you a horse and get you out of here." Wulfgar said, patting him on the shoulder.

"No, I am staying here. You spoke to me about the years of preparation which my father and foster father have invested in me. If I have taken one thing from them it is a sense of honour. A warrior's reputation and honour count more to him and his family than his life. If my fate is to die here with you then that is what the norns have decreed. How could I face them knowing that I ran away from a fight. I would rather be dead if that is the choice."

To his surprise Wulfgar's face broke into a weary smile.

"I thought that would be your reaction, I just wanted my reply to be ready when they confronted us at our bench in Valhall. If I am to die here I would be honoured to die with a man like you."

"And I you, Wulfgar," he replied.

Wulfgar refilled their horns with ale.

"Come my friend, we have much to do."

Draining their ale they ducked out of the tent and regarded their forces.

"Very much," he sighed.

THEY WORKED THROUGH THE NIGHT.

Torches were placed at intervals, illuminating the floor of the gorge with a pale flickering light, casting spectral shadows which danced upon the milky white walls. By the time that the pale blue-grey glow of the pre dawn began to cast its wan light to the east every man knew his position in the Geat line and knew the men who he was to fight alongside.

Beowulf had walked the line and insisted that the men introduce themselves and give a brief description of their work and responsibilities so that in the fight ahead they would not be strangers to one another. Knowing even a few details of each other would help to bind them as a group, he reasoned. He knew that the common soldiery tended to fight more for their friends or to protect immediate loved ones than out of any sense of duty to king or nation, so even this superficial level of familiarity with their companions should help them fight for one another he hoped.

He had been joined in the night by Gunnar who had been his right hand man in the shield wall at the river.

Wulfgar had acted as witness as he had formally offered to take Gunnar into his hearth troop. Gunnar had accepted and placed his hands inside Beowulf's, before giving him his oath, despite the fact that Beowulf had warned him that the chances were that he might soon hold the record for the shortest time anyone had been a warrior.

To the rear an ox had been slaughtered and it was already being spitted and suspended above a fire pit. Soon the smell of roasting meat filled the gorge and the men cast hungry glances at the carcass as it turned lazily, the fat sizzling and spitting as it ran down the sides of the beast to fall into the fire below. Bjorn organised a rotation of the men from their positions at the wall, ensuring each man had his fair share of meat, bread, cheese and ale.

As the sun cleared the eastern horizon Beowulf and Wulfgar found a large flat stone to sit on and enjoy their breakfast. It had been a long night but they were agreed that they had done all that they could.

A shield wall had been organised stretching from one side of the gorge to the other. By spreading the line extremely thinly they had managed to form a second line behind the first to lend the defence an appearance of depth but they were both experienced enough to realise that they would not last long against a determined attack by well led warriors.

Beowulf had asked if the gorge narrowed at any point to the rear, hoping that they could retreat there and shorten the line, but of course the width of the gorge was constant along the whole of its length, as he had seen when he travelled along it with Kaija.

In truth he already knew the answer before he had asked the question. If anyone knew the area it would be Wulfgar. Not only was he the ealdorman but he frequently hunted here.

No, it was a good defensive position he admitted to himself. The problem was lack of men and without a miracle it looked as though this was all they would have.

As if to confirm his fears, two of the men who had met him on the road the night before appeared, pounding along the road from the direction of the Swedish forces.

Their approach caused the men to cast worried looks in their direction. It was obvious to all that it could only be bad news. Beowulf flung has food to the grass and, standing, stretched his muscles.

When was the last time he had slept?

It was the night he had returned from the outskirts of Skovde with Kaija when they had first seen the Swedes he decided.

How long ago was that? Was it yesterday? The day before?

He realised that he had no idea. He suddenly felt very weary.

The riders spotted them and used their mounts to force their way through the press of men who looked up at them, expectantly. Dismounting a short distance away they let their reins drop to the floor and approached them, breathlessly.

"They have broken camp lord, and are dismantling the barrier. They will be here soon. Wæl and Oslaf are keeping half a mile in front of them so we will know when their arrival is imminent."

Wulfgar nodded.

"Go and grab yourself some food and ale. It looks like we are going to be very busy soon."

"Thank you, lord."

Wulfgar turned to Beowulf.

"Well, what do you think, have we done all that we can?"

"I think so lord, where do you want me?"

"I will take the centre," Wulfgar announced, "and I want you on my right. Wulf can take the left. If you surround yourselves with the best men you will both have a chance of surviving the rout."

Wulfgar took Beowulf by the arm and led him to one side.

"We both know we cannot win here today. The best we can do is to try and survive and keep the best of our men alive with us so that we can fight another day. When the shield wall breaks wheel your men back against the gorge sides. I will tell Wulf to do the same over there. Whichever side I think that I have the best chance of reaching with my men I will make for. A lot of men will die but it can't be helped. Good luck."

With a nod Beowulf turned and made his way to his place in the line. Gunnar came from Wulfgar's tent as he passed. Wulfgar had sent him off with Ulf to find arms and armour more appropriate to a member of a hearth troop. More practical training would be arriving very soon he had joked.

"I feel safer already!" Beowulf called across with a grin as he noticed Gunnar.

Gunnar beamed with pride at his new appearance, and Beowulf hoped that his confidence in him was not misplaced. Beowulf took his place in the front of the line. He still wore his gashed helm from the previous days fight. Wulfgar had offered to find him a replacement but he had refused. It was a family heirloom, a gift from his father. He would have it repaired when he got time. Wulfgar had insisted that he remove his armour and have it polished, 'in case the Swedes think that we are being led by farmers straight from the fields'.

At least he once again looked like a Geat lord, dressed in his war splendour, even if he felt rather less so.

He glanced behind him once again, checking the supply of throwing spears were in place and within easy reach. One benefit of having so few men, he thought grimly, was that there were more than enough angon to go around.

An oppressive silence fell on the gorge as they waited for Wulfgar's men, Wæl and Oslaf, to appear around the bend in the road. Beowulf could sense that every pair of eyes in the Geat spear hedge was fixed on the point at which they must soon appear.

Even the weather seemed to be adding to the tension. Despite the early hour, an oppressive heat had descended on the gorge, and, as if covering the advance of the Swedish raiders like a monstrous cloak, a thick band of charcoal grey clouds rolled in from the east. Soon the distant rumble of thunder carried to the waiting Geats and the heart of the clouds flashed and flickered as lightning bolts cracked and fizzed among them.

Men began to cast nervous glances at their neighbours as the storm grew nearer, clearly wondering if the gods had deserted them and chosen to side with their enemies. Men instinctively reached inside their shirts and withdrew their lucky talismans. Many of them wore the hammer of Thunor and they rubbed and kissed them in devotion. Thunor was the god of thunder and it was the sound made by the passage of his chariot through the sky which was the cause of the rumbling which men called thunder, while the bolts of light-ning marked the passage of his thrown hammer.

A sudden, mighty, boom shook the ground and seemed to resound off of the walls of the gorge.

As if responding to a prearranged signal, Wæl and Oslaf appeared on the road, their cloaks flying in their wake.

Seeing Wulfgar's standard flying at the centre of the line they made straight for their lord to report on the arrival of the enemy. Beowulf watched as the Geat line opened up and swallowed the men.

A cool breeze got up and began to blow directly in the faces of the Geat warriors. The storm was practically overhead now, the thunder claps no longer boomed but crashed and cracked and the lightning bolts arced out of the boiling mass of leaden clouds almost simultaneously. Thick, fat, raindrops began to fall from the clouds, slowly at first, but within moments they had increased to a torrent, the wind whipping them, painfully, straight into the faces of the waiting men.

From its midst they appeared.

Emerging from the forest like a monstrous silver serpent, the Swedish column uncurled itself to its right and lined up facing them. Beowulf tried to count the number of lines that the enemy formed but found that, even screwing his eyes up against the severity of the storm, he could not make it out.

"Gunnar, how…"

"Six, lord," he interrupted.

"Plus the hundred warriors who remain mounted at the mouth of the gorge."

Beowulf watched as Ohthere, Onela and the Troll rode along the front of their warriors, encouraging them and calling out to individuals in the front row.

Good leadership.

Thank the gods that Wulfgar had had the foresight to place sharpened stakes in front of their position otherwise they would clearly have come straight on and ridden them down.

These boys were not in the mood to talk. They were going to hit us hard and be on their way.

He felt a small surge of hope.

Maybe they had found out that the Geat relief force was near and were trying to finish it quickly?

He hoped that he was right.

The Swedes were clearly shouting and clashing their spears against their shields as the three riders left the field to Beowulf's right but the noise was completely drowned out by the crashing and rumbling of the storm which was now directly overhead.

The field ahead passed in an instant from darkest night to brightest day as lightning snaked its way overhead.

And then the Swedes attacked.

AS IF PART of some divine plan to crush the Geat forces, the rain seemed to double in intensity the moment that the Swedish advance commenced.

Despite screwing up his eyes and continually blinking, Beowulf could barely make out the line of polished iron as it came on towards them. Flicking a glance along the Geat line, he could see that men were trying to cope with the blinding deluge as best they could. Some had lowered their faces or turned their heads to the side while others were continually closing their eyes for long periods.

The enemy of course had the wind and rain at their backs and would be further encouraged by the Geat discomfort Beowulf thought, grimly.

When the Swedish line reached a position a short bow shot from them a horn sounded, distantly, from Beowulf's right.

Immediately the enemy line broke into a run at two points. Beowulf watched as two boar snouts developed, each clearly led by elite warriors. To his consternation Beowulf realised that the Swedish attacks were aimed at the two weakest points in the Geat shield wall, midway between himself and Wulfgar and on the other side midway between Wulfgar and Wulf.

It could only have one outcome and Beowulf watched, a virtual spectator, as the Swedish charge surged towards the line to his left. A dozen paces from the wall the leading group of Swedish warriors drew back their arms as one and released a deadly shower of francisca throwing axes. Beowulf watched, spellbound, as the axes spun through the air before disappearing into the ranks of the Geat warriors.

The Swedes had deliberately aimed the franciscas low, straight at the unprotected legs of the defenders who screamed in pain and fear as they tore into them.

Moments later the boar snout hit the still reeling shield wall with a crash which echoed around the walls of the gorge like a winter wave crashing on the shore. Thinly spread, blinded and stung by the driving rain and crippled by the franciscas, the Geat line wavered for a moment and then burst open like an overripe pear.

Beowulf could only watch as the Swedes roared in triumph and began to move away from the positions in front of him, funnelling into the rapidly widening gap in the Geat position.

The overwhelming success had inadvertently handed Beowulf the chance to hit them back and he seized it.

"Angon now, into their flank!"

Moments later a cloud of deadly missiles arced into the unprotected sides of the attackers. Concentrating on the battle ahead of them the first strike took them completely by surprise. Beowulf watched as the shafts buried themselves deeply into the heads and bodies of the nearest Swedish warriors. Despite the cries of their companions most of the

Swedes still seemed unaware of the new threat to their flank.

Elated, Beowulf ordered that every man launch as many spears at the enemy, as quickly as possible, before they realised what was happening and turned to face them.

Overhead the storm still raged, thunder and lightning crashed and flickered, helping to conceal the cries of the injured and dying in the Swedish ranks.

Slowly the Swedes became aware of the danger to their left.

The nearest two ranks of the Swedish wedge began to turn their way and form up in a defensive wall. Risking a glance over to his left, Beowulf was horrified to see that the Geat shield wall had completely given way at both points of attack.

Wulfgar and his hearth warriors remained at the centre of the battlefield, clustered around his standard, but hundreds of Swedish warriors were streaming around them.

A bizarre image flashed into Beowulf's mind of the stream behind Hygelac's hall rushing and babbling around a great rock which sat at its centre.

Over to far side of the gorge he could see Wulf's hearth warriors clustered around their lord. It looked to Beowulf that he was already beginning to pull in the wings of his remaining shield wall prior to retreating to the gorge sides.

Beowulf was torn as he watched the disintegration of their forces. His instinct screamed at him to take his remaining warriors and fall on the lightly defended flank of the enemy. He knew that he could cause havoc there for a while before the Swedes regrouped and counter attacked him but to his surprise he hesitated.

He had no doubt that he would have rushed straight into

the attack just a few days ago without a thought, bent on glory and renown.

Now that he had experienced battle first hand and had seen men kill and be killed at close quarters, indeed suffered wounds himself, he found that a new desire to preserve the lives of the men under his command had arisen in him.

Anyhow, he reflected, already his hesitation had probably cost them the chance.

Looking back to his front he saw that hundreds more of the enemy were rushing to the aid of those which had formed up against him.

The Geat wall had broken and its remnants were streaming from the field, back down the gorge towards Edet.

Beowulf watched as the Swedish mounted warriors swept through their old position in pursuit, cutting down the fleeing Geats from behind.

Released from the task of chasing off their opponents those on foot were now beginning to regroup and mass against the three remaining islands of Geat resistance. The sound of heavy fighting was still coming from his left, as those men, in what had now become his left wing, fought ferociously against becoming overwhelmed.

He had to help.

Taking several steps back from the wall he addressed his men.

"We need to retreat in good order to the sides of the gorge. Those of you on the right flank…" he shouted. "Anchor yourselves against the gorge wall, everyone else, wheel back alongside them. Keep your formation at all times. You saw what will happen if you break. Keep your discipline and we will survive this."

Beowulf walked quickly along the line.

"You…you…you..." he called out a dozen times, clapping

some of the most useful looking warriors on the shoulder as he did so. "You boys come with me, we have work to do. Gunnar!" he called. "Let's go!"

Beowulf led the group quickly towards the end of the line, hoping that he would reach it before it was turned by sheer force of enemy numbers.

Once the Swedes broke through into their rear the line would be attacked from both sides and the end would follow soon after.

Ahead of them the Geat wall was just holding its own against the push of attackers in heavy hand to hand fighting.

As he drew near he saw the blade of a framea emerge from the neck of the man he was approaching. As the man fell away, his place was immediately taken by his killer who forced his way into the gap in the Geat shield hedge and stamped on his victim's face as he attempted to remove the embedded weapon.

"Swords lads, let's push these bastards back!"

At the last moment the triumphant Swedish warrior looked up from his mortally wounded victim, straight into the face of a charging Geat lord.

With a yell Beowulf raised his sword and drove it deep into the man's gaping mouth, shouldering him aside as he crashed through, deep into the ranks of the enemy. Thrusting at the left hand side of the Swedish wall with his shield, he struck out with his sword to left and right at any unprotected arm, leg or torso which came within range.

Frantically the nearest Swedes attempted to scramble away from him.

Moments ago they had been on the verge of over-whelming men of the Geat levy and were gripped by the excitement of imminent victory.

Suddenly a giant, armour clad, sword swinging lord had appeared in their midst and they recoiled in confusion.

Beowulf glanced to his right.

All along the line the enemy were pulling back in panic as a result of their frenzied attack.

Beowulf turned and screamed at the Geat shield wall,

"Run as fast as you can to the position up beside the gorge wall and reform on my men there, fast!"

He could not spare the time to see if they were doing as he had ordered. He had given them this one chance to live. If they were too slow or stupid to take it they would die, it was as simple as that.

With a yell he threw himself once more at the men opposite him. He was moving smoothly now, his brain and body reacting instantaneously to counter any threat or to take advantage of any opportunity which presented itself.

A face appeared over the top of a shield rim for a moment and he watched in semi detachment as his sword flicked out to take its owner before he could duck away. He almost casually knocked away a framea which had been directed at his head and saw the terror in the man's eyes as he fixed his gaze upon him.

With a final roar he charged at the enemy, scattering them.

Quickly he began to pace backwards towards the relative safety of the gorge walls.

"Geats, converge on me."

Once clear of the Swedish line he could see the results of their work. A quick glance revealed a score or more bodies lay among the puddles of the rain lashed grass floor of the gorge. Some of these would have been from the previous fighting but he had no doubt that a considerable number of them had been caused by his group's attack.

"Are we all here?" he called as they backed together, facing the enemy.

"Ottar fell. They were all over him like a pack of dogs once he went down. They skewered him like a stuck pig, the bastards."

"That's enough! Anybody else? Injuries?" Met with silence he went on. "We did well, let's keep it that way. We make our way back to our line as quickly as we can. Stay together, facing them, and we will be fine. They have tasted our steel and know how good we are so they won't be in a hurry to close with us again. I didn't notice many heroes in their ranks did you? Half of you grab a framea from the floor and we will hold them at bay. If any of them get close enough, use your sword. *Let's go!"*

They started to back up as quickly as they could, shadowed by the Swedes who started to move up either side of them. Beowulf knew that if they managed to get behind them their retreat would be ended and they would be overwhelmed.

He considered making a lone attack into the Swedish line to give his men more time to get back but discounted it. They were stronger together and he would only weaken the collective defence.

"How far left to go?"

"About fifty paces, lord." Gunnar replied from the rear of the group.

As they neared safety Beowulf could sense the agitation amongst the Swedish ranks increase as men wrestled with their consciences. To allow this tiny group of outnumbered warriors to escape unharmed was shameful, and a thing which they would regret for the rest of their lives, but to attack them seemed to offer only certain death.

"Ready, one or more of them will attack us any time now," Beowulf murmured.

Within moments a large warrior, naked to the waist, and with a shock of hair the colour of blood, let out a cry and lumbered towards them, swinging a huge battle axe around his head.

Beowulf knew that he must deal with him quickly and effortlessly otherwise, encouraged, the rest of the pack would descend on them and tear them apart.

The man was big, heavy set and obviously powerful but he moved more like an ox than a bull, Beowulf decided. He dropped his shield and ran towards the man.

Grinning, his opponent unwound his body and swung his axe in a scything arc towards Beowulf's legs. Although powerful, the effort was clumsy, and Beowulf had no trouble in avoiding the strike. At the last moment he jumped high, easily clearing the sweeping blade. In one fluid movement his sword flashed out.

Landing beside the immobile giant, Beowulf calmly trotted back to his position and took up his shield.

The Swede stood as if transfixed before them as they resumed their retreat to the safety of the Geat line.

The other Swedish warriors looked to one another in confusion as their man seemed to watch the retreating Geats but make no further attempt to attack them.

Suddenly his legs seemed to buckle and he started to fall. As he fell to his knees a thin red line appeared at his neck.

Tumbling slowly to one side, the man crashed down.

As he did so his head came cleanly off and rolled across the sodden grass towards his companions.

A gasp of shock escaped the watching Swedes, followed by a low moan as they began to take in the demonstration of swordsmanship which they had just been privileged to witness.

All the time Beowulf and his group were moving closer to safety.

When a safe distance had opened up between them and the Swedish forces a whistle from above told him that the Geatish line was now close enough for them to support their retreat with volleys of spears. Although they fell short, it was enough for the following Swedes who knew they had now lost any chance of overtaking the men. Still clearly in awe of Beowulf's prowess, they moved back to a safer distance.

As they regained their shield wall they were met by cheering faces, whoops and clashing spears.

Beowulf smiled. A small victory had been taken from the day, but they still faced certain annihilation if help from the South didn't arrive very soon. Looking across the gorge he could see that the other two Geat groups, those of Wulfgar and Wulf, were still intact and holding out, swamped in a sea of enemy warriors.

Over to his left, the last of the mounted warriors were returning from their grisly hunt.

He realised for the first time that the sun was shining.

The storm had moved on and the air felt fresh and clean, the earlier clamminess washed away. He was pleased to see that Gunnar had remained faithfully at his side. He had all the makings of a fine hearth companion.

He was suddenly struck by a thought.

"Have you ever used a sword, Gunnar?"

Gunnar grinned impishly.

"Yes, lord, just now."

He chuckled at the man's matter-of-fact answer. He was certain that he had chosen wisely.

"It's lucky those Swedes didn't know that!"

17

"Smoke!"

Beowulf followed the warrior's gaze southward. Angry, black, smoke was beginning to billow above the southern end of the Troll's Hat as the town of Edet suffered the agonies of pillage and destruction. He could tell from the anguished faces of many of the men which ones still had loved ones in the town and felt a pang of sympathy for them, but he couldn't let it affect their morale.

"That is just a few buildings burning." He shouted. "If we had not been here all these bastards in front of us would have been there by now. What you can see is just a quick 'grab what you can' raid by a few horsemen, they won't have the time to bother with women and children. The longer we hold them here the safer your loved ones will be."

Beowulf watched as the frowns turned to pensive smiles as their friends backed up his words. He could almost read their thoughts as they tried to reassure themselves that all would be well.

"Of course he's right, he's a lord. The Swedes are still here because of us. Anyone who could cut the head off an

enormous great ginger troll must know what he is talking about!"

Beowulf looked back at the Swedish warriors facing them. They seemed undecided about what to do next. While they were milling around waiting for someone to tell them he would use the time to make their task as difficult as possible, he decided. The ground rose slightly to the gorge sides. Along the base of the sheer walls, rocks and stones of all sizes had fallen and collected over the years.

They could be useful.

He looked at the line of warriors. They were still strung out, two deep, for the most part. The first thing to do was organise the wall properly, he decided. He called for their attention. "When I say so, I want the line shortened to a length of sixty men, stretching from that boulder, in an arc to curve back onto the wall. Experienced, fully equipped warriors will make up the front row and as much of the second row as possible. The rest of you lads make a further two or three lines behind them. They won't be coming through that in a hurry will they?" he grinned encouragingly at them.

To his relief he saw hope begin to illuminate the faces of the men again. Hygelac's words came back to him as he watched.

'*So long as there is a plan to follow, most men will be happy.*'

"Right, do it *now!* Quick as you can, before those bastards see that we are in disarray."

To his delight and relief the manoeuvre was largely executed in a few moments. The warriors had already naturally gravitated to the front of the line. Those on the ends simply filed in front of those in the centre in one quick, fluid, movement, much to the disgust of their comrades who suddenly found themselves removed from the position of most honour. Naturally the men of the levy lost no time in gratefully removing themselves to the safer positions to the rear of the shield wall. Before the watching Swedes could take advantage of the confusion the move was completed.

Beowulf looked on at the new formation with pride.

A solid wall of shields and framea would face any attacker, all of which were wielded by experienced warriors. Behind them they faced three full rows of framea wielding men of the levy. The very fact that they had survived the earlier rout suggested to Beowulf that these were probably the pick of those men. Not only that, they would be fighting to avenge the sack of their town and were worried about the fates of their families there. The Swedes could expect to be granted no quarter from that direction either, he smiled to himself. Behind them lay the solid walls of the Troll Gorge. There was no chance that they would be enveloped this time even if they did break through.

Yes, it was a strong position. Could he make any better?

"Gunnar, let's have a look around and see what we have here."

Beowulf was pleased to see that the men seemed to be in good spirits despite the defeat they had experienced earlier. They were intelligent enough to realise that they had simply been too few in number to stop the Swedes from breaking through their shield wall. Once that had happened very few armies can recover. Now they felt secure in a strong defensive position with their best warriors to the fore and a solid wall of rock to their rear. Most had the imagination to realise that they must look a formidable nut for the Swedes to crack.

"How about a few words of sympathy for the wounded, lord?"

Beowulf looked at the line of men laid out at the rear of the formation.

"Ulf!" he exclaimed. "How did you get here?"

"Help me up and I will tell you, lord."

Ulf struggled to his feet as Beowulf and Gunnar supported him. His right thigh was bound tightly with a bloody strip of cloth but otherwise he seemed to be unharmed.

"I caught one of those Franciscas, right at the start of the attack. I hardly had time to recover my balance before they were all over us. I managed to stab up at a couple from the ground as they stormed through and thought that I was about to join Woden, but a couple of my lads found me in time and managed to drag me out. They supported me as we fought our way over to your position and joined your boys. There was nothing I could do down there but die. Our line had disappeared by the time I was back on my feet, all I could see were Swedes. Luckily they were more interested in pouring into our rear than stopping to finish us off. I saw a few look at us and think about it, but we were obviously experienced warriors so they moved on to easier meat. I watched your little band retreat up to us though. Nice sword work lord, the best entertainment that I have had all day."

"It's good to see you here, Ulf," Beowulf smiled, clapping him affectionately on the shoulder.

Ulf grimaced. "Have we seen our last sunset, lord?"

"No!" Beowulf responded confidently. "They had their chance when we were down there. Even if there is no Geat force coming to our aid why would they waste the lives of their men to wipe us out. We now have our best men in good defensive positions and the only riches to be had would be those we are wearing. Any gain would not be worth the price they would have to pay. No," he continued, "they will treat with us and try to leave us with the impression that they spared our lives while we were at their mercy, but I suspect the truth is that they want to be away from here as quickly as possible. They have had their revenge on us for the humiliation at the border. That will be enough for them."

Beowulf realised that Ulf had propped himself up against a wagon. He hadn't noticed it before while he was busy organising the shield wall.

"What is in the wagon?"

"My surprise gift to you, lord," Ulf smiled as he threw back the covering.

Inside, stacked high, were hundreds of throwing spears. Beowulf gasped at the sight. They would make all the difference if the Swedes attacked.

"Where did you find them?"

"When you lot ran off to rescue our left wing it drew the attention of those attacking us. I used the time to organise a quick sweep of the ground in front of us, gathering up the angon' and any other weapons that we could see strewn about and drawing the wagon into our rear. There is not much future to be had in handing your enemy piles of weapons that he can use against you, lord!"

Beowulf laughed. "You may only have one good leg, Ulf, but there's nothing wrong with your head is there."

"There is not much more we can do but wait now, is there lord?" Gunnar put in.

"Maybe one more thing," he murmured, "get together a dozen of the levy for me."

ONCE THE MEN WERE ASSEMBLED, Beowulf explained their role to them.

"All those rocks you can see at the base of the cliff. I want them sorted into different piles, by size. The larger rocks I want you to spread randomly, five to ten paces in front of our position."

Beowulf noticed the men's shoulders slump in disappointment.

"I know, it is hard unglamorous work, but if you can disrupt their attacks in any way, you can really help our warriors in the front line. Believe me, I have stood there and they will be grateful to you for any advantage that you can provide for them."

Beowulf was pleased to see that their mood brightened as the importance of the work was explained to them.

"The smaller rocks I want to be big enough to be thrown over the heads of our lads and onto the heads of the enemy. It will make them keep their shields high. They will already be dodging our spears and they may miss something as small as a rock. It could cause them real problems. Let's get it done as quickly as possible. They can't delay much longer if they intend to attack."

The rocks were scattered where Beowulf had ordered and food and ale was distributed among the men. They ate and drank at their stations in the shield wall.

Facing them the Swedes had gathered in their hundreds, and stood just out of spear shot watching them like hungry wolves.

Beowulf jumped onto the back of the wagon and peered over their heads at the other Geat formations. Wulf's formation on the far side of the gorge mirrored his own, while hunkered in the middle of the pass the white boar standard of Geatland still curled proudly above of a ring of brightly painted shields.

Time to create more trouble, before the men start to get nervous again.

"Ulf, I am going to stir them up. If I don't come back, take command," he ordered.

Jumping down from the back of the wagon he took up his shield and refastened his helm. As he adjusted it his fingers ran over the ragged hole which had been cut into one of the plates by the sword blade at the river crossing.

"Gunnar, if I die, I want you to make sure that this helm and my sword get returned to my family."

"Yes, lord."

Beowulf edged through the crowd of men, rolling his shoulders as he did so.

All faces were turned to him as he emerged from the front of the Geat shield wall and continued walking towards the enemy.

The Swedish line seemed to quiver as they became aware of his approach. Conversations trailed off in mid sentence as men involuntarily gripped their weapons tighter and regarded this approaching madman. He had cast his die and would certainly make his reputation as a warrior in the next short while.

Whether that reputation was to ring down the ages as an example of bravery or idiocy would be decided in the coming moments.

He concentrated on the sliver of Hrani's, Woden's he now knew, staff, but it still remained cool to his skin. To his surprise it had remained so over the last few days of fighting. Either he had never been in any real danger or Woden had abandoned him as Kaija had warned he might. Well, there was one way to find out, he told himself. His eyes searched the rapidly approaching Swedish line.

There he is, that's the one.

Slightly off to the right of his approach, the largest enemy warrior towered above their shield wall.

He could sense the big warrior's confusion as he realised that the mad Geat lord was heading directly for him. He could also sense the excitement beginning to build amongst his comrades as they began to realise what was about to happen.

Beowulf was thrilled as the sounds of chanting and cheering began to build from the Geat position to his rear, intermixed with the clatter of sword hilts and spear shafts on shields.

Men further down the Swedish line broke ranks and moved forward to get a better view as Beowulf finally reached his objective and locked eyes with the brute.

"Fight me." Beowulf calmly commanded the Swedish giant.

Bewildered, the man looked to left and right, seemingly for confirmation that he had heard correctly.

Slowly the warrior's face broke into a, largely toothless, grin.

Beowulf fought to maintain his composure as the Swede's onion and crow garlic tainted breath washed over him. Beowulf was taller than almost every man he had ever met, but this giant of a man stood a full head taller than him, even in his battle helm. His bulbous, reddened, nose was framed by greasy brown plaits which hung limply either side of a badly pockmarked face. Mixed together with the smell of his last meal and the various odours which tended to cling to a man who had been on campaign for several weeks, Beowulf began to wish that he had chosen another opponent.

Still the man hesitated.

Exasperated, Beowulf took several paces back and addressed the Swedish line.

"Have none of you *nithing's* the balls to fight me?"

He began to suspect that the word had been passed around that this was the Geatish lord who had dispatched the last Swedish warrior to fight him with such ease. He began to grow uneasy. If no volunteers came forward he would be placed in an embarrassing position. He could seek to provoke them by striking one of them down in cold blood, and although the two sides were technically still fighting, it would hardly be seen as an honourable action by one of his rank against a common warrior. Or he could abandon the whole idea and return to the Geat position. He cringed inwardly at the thought of retracing his steps without a victory, no doubt accompanied by the mocking jeers of the Swedes. His mind raced. *Why won't they fight me?*

"They have been ordered to stand their ground and not react to any taunting."

A voice carried over the heads of the enemy as they began to move respectfully apart. Beowulf caught glimpses of highly polished armour as the owner of the voice made his way through the grimier ranks of the common soldiery.

Beowulf declined his head slightly in deference to the ætheling's rank.

"Ohthere."

"Beowulf," he smiled, in response. "We meet at last. I hoped that you would survive."

"I hoped that I would kill you, lord," he snarled in reply.

Beowulf was finding it difficult to adjust, mentally, to the new situation. Moments ago he was contemplating a one man attack on hundreds of Swedish warriors and now it seemed he was about to engage in polite conversation with a leading member of their royal family. Ohthere smiled again.

"You can stop waving it around now Beowulf, you are frightening the horses."

Taking his arm he motioned that he follow him to the dead ground between the two forces.

"I need to talk to you privately Beowulf, if you would be so kind. I would consider it a great personal favour if you would hear me out."

Intrigued, Beowulf walked alongside Ohthere to a point out of earshot of either force. He flicked a glance up at the men of the Geat shield hedge. They had slowly grown silent and watched in confusion as the pair made their way towards them. They too seemed to be having trouble adjusting to the events unfolding before them. When safely out of earshot, Ohthere stopped and looked up at the Geat position.

"Impressive, I like your use of rocks to disrupt the cohesion of the charge. I must remember that one. Not as impressive as the use of a beaver dam though, I nearly broke my neck trying to get through that morass!" he laughed. "Don't be so impulsive though," he continued. "There was no need for you to leave your defences and challenge everyone to a fight. It lacked maturity and made you look foolish, and it would seem that I need you to live a long life."

Now thoroughly bemused, Beowulf waited as Ohthere paused and stared into the distance. Clearly he had something important to say and was having trouble finding the right words. Finally the ætheling found his tongue.

"We have a holy man with us, a wizard. Smelly bastard, lives in the same rags which I remember him wearing when I was a child. Anyway, he may smell like a troll's outhouse, but there is no denying that he has the ears of the gods. He talks to them and they talk through him, Beowulf, and when they do I tend to believe what they say. He has rarely been mistaken in his interpretations of their messages. He said that it was unclear whether you would survive this day because you have recently upset one of Woden's maidens and he had removed his protection from you as punishment."

Beowulf looked at him in shock as his hand moved to the shard of wood which Hrani had gifted him. He understood now why it had remained cool throughout the heavy fighting.

"I can see from your face that that obviously meant something to you, so you should believe me when I ask this favour of you." Ohthere continued. "It would seem that should you live through this day, at some time in the future my sons Eanmund and Eadgils will need to seek the protection of your cousin Heardred and yourself. I have seen what type of man you are so I am confident that you will act with honour. Our fates seemed to be linked in some way and I regret that we cannot fight on the same side. Maybe when peace returns between our people you would honour me with a visit to my hall to meet the boys, they are about your age. You can hunt in my forests and fill my stores with boar and venison!"

"I would be honoured, lord," Beowulf replied.

"Thank you Beowulf, I am in your debt." Ohthere smiled and nodded at the big Geat.

"We are leaving now," he continued. "It seems that you told the truth at the river. Your king had not sailed to Jute Land yet after all. He is an hour or so away from here with his host, according to my scouts, so we must be on our way." Ohthere started to leave before pausing and looking back. "Oh, there was one other thing that the wizard said. He told me that you would cross the sea to fight a creature that could not be killed or harmed by metal blades. So that is something for you to look forward to!" he smiled.

Beowulf watched as Ohthere strode back to the watching Swedish warriors. "Back to your mounts boys," he called with a sweep of his arm, "let's get going, we have done our work here." With a cheer and clashing of weapons they turned as one and began to make their way to the horses which were beginning to be brought up to their rear.

Beowulf watched as they mounted and, forming columns, quickly began to leave the field. Soon the last of the Swedish force were disappearing back along the road which led to the border.

After the noise and confusion of the day, an eerie silence seemed to descend on the gorge.

Beowulf stood and regarded the battlefield, now revealed before him. A sad line of broken and blood stained bodies marked the position in the original Geat shield wall where the Swedish attack had punched through. A smattering of bodies lay where they had fallen as they attempted to flee from the carnage, only to be run down by the Swedish mounted warriors. Occasional heaps of bodies marked the positions where groups of men had tried desperately to rally and face the onslaught.

The field itself had been churned into a sea of mud by the hundreds of feet and hooves which had traversed its length as the fighting ebbed and flowed in the driving rain. Several horses lay impaled on the stakes which had been driven into the ground in front of the Geatish wall for just that purpose.

Beowulf looked at the small force surrounding Wulfgar in the centre of the gorge. Still in their defensive position they looked like a giant hawthorn he thought to himself.

Over on the far side he could see Wulf's men beginning to relax and leave their shield wall.

He looked back at his own men. Despite the fact that the enemy had left the field they remained in their positions, arms to the fore, faithfully fulfilling the last order they received from their lord.

Slightly ashamed, he recalled Ohthere's words to him about maturity. He *had* been foolish. He must learn to control his impulses. Wearily he indicated that the men come down and join him.

Together, with heavy hearts, they tramped across the mire to join the rest of the survivors. They had survived the onslaught but there was no disguising the enormity of their defeat. Beowulf estimated that nearly half the men who had stood with him at the beginning of the day now lay broken and bloody around him.

The Troll's Hat had become the Hreosnahill.

Sorrow Hill.

THE FIRST OF the Geat relief force arrived, as promised, within the hour.

A score of horsemen were the first to come into view, led, Beowulf saw to his great joy, by his father, Ecgtheow.

The survivors had now consolidated their position at the centre of the gorge and although the danger had passed, their warrior's pride had led them to maintain a sound defensive position until the relief force arrived.

Wulfgar, Wulf and Beowulf emerged, wearily, from the defences as Ecgtheow and his men reined in.

"You are a very welcome sight, but I am afraid we have already seen them off!" Wulfgar called as they approached, his men proudly cheering and clashing their shields behind him.

Ecgtheow dismounted and embraced Wulfgar. "I am sorry we took so long old friend." He began. "We were all but on the ships before word reached us of the attack. Hythcyn should be passing through the town by now with the army, they will be here soon."

Beowulf noted that his father had called the king by his

name and not his title. He also saw that it had not gone unnoticed by Wulfgar and Wulf. He had been away from the intrigues in the South for a while and was thankful for it. He was surprised that his father had been so loose with his words. Either Ecgtheow was growing clumsy with age, which he doubted very much, or something was going on here which he was not as yet party to. He would make sure that he approached his father about it when the opportunity arose.

Ecgtheow nodded to Beowulf and Wulf in greeting. "Woden's eye!" he exclaimed as he looked around the battlefield. "It must have been some fight, how many of them were there?"

"Six, seven hundred?" Wulfgar guessed. "We were a bit too busy for an accurate count!" he laughed. "Luckily I had thought to send a force to the border to delay them there for as long as they could. It enabled me to gather as many men as I could for the main defence here. I sent Beowulf along there as well to gain experience."

For a moment Beowulf thought that he must have misheard as he listened, aghast, as Wulfgar claimed the credit for the fight at the river. It had been his plan and he had commanded the forces there. In fact he had had to almost beg Wulfgar for any men for the enterprise.

"Well done Beowulf! I am pleased that you are learning to fight under men like Bjorn, he is a good warrior." His father stood, beaming, in front of him. "Let me look at you. You certainly seem as though you saw some action, what happened to your helm?"

Beowulf fought against the conflicting emotions of confusion and anger which were fighting for control of him. He flicked a look at Wulfgar who was continuing to describe the battle as if he had been there.

"A sword strike lord, I managed to duck inside the blow, as you taught me once," he stammered.

"Well done!" Ecgtheow gave him an affectionate hug. "We'll have to get that plate replaced before you see your mother though!" he quipped.

Wulfgar and Ecgtheow moved off to inspect the battle-field. Already crows and ravens were worrying the corpses. Overhead a pair of golden eagles circled in the evening sky. Soon it would be dark enough for the foxes and wolves to emerge from their hiding places to gorge on the dead.

Anger suddenly coursed through Beowulf's veins like liquid fire. With a snarl he turned and sucked in a breath to shout a repudiation of Wulfgar's version of the events of the last two days. Before he could act, a strong hand gripped him by the arm and pulled him to one side.

"Forgive me, lord. Now is not the time or place to make a scene. Let the old warrior have his moment of glory. Walk with me for a moment and I can help you."

Beowulf jerked around ready to strike whoever had laid a hand on him. To his surprise Bjorn had emerged from the line of warriors and was gesturing, pleadingly, with his arm. Beowulf shrugged Bjorn's hand away and made to confront Wulfgar.

"Please, lord. Let me explain."

The slight delay had been enough to allow the first rush of anger to abate slightly. He regarded Bjorn. He had fought with him and thought that he earned the right to be granted this one, small, request.

"Make it quick!" he stormed as he walked briskly away from the others.

"Thank you, lord," Bjorn began when they paused after a few moments.

"May I speak plainly, warrior to warrior, lord?"

Beowulf stared ahead, his lips still pursed in anger. Finally he gave a curt nod.

"If you listen to what I am about to say you can become a better warrior and an even better lord. We have fought together and you know that I am a straightforward and honest man and that I will speak the truth to you. You have had a privileged upbringing compared to the rest of the men here. The son of an ealdorman, fostered with an ætheling and the grandson of the king. You have learnt about how to fight and command, that much is clear," he smiled, "but you have not had to learn about how to follow. Every one of the warriors here knows that the fighting at the border was your plan and that you led the forces there. They even know of your pledge to the men that you would be the last to leave and that you kept that promise. It means a lot to them that you value their lives so highly. You have built a reputation to be proud of over the last few days. Likewise every warrior knows that he fights for his lord, and his lord fights for victory. Wulfgar is ealdorman here not Beowulf. *You* fought for him but *he* had the victory. Every detail of what happened here will soon become common knowledge, from the lowliest swineherd to the king himself. These men," he indicated with a sweep of his arm, "will be plied with ale and begged to regale every gathering they attend from now until they lay on their funeral pyre with the tale of these battles, and the tale they tell will be of Beowulf and Wulfgar, not just Wulfgar. If you can learn to keep your composure your reputation will grow even greater."

Beowulf's gaze drifted across the broken and bloody corpses as he listened to Bjorn's words.

It was the second time that day that he had been told that he was acting like a spoilt child he reflected, both times by men he respected.

He realised that he was fortunate that men of their calibre had taken the time to offer him their advice.

"Thank you, Bjorn. I appreciate what you have said. It must have been difficult for you to approach someone of higher rank and say those words."

Bjorn gave a relieved smile. "It does you credit lord, that I felt able to."

A cheery call came from their right. "Have you been fighting again?"

Beowulf turned towards the voices. Standing ten feet away, hands on hips and smiling broadly, stood Ecgtheow's hearth warriors Bjalki and Orme. Beowulf grinned. He had known both of them since he was a boy, and being the privileged son of an ealdorman, Bjalki in particular had been the closest he had had to a friend in his earliest years.

"Look Bjorn, there are two warriors! Look at their shiny armour and sharp blades. I wonder if they have ever had the chance to use them." He teased. Orme shook his head as he looked Beowulf over with a practised eye.

"You look like shit, lord!"

Beowulf laughed. It was good to back amongst old friends.

"Thanks, Orme. I feel even worse."

KING HYTHCYN ARRIVED SHORTLY after with the main Geat army.

Initially Beowulf and Wulfgar greeted the king, but it soon became clear that Beowulf was exhausted.

Red eyes stared dully from twin dark circles on his lined and grimy face. His clothes and armour were encrusted with mud, blood and gore from the fighting.

"When was the last time you slept kinsman?" Hythcyn had asked, concerned by his haggard appearance when he saw him.

Beowulf tried to think but it was becoming beyond his capabilities. Eventually Wulfgar volunteered an answer for him.

"It has been two full days since he has had any rest and three since he had a regular night's sleep. He has fought two battles, one each day, lord."

Hythcyn stepped forward and put an arm affectionately around his nephew's shoulder. "You have done more than your duty to me and our people. Go and rest now. Ealdorman Wulfgar can describe the events here. We will talk again when you wake."

A small part of Beowulf's brain told him that he should remain and ensure that the king got the true version of events but he really was too tired to care. He was sure that Bjorn was right. The truth would find its way out eventually. He had increased his reputation amongst the Geat warriors and had become known as a leading Geat warrior amongst the Swedes. If that was all the recognition he gained for his efforts of the last few days, it would be enough.

As he left the king and his entourage he spotted Ulf hobbling along, supported by one of his men.

"Beowulf, have some ale, you deserve it!" he called.

"I deserve sleep more!" he countered, wearily. "Have you seen my man, Gunnar?"

"He said he had left something over by our wagon," he replied, indicating their old defensive position by the gorge wall.

Wearily Beowulf trudged the hundred yards over to the place. He called Gunnar's name but there was no reply.

Exasperated he was about to leave when he heard the

sound of soft breathing coming from the floor of the wagon. Peering over the side he saw that Gunnar had collapsed, exhausted, onto the stack of spears and was sleeping deeply.

Managing a smile, Beowulf picked up a discarded cloak and threw it over the sleeping form of his hearth warrior. He turned to go but the distance back to the tents seemed to have grown enormously and he was suddenly overwhelmed by the crushing need to sleep. Physically and mentally spent he managed to drag himself up onto the pile of spears and lay down next to Gunnar.

Drawing his cloak about him he closed his eyes and was swallowed by the darkness.

18

"*L*ord...lord.*" A voice, remote but insistent, entered his thoughts.

"I have brought you some food and drink. The king is asking for you."

Beowulf rolled on his back and exhaled. Flinging back his heavy cloak, he winced as the strong sunlight fell across his upturned face. Reaching up he rubbed his face with his hands, hoping that it would help him to focus on the intruder's words.

He had been in a deep sleep and his body was struggling to return to the blissful state. His eyes were still warm and heavy and he longed to close them again and pull his cloak back around him.

"Lord, King Hythcyn wants you. He sent me to fetch you."

Beowulf surrendered with a sigh.

"Gunnar?"

"Yes, lord, the kin…"

"Yes, I know the king wants to see me. How long have I been asleep?"

"Well the Yule celebrations went off well and…"

"Gunnar, don't arse about," he grunted. "You have just woken me from a blissful sleep and I am surrounded by very sharp spears."

"Sorry, lord. Getting on for a full day. It is late in the afternoon and the king is asking for you."

"Is he, well he will have to wait until I take a leak."

Swinging his legs down from the wagon, Beowulf sighed as he relieved himself against one of the wheels.

"That's better, give me some ale Gunnar and we can go and make the king happy."

Taking up his arms from the place he had stacked them the previous evening Beowulf and Gunnar made their way back across the valley floor to King Hythcyn's tent which had now been erected near Wulfgar's old defensive position.

Beowulf noticed that men had been busy while he slept.

The bodies of the enemy warriors burned on a pyre at the far side of the field. The Geat dead had been collected, cleaned as best they could, and laid out along the far wall of the gorge. Word had been sent to Edet and the surrounding settlements that any families who feared that their men had perished in the fighting would be given three days in which to come and claim the bodies. Thereafter they would have to be burnt individually and interred at the king's expense.

Already, fearful looking women and children were beginning to arrive from the town, he noticed, sadly.

The bodies of several foxes and crows lay strewn across the field, the arrows puncturing their bodies telling their own tale. Ravens still picked at will at these last windfalls. Ravens belonged to Woden and no warrior in his right mind would harm one unless he wanted to spend eternity with Hel, the half decayed goddess of the underworld.

Beowulf spotted Hythcyn surrounded by a coterie of warriors near the tents.

"Beowulf, there you are!" he hailed him as he caught sight of his approach. "The gods man, you look as though you've been in a war!"

The group of finely attired warriors around him laughed at his weak joke, as Beowulf ran a contemptuous eye over them.

Nithings.

Beowulf looked at himself for the first time. His hands were the colour of the earth, his fine clothes lay in tatters and his mail byrnie was still encrusted with blood and, it looked like, brains. His heavy leather battle coat was smeared with various substances which he had no wish to examine more closely, and his metal arm guards and byrnie were beginning to show the first misting of rust where they rubbed together, a result of the fighting at the river and the effects of the downpour during the thunderstorm. He knew that his helm had a great jagged hole on the top and was no doubt just as battered and grimy as the rest of his armour.

"They are marks of honour, Beowulf," Hythcyn smiled, "but there is no need to wear them forever."

The watching warriors smiled again.

"I have heard all about your efforts, both at the border and here, from several people and they all agree that you fought bravely."

"And commanded!" Beowulf snapped.

The king smiled and laid a hand on Beowulf's arm. "Rest assured that I know everything, kinsman. I am the king. It is my duty to know who fights well for me so that they can be justly rewarded. My steward will find some clean clothes for you while you clean yourself up. The armourers will clean and repair your other equipment and have it ready for you.

We will talk then. I have an important task which I want you to perform for me. There is a pool over there where you can wash yourself. Heardred is over there I believe," he smiled.

Beowulf and Gunnar swiftly made their way over to the place which Hythcyn had indicated. Heardred was sitting on a rock, grinning, as they approached. Beowulf tried to hug his cousin in greeting but he managed to scramble out of the way.

"You are not touching me, you filthy bastard!" he called back with a laugh.

Beowulf removed his armour and clothes and tossed them to the waiting steward. Grinning, he spread his arms wide.

"Cousin!"

"I am definitely not hugging you now!" Heardred exclaimed. With a yell Beowulf jumped into the pond, surfacing with a gasp. "Shit, that's cold!"

"Sorry, we tried to find you a warm pond, but this was the best we could do." With a flick of his head Heardred indicated two heavily armed men who stood nearby. "These are my Bronding minders."

"Lord." They nodded, respectfully.

Beowulf threw Heardred a questioning glance.

"It seems that my father had already sailed to take on the Jutes when the message about the Swedish attack reached Miklaborg. A ship was sent after them but they haven't returned yet. These boys are here to make sure that I don't go and join him I guess. I don't know what Hygelac is up to but he wouldn't abandon my mother, so your guess is as good as mine where he has got to."

Beowulf pondered the situation.

What was Hygelac up to?

A wicked thought came to him as he vigorously rubbed the grime from his body.

"I hope that neither of you boys hail from Skovde?" he called across to the Bronding warriors.

"Lord?"

"I watched it burning from a ridge three or four days ago."

The pair exchanged a shocked look.

"Clearly they have not been let in on the news yet," Heardred grinned delightedly.

"You are nothing but trouble, Beowulf. I have missed you. Tell me about the fighting and I won't throw these great big rocks into the water!" he laughed.

BEOWULF AND GUNNAR retraced their steps to King Hythcyn's tent. The steward had returned with new clothes but the arms and armour were still being repaired and polished he was told.

Beowulf felt reinvigorated after his long sleep and his immersion in the ice cold water of the pond. He was back to himself, he felt, practically fizzing with energy. He had felt a pang of remorse at leaving Heardred under virtual guard but he realised that there was not much he could do to help his cousin at the moment. He decided to bring the matter up with the king if the opportunity arose. Hythcyn emerged from the tent just as they arrived. He smiled broadly at Beowulf, motioning that he follow him.

"I need to discuss our plans with my kinsman," he announced to the throng of warriors which trailed along in his wake, "would you be kind enough to allow us some privacy?"

They all nodded their assent and returned, no doubt, Beowulf thought, to draining the king's ale.

He was pleased to see that Gunnar had heard the king's

words and already moved away. Beowulf was pleased with him. He was not only intelligent and brave but he did not always have to be told what to do.

"You have had a hard few days but you survived and grew from the experience. You look older than when you left Miklaborg last week." Hythcyn began. They were slowly pacing the ground between where the Geat shield wall had stood, all too briefly, and the position from which the Swedes had launched their attack. Very little now distinguished the area from any other in the gorge, Beowulf noticed. Already the grass had begun to recover from the pounding it had received that day. With the removal of the bodies, stakes and stray weapons it was already becoming difficult to imagine it as a place of slaughter. Soon the rains would wash away the last traces of blood from the grass and the battle will exist only in the minds of the combatants and the scops, those who recounted the great deeds of the past.

Hythcyn paused and surveyed the scene, as if imagining the battle. His expression hardened, and Beowulf saw the mask of amiability which Hythcyn had perfected over the last months slip away and be replaced with the look of cold anger and hatred which he remembered from the past. He had had a momentary glimpse of the old calculating Hythcyn and it had, he had to admit to himself, unnerved him. Hythcyn continued, his gaze still distant,

"We are taking the fight back to them Beowulf. Who do these æthelings think that they are, that they can come to our land and use it and its people for sport while we are away?"

Beowulf was shocked. To his knowledge no Geat army had ever before invaded Swede Land. They were simply too small since their cousins, the Goths, had crossed the sea to the south and gone in search of new lands.

"I see from your expression that you are surprised kinsman." Hythcyn smiled, his composure regained. "That is why we will succeed! They will not be expecting it either, but this can only be the work of the gods. We have a large, fully equipped army, already mobilised and gathered for war, completely provisioned for an extended campaign in a foreign land. We have a steadfast, and now outraged, ally in the Bronding king, Hrothulf."

"If he lives, lord," Beowulf put in. "I saw the Bronding capital burning with my own eyes. Surely Hrothulf would have stayed and fought. He may well be dead."

"It will make no difference. Whoever their king is, they will fight with us. Ealdorman Alfhelm accompanied the Bronding ætheling, Wigmund, to Skovde early this morning with his hearth warriors while you were still sleeping. He will rejoin us on the march, with or without his father's blessing, if, as you rightly point out, he still lives. Your father, Ecgtheow, left with a strong force to shadow the Swedes and ensure that they are intending to return home and not double back and hit us again elsewhere. I am going to wait here a further ten days to give the rest of the army and the provisions time to travel here from the coast."

Hythcyn turned and, to his surprise, gripped Beowulf by the shoulders.

"I have a special task for you Beowulf. The king of the Swedes, Ongentheow, must move with his army against me when I invade his lands and that will present us, you, with an opportunity which is too great to miss. I want you to take the fleet which was assembled to attack the Jutes and sail to the Swedish capital at Uppsala. Burn it for me. Let them know that if they attack and burn our towns then we will attack and burn theirs. Take fire and sword to the lair of the beast and burn his black heart out!"

Beowulf struggled to accept the dramatic change in his

position over the course of the past few days. The last time he had seen the king he had been the barely trusted son of a potentially mutinous lord, practically a hostage. Now it seems he was to command one of the most audacious raids in the history of his people.

"May I ask one favour of you, lord?"

"Of course, name it and I will fulfil it if it is in my power to do so." Hythcyn smiled.

"I would like Heardred to accompany me."

Beowulf watched as the king's smile fell from his features.

"I know the situation with his father, your brother Hygelac, but I have spoken to him and I am convinced that he feels that his father would never abandon his mother. I don't know what Hygelac is up to any more than you do, but I would be surprised if it was not for the benefit of our folk."

"You ask a lot," Hythcyn finally replied. "Together they could pose a powerful threat to my position as king if they had a mind to."

"I will give you my word that I will return to you at the end of this campaign. I would insist that Heardred also gave his word."

Hythcyn pursed his lips as he thought.

Beowulf watched hopefully as the king deliberated.

"You have earned the right to my trust Beowulf. If Heardred gives such an undertaking he would be free to join you. He *is* experienced in such operations after all. He could be a great asset to you. Come, I have an old friend of yours drinking my ale at the moment. I am sure that you will be glad to see him again."

They crossed the last few yards to the tent and stepped inside. The familiar smells of warriors on campaign washed

over them, ale, meat, oiled leather and sweat. Beowulf immediately felt at home.

As his eyes adjusted to the light he noticed a big man rise
from one of the benches with a grin.

"Are we to sail together again, lord?"

He smiled as the man approached him, taking the proffered horn of ale.

"It would seem so Hudda."

"I KNEW that I could count on you, you wily old fox!"

Beowulf and Heardred rode abreast of each other as the
column of warriors made their way along the gorge which led
back to the town of Edet. Ahead of them rode Wulfgar and
Bjorn. With his forces depleted by the fighting, Wulfgar had
been entrusted with the safety of the Geat kingdom while the
king was campaigning in Swede Land. Wulfgar and Bjorn
were to travel on to Miklaborg while Ulf remained at Edet to
recover from his leg wound.

Despite his new prominence in the Geat forces he had
insisted that Wulfgar and his leading warrior lead them back
into his home town, the town which they had shed so much
blood to defend. Bjorn had caught his eye as they had
mounted their horses outside the king's headquarters and had
subtly inclined his head to Beowulf in thanks for the gesture.
Beowulf had returned the smile. The more he had thought on
the advice that Bjorn had offered him the day that his father
had arrived, the more he had come to appreciate it. It was
obvious to him that his reputation amongst both the men and
their leaders alike had only increased through his, apparent,
self control, and still the full story of the fighting had become

common knowledge. His promotion to head of the fleet was proof of that.

Behind Beowulf and Heardred rode Hudda and Gunnar who seemed to have become almost inseparable since they had found out that they were both sailors. Eventually the others had grown tired of their continual 'you call that a wave! I remember once…' tales and they had been banished to the rear of the column.

As they neared the outskirts of the town the first signs of destruction appeared. A few of the outlying huts which lined the road lay blackened and burnt, their skeletal structures lying haphazardly where they had finally collapsed. Beowulf noticed that all the animal pens had been emptied and there was not a horse in sight. There was certainly going to be no shortage of horses in Swede Land when the raiders returned. They had also rounded up and driven before them all of the mounts which the Geat warriors and levy had corralled to the rear of their position in the gorge, including his own which had contained all his spare clothing and other belongings. Luckily he had been wearing his armour and weapons, which now, newly repaired and polished, shone like new. Still, the only shirt and trousers which had been fine enough for one of his rank were too small and every discomfort he felt reminded him of the ignominy of their defeat.

"It doesn't seem as though the townsfolk tried too hard to extinguish the flames of your toll booth over there!" Heardred quipped.

"They won't feel so clever when I raise the duties to pay for a new one," Wulfgar frowned in response, much to Beowulf and Heardred's amusement.

Entering Edet they were pleased to see that the damage was really quite slight. A few of the better class buildings had obviously been ransacked for any easily moveable wealth by the marauding Swedes and a few of them had had their thatch roughly pulled off, but, as it lay spread in piles against the walls of the buildings it should be reusable he thought. It was a common place for people to hide valuable objects and the thatch was often one of the first things to be pulled apart in any sack. Wulfgar's mood lightened considerably when he saw that only the halls of the richest merchants seemed to have been touched.

"Serves them right, the tight bastards," he beamed. "I only wish that I could have joined in!"

The townsfolk had already largely repaired any damage in the short time since Hythcyn's arrival and they stopped to watch the arrival of their ealdorman. Beowulf watched as tears of pride filled Wulfgar's eyes when the population of the town broke into spontaneous applause and cheering as they passed through on the way to his hall where they would spend the night. It was possibly the proudest moment in the old man's life and Beowulf was pleased that he had had the opportunity to contribute to it.

"You go on up with the others, cousin," Beowulf remarked to Heardred, "I have something to attend to in the town before I join you."

Heardred raised his eyebrows in surprise and smirked. "Is she pretty?"

Beowulf chuckled before adding cryptically. "She could be given the chance. But I need to find her a mother first."

GUNNAR ASKED amongst the townsfolk if there were any of the women from the dock area still in the town. Unsurprisingly they seemed to have returned home once the Swedish riders had left and the Geatish army had arrived. They were about to leave the town and retrace their steps to the docks when a woman came running behind them, calling out to them. They curbed their mounts and waited for her to reach them. Beowulf and Gunnar watched, amused, as the woman continually nodded her head in deference and attempted to speak. Holding her sides and blowing hard from the effects of the short run she eventually managed to gasp out, "the girl… lord… she is in there," waving a flabby arm towards a barn which lay off to one side of the road.

Tossing the woman a silver coin, Beowulf and Gunnar dismounted and allowed the woman to lead the way as she slowly recovered from her obviously rare bout of physical exertion.

"My sister has her, lord. She looked after her just as you ordered, she's been well treated and well fed, you'll see."

Arriving at the barn the woman disappeared inside and re-emerged moments later with her sister and Ursula.

The young girl tried to hide behind the skirts of the woman as she saw Beowulf and Gunnar.

Beowulf cursed himself for being so thoughtless. Why hadn't he thought to bring one of the women from Wulf-gar's hall to take care of the traumatised girl? She was bound to feel threatened by them after the experiences she must have suffered at the hands of the watchman and his cronies.

"Do you remember me, Ursula?" he asked, gently.

She nodded shyly and whispered. "You are the lord who killed my master."

"Do you remember Gunnar? He was a sailor at the dock."

She gave a nod and a slight smile.

"I don't remember seeing her, lord." Gunnar muttered to Beowulf.

"That doesn't matter Gunnar. She doesn't seem to be

afraid of you and that is all that is important at the moment," he murmured back.

"Would you let Gunnar take you to the ealdorman's hall where some of the women there could look after you?"

Ursula's face relaxed slightly and she gave a small nod.

"Come on then, you can ride on my horse and I will walk alongside you and make sure that you don't fall off." Gunnar smiled encouragingly at the girl.

She shuffled forward and Gunnar helped her up into the saddle. Beowulf tossed the woman a pouch of silver for her trouble. He had wanted to ask her why none of the women or men at the dockyard had intervened to stop the abuse but he decided that he really didn't want to learn any more details of the people there than was necessary. The whole business had left him feeling dirtier than he had after the battle and he just wanted to put as much distance between himself and them as possible, as quickly as possible.

Obviously there were some decent people there. Gunnar was based there on occasion, although he would have slept on the boat and not seen what was going on, so they must have been afraid to challenge the gang, he decided. He resolved to mention the situation at the dock to Wulfgar and Ulf. They needed to maintain a greater presence there to stamp on any wrongdoing.

As they walked through the town Beowulf listened as Gunnar talked in his friendly, relaxed manner. Slowly Ursula became less guarded in her replies.

As they led the horses up the shallow rise which led to Wulfgar's hall, Beowulf felt as if he was climbing up into a cleaner, more wholesome world.

THEY LEFT Wulfgar's hall after a late breakfast.

The previous evening had been given over to a riotous celebration of life, as the warriors who had fought in the battle reacquainted themselves with the pleasures of the hall. It had been a defeat of sorts but they had succeeded in keeping the vast majority of the enemy away from the town and the interior of the kingdom. They knew that they had only been overwhelmed by superior numbers and their bravery and honour had never been questioned.

Beowulf and Gunnar had arranged for Ursula to spend the night in the care of the wives of some of the warriors. A few of Wulfgar's warriors had been with him long enough to have been given permission to start a family and Wulfgar had built quarters for the men to enable them to have a semblance of a normal family life.

One of the women had approached Beowulf earlier that morning and asked if she might accompany the child until she was settled. Beowulf had gratefully accepted the offer. He had considered asking if the child could remain with one of the families there but decided that it would be asking too much of a warrior to take on another man's child, whatever the circumstances, and it would place them in an embarrassing position if he asked.

Once they had left the immediate vicinity of the town the traffic on the road south quickly diminished. Slowly they left the sounds of the waterfall and rapids behind them as they moved on into the soft heart of the kingdom.

The valley of the Geat River lay before them, seemingly dozing in the sultry heat of midday, when they decided to rest. The day was hot and they were in no great hurry. Beowulf had several days to accomplish the visits he had planned before he sailed with the fleet. They relaxed awhile in the shade before moving on. He watched as the woman and girl sat on the bank cooling their feet in the tumbling waters of the river. Near the opposite bank a heron stood, immobile, its eyes focused on the water for any sign of movement beneath the surface. Ursula squealed in delight as a dragonfly skimmed the surface of the river before it darted along the bank and became lost from view.

Moving on they soon came to the small hamlet of Little Edet. The others rode on and waited at the far side of the village. Beowulf dismounted and led them to the farm on the outskirts, alongside which stood the familiar enclosure with its now healthy cow. Screams and cries coming from high in the trees to the rear of the farm confirmed that he had come to the right place.

"Hello? Is there anyone in there?" Beowulf called from the courtyard.

The couple came out of their home and lowered their heads respectfully as they saw him.

"How's the cow?"

"She is fine now, lord."

He could sense their confusion. It can't be every day that a lord comes around enquiring about the health of their cow. He almost laughed aloud at the idea. "I have a proposition to put to you. I will pay you for your help and be in your debt. Are you interested?"

The couple shot each other a nervous glance. "We will do your bidding whatever you order us to do, lord. We are loyal Geats and we are already in the debt of you and the holy woman."

"This is not an order. I will only enter into this agreement with your honest and full support, do you understand? There will be no consequences to you if you do not wish to do this. You are completely free to say no to me."

"We understand, lord."

"Those *are* your children? Henrik and Hanna, the ones I paid to hold my horse last time I was here."

The couple nodded, glumly. *What have they done now?*

"I like their spirit. They look happy and healthy. They are a credit to you both." Beowulf smiled at them as they visibly relaxed. "I have a girl of about their age who I need to find a loving home for. She has had a bad time but I think that she would be lucky to grow up in a family like yours. In return I would pay you a regular amount until she reaches adulthood." Beowulf paused to let his offer sink in. "I will bring her over and you can decide."

Beowulf went over to the woman's horse. As he did so the children ran, noisily, into the courtyard. Seeing him standing there they slid to a halt in a cloud of dust.

"Where have you been Henrik?" he asked.

"We were swinging in the top of a tree when we saw you come down the road with the other warriors, lord. We were coming to watch you go past." He paused before narrowing his eyes shrewdly. "I have spent the silver, lord."

Beowulf laughed. "I don't want the silver back Henrik, or yours Hanna. It was honestly earned." He looked back at the farmer and his wife. They were smiling.

"We would be happy to add her to our family, lord, what is her name?"

"Ursula," he replied.

HE PAUSED JUST before the farm was lost to view around a bend and tried to fix the scene in his memory. The hall nestled against the side of the valley. White lime washed walls and brown thatch.

Beowulf watched as the mother gave her three children

something to drink before two of them raced back into the woods, calling on the other one, the skinny one, to follow. He watched as she hesitated before slowly following them. By the time that they were disappearing into the tree line she had summoned up her courage and was racing after them. He was almost overwhelmed with happiness. To his surprise he found that of all the things which he had accomplished over the last few hectic days, finding a little girl a home had given him the most pleasure.

He urged his horse on and cantered after the others.

"You were successful then," Wulfgar observed as he drew up with them.

He nodded, not wishing to speak in case his emotions gave him away. They seemed to realise anyway.

"It was a good thing, lord," Gunnar added. "There's no room for a young girl where we are going."

A splash came from the river on his right. Midstream an otter lay on his back, watching them as it gnawed hungrily on the head of a fish.

Is that the same otter that I watched with Kaija?

The events of the last few days came flooding back into his memory. Skovde burning, the fight at the river, beheading the giant Swedish warrior, Ohthere's strange warning,

He told me that you would cross the sea to fight a creature that could not be killed or harmed by metal blades.

"Beowulf…cousin?"

"Yes, Heardred?"

"We need to leave now if we are to make Miklaborg by evening."

He flashed them a grin, crying out. "Well, why are we waiting here then?"

Urging his horse into a gallop, he laughed as he heard the whoops and shouts as they urged their mounts after his. He was a lord of men, good fighting men. He had out-thought a cunning and powerful enemy and been rewarded by his king on the field of battle with command of the largest, best equipped fleet the Geats had ever prepared.

He was on his way to his enemy's lair to burn out his black heart with fire and sword!

AFTERWORD

The Beowulf poem is rightly considered a jewel of Anglo-Saxon England. If that fabulous jewel can be said to contain a flaw for the general reader today it could be argued that it lies in the very framework upon which the poem is built. Written down over one thousand years ago and dealing with events which were even then hundreds of years old, the original *scop* had woven a tale to appeal to an audience more familiar with concepts of honour and reputation. Likewise there are references to ideas, values and historic events which must have been familiar to the original audiences but are now lost to us.

For this, and the following novels in this trilogy, I have endeavoured to anchor the story to key events mentioned throughout the original poem. For example when the adult Beowulf's arrival is announced to King Hrothgar he replies, "I used to know him as a young boy," from which statement I developed the episode of the journey to, and adventures in, Hleidra, modern day Ljeira. Likewise the Danish port at Roskilde becomes the more ancient Hroars Kilde.

Other episodes in Beowulf's youth are recalled throughout the poem, the swimming match with Breca, the fight with 'sea monsters' and his boast of killing trolls, an episode which will appear in book two, Wræcca. Although there is no evidence that Beowulf, if he actually existed at all, was ever fostered with his uncle Hygelac, this would have been an entirely plausible arrangement. Heroic Germanic society attached a special relationship between a man and the son of his sister and fostering helped to reinforce ties of kinship and obligation.

Although the location of the Geat kingdom seems to wander over much of modern day southern Sweden according to which book you read, I have chosen to centre it on the modern town of Kungalv in Vastra Gotaland. Situated, as described, at the juncture of two rivers it was ideally placed to control access to the interior and was the location of the fortress of Miklaborg. The main port in the area I have chosen to call Geatwic, which means 'Market place of the Geats', now known as the port of Gothenburg. Edet is the former name of Trollhattan, to the north of which lies the mountain known as the Troll's Hat. From here the Gota River, which I have changed to the Geat River, flows south, past Miklaborg/Kungalv to the sea. Ecgtheow's hall lies near the town of Skansen, modern day Kungsbakka.

I chose to use the older Germanic names for the deities than the more familiar, later, names which were recorded by Christian chroniclers in Viking times. Thus Odin becomes Woden, Thor becomes Thunor etc. I felt that this was not only more accurate for the time in which our tale is set but will better reflect the growing links which will become more apparent between the Geat homeland and the new Anglian kingdom, centred on their great port at Gippeswic (Ipswich), which was developing on the other side of the North Sea, as our story progresses.

One area of my tale which may have been controversial

not so long ago is the use of sails, masts and figureheads. It used to be an 'Established Fact' that the ships of this period were too weak to use masts and sails and were in effect large rowing boats awaiting the development of the heavy keel during the Viking age. However more recent research, both theoretical and practical, has proven that this was not the case. Indeed the flat bottomed, leaf shaped, design of these hulls were ideal for use in the rivers and shallow waters of the North Sea and Baltic. Not only were they more practical while on the move but they were able to be beached easily without tipping onto one side. Several carved figure heads dating from this period and earlier have been recovered from the River Scheldt in present day Belgium and there is written evidence from Roman sources of the Franks using such vessels, with sail, dating from at least 250A.D. The Beowulf poem of course describes how the Geats...

"...sailed from Denmark. Right away the mast was rigged with its sea-shawl; sail-ropes were tightened...."

The only area in which I may have knowingly strayed is in the use of the term Dracca, Dragon, for the warships of the period. It was just too descriptive not to use and perhaps it would be surprising if the people of that time, given the evidence contained within the Beowulf poem and other examples of their work, did not call their vessels at least something very similar.

Hythcyn may or may not have killed his brother by accident but it seems as certain as our scant sources allow us that he was in fact responsible for this act and that it lead, indirectly, to the old king's death. Herebeald would not be the first, or last, heir to the throne to die in suspicious circumstances. If I have wrongfully besmirched his character I can but apologise to his spirit.

In the following volume Beowulf leads the Geat fleet to

the Swedish capital at Uppsala as the Geats strike back at their enemy. Amid the fighting which sweeps across the land, kings rise and fall and reputations are won and lost.

Meanwhile the first stories of a Night Horror in Dane Land begin to reach the North.

Cliff May
East Anglia
March 2013

CHARACTERS

ALFHELM - Ealdorman of Geatwic.

ASTRID - Daughter of Hygelac. Beowulf's cousin.

BEOWULF - Son of Ecgtheow. Grandson of King Hrethel.

BINNI - A one armed veteran at Miklaborg.

BJALKI – Ecgtheow's leading hearth warrior.

BJORN - Wulfgar of Edet's leading hearth warrior.

BRECA - Bronding foster son of Hythcyn. Beowulf's opponent in the skating race and the swimming match.

COLA - Guard at Eadgar's workshop in Geatwic.

EADGAR - Craftsman at Geatwic.

EADGILS - Younger son of Ohthere, brother of Eanmund. A Swedish prince.

EALHSTAN - Hygelac's hearth warrior.

EANMUND - Eldest son of Ohthere and brother of Eadgils. A Swedish prince.

EDITH - Cola's sister and wife of Eadgar.

EOFER - An Engle. Marries Astrid, Beowulf's cousin.

FINN - Saves the life of Beowulf during the swimming race.

GUNNAR - A sailor. Becomes Beowulf's first hearth warrior after the fighting at Sorrow Hill.

GUNNAR (2) - Hygelac's ship master at Marstrand.

HANNA - Girl at Little Edet. Sister of Henrik.

HARALD (1) - Danish reeve at Hroars Kilde.

HARALD (2) - Hygelac's ship master.

HARALD (3) - Leader of the bowmen at the river fight.

HEARDRED - Son of Hygelac. Beowulf's cousin.

HEATHOLAF - Wuffing leader killed by Ecgtheow during his youth.

HENRIK - A boy at Little Edet. Brother of Hanna.

HEREBEALD - Eldest son of King Hrethel. Killed by his brother Hythcyn during a hunt.

HILD - Wife of Herebeald.

HRANI - The god Woden.

HRETHEL - Son of Swerting. king of Geats and Beowulf's grandfather.

HROMUND - Hygelac's thegn.

HROTHGAR - King of the Danes.

HROTHULF - King of the Brondings.

HUDDA - Ecgtheow's ship master.

HYGD - Hygelac's wife

HYGELAC - Son of King Hrethel.

HYTHCYN - Son of King Hrethel.

KAIJA – A volva at the temple of Gefrin. She accompanies Beowulf on the journey which leads to Sorrow Hill.

ONELA – Youngest son of King Ongentheow.

ONGENTHEOW – King of the Swedes.

OHTHERE – Eldest son of King Ongentheow.

ORME - Ecgtheow's hearth warrior.

ORME - (2) A warrior killed during the fight with raiders.

OSLAF – Wulfgar's hearth warrior.

RANNULF – Heardred's hearth warrior.

RATTY – Hudda's crewman. Later lost at sea.

SIGRID - Beowulf's mother. Daughter of King Hrethel.

SVIP – Ecgtheow and later King Hrethel's falconer.

SWEGN – Danish reeve at Hroars Kilde.

SWERTING - Beowulf's great-grandfather. The founder of the dynasty.

THURGAR – Hygelac's hearth warrior.

THORFINN – Hygelac's hearth warrior.

TINY – Hudda's crewman.

TOFI – Hygelac's hearth warrior.

UCCA – Hudda's crewman.

ULF – Wulfgar's hearth warrior.

ULFGAR – Hygelac's thegn.

UNFERTH – Nephew of Danish King Hrothgar.

URSULA – A young girl rescued by Beowulf.

VOISLAV – Slavic thrall freed by Hrothgar at
    Beowulf's request.

WÆL – Wulfgar's hearth warrior.

WEALHTHEOW – Wife of King Hrothgar.

WIGMUND – Son of the Bronding King Hrothulf.

WULF – Hygelac's hearth warrior.

WULF (2) – Wulfgar's thegn. Leads the Geat left
    flank at Sorrow Hill.

WULFGAR – Ealdorman of Edet. Leads the Geatish
    forces at Sorrow Hill.

PLACES/LOCATIONS

ANHOLT – An island in the Kattegat.

BRITANNIA – The former Roman province.

EDET – Trollhattan, Vastra Gotaland.

GEAT RIVER – Gota Alv, Vastra Gotaland.

GEATWIC – Gothenburg, Vastra Gotaland.

HESSELO – An island in the Kattegat.

HLEIDRA – Ljeira, Sjaelland, Denmark.

HROARS KILDE – Roskilde, Sjaelland, Denmark.

LITTLE EDET – Lilla Edet, Vastra Gotaland.

MARSTRAND – Vastra Gotaland.

MIKLABORG – Kungalv, Vastra Gotaland.

NORTH RIVER – Nordre Alv, Vastra Gotaland.

RIVER FIGHT – North of Grastorp, Vastra Gotaland.

SARO – Near Kungsbakka, Halland.

SKANSEN – Kungsbakka, Halland.

SKARA – Near Tjuvkil, Vastra Gotaland.

SKOVDE – Vastra Gotaland.

SPIRIT LAND – Sjaelland, Denmark.

TROLLS HAT/SORROW HILL – Hunneberg, Near
   Trollhattan, Vastra Gotaland.

ABOUT THE AUTHOR

I am writer of historical fiction, working primarily in the early Middle Ages. I have always had a love of history which led to an early career in conservation work. Using the knowledge and expertise gained we later moved as a family through a succession of dilapidated houses which I single-handedly renovated. These ranged from a Victorian townhouse to a Fourteenth Century hall, and I added childcare to my knowledge of medieval oak frame repair, wattle and daub and lime plastering. I have crewed the replica of Captain Cook's ship, Endeavour, sleeping in a hammock and sweating in the sails and travelled the world, visiting such historic sites as the Little Big Horn, Leif Erikson's Icelandic birthplace and the bullet scarred walls of Berlin's Reichstag.

Now I write, only a stone's throw from the Anglian ship burial site at Sutton Hoo in East Anglia.

ALSO BY C.R.MAY

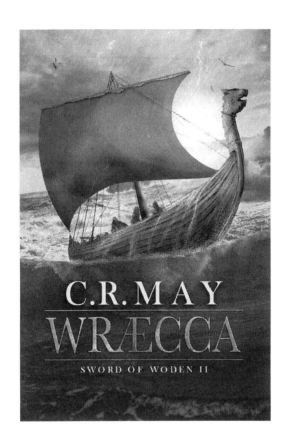

WRÆCCA

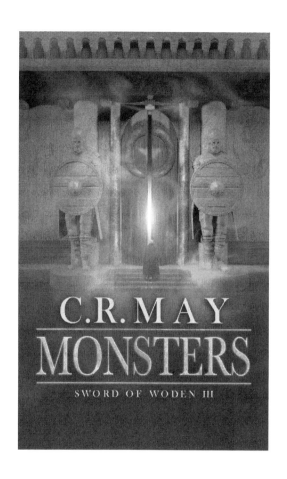

MONSTERS

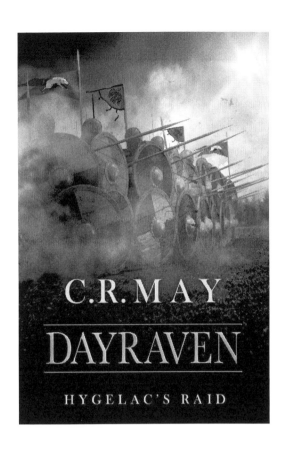

DAYRAVEN

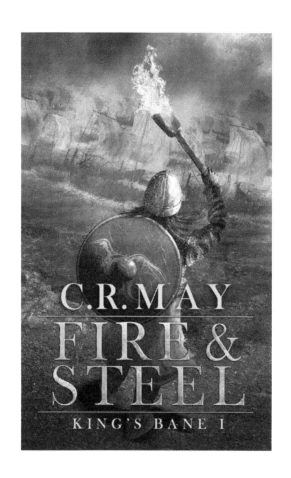

FIRE & STEEL

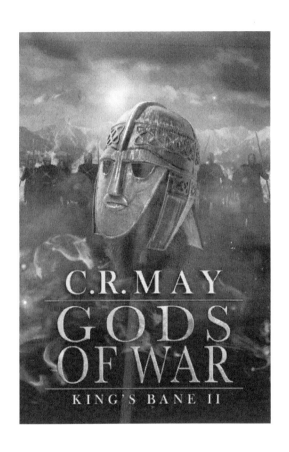

GODS OF WAR

THE SCATHING

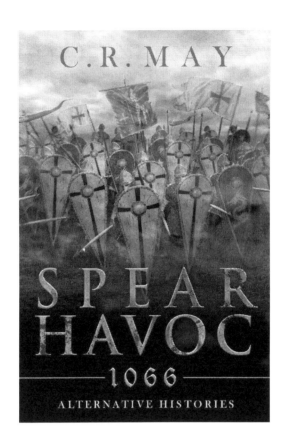

SPEAR HAVOC

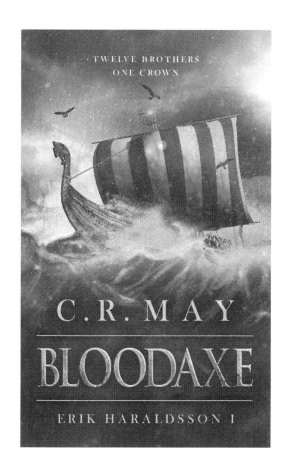

TWELVE BROTHERS
ONE CROWN

C. R. MAY

BLOODAXE

ERIK HARALDSSON I

BLOODAXE

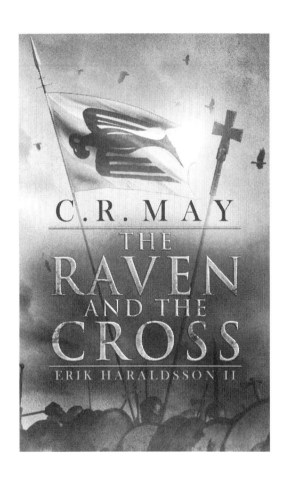

THE RAVEN AND THE CROSS

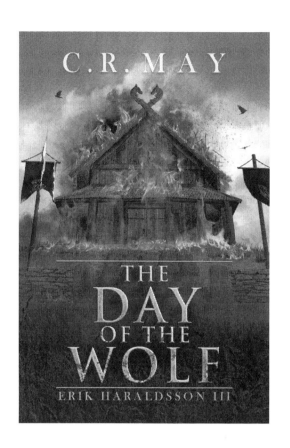

THE DAY OF THE WOLF

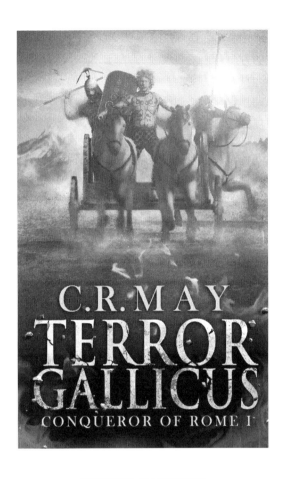

TERROR GALLICUS

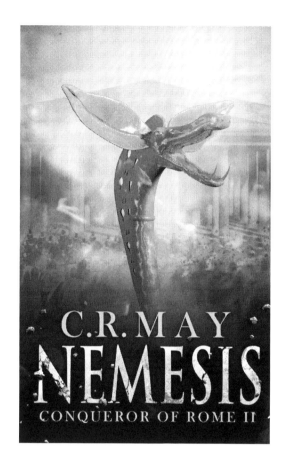

NEMESIS

Printed in Great Britain
by Amazon